MICHAEL STEPPED INTO THE BARN . . .

He waited, half-expectantly, as the darkness seeped into him, enveloping him within its folds. And then something reached out of the darkness and touched him.

Michael started but stood his ground, oddly unafraid. And then he heard a voice, flat, almost toneless, drifting hollowly from somewhere in the depths of the barn.

"Michael."

Michael froze.

"I knew you'd come." There was a pause, then the voice went on. "I have been calling you. I wasn't sure you heard me."

"Who are you?" Michael asked. His eyes searched the darkness but could find nothing. Nor could he be certain just where the voice came from. As the silence lengthened, he began backing toward the door. "Tell me who you are," he said, more loudly this time.

"I am Nathaniel," the voice said. "I am Nathaniel. . . ."

NATHANIEL
The New Novel of Endless Fear
by the multimillion-copy bestselling author
JOHN SAUL

BY JOHN SAUL

NATHANIEL

John Saul

BANTAM BOOKS
TORONTO · NEW YORK · LONDON · SYDNEY · AUCKLAND

NATHANIEL
A Bantam Book / July 1984

ISBN 0-553-24172-9

Published simultaneously in the United States and Canada

Bantam Books are published by Bantam Books, Inc. Its trademark, consisting
of the words "Bantam Books" and the portrayal of a rooster. is Registered
in U.S. Patent and Trademark Office and in other countries. Marca Registrada.
Bantam Books, Inc., 666 Fifth Avenue, New York, New York 10103.

PRINTED IN THE UNITED STATES OF AMERICA

H   0 9 8 7 6

PROLOGUE

The night closed in like something alive, its warm dampness imbuing the house with an oppressive atmosphere that seemed somehow threatening to the child who sat in the small front parlor. There was something in the air she could almost touch, and as she sat waiting, she began to feel her skin crawl with the peculiar itching that always came over her late in the summer. She squirmed on the mohair sofa, but it did no good—her cotton dress still clung to her like wet cellophane.

Outside the wind began to rise, and for a moment the girl felt relief. For the first time in hours, the angry sound of her father's voice was muted, covered by the wind, so that if she concentrated hard, she could almost pretend that that sound was a part of the rising storm, rather than a proof of her father's fury and her mother's terror.

Then her father was looming in the doorway, his eyes hard, his anger suddenly directed toward her. She cringed on the sofa—perhaps if she made herself smaller he wouldn't see her.

"The cellar," her father said, the softness of his voice making it no less threatening. "I told you to go to the cellar."

"Father—"

1

"Storm's coming. You'll be safe in the cellar. Now go on."

Hesitantly, the child stood up and began edging toward the kitchen door, her eyes flickering once, leaving her father's angry face to focus on the door behind him, the door beyond which her mother lay struggling with the pains of labor. "She'll be all right," he said.

Not reassured, but knowing argument would only increase her father's wrath, the girl pulled a jacket from a hook and struggled to force her arms through its tangled sleeves. Then, shielding her eyes from the driving wind with her right arm, she left the house and scuttled across the yard to the cyclone cellar that had been carved out of the unyielding prairie earth so many years ago. Once she glanced up, squinting her eyes against the stinging dust. In the distance, almost invisible in the roiling clouds, she could barely make out the beginnings of the storm's angry funnel.

More terrified now of the storm than of her father's anger, she grasped the heavy wooden door of the cellar and hauled it partway open, just far enough to slip her body through the gap. She scrambled down the steep steps, letting the door drop into place behind her.

For what seemed like an eternity, she sat in the near-total darkness of the storm cellar, her ears filled with the sounds of the raging winds.

But sometimes, when the howlings of the storm momentarily abated, she thought she could hear something else. Her mother, calling out to her, begging her to come and help her.

The girl tried to ignore those sounds—it was impossible for her mother's voice to carry over the storm. Besides, she knew what was happening to her mother and knew there was nothing for her to do.

When the baby came, and the storm had passed, someone—her father or her brother—would come for her. Until then, she would stay where she was and try to pretend she wasn't frightened.

She curled herself up in a corner of the cellar and squeezed her eyes tight against the darkness and the fear.

She didn't know how much time had passed, knew only that she couldn't stay by herself any longer, couldn't stay alone in the cellar. She listened to the wind, tried to gauge its danger, but in the end she wrapped the jacket close around her thin body, and forced the cellar door open. The wind caught it, jerked it out of her grasp, then tore it loose from its hinges and sent it tumbling across the yard. It caught on the barbed wire fence for a moment; then the wire gave way and the wooden door hurtled on, flipping end over end across the plains, quickly disappearing into the gathering dusk. The girl huddled at the top of the steps for a few moments. There was a light on in the house now, not the bright lights she was used to, but the glow of a lantern, and she knew the power had gone out. The flickering lamplight drew her like a moth, and she braced herself against the driving wind, leaning into it as she began making her way back across the yard. She was disobeying, she knew, but even facing Pa's anger was better than staying alone any longer.

Still, when she reached the house, she couldn't bring herself to go in, for even over the howling wind she could hear her father's voice. His words were unintelligible but his anger was terrifying. The girl crept around the corner of the house, crouched low, until she was beneath the window of the room in which her mother lay.

Slowly, she straightened up, until she could see into the room. On the nightstand stood an oil lantern, its wick turned low, its yellowish light casting odd shadows. Her mother looked almost lifeless, resting against a pillow, damp hair clinging to sallow skin, her eyes wide, staring balefully at the towering figure of her father.

And now she could hear the words.

"You killed him."

"No," her father replied. "He was born dead."

The little girl watched as her mother's head moved, shaking slowly from side to side as her eyes closed tight. "No. My baby was alive. I felt it moving. Right up until the end, I felt it moving. It was alive, and you killed it."

A movement distracted the girl, and her eyes left her mother's tortured face. Someone else stood in the corner of the room, but until he turned, the girl didn't recognize him.

It was the doctor, and in his arms he cradled a tiny bundle wrapped in a blanket. A fold of the blanket dropped away; the girl saw the baby's face, its eyes closed, its wizened features barely visible in the flickering lantern light.

By its stillness, she knew it was dead.

"Give it to me!" she heard her mother demand. Then her voice became pleading. "Please, give it to me . . ."

But the doctor said nothing, only refolding the blanket around the baby's face, then turning away once more. Her mother's screams filled the night then, and a moment later, when the girl looked for the doctor again, he had retreated from the room. Now that they were left alone, her father was regarding her mother with smoldering eyes.

"I warned you," he said. "I warned you God would punish you, and He has."

"It was you," her mother protested, her voice weakened by pain and despair. "It wasn't God punishing me, it was you." Her voice broke, and she began sobbing, making no attempt to wipe her tears away from her streaming eyes. "It was alive, and you killed it. You had no right— you had no right . . ."

Suddenly the girl saw the door open, and her brother appeared. He stood still for a moment, staring at their mother. He started to speak, but before he could utter a word, their father turned on him.

"Get out!" Then, as the girl watched, her father's fist

rose into the air, then swung forward, catching the side of her brother's head, slamming him against the wall. Her brother crumpled to the floor. For a time that seemed endless to the watching girl, he lay still. No one spoke. Then, slowly, he rose to face their father.

He opened his mouth to speak, but no words came out. His eyes glowed with hatred as he stared at his father; then he turned away and stumbled out of the little room.

The girl backed away from the window, unconscious now of the wind that still battered at her, her mind filled only with the sights and sounds she instinctively knew she should not have witnessed. She should have obeyed her father and stayed in the storm cellar, waiting for someone to come for her.

She started back toward the storm cellar. Perhaps, if she tried very hard, she could blot all of it out of her mind, pretend that she had seen and heard none of it, convince herself that she had never left the cellar, never witnessed her mother's pain and her father's fury. And then, ahead of her, a few feet away, she saw her brother and cried out to him.

He turned to face her, but she knew he didn't see her. His eyes were blank, and he seemed to be looking past her, looking out into the storm and the night.

"Please," the girl whispered. "Help me. Please help me . . ."

But if her brother heard her, he gave no sign. Instead, he turned away, and as if he was following the call of some other voice the girl couldn't hear, he left the house and the yard, disappearing into the prairie. A moment later he was gone, swallowed up by the storm and the night. Alone, the girl made her way back to the cyclone cellar.

She crept down the steps through the gaping hole where the door had been, and went back to her corner. She drew the jacket tightly around herself, but neither the jacket nor the doorless cellar could protect her.

Through the long night she huddled there, the storm and the scene she had witnessed lashing at her, torturing her, boring deep within her soul.

After that night she never spoke of what she'd seen or what she'd heard. She never spoke of it, but she never quite forgot.

CHAPTER 1

"Are you my grandpa?"

Michael Hall gazed uncertainly up into the weathered face. He had never seen the man before, yet he recognized him as clearly as if he were looking into a mirror. He tried to keep his voice steady, tried not to shrink back against his mother, tried to remember all the things his father had taught him about meeting people for the first time:

Stand up straight, and put your hand out.

Look the person in the eye.

Tell them your name. He'd forgotten that part.

"I—I'm Michael, and this is my mother," he stammered.

He felt his mother's grip tighten on his shoulders, and for just a moment was afraid he'd done something wrong. But then the man he was talking to smiled at him, and he felt his mother's hands relax a little.

He looks like Mark. He looks just like Mark. The thought flashed through Janet Hall's mind, and she had to make a conscious effort to keep from hurling herself into the arms of the stranger who was now moving closer to her, an uneasy smile failing to mask the troubled look in his eyes. Barely conscious of the airport crowd that eddied around her, Janet found herself focusing on the lean angularity of her father-in-law's figure, the strength in his face, the aura of calm control that seemed to hover around him as it had around his son. Unconsciously, her hand moved to her waist and she smoothed her skirt in a nervous gesture.

It's going to be all right, Janet told herself. *He's just like Mark, and he'll take care of us.*

Almost as if he'd heard Janet's private thought, Amos Hall leaned down and swung his eleven-year-old grandson off his feet, his farmer's strength belying his own sixty-seven years. He hugged the boy, but when his eyes met Janet's over Michael's shoulder, there was no joy in them.

"I'm sorry," he said, dropping his voice to a level that would be inaudible to anyone but Janet and Michael. "I don't know what to say. All these years, and we only meet when Mark—" His voice faltered, and Janet could see him struggling against his feelings. "I'm sorry," he repeated, his voice suddenly gruff. "Let's get your baggage and get on out of here. We can talk in the car."

But they didn't talk in the car. They drove out of North Platte and into the vast expanse of the prairie in silence, the three of them huddled in the front seat of Amos Hall's Oldsmobile, Janet and Amos separated by Michael. The numbness that had overcome Janet from the moment the night before when she had been told that her husband was dead still pervaded her, and the reality of where she was— and the why of it—had still not come fully into her consciousness. She had a feeling of being trapped in a nightmare, and every second she was waiting for Mark to awaken her from the dream and assure her that everything was all right, everything was as it had always been.

And yet, that was not to be.

The miles rolled past. Finally, Janet made herself glance across to her father-in-law, who seemed intent on studying the arrow-straight road ahead, his eyes glued to the shimmering pavement as if, by concentration alone, he, too, could deny the reality of what had happened.

Janet cleared her throat, and Amos's eyes left the road for a split second. "Mark's mother—"

"She never leaves Prairie Bend," Amos replied, his gaze returning to the highway. "Rarely leaves the house anymore, if truth be known. She's getting along, and the years—" He paused, and Janet could see a tightness forming in his jaw. "The years haven't been as kind to her as they might," he finished. Then: "Funeral's gonna be tomorrow morning."

Janet nodded mutely, relieved that the decision had been made; then, once more, she let herself fall into silence.

An hour later they arrived at the Halls' farm. The old two-story house was not large, but it seemed to Janet to have a sense of itself, sitting solidly on its foundation, surrounded by a grove of elms and cottonwoods, protected from the vast emptiness of the plains that stretched to the horizon in every direction save one, where a stand of trees marked the route of a river making its way eastward, to flow eventually into the Platte.

"What's the name of the river?" Michael suddenly asked, and the question pulled Janet's attention from her father-in-law.

"The Dismal," Amos replied as he brought the car to a stop in front of the house. A moment later he was taking Janet's baggage out of the trunk. With a suitcase in each hand, he mounted the steps of the front porch, Janet and Michael trailing behind him. Suddenly the door opened and a figure appeared on the threshold, a woman, gaunt and hollow-cheeked, as though her life had been spent in constant battle with the unrelenting prairie.

She was seated in a wheelchair.

Janet felt Michael freeze next to her, and took him by the hand.

"We're back," she heard Amos Hall saying to the woman. "This is Mark's Janet, and this is Michael."

The woman in the wheelchair stared at them in silence for a moment. Her face, worn with age and infirmity, had a haggard look to it, and her eyes, rimmed with red, seemed nearly lifeless. But a moment later she smiled, a soft smile that seemed to wash some of the years away

from her countenance. "Come here," she said, spreading
her arms wide. "Come and let me hold you."

The numbness Janet had been feeling since last night;
the numbness that had insulated her every minute today
and allowed her to maintain her self-control as she packed
their bags, ordered a cab, and got herself and Michael
from Manhattan to the airport; the numbness that had
sustained her through the change of planes in Omaha, the
arrival in North Platte, and the drive to Prairie Bend,
drained away from her now.

"He's dead," she said, her voice breaking as for the
first time she truly admitted to herself what had happened.
Dropping Michael's hand, she stumbled up the steps and
sank to her knees next to Anna Hall's wheelchair. "Oh,
God, what happened to him? Why did he die? Why?"

Anna's arms encircled Janet, and she cradled her daughter-
in-law's head against her breast. "It's all right, child,"
she soothed. "Things happen, sometimes, and there's nothing we can do about them. We just have to accept them."
Over Janet's head, her gaze met her husband's for a
moment, then moved on, coming to rest on Michael, who
stood uncertainly at the foot of the steps, his eyes riveted
in worried fascination on his mother. "You, too, Michael,"
Anna gently urged. "Come give Grandma a hug, and let
her take the hurt away."

The boy looked up then, and as his eyes met her own,
Anna felt a flash of recognition surge over her frail body.
In the boy, she saw the father. And as she saw her son in
her grandson's eyes, she began to feel fear.

Amos Hall led Janet and Michael up the narrow staircase to the second floor, where three large bedrooms and a
generous bathroom opened off the hallway that bisected
the house. He opened the door to the first bedroom, then
stood aside to let Janet pass him. "You'll be in here. Used
to be Laura's room."

"Laura?" Janet echoed, in a voice that sounded dazed
even to herself. "Who's Laura?"

Amos frowned, his eyes clouding. "Mark's sister. Until she got married, this was her room." He paused a moment, then, as if he felt an explanation was necessary, spoke again. "I was going to turn it into a den, or a study. I just never got around to it."

Janet gazed at the room, taking in its details with apparent calm, while she frantically searched the corners of her memory for the information she knew must be there, that had somehow slipped away from her.

The name Laura meant nothing to her.

The whole idea of Mark having had a sister meant nothing to her.

But that was ridiculous. If Mark had had a sister, he *must* have talked about her sometime over the years. She'd simply forgotten. Some kind of amnesia, maybe: somehow, during the last few hours of shock, it must have been driven from her mind.

"It's just fine," she said at last, careful not to let her voice betray her confusion. She glanced around the room once more, this time forcing herself to concentrate. There was nothing special about the room; it was simply a room, with a bed, a chair, a nightstand, and a dresser. A chenille bedspread covered the slightly sagging mattress, and there was a braided rug covering most of the pine floor. Ill-fitting curtains hung at the window, and an image of a Sears catalog suddenly came into Janet's mind. A second later, she made the connection: the curtains were identical to the ones she had had in her own room when she was a little girl, the ones her mother had ordered from the Sears catalog, in a size close to, but not quite right for, the windows. Her mind churned on, and the rest of the memories flooded back, the memories she'd deliberately suppressed, hoped never to look at again:

The fire, when the old house she'd been born in had burned to the ground, consuming everything she loved— her parents and her brother, too—leaving her to be raised by a series of aunts who somehow had always found reasons to pass her on to someone else until, at last, she'd turned eighteen and gone to live by herself in New York. A year later, she'd married Mark.

And now, once again, here were those mail-order curtains, bringing back those memories. She sank onto the bed, one hand reflexively coming up to cover her eyes as she felt them fill with tears.

"Are you all right?" she heard her father-in-law ask. She took a deep breath, then made herself smile.

"I'll be fine. It's just that—that—"

But Amos Hall stopped her. "Lie down for a little while. Just lie down, and try to go to sleep. I'll take care of Michael, and later on we'll talk. But for now, just try to get a little sleep." Taking the boy firmly by the hand, Amos left the room, closing the door behind him.

For a long time, Janet lay on the bed, trying to make herself be calm, trying to put the memories of the past to rest and cope with the problems of the present.

Laura.

She would concentrate on Laura.

Somewhere in her memory, there must be something about Mark's sister, and if she concentrated, it would come back to her. It just wasn't possible that Mark, in their thirteen years together, had never mentioned having a sister. It wasn't possible. . . .

And then the exhaustion of the last hours caught up with her, and she slept.

Michael stared in awe at the room his grandfather had shown him into. It was a boy's room, its walls covered with baseball and football pennants. Suspended from the ceiling were four model airplanes, frozen in flight as if they were involved in a dogfight. Over the bed there was a bookshelf, and Michael could recognize some of the books without reading the titles: identical volumes sat on his own bookshelf back home in New York. "Was this my father's room?" he asked at last.

"This is all the stuff he had when he was a boy," his grandfather replied. "All these years, and here it is. I suppose I should have gotten rid of it, but now I'm glad I didn't. Maybe I was saving it just for you."

Michael frowned, regarding his grandfather with suspicious eyes. "But you didn't know I was coming."

"But you would have, wouldn't you?" Amos countered. "Someday, wouldn't you have come to visit your grandparents?"

Michael shook his head. "I don't think Dad wanted to come here. I don't think he liked it here."

"Now what makes you say a thing like that?" Amos asked, lowering himself onto the studio couch that served as a bed, and drawing Michael down beside him.

" 'Cause every time I asked him if we could come here to visit, he said maybe next year. That's what he always said, and whenever I told him that's what he said last year, he always said he'd only said maybe. So I guess he never really wanted to come, did he?"

"Maybe he could just never find the time," Amos suggested.

Michael shrugged, and drew slightly away from his grandfather. "He always took us on a vacation. One year we went to Florida, and twice we went camping in the mountains." Suddenly he grinned. "That was neat. Do you ever go camping?"

"Not for years. But now that you're here, I don't see why we couldn't go. Would you like that?"

The grin on Michael's face faded. "I don't know. I always went camping with my dad." He fell silent for a moment, then turned to look up into his grandfather's face. "How come my dad died? How come he even came out here without bringing us with him? Or even telling us he was coming?" Anger began to tinge his voice. "He said he was going to Chicago."

"And he went to Chicago," Amos replied. "Then he came here. I don't rightly know exactly why."

Michael's eyes narrowed. "You mean you won't tell me."

"I mean I don't know," Amos said gruffly, standing

up. He paused, then reached down and took Michael's chin in his rough hand, forcing the boy to face him. "If you mean I'm not telling you something because I think you're too young to know, then you're wrong. I don't hold with that sort of nonsense. If a boy's old enough to ask a question, he's old enough to hear the answer." His hand dropped away from Michael's face but he continued to regard his grandson with an unbending gaze. "I don't know why your father came out here," he said. "All I can tell you is that he got here yesterday, and last night he died."

Michael stared at his grandfather for a long time, and when he finally spoke, his voice was quavering. "But how come he died? He wasn't sick, was he?"

"It was an accident," Amos said shortly. "He was in the barn, up in the loft. He must have tripped over something."

The suspicion came back into Michael's eyes. "What?" he demanded.

Amos stiffened slightly. "I don't know—nobody does. Anyway, he fell off the edge of the loft, into the haybin."

Michael frowned. "What's a haybin?"

"On a farm, you keep the hay in bales up in a loft. Then, when you want to feed the animals in the barn, you pitch some of the hay down from the loft into the haybin."

"But how far is it?"

"Maybe ten feet."

Michael's frown deepened. "I fell that far once, and all that happened was that I twisted my ankle."

Amos hesitated, then spoke again. "But you didn't fall onto a pitchfork, did you?"

Michael's eyes widened. "A pitchfork?"

Amos nodded. "It's a big fork, with four tines. It's what you use to move hay around with. It was lying in the bin, and your dad fell onto it."

Suddenly Michael was on his feet, his face contorted with fury. "No! That's not what happened!" His voice rose as his angry eyes riveted his grandfather. "My dad didn't fall—he wouldn't have! Somebody must have pushed him. Somebody killed him, didn't they? Somebody killed my father!''

Michael's fists came up, ready to begin pummeling at his grandfather, but Amos reached out, putting one large hand on each of Michael's forearms. As his strong fingers closed, Michael found himself held immobile.

"Now you listen to me, young man," he heard his grandfather say. "What happened to your father was an accident. Nobody pushed him, and nobody killed him. It was an accident, and it's over with. Do you understand?''

Michael stared at his grandfather, then started to speak, but something in the old man's eyes made him remain silent. He swallowed hard, then nodded his head. His grandfather's iron grip eased, and his arms dropped to his side.

"And another thing," Amos added, his voice softer now, but no less commanding. "If I tell you something, you can count on it being the truth. So I don't ever again want to hear you arguing with me. Is that clear?''

"But—"

His grandfather interrupted, "You're not a baby anymore, and you mustn't act like one. You asked me what happened, and I told you." He was silent for a moment, then: "If you don't want an answer, don't ask a question. And don't ever argue with me. I'm older than you, and I'm wiser than you, and I don't hold with children not respecting their elders. All right?''

For several seconds Michael said nothing, but then, from the depths of his subconscious, the right words rose to the surface. "Yes, sir," he said softly. His grandfather smiled.

"Good. We're going to get along just fine, you and I. Now, you get settled in here, and when you're ready, come on downstairs, and I'll show you around the place. And I bet your grandma will have something good in the oven. You like apple pie?''

Michael nodded, but said nothing.

"Well, I'll bet you've never tasted anything like your grandmother's apple pie." He started out of the room, but stopped when Michael suddenly spoke again.

"Grandpa, how come Grandma can't walk?"

Slowly, Amos Hall turned back to face the boy. "I was wrong a couple of minutes ago," he said after a long silence. "I won't answer all your questions, because some questions just don't have answers. And that's one of them. I don't know why your grandma can't walk, Michael. It's just something that happened a long time ago." He turned, and left Michael alone in the room that was filled with all the things that had belonged to his father.

Anna Hall looked up from the kitchen table where she sat in her wheelchair, shelling peas for that evening's dinner. "Well? Are they getting settled in?"

Amos lowered himself into the chair opposite her. "If you can call it that. The girl's taking it hard, I think."

Anna stopped working for a moment, but still avoided her husband's eyes. "We can't expect her not to, can we? For us, it's a little different. We hadn't even seen him for twenty years. It was almost as if he was already dead—"

"He *was*," Amos replied, his voice bitter. "As far as I'm concerned, he was as good as dead the day he walked out of here."

"Don't say that, Amos," Anna pleaded. "Please don't say that, not anymore. What if Janet hears you? What would she think?"

"What does she think anyway? What do you suppose Mark told her about us? You don't think he didn't talk about us, do you?" When Anna remained silent, his voice rose. "Do you? Do you really think he wouldn't have told her all about that night, and what he thought he saw?"

Anna's eyes narrowed. "If he did, then why is she here? Why didn't she tell us to ship Mark's body back to New York? I don't think he told her anything. Nothing at all."

Amos sighed and stood up. "Well, it doesn't matter. The important thing is that she came back and brought the child with her."

"But that doesn't mean she'll stay, Amos."

"She'll stay," Amos replied grimly. "She needs us right now, and we'll be here for her. She'll stay. I'll see to it."

As Amos strode through the back door, Anna regarded her husband's erect spine with bitterness. It was true, she realized. If Amos wanted Janet and Michael to stay in Prairie Bend, they would. And she, who had never been able to defy her husband in all the years of their marriage, would not defy him now.

Janet Hall awoke from a restless sleep. The nightmare had come back, the one she hadn't had since she'd married Mark. Now, as she came out of the dream, she felt disoriented, and the acrid smell of smoke lingered in her memory. For a moment she listened for the familiar sounds of the city at night, but heard only the silence of the prairie. And then, in the silence, there was something else: a whimpering sound, mixed with soft moanings.

Michael, in the grip of his own nightmare.

Shaking off the last vestiges of sleep, she got out of bed, slipped into the flannel robe Anna had given her, and made her way through the darkness to the room next door, where Michael slept. She found him tangled in the sheets, his arms moving spasmodically, his hands bunched into tight fists.

"Michael—Michael, wake up. You're having a nightmare."

Michael's eyes flew open. He stared at his mother without speaking, then his arms went around her neck, and he buried his face in her breast. She drew his quivering body close, cradling him. "He's not here," he sobbed. "He's gone, Mommy. I saw someone push him, and then he fell off the edge. He fell, and he fell, and then there was a—a pitchfork. I saw it, Mom. I tried to warn him, but I couldn't. And then—and then—''

"Hush," Janet soothed. "It was only a dream, sweetheart. You just had a bad dream." The shaking subsided, and Michael relaxed his grip on her, but Janet hugged him closer. "Would you like to come and sleep with me tonight?"

Now Michael wriggled out of her arms and drew slightly away from her, shaking his head. "I'm too old for that," he said.

"I know," Janet agreed. "But sometimes people get lonely, or frightened, and they need to be close to someone. I just thought maybe tonight you might want—"

"I'm okay," Michael interrupted. He sat up in bed and began straightening out the sheets, and Janet rose uncertainly to her feet.

"If you're sure you're all right—"

Michael nodded vigorously. "I'm fine, Mom." He lay back down, pulling the sheet up to his chin.

Janet leaned down and kissed him on the forehead. "All right. Sleep tight. If you need me, I'm right next door. Okay?"

Michael nodded, turning away from her to curl himself up into a tight ball. Janet watched him for a moment; then, reluctantly, she left him alone and started back to her own room. In the hall, standing at the head of the stairs, she found Amos. Startled, she tripped over the hem of her robe. Instantly, Amos put out a hand to steady her.

"Are you all right?"

"A nightmare. Michael just had a nightmare."

Amos nodded. "I heard something. I was coming up to see what was wrong."

Janet nodded. "I guess I wasn't sleeping very well anyway. I—I just feel all confused. It's as if everything's a dream, and I keep thinking I'll wake up, but then I know I won't."

Wordlessly, Amos led her into her room and guided her back into bed. "It'll take time," he finally said. "You have to give yourself time to get used to it. But you'll be all right, Janet. You and Michael will both be all right. We're here, and we love you, and we'll take care of you for as long as you need us. All right?''

In the dim moonlight that filtered into the darkened room, Janet looked up at her father-in-law. There was so much of Mark in his face, so much of Mark's strength in his eyes. "I—I just feel so helpless—''

"And that's all right, too,'' Amos assured her. "Just try to go back to sleep, and try not to worry.''

He stayed with her, sitting in the chair near her bed, until once more she drifted into sleep.

Michael lay still in bed, listening first to the soft mutterings of his grandfather and his mother talking, then shifting his attention to the sounds of the night. Crickets chirped softly, and the lowing of cattle drifted through the darkness. His eyes searched out the model airplanes, and he began thinking once more about his father.

He couldn't *feel* his father.

That, he decided, was what was strange about this room. Even though it was filled with his father's things, he couldn't feel his father.

That was something he'd never experienced before. Always, for as long as he could remember, he'd been able to sense his father's presence near him, even when Mark wasn't at home. It was as if any place his father had been, he'd left something of himself behind, something for Michael to hold on to. It was something special between himself and his father, and even though they'd never talked about it, Michael was sure his father had felt it too.

And yet, in this room, with all his father's things around him, Michael couldn't feel him.

He'd felt him in the dream, though.

In the dream, he'd seen his father standing in the hayloft, and he'd seen someone else, someone he couldn't quite make out, near his father.

And then there'd been a flash of movement, and suddenly his father was over the edge, falling.

It was as if Michael himself was falling, but even as he felt himself tumbling endlessly toward the haybin, he'd also watched as his father's body plummeted toward the darkness below.

He'd seen the pitchfork, its handle buried in the hay, its four gleaming tines pointed straight upward, waiting for him, waiting for his father.

He'd tried to cry out, tried to scream, but no sound would come from his throat.

And then he could feel the cold, knife-edged steel plunging into his flesh, but even as the pitchfork pierced him, he could see that it wasn't himself falling onto the dangerous tines, but his father. Yet even knowing it was not he who was dying, Michael could still feel the pain, feel the agony shooting through his father's body, feel the death that had come for his father.

And above, watching, there was someone else. . . .

It was only a dream, and yet deep within himself, Michael knew it was more than his mind's imaginings.

It was real.

CHAPTER 2

No matter how hard she tried, Janet Hall couldn't focus her mind on the reality of what was happening. There was a sense of wrongness to everything, and she found herself grasping at inconsequentials. Suddenly, in the warmth of the spring morning, she saw herself as she should have been right now, striding down Madison Avenue, past the Carlyle Hotel toward American Expression, the boutique that was the usual focus of her Wednesday morning shopping expeditions.

And Michael should have been sitting in his classroom at the Manhattan Academy, pretending to be paying attention to his teacher. He wouldn't be, of course. Instead, Michael would be gazing out on the bright and sunny morning and dreaming of spending the weekend camping with Mark in the Berkshires.

And Mark. Mark should be facing his eleven o'clock class, polishing his glasses and filling his pipe while he glanced over his notes on The Effects of the War in Viet Nam on the Middle-class Family.

That was the way it should be. A typical family—if not the almost laughably stereotypical family Mark had once called them—going through the routines of their normal, stereotypical lives. But things were rarely as they should be, and today *nothing* was as it should be.

21

Everything was wrong; everything was unreal.

Mark was *dead*.

That was the thing she had to accept; when she could understand that, then everything else would fit, and she would be able to orient herself to her surroundings.

She forced herself into reality, yanked herself out of New York and back into Prairie Bend, and fixed her eyes on the coffin that stood next to the open grave. That's Mark, she told herself. That's all that's left of him, and in a few minutes, they are going to put him in the ground, and cover him up, and then he will be gone. *Gone*. She repeated the word to herself, but it still had no real meaning for her. Mark couldn't be gone, not forever. It wasn't fair. And that, she realized in a moment of sudden clarity, was the key to it all. *It wasn't fair*. There hadn't been anything wrong with Mark, except perhaps that odd daredevil streak in him that had never fit with his professorial personality, those sudden, inexplicable urges to thrust himself into danger that had, apparently, finally killed him.

It hadn't always been that way. When they'd first gotten married, he'd been what she'd always dreamed of: a quiet man living a quiet life. And then, a year into the marriage— eleven years ago—two things had happened: Michael had been born, and Mark had bought a motorcycle. Though Mark had denied it, Janet had always been sure there was a connection between the two events. It was as if Mark wanted to prove to his son that he was more than a milquetoast professor, that he was some kind of he-man, or at least his own image of a he-man. The motorcycle had been just the beginning.

Finally, there had been the skydiving. He'd taken that up two years ago, after a year of dragging his family out to the Jersey meadows every weekend to "watch." From the beginning, Janet had been sure that her husband would not be content to stay on the ground, and she had been right. Six months after he started watching, he started jumping. Of course, he'd been careful, as he was careful about everything.

And there, she realized, was the irony. Two years of skydiving, two years of risking his life from thousands of feet in the air, only to die in what couldn't have been more than a ten-foot fall.

It simply wasn't possible—not possible that he was dead, had left her alone to raise Michael—Michael, and the baby. She had not told the Halls yet about the baby, and they hadn't seemed to notice. But soon she would have to face telling them. And telling Michael.

And the guilty, disloyal thought came into her head once more: it was all Mark's own fault. If he'd come straight home from Chicago, as he'd planned to do, none of this would be happening. He hadn't been back to Prairie Bend in years. Not, in fact, in all the years she'd known him. So why had he gone back now?

It didn't make sense.

A wave of nausea swept over her, a twinge of the morning sickness that had plagued her far past the time when it should have ceased. Janet steeled herself against it, refusing to give in to it. *I won't be sick,* she told herself. *I won't be sick at Mark's funeral. I'll get through this.* Suddenly she felt a steadying hand on her elbow, and looked up to see Amos Hall watching her intently, his blue eyes—so like Mark's eyes—filled with concern. Shutting everything else out of her mind, she clutched her father-in-law's hand and forced herself to watch as they lowered her husband's coffin into the ground.

Michael stood quietly next to his mother, doing his best to keep his mind on what the minister was saying about his father. If he listened hard to the words, then maybe his headache would go away. But try as he would, he couldn't concentrate, for what the minister was saying didn't seem to be about his father at all. At least, not the father he had known. The minister kept talking about the importance of being at home and living and dying among your own, and Michael couldn't really see the connection between the words and his dad. Did the minister mean that if his father hadn't ever left Prairie Bend, then he wouldn't have died? But that didn't make sense—he'd been in Prairie Bend when he died.

Died. The word hadn't really had any meaning to Michael before yesterday. People died, but not people you knew, much less your own father. And yet it had happened. He stared at the coffin, knowing this was the last he would ever see of his father, but even as he watched it, he still couldn't believe that his father was really inside that wooden box, was really being buried in the ground, was really gone forever. He couldn't be . . .

He let his eyes wander away from the coffin, to scan over countless unfamiliar faces that all seemed to look alike, and then gaze out toward the horizon. Never in his life had he been able to see so far. The town, more like a village really, was behind him, and beyond the low stone wall of the cemetery, the plains stretched endlessly to the horizon, broken only by the slowly flowing river that curved around the town, giving the community its name, and the farmhouses, scattered here and there in the emptiness, each of them surrounded by a few huddled trees planted as protection against sudden prairie winds. And above it all the enormous sky, not the flat kind of sky he was used to, but a three-dimensional sky that seemed to cover the world like an enormous blue bowl. It was all so much larger than anything at home. At home, the city was always close around you, and even when you were out of the city there was a smallness to the countryside, with the forests crowding in and the profusion of low hills cutting off the view in every direction. But out here, on the plains, everything was open. He felt as though he could breathe more deeply than he ever had before.

He sensed movement next to him and felt his mother's hand squeezing his own. The service was ending. The minister had stooped down to pick up a clod of the black earth, which he was now holding over the open grave. It was all over, and his father was gone.

"Ashes to ashes, dust to dust . . ." Strong fingers

squeezed the clump of earth, and as Michael stared, it broke up, dirt drumming onto the casket with a hollow sound that made Michael's throat constrict. A snuffling next to him told him that his mother was crying, and suddenly his eyes, too, filled with tears. Self-consciously, Michael let go of his mother's hand, pulled a handkerchief from his hip pocket, and blew his nose. He felt his mother's hand on his shoulder, pressing gently. Then it was over. He turned away from his father's grave.

And as he turned, something caught his attention. A glint. A movement. At first he wasn't sure what it was, but as his eyes scanned the plains again, he realized it must have been the sun flashing off the weathervane that stood perched high on the ridgepole of a weathered barn about a half mile away. Yet, as he watched it, he realized that there was no wind today. The vane wasn't moving. Then what had flashed? Maybe it was just his imagination. He started to turn away once more, to follow his mother toward his grandfather's car, but once again his attention was caught by the flash. No, not quite a flash. It was something else, something he couldn't quite focus on. He examined the farm and frowned. There was something different about it, something he couldn't quite figure out. He cocked his head, shading his eyes with his hand, and then felt an unfamiliar touch on his shoulder. He looked up to find his grandfather frowning at him.

"You all right?" Amos Hall asked.

Michael nodded. "I thought I saw something. Out there."

The older man followed his gaze, then shrugged. "That's Ben Findley's place. Not much to see out there. Man doesn't keep it up like he should. It comes of living alone."

"Doesn't he have a wife?" Michael asked.

His grandfather hesitated, then shook his head and started leading Michael away. "Had one years ago, but she left. And you'd do well to stay clear of that place."

Michael stopped, turning back to stare once more at the

farm which had suddenly become fascinating. "How come?"

His grandfather offered him a faint smile. " 'Cause Ben Findley doesn't like kids," he said. "He doesn't like anybody, but especially, he doesn't like kids." Then his voice softened, and he took Michael's hand. "Now come on, son. Let's get back to the farm. This is all over here, and we've all got to get back to living." He started walking slowly away, and his arm fell across Michael's shoulders. He was silent as they moved through the sunshine, but before they got to the car, he paused and turned to face Michael.

"You sure you're all right?" he asked, and Michael knew that this time Amos was talking about his father.

"I think so," he said uncertainly. "I—I just can't get used to it. I keep thinking he's going to come back, even though I know he's not."

His grandfather glanced back toward the grave, then pulled his handkerchief from his jacket pocket and wiped at his eyes. "He should have come back a long time ago," he said in a voice that made Michael wonder if he was supposed to be listening or if the old man was talking to himself. "All of you should have. But now that you're home, we'll see that you stay here."

Then, once more, he moved toward the car, where Anna, brushing off Janet's attempts to help her, had swung herself out of her wheelchair and into the back seat of the Olds, then folded up the chair and pulled it in after her.

"See?" she asked Janet when she was done. "It's just a matter of deciding what you have to do, then doing it." A few moments later, when Janet had joined her in the back seat, and Amos, with Michael beside him, had pulled away from the little cemetery, she reached out and took Janet's hand. "That's what you're going to have to do now," she said. "Decide what to do, then do it. But don't you fret about it, dear—we're all here, and we'll all help."

Janet lay her head back against the seat, and closed her

For the Bitch and Moan Society

eyes, offering a small prayer of gratitude for the family Mark had left behind him. He may not have needed them, she thought, but I do. Dear God, how I need them . . .

Janet glanced at the clock in the corner of the living room and wondered how much longer it could go on. It was already four-thirty, and it was becoming harder and harder to fight off the exhaustion of the day. The room was hot and stuffy, and overfilled with people, and Janet was beginning to think the situation, for her, was hopeless. She could remember the names of Mark's sister, Laura, and her husband—Buck Shields—and their son, Ryan, who seemed to be about Michael's age, but that was all. And the introduction to them had been terribly awkward, for she hadn't even been able to utter a polite "I've heard so much about you." She'd hoped that when she saw Laura, she'd recognize her, that something about her would jog her memory, but it hadn't. What *had* struck her immediately, though, was the fact that Laura, like herself, was pregnant, but much further along. Though Janet had not commented on it, and was relieved that Laura had not seemed to guess, the coincidence had made her feel an immediate bond to the delicate-looking woman who was her sister-in-law. Nevertheless, Janet had finally come to the conclusion that in all their years together, Mark had never mentioned his sister to her.

Why?

Each time she saw Laura—an ethereal wisp of a woman whose eyes, even when she smiled, seemed oddly haunted— the question of why Mark had never spoken of her came into Janet's mind. Each time, she rejected it, shifting what was left of her concentration to someone else.

But there was only a sea of nameless faces, people whom she hoped were not offended by her inability to greet them with the same familiarity with which they greeted her:

"So you're Mark's Janet."

Mark's Janet.

Over and over again, the same two words. *"Mark's Janet."* At first it had upset her, the casual reference to herself as if she were nothing more than her husband's possession, but as the afternoon wore on she had grown used to it, discovering that the phrase wasn't truly offensive; indeed, there was a strangely comforting quality to it. It wasn't that she had been owned by Mark, it was simply that she was a part of him. To these people—so different from her New York friends—she and Mark had, upon their marriage, ceased to be individuals. Had these been her family instead of Mark's, had Mark been here instead of herself, the words would simply have been reversed.

This day, Janet was finding comfort in that lack of individuality. It meant that she did not have to put herself out to define herself to these people, did not have to expose herself to them or make them understand her. They already knew who she was.

"Are you all right?"

Startled, Janet looked up. She recognized the man as someone to whom she'd been introduced, but as with all the others, she could not put a name to the face.

"Potter. Dr. Charles Potter."

He was, she judged, in his late fifties—maybe his early sixties—and he looked exactly like what he was, a country GP. His hair was white, and his manner was what would once have been described as courtly. And, though she could hardly believe it, he was wearing an ice-cream suit.

"I beg your pardon?" Janet blurted.

"Are you all right?" Potter repeated. "You look a mite peaked."

"I'm fine," Janet assured him, and then realized that the room was much too warm, and she felt flushed. She tried to stand up, and discovered she couldn't. "Well, I guess I'm not all right after all," she said weakly. "How do I look?"

Potter grinned, losing a bit of what Janet was certain was a carefully cultivated image. "As I said, a mite peaked. Which, around here, covers most conditions not covered by 'right fit.' And you certainly don't look right fit.'' Then, as he continued speaking, his voice turned serious. ''Which isn't remarkable, under the circumstances. I said it at the funeral, and I said it earlier this afternoon, but I'll say it again. I'm sorry about Mark. He was a good man.''

Janet nodded automatically, suddenly aware of a strange dizziness and a surge of nausea. ''I wonder if maybe I ought to lie down,'' she suggested, and Potter was immediately on his feet, signaling to Amos Hall, who hurried over.

''I think we'd better get her upstairs,'' Potter said. ''It all seems to have been a bit too much for her.''

Suddenly everyone in the room seemed to be staring at her. ''No—please—I'll be all right, really I will,'' Janet protested, but Amos, still powerful despite his years, picked her up and carried her up the stairs, Dr. Potter following close behind.

In her room, Amos laid her gently on the bed, then smiled at her. ''Doc will have a look at you, and Mama and I'll get rid of the mob downstairs. They all should have left hours ago anyway, but you know how these things are. Doesn't matter that everyone sees everyone else every day of the year. You put them together for whatever reason, and they just keep on talkin'.'' Then he was gone, and Potter was sitting on the edge of the bed, taking her pulse. A moment later a thermometer was in her mouth, and Potter was asking her what seemed to be an unending series of questions about the state of her health. Finally he got to his feet, pulled a blanket over her, and instructed her to get some sleep.

Janet looked at him curiously. ''But I'm not sleepy,'' she protested. She paused, then: ''I just had a bad moment, because of the heat downstairs.''

Potter peered at her over the tops of his glasses, taking in her condition.

''Are you sure?'' he asked pointedly.

Janet sighed. Though she was barely starting to show,

the doctor seemed to have guessed the truth with one shrewd glance. Still, he seemed to be waiting for her to acknowledge it. When she only smiled wanly, he shrugged.

"It's probably the stress of the last few days," he said, adding, "On the other hand, it could be something else, a touch of the flu or some bug or other. I'll tell you what you do. You get some sleep, and tomorrow I want you to come to my office and we'll take a look. All right?"

Janet lowered herself gratefully into the pillows, as Potter closed the door behind him. She *was* tired, she *didn't* feel good, and if she at least feigned sleep, then she would be left alone. Otherwise—

She had a vision of all the women of Prairie Bend, each one just like all the others, parading through her room, clucking over her, fussing at her, offering her homemade soup.

But even that vision, like the phrase "Mark's Janet" a little earlier, was somehow comforting. Totally alien from her life in New York, but nonetheless comforting. Slowly, she let herself drift into sleep.

"When are you going home?" Ryan Shields asked his cousin. After some initial suspicious circling of each other, the two boys had formed an alliance as the day had gone on, and after Michael's mother had been taken upstairs, they had finally escaped from their grandmother's living room. Now Ryan, ignoring the fact that he was wearing his Sunday suit, sprawled on the patchy green beneath the immense elm tree that shaded the yard between the house and the barn. He stared curiously up at Michael. Even though Michael was a year younger than himself, and three inches shorter, Ryan wasn't at all sure he could take him in a fight. Indeed, an hour ago he'd given up even considering the possibilities, after Michael had rescued him from the clutches of his Grandmother Shields, who never failed to treat him as if he were still four years old.

From his perch on the rotting rope swing, Michael gave

an experimental kick that barely set the device in motion. "I don't know," he replied. "I guess in a few days."

Ryan frowned. "That's what my dad said you'd do. But I think my mom wishes you'd stay here."

Michael cocked his head. "Why would she want that?"

"Search me," Ryan replied. "All I know is that they got in a big fight about it on the way over here. Well, it started to be a fight, anyway." He paused and looked down, studying a blade of grass he'd plucked from the lawn as if it fascinated him. Not looking at Michael, he said, "Did your mom and dad fight?"

Michael shook his head. "Hunh-unh. At least not when I was around. Do your folks fight a lot?"

Ryan nodded. "Mostly about this place. Mom hates it here. Today, she said your dad was right to leave when he did."

Suddenly Michael brought the swing to a halt, and joined his cousin on the ground. "Did she ever say how come Dad left?"

"Hunh?"

Michael, in unconscious imitation of his cousin, plucked a blade of grass and stuck it between his teeth. "I always thought Dad just didn't want to be a farmer. But that seems kind of stupid. I mean, just because he wasn't a farmer isn't any reason not to come and visit, is it?"

"Nope," Ryan agreed. "My dad doesn't farm. What does that have to do with it?"

Michael rolled over and stared up into the elm tree, and for a long time the two boys were silent. When at last he spoke, Michael's voice trembled. "Did—did you ever think about your dad dying?"

Ryan shifted uncomfortably, then glanced away from Michael. "Sure. Doesn't everybody? Except—"

"Except what?" Michael asked.

"Well, I guess I only thought about it 'cause I knew it wasn't really gonna happen."

Suddenly Michael sat up, and his eyes fixed on his cousin. "I used to think about my dad dying when he went skydiving. That's like falling. Do you think me thinking about it could have made it happen?"

"That's crazy," Ryan replied. "You can't make something happen just by thinking about it. Besides, what happened to your dad was an accident, wasn't it?"

Michael nodded, but his eyes were uncertain.

"Then it wasn't your fault." Suddenly both boys sensed a presence nearby, and looked up to see their grandfather looming over them. They scrambled to their feet, self-consciously brushing the dust and grass from their clothes.

"That'll make your mothers real thrilled with you," Amos Hall commented. "What's going on out here?"

"We were just talking," Ryan told him.

"About what?"

The two boys glanced at each other. "Things," Michael replied.

"Things," Amos repeated. He fixed his eyes on Ryan. "You know what I was just saying to your grandma a couple of minutes ago? I was saying that I'll bet those two boys are sitting out there discussing 'things.' And do you know what she said?"

Ryan regarded his grandfather suspiciously, sure he was about to fall into a trap, but in the end his curiosity got the best of him. "What?" he asked.

Amos grinned at the boy. "Well, why don't you just go find her and ask her yourself? And while she tells you, you can help her with the dishes." Then, when Ryan had disappeared through the back door of the house, he lowered himself to the ground and gestured for Michael to sit down beside him. "Everybody's gone home," he said, "so you can go back in without having to worry about them all poking at you and telling you how cute you are, and how much you look like your father, or your mother, or your Uncle Harry, if you have one. It's all over." He paused, then: "Do you understand?"

Michael hesitated, then nodded unhappily. "The funeral's over."

Amos Hall's head bobbed once. "That's right. The

funeral's over, and now we all have to get on with life. Your mother's still in bed—''

''Is she all right?'' Michael broke in.

''She's probably just tired. It was hot as blazes in there, so we put her to bed. When you go inside I want you to be quiet so you don't wake her up. Go on in and change your clothes, and then come out to the barn. There's still a lot to be done, and we only have a couple of hours of light left.'' He stood up, then offered Michael a hand. For a moment, he thought the boy was going to refuse it, but then Michael slipped his small hand into Amos's much larger one, and pulled himself to his feet. Still, instead of heading for the house, Michael hesitated. Amos waited for him to speak, then prompted him.

''What is it, boy?'' he asked, his voice gruff, but not unkind.

Michael looked up at his grandfather, his eyes wide. ''What—what's going to happen now, Grandpa?''

Amos Hall slipped an arm around his grandson, and started walking him toward the house. ''Life goes on,'' he said, and then in a tone meant to be reassuring, ''We'll just take it one step at a time, all right?''

But Michael frowned. ''I guess so,'' he said at last. ''But I wish dad were here.''

''So do I,'' Amos Hall replied, but the gentleness had gone out of his voice. ''So do I.''

Janet awoke to the setting sun, and for the first time since she had been married, did not reach out to touch her husband. The funeral, then, had accomplished that much. Never again, she was sure, would she awaken and reach out for Mark. He was truly gone, and she was truly on her own now.

She sat up and began tentatively to get out of bed. The nausea was gone, and the flushed feeling with it, so she put her feet into a pair of slippers and went into the bathroom, where she splashed her face with cold water. Then she went back to her bedroom, took off the clothes she had been sleeping in, and put on a robe. At the top of the stairs, she listened for a moment.

There was a murmuring of voices from the kitchen but only silence from the living room. Running a hand through her hair, she started down the stairs.

The family was gathered around the kitchen table, and as she came upon them she stopped, startled. It was as if they belonged together, the elderly couple at either end of the table, and Michael, so obviously *theirs,* between them. It must, Janet realized, have been what the family looked like twenty years ago, except that instead of Michael between them, it would have been Mark. And Laura.

Almost abstractly, she noted that there was no place set for her at the table.

Michael saw her first.

"Mom! Are you okay?"

"I'm fine. I was just tired, and it was so hot—well, I'm afraid your old mother had what they call a fainting spell."

"Are you sure you should be up, dear?" Anna Hall asked, her voice anxious. "Why don't you go back up, and I'll fix a plate for you. It's just leftovers from the reception, but we're making do with it. Or I could fix you some soup. There's nothing like good homemade—"

"I'm fine, Anna," Janet insisted. "If I could just sit down, I'll—"

"Get your mother a chair, Michael."

As his grandfather spoke, Michael got up from the table, ducked around his mother, and disappeared into the dining room. A moment later he was back, bearing one of Anna's needlepoint-seated lyre-back "Sunday" chairs.

"Now why can't I ever get action like that at home?" Janet asked as she settled herself at the table. "It would have taken me ages just to get his attention, and then there would have been a chorus of 'Aw, Moms,'—"

"Aw, Mom . . ."

"See what I mean?"

Amos glared at her. "Children do what's expected of

them,'' he stated, his tone indicating that there was no
room for discussion.

''Or perhaps it's just novelty,'' Anna hesitantly suggested.
Amos turned, about to speak, but she ignored him, wheel-
ing her chair away from the table. A moment later she
handed Michael some silverware and nodded toward Janet.
''Set your mother a place.'' She shifted her attention back
to Janet. ''It's a known fact that children behave better in
other people's houses than they do in their own. As for
expectations,'' she added, turning to her husband, ''what
about Mark? We expected Mark to stay in Prairie Bend
forever, and you certainly made that expectation clear to
him. So much for *that* theory.''

An odd look came into Amos's eyes, one that could
have been either hurt or anger. In the tense silence that
followed, Janet reached out to squeeze the old man's hand.
''I hadn't known Mark was supposed to come home after
college,'' she said. ''What would a sociologist have done
here?''

Though she'd directed the question at her father-in-law,
it was Anna who answered.

''At first, after he . . . left,'' she said in a near whisper,
choosing her words cautiously, ''we didn't even know
he'd gone to college. We didn't know where he'd gone.
All we knew was that he wasn't here. But we thought he'd
come back.'' She shrugged helplessly, avoiding Amos's
silent stare. ''By then, we just didn't know him anymore.
And you don't need a degree to run a farm. I guess he was
never interested in farming. Not this farm, and not his own
farm, either.''

Janet's fork stopped halfway between her plate and her
mouth, and she stared at Anna. ''*His* farm? What are you
talking about? Mark never had a farm.''

''Of course he had a farm,'' Anna replied, her expression clearly indicating her conviction that Janet must be
suffering a momentary lapse of memory. Then, as Janet's
demeanor failed to clear, her eyes shifted to her husband,

then back to Janet. "You don't mean to tell me he never told you about the farm, do you?"

Janet, feeling a sudden panic, turned to Michael for support. Was the same thing that had happened when she'd heard about Mark's sister about to happen again? "Did daddy ever say anything to you about a farm? About owning a farm, I mean?"

Michael shook his head.

"But that's not possible," Amos interjected. "You must have known. The taxes, the estate—"

"The estate?" Janet asked. What on earth was he talking about? Slowly she put down her fork, then looked from Amos to Anna. At last her eyes came to rest on Michael. "I think perhaps it's time you went up to your room."

"Aw, Mom . . ."

"Do as your mother says," Amos snapped, and after a moment of hesitation, Michael got up and left the table. Only when his footsteps had stopped echoing in the stairwell did Janet speak again. When she did, her voice was quavering.

"Now what is all this about?" she asked. "I thought you meant that Mark owned a farm a long time ago, before I met him. But when you mentioned taxes, and the estate—"

"He's always owned a farm," Amos said. "It was a wedding present, just as half of Laura and Buck's farm was a wedding present to them. Buck's parents gave them the other half. They don't live on it, but they still own it and take the responsibility for it. And if Mark had married a local girl—"

But Janet had stopped listening. "A wedding present," she whispered. "But you sent us silverware—"

"Well, of course there was that, too," Anna replied.

"But that was *all* there was," Janet insisted, her voice growing shrill in spite of herself. "If there'd been anything else, Mark would have told me. Wouldn't he? *Wouldn't he?*"

Amos reached out and took her hand. "You really don't know anything about it, do you?"

Mutely, Janet shook her head.

"It's forty acres," Amos said. "It was deeded to Mark on your wedding day, and he's owned it ever since. I know, because I was afraid he might try to sell it, so I've kept track. I always hoped he'd come and live on it someday, but I guess I always knew that wouldn't happen. Not ever, not the way he felt. But he did pay the taxes on it. As far as I know, he never tried to sell it."

"But what's happened to it?" Janet asked. "And why haven't I ever heard of it before?"

"I don't know why you've never heard of it," Amos replied. "But it's still there. It's yours now."

For a long moment, Janet stared at her husband's parents, her mind churning. When at last she spoke, it was without thinking.

"He hated you very much, didn't he? All of you."

Amos Hall's eyes flashed with anger, but Anna only stared ahead, looking into space.

"Yes, I suppose he did," Amos finally said, the anger in his eyes disappearing as quickly as it had come. "But he's dead, now. All that's behind us, isn't it?"

CHAPTER 3

Though she went to bed early that night, Janet Hall did not go to sleep. She sat up, staring out over the moonlit prairie, her robe drawn tightly around her as if it could protect her from her own thoughts. For a while she tried to concentrate on the stars, laboriously picking out constellations she hadn't seen so clearly since her childhood, but then, as the night wore on, her thoughts bore in on her.

It wasn't just his sister Mark had never mentioned.

There was a farm, too.

All along, there had been a farm.

Painfully, she made herself remember all the talks they'd had, she and Mark, all the nights—nights like this—when they'd sat up talking about the future.

For Janet, the future had always held a farm.

Nothing concrete, nothing real. For Janet, the farm of her dream was something from a child's picture book—a small place, somewhere in New England, with a white-washed clapboard house, a bright red barn with white trim, an immaculate barnyard populated with hens and tiny fuzzy chicks, the whole thing neatly fenced off with white post-and-rail. There would be stone walls, of course, old stone walls meandering through the pastures, but the borders, the limits of her world, would be edged in white. And there they would live, their small family, released at last from the congestion of the city, their senses no longer dunned by the smells of garbage and exhaust, the sounds of jackhammers and blasting horns, but expanding to the aroma of fresh-mown hay and the crowing of roosters at dawn.

All idyllic, all a dream, and all of it, always, gently derided by Mark. All the reasons why it was impossible, all the excuses that they continually debated: They were city people, though they both had been born in the country, and New Yorkers by choice, Mark would insist; choices could still be made, Janet would counter. Mark was a teacher, not a farmer; there were colleges in New England, everywhere you looked—he could still teach, and they could hire someone to run the farm. Michael was happy in his school, Mark would point out; children change schools all the time, and there's no proof, Janet would argue, that city schools are better than small-town schools.

In the end, however, it had always come down to the one argument for which Janet had no answer.

They couldn't afford a farm, couldn't manage to save enough even for a half-acre in the suburbs, let alone a farm.

Now, Janet realized that it had all been a lie. From the day they were married, the lie had been between them, and she had never felt it, never faintly suspected it. There had even been times when Mark had seemed to join in her dream.

They had been in Millbrook, and they had come around a curve in the road, and there, spread out before them, was Janet's dream. It had been Mark who had noticed it first; Janet had been studying a map, trying to match the route numbers to the street names that seemed to be posted only every five miles and then changed with every village they passed through. Suddenly Mark had stopped the car and said, "Well, there it is, and even I have to admit that it's pretty." She'd looked up, and across a pasture that sloped gently away from the highway, she had seen her farm— white clapboard house, red barn, white post-and-rail fence, even a stream, dammed to form a millpond. And it was for sale.

They'd talked about it all weekend, even going so far as to investigate the possibility of Mark's finding a job in Poughkeepsie. But in the end, on Sunday night as they drove south on the Taconic Parkway, they'd faced reality.

They had no money, and they couldn't buy the farm without money.

But it had been a lie. And Mark had known it was a lie.

What else was there? How much had this stranger with whom she had spent thirteen years of her life kept hidden from her? What else would she find as the days went by and she learned more about the man she had married?

Anna. Had Mark known his mother was confined to a wheelchair? It seemed impossible that he hadn't, and yet it seemed equally impossible that he had never said anything to her about it. But he hadn't.

When Janet had asked her mother-in-law about it just before coming upstairs that night, Anna had only shrugged, a look of philosophical resignation in her eyes. "I suppose he must have known," she'd said. "It happened after he went away, but I think Laura must have told him about it."

"But he never heard from Laura," Janet had protested. "He never even *talked* about her. Until yesterday, I didn't even know Mark had a sister."

Anna's eyes had flickered with pain for a moment. "You have to understand," she'd finally said. "There were some things Mark just wanted to shut out of his mind. He always did that, even when he was little. I remember he had a puppy once—a little black shepherd— but it got sick, and Amos had to put it down. Afterward, I tried to talk to Mark about it, but he wouldn't admit the puppy'd ever even existed. Just shut it out completely." She sighed, weariness spreading across her features. "I suppose that's what he did when he left Prairie Bend. Shut us out, just like that dog."

"But why? Why did he leave?"

And for that, there had been no answer. "It doesn't matter anymore," was all Anna would say. "It's all in the past. There's no use dredging it up now. It would only cause pain." She'd looked beseechingly at Janet. "I've had enough pain, dear. Can't we leave this alone?" Then she'd held out her arms, and Janet, her throat constricting with feeling, had leaned down, clumsily embracing this fragile woman she hardly knew.

As she sat in the darkness that night, trying to concentrate on the stars, Janet felt the props of her life slipping away from her, felt the rock of trust she'd always had in Mark dissolving into sand. Already, it was slipping through her fingers, leaving her with nothing to cling to.

By the time the horizon edged silvery-gray with dawn and she drifted into an uneasy sleep, Janet's grief over the death of her husband had begun to change into something else. An odd fear had begun to pervade her, a fear of what else she might discover about Mark, what other secrets might have lain hidden from her during all the years of her marriage.

When she awoke several hours later, she could feel a difference in herself. It was as if uncertainty had gathered around her, crippling her. She lay still for a long time, unable to make up her mind to get up, unsure whether she could face the day.

She closed her eyes for a few moments, and suddenly she saw an image of Mark's face, but his features were slightly blurred, and there was something in his eyes—a secretiveness—that she'd never seen before. And then the image changed, hardened and sharpened into the visage of Amos.

His eyes were clear, his features strong. And he was smiling at her, offering her the strength she could no longer get from Mark or find within herself.

She rose from her bed and went to the window. Below her, in the barnyard, she watched Michael feeding the chickens. A moment later Amos emerged from the barn, and as if feeling her gaze, looked up; she waved to him; he waved back to her.

And then the nausea hit her. Turning away from the window, she hurried to the bathroom, threw up in the toilet, and waited for the sickness to pass.

What's going to happen to us? she wondered a few minutes later as she began dressing. *What's going to happen to us now?*

Ryan Shields pedaled furiously through the village, then east on the highway toward his grandparents' farm. He didn't slow down until he'd made the turn into the driveway, but by the time he got to the front yard, he was coasting, his feet dragging in the dust as makeshift brakes. He came to a dead stop, expertly dropped the kickstand with one toe, then balanced on the leaning bike, his arms crossed, only his slouching posture preventing the bike from tipping over. It was a technique he'd learned only a month ago, and it had quickly become his favorite pose. He cocked his head, squinting in the brightness of the sun, peering at the house. "Hey! Anybody home?"

A moment later the front door opened, and Michael came out on the porch. "Hi."

"Hi. Whatcha doin'?"

"Nothing. Everybody's gone into town to Dr. Potter's."

Ryan swung his leg over the handlebar, and stepped off the bike, which promptly fell over into the dust of the driveway. "Shit." He picked up the bike, carefully balanced it on the kickstand, then mounted the steps to the porch. "Is your mom still sick?"

Michael shrugged. "I don't know. I guess not. Anyway, it didn't seem like it this morning, and she was okay last night." Then he frowned. "How come you're not in school?"

"School's out."

"At home, we don't get out for another three weeks."

"We always get out early here. Most of the kids have to help their dads with planting. Can I come in?"

Michael's expression became guarded. "There's nobody home."

"You're home."

"But I'm not supposed to let anybody in the house when I'm by myself."

Ryan stared at him in disbelief. "Why not?"

" 'Cause you never know who might come to the door. There's all kinds of crazies in the city. What can you do?"

"Well, I'm not crazy, and this is my grandparents' house, and I can come in if I want to." Then, seeing Michael suddenly tense, he grinned. "Stop worrying. Grandma and Grandpa won't care, and it's their house, not yours. I come out here all the time." He brushed past Michael and went inside, then called back over his shoulder, "You want a Coke?"

Michael hesitated a moment, then decided that Ryan was right. This wasn't New York, and Ryan was his cousin. "There aren't any," he said, following Ryan inside and letting the screen door slam behind him. "I already looked."

"Where'd you look?"

"In the 'fridge."

"Grandma keeps them in the laundry room. Come on."

A moment later, each of them armed with a warm Coke, they wandered out into the backyard. "Hey, have you been down to the river yet?"

Michael shook his head. "I haven't been anywhere."

"Well, come on," Ryan told him. "The river's the best part of Prairie Bend." With Michael following him, Ryan headed around behind the barn, then across the pasture toward the strip of cottonwoods that bordered the river. Five minutes later, the two of them stepped out of the sunshine into the deep shade of the trees. In contrast to the openness of the prairie, the woods were choked with underbrush. The canopied branches overhead created a closed-in feeling that made Michael shiver.

"Where's the river?" he asked.

"Down the trail. Come on."

A couple of minutes later the path made a sharp right, then opened out onto the river. Here the bank was low, and Ryan scrambled down onto the beach that separated the woods from the water. "You should have seen it last month. It was full, and the whole beach was covered. Right here, the water must have been six feet deep."

"How deep is it now?" Michael asked. They'd crossed the beach and stood at the water's edge. The river was moving lazily, the current only rippling the surface near the far bank, but it was murky, its waters stained by the silt it carried.

"Only a couple feet on this side. You could wade almost all the way across, but it gets deep over by the other bank."

"Can we go swimming?" Michael asked.

Ryan looked doubtful. "I don't know. It's still kind of early, and the water's pretty cold."

"Aw, come on," Michael urged. "You said it was shallow."

But Ryan still hesitated. "Nobody ever goes in this early. It's too dangerous. You can't see where the holes are, and the current can grab you."

Michael stared out at the river. "You chicken?" he finally asked.

That did it. Ryan scowled at his cousin. "There's a swimming hole down near the bend. Come on."

They started downstream and in a few minutes came to the point where the river began the first of the curves that would take it around the village. Here, the spring floods had eroded the bank, creating an inlet where the water seemed almost still. A huge cottonwood stood by the inlet, its roots half exposed, one enormous limb reaching out over the water. From that branch, a rope hung, an old tire tied to its free end. Michael knew immediately what it was for.

"How do you get to it?"

"You have to climb the tree, then go down the rope,"

Ryan explained. "Once you're on it, you get it swinging, then dive off it."

"You wanna go first?"

Ryan stared at him. "Are you crazy? Nobody's been in swimming yet. There could be rocks in there, and it's cold, and you don't know how deep it is. None of the kids go off the tire until someone's been down there to make sure it's safe."

"What could happen?" Michael asked.

"You could break your neck, that's what," Ryan replied.

"Bullshit."

"Bullshit, nothin'! It's happened."

"Well, it won't happen to me," Michael said. He set his half-drunk Coke down and started stripping off his clothes. A moment later, naked, he scrambled up the cottonwood and began making his way out onto the limb that overhung the swimming hole. From the shore, Ryan watched him anxiously.

"Don't start down the rope 'till you check it out. It might be rotten."

Michael nodded. A few seconds later he came to the rope, and straddling the branch, grasped the loop with both hands. He gave it an experimental tug and, when it held, began pulling harder. Satisfied that it wouldn't break, he reached down and took hold of the hanging section. Finally he rolled off the trunk, and began letting himself down the rope until his feet touched the tire. When he was standing on the tire, he grinned at Ryan, then began slowly pumping to get the tire swinging.

"You're supposed to sit on the tire," Ryan yelled.

Michael ignored him. The makeshift swing began to move, with Michael maneuvering it so that soon it was arcing back and forth, over the bank on the backswing, and out over the center of the swimming hole on the forward swing. When he had it going as high as he could, he crouched on top of the tire, waited for the crest of the forward swing, then released his grasp on the rope and sprang away from the tire, flipping himself into a back dive. Just before he hit the water he took a deep breath, and listened with satisfaction to the scream that had burst out of Ryan. Then he plunged into the icy water.

From the shore, Ryan stared at the spot where Michael had disappeared into the murk, unconsciously holding his breath and counting the seconds. Time seemed to stand still as he waited for his cousin's head to reappear.

Ten seconds went by, then fifteen.

Twenty seconds.

Thirty.

His breath bursting out of his lungs, Ryan began to panic. Should he jump in after Michael, or run for help? But run where? No one was home at his grandparents', and the village was too far away.

"Help! Somebody help us!"

And then, just as he was about to jump into the dark water, the surface broke, and Michael's grinning face appeared. With three strong strokes, he made it to the shore and scrambled out.

"It's neat!" he cried. "You want to try it?"

Ryan ignored the question. "What the hell are you doing? I thought you'd hit a rock!"

"I coulda stayed under for a whole minute," Michael said, flopping down on the ground. He was barely even panting, and his eyes were sparkling. "Did I scare you?"

Ryan glared down at his cousin and again ignored the question. "You coulda gotten killed."

"I scared you, didn't I?"

Ryan finally nodded his head. "So what?"

"Betcha thought I wouldn't do it."

Ryan shrugged elaborately. "So you did it. What's that prove, except that you're stupid?"

"It wasn't stupid—it was fun. Go on—try it!"

But instead of peeling off his clothes, Ryan only sat down and reached for his Coke. "I'm not gonna try it, and if you want to think I'm chicken, go ahead. There's rocks down there. You were just lucky you didn't hit one."

Michael took a sip of his Coke and thought about it. He'd

known there were rocks beneath the surface—at least, Ryan had told him so, and he hadn't thought Ryan was lying. And yet, while he'd been swinging on the rope, he hadn't felt frightened. He'd felt excited, and knowing he was taking a risk was part of the excitement. But he hadn't really thought about getting hurt. Or had he? He tried to remember, but couldn't. All he could remember was the thrill of swinging out over the river, then letting go and plunging toward the cold water, not knowing exactly what was under the surface.

Suddenly a vision of his father came into his mind, plunging through the air, then slowing as his chute opened. Always, the chute had opened. But what if it hadn't?

Was that what his father had loved about skydiving? The risk? Knowing that each time he tried it, the parachute might not open? And yet, even as he'd dived, Michael had known nothing was going to happen to him. He'd *known* it. But how?

He began pulling his clothes back on, and a few minutes later the two boys started back toward their grandparents' house. It wasn't until they'd emerged from the woods and started across the pasture, though, that Michael finally spoke.

"I wasn't going to hurt myself."

Ryan glanced at him, but kept walking. "How do you know?"

Michael shrugged. "I just know."

Now Ryan came to a halt and stared at Michael. "What are you, some kind of nut?"

"N-no," Michael stammered. "But when I dove, I knew I was going to be all right. I just knew it." Unconsciously, his hand went up and rubbed the back of his neck, and Ryan suddenly grinned.

"If you didn't get hurt, how come you're rubbing your neck?"

Michael dropped his hand to his side. "It's not my neck. I just have a headache, that's all."

"Yeah," Ryan agreed, his voice mocking now. "Just a

headache. You *did* hit a rock, didn't you. Lemme see your head."

Bending, Michael let his cousin examine the back of his head. "Is there a cut?" he asked, his voice half curious, half challenging.

"Unh-unh. Is it sore?"

"Not like I hit it. It's just a headache." Suddenly he frowned, wrinkling his nose. There was a strange odor, as if something was burning. "What's that stink?"

"Stink? What stink?" Ryan sniffed at the air, then shook his head. "I don't smell anything."

"It's like something's on fire." He scanned the horizon, sure he would see a plume of smoke nearby, but there was nothing. He turned back to Ryan. "Don't you smell it?"

Ryan scowled. "I don't smell anything, 'cause there's nothing to smell. What are you, some kind of nut?" he said again.

A flash of pain shot through Michael's head. "Don't you call me crazy," he flared.

Ryan's expression darkened. "I'll call you whatever I want to! What are you gonna do about it?"

Michael stood still, sudden fury toward his cousin mounting inside him as his head throbbed with pain. "Drop dead," he heard himself whisper. "Why don't you just drop dead?"

Ryan's eyes began to dance, and the beginnings of a grin spread over his face. But then, as Michael glared at him, the grin faded, and the color drained from Ryan's face as his hands clutched at his stomach. He began backing away from Michael, then turned and began running across the field.

A moment later Michael was alone, and his headache began to ease. As he started walking back toward his grandparents' house, he tried to figure out what had happened. But no matter how hard he thought about it, it still didn't make sense. All he'd done had been to tell his cousin to drop dead. Everybody did that, and everybody knew it was only words. And yet, for a few seconds, it had almost looked like Ryan really *was* going to drop dead.

But they were only words, and they weren't even his words. They'd just sort of tumbled out of his mouth, almost as if someone else had spoken them.

But there was no one else. . . .

Janet emerged from Dr. Potter's small consultation room into the parlor that served as reception area during the day and Potter's living room at night. Amos Hall rose from his position on the Victorian sofa that stood in the bay window, but Anna remained still in her chair, her hands folded in her lap, her posture expressing a calmness that her anxious eyes belied. "Well?" she asked.

Janet's mouth curved into an uncertain smile. Now or never. She had to tell them, and through a sleepless night she had decided that the examination would provide the perfect moment. "Well, I'm pregnant," she said.

A sigh emerged from the older woman, and she slumped in her chair. "So," she said at last, her eyes shifting away from Janet to glance warily at her husband. "I suppose that's some kind of blessing, isn't it?" she said.

"I don't know," Janet replied, too involved in her own emotions to notice her mother-in-law's reaction to the news. "I'm afraid I'm going to have to do some thinking about it."

"Thinking?" Amos Hall strode across the room and took Janet's coat from a hook, holding it for her as she slid her arms into its sleeves. "What's there to think about?"

Janet swallowed, wondering if she should tell them that her first thought on having the pregnancy confirmed was that she should have an abortion as soon as possible. She had known she was pregnant for several weeks and had kept her suspicions to herself, hesitating even to tell Mark. There had been no real notion in her mind then that she would not have the baby—she loved Mark too much to deny him a second child, despite the upheavals it might cause in their lives. After all, Michael was already nearly twelve—almost a teenager—and their small family was settled, comfortable. But now Mark was dead. Everything had changed.

"I'm not at all sure I should have it," she said in a carefully neutral voice. "I'm not as young as I could be—"

"Not have it?" Anna cried. "Not have Mark's baby? Oh, Janet, you can't be serious. Why, that would be— well, to start with, it would be murder!"

"Now, Mama, don't get yourself worked up," Amos Hall cautioned his wife, though his eyes never left Janet. "Things have changed. Not everyone thinks the way you and I do anymore."

"If the baby's healthy, it has a right to live," Anna declared, her eyes flashing with anger. Then, softening a little, she turned to Janet. "I'm not an old-fashioned woman, dear, whatever Amos says. I can certainly see that there might be circumstances where it could be better for a baby not to be born." She eyed Janet's midsection critically, its slight swelling apparent to her now. "Besides, it's too late, isn't it?"

"Almost," Janet conceded. "But what about my feelings? Don't my feelings count?" she added, then wished she hadn't.

"Your feelings?" Anna asked. "What do you mean? Do you mean you don't *want* the baby?"

Janet shook her head. "That's not it at all, Anna. It just seems like—" She stopped short, suddenly realizing she didn't have the slightest idea of how she felt about anything. All she felt was confused. If only she could talk to Mark. . . . But she couldn't, not ever again. And, she remembered with a shudder, the Mark she had thought she'd known was a different man from the one she was discovering since she'd arrived in Prairie Bend. She appealed to Amos. "Would you mind if I walked home?" she asked. "I really think I need to walk a bit. I need to get used to things. There's so much to sort out."

Amos frowned. "Are you sure? I'm not sure how much exercise—"

Janet put up a protesting hand, and made herself smile with a confidence she wasn't feeling. "Times have changed, Amos. And I really do need to be by myself, just for a little while." Without waiting for a response, she opened the door and stepped out of Dr. Potter's office into the bright noontime sun. She glanced around, orienting herself, and then set out for the center of the village.

Prairie Bend, she realized, was truly no more than a village, and it seemed, as she walked the single block from Potter's house to the main street, oddly familiar. It wasn't until she'd walked a bit further, though, that she realized just what it was about the town that she recognized. It was like the country village of her dreams, the picturesque town she'd imagined whenever she'd envisioned the peaceful little farm that would someday be hers.

Prairie Bend was more than a century old, but it appeared that it had reached its full size shortly after it had been founded.

It had been carefully planned in the shape of a half wheel, with four spokelike streets radiating out from the square at the hub, and three more streets, each of them paralleling the curve of the river, sweeping around those spokes. The lots had been carefully laid out, with obvious foresight, but then, apparently, the planned-for population had never materialized, for most of the lots were still empty, though none of them was uncared for, and the wide green lawns, bordered by trees and occasional gardens, created a parklike, spacious feeling.

Nowhere was there a building that looked new, yet nowhere was there a building that was in disrepair. The village was small: a general store, the post office, a drugstore which did double duty as the only café in town, two gas stations—one of which had a garage—a tiny school, and the church. All of it neatly arranged around the little square, all of it shaded by immense old trees, and all of it cradled in the bend of the river.

Janet paused in the square and tried to reconcile what she was seeing with what Mark had told her about Prairie Bend. But slowly, she began to realize that he had never said much about it at all—only that he hoped never to see it again.

But why?

There was nothing threatening about it, nothing out of the ordinary, really, except for its loveliness.

Then what was it that Mark had hated so much?

And why had Prairie Bend never grown?

Why had a place so lovely stayed so small?

She didn't know, and she probably never would know.

Unless she stayed.

It was the first time she'd let herself fully face the idea that had been niggling at her mind all morning, but now, in the quiet and peace of the spring noontime, she began examining the idea, making a mental ledger of its advantages and disadvantages.

She had family, albeit in-laws, in Prairie Bend; none in New York.

She had little money in either place, and nothing much in the way of professional skills.

She would be able to keep her apartment in New York for the moment, but only for the moment. Eventually, she would have to find a cheaper place to live.

In Prairie Bend, she owned a farm.

Mark had hated Prairie Bend, but had never told her why. Perhaps there had been no reason, or at least no good reason.

She thought about her in-laws. Good people, kind people, who wanted to take care of her. But why? Who was she but the widow of the son who had rejected them? Why should they care about her?

Yet, even as she asked herself the question, she was sure she knew the answer. They cared about her because they were warm and loving people who didn't hold their son's actions against her or her child. No—they wanted her, and they wanted Michael. And for a while, at least, she wanted to rest in the refuge of Prairie Bend and the love of Mark's parents.

As she left the square and passed through the rest of the village, then started out toward the Halls', she knew her mind was made up.

Forty minutes later she walked into Anna Hall's kitchen and sat down at the table. Her mother-in-law glanced disapprovingly up from the cake batter she was stirring, then away.

"Did you get your thinking done?" she asked in a voice that implied a sure knowledge of the outcome of that thinking.

"Yes, I did," Janet said quietly. "I'm going to keep my baby, and I'm going to keep my farm. Michael and I are going to live here."

Anna Hall put down the spoon, then held her arms out to Janet, who slipped willingly into her embrace.

"If that's what you want," Anna whispered. "If you're sure that's what you want, then you're welcome here. More than welcome. But I warn you," she suddenly added. "Once you become a part of Prairie Bend, you'll never be able to leave."

A shiver passed through Janet, but a moment later she had forgotten it.

CHAPTER 4

"We're not going home at all?" Michael's voice clearly reflected his bewilderment. "But why?"

He was sitting with his mother in Anna Hall's rarely used living room, and while Janet perched nervously on the edge of a sofa, Michael himself rocked furiously on a bentwood chair.

"Lots of reasons, darling," Janet replied, forcing herself to meet Michael's angry eyes. "For one thing, we have a home here—a place to live that's all our own. Wouldn't you rather live in a house than an apartment?"

"I don't know," Michael answered, too promptly. "Dad never wanted to live on a farm. I bet if Dad were here, we'd be back home."

"I know," Janet sighed. "If your father were here, everything would be the way it always was, but he isn't here, and everything has changed. I know it's hard, and it's going to get harder, honey. Now it's up to me to figure out what's best for us, and I think it's best that we stay here."

"But *why?*"

"For one thing, we don't have much money, and living in New York is very expensive."

"Why don't you get a job?" Michael asked with the serene innocence of his years.

"I might be able to," Janet agreed. "But it wouldn't be much of a job. And what would you do? I can't leave you by yourself every day, and we'd never be able to afford someone to come in."

"I can take care of myself," Michael replied. "I'm not a baby anymore."

Janet smiled at her son. "Of course you aren't. And if we weren't living in New York, I wouldn't worry at all. But in the city I'd worry about you all day, every day. Besides, right now, I don't think I could get any kind of a job at all."

Michael stared at her, and suddenly stopped rocking. "Why not?" he asked, the sullenness in his eyes fading slightly.

"Well," Janet said, "it seems our family is going to get a little larger."

There was a silence, and then Michael realized what she was saying. "You mean you're going to have a baby?"

Janet nodded. "So you see, I'd have to leave whatever job I got in a few months. And most people wouldn't hire me to begin with, right now."

"Why tell them?" Michael asked. "You don't look pregnant."

"I don't lie," Janet spoke quietly. "And I don't ever again want to hear you suggest such a thing. Is that clear?"

Michael squirmed and his eyes shifted away from hers. "I didn't mean you should lie . . ." he began, but Janet didn't let him finish.

"Not telling the truth is lying, Michael. It doesn't matter if someone doesn't ask you a question. If you know something that's important to a situation and don't say anything about it, that's lying. And you know it, so let's end it right there." She paused for a moment, and settled herself back into the sofa. "The point of all this is that I can't get anything more than temporary work right now, and won't be able to for at least a year, maybe more. And we can't live in New York without me working. Can you understand that?''

There was a long silence, and then Michael nodded. ''I guess so.'' Then, a moment later: ''But what about all my friends?''

''You'll make friends here,'' Janet assured him.

Michael left the rocking chair, and went to gaze out the window. ''What if I don't?'' he asked, and in his voice Janet heard all the doubts that she herself had not yet been able to put aside.

''But you *will*,'' she insisted, and immediately wondered if her reassuring words were for her son or for herself.

For a long time, Michael stared silently out the window, and then abruptly turned to face her with the question she had least expected. ''Why didn't Daddy ever tell us we had a farm?''

Janet searched for an answer, but found none. None, at any rate, that wouldn't tarnish Michael's memory of his father, and she wasn't willing to do that. ''There was no reason to, really,'' she said at last. ''Daddy wasn't a farmer, and never wanted to be. And there aren't any universities around here where he could have taught.'' She brightened, as an idea came to her. ''Perhaps it was his idea of insurance, in case anything ever happened to him. Something to leave us. Not only a home, but a family, too. What if he'd told me?'' she improvised. ''I'd have talked him into selling it, and buying something closer to New York, and now, instead of having something we own, we'd have a mortgage to pay, and no family around to help us. Maybe Daddy was smart never to tell us about the farm.''

If only, she thought to herself, I could believe that. But I don't. Not a word of it.

Michael, however, seemed to accept her words at face value. ''Where is it?'' he asked.

Janet stared at her son, then burst into laughter for the

first time since Mark had died. Michael looked at her oddly, then glanced uneasily away. "What's so funny?"

"You know what?" Janet gasped. "I don't even *know* where it is! Here I've made up my mind to move us onto a farm, and I never even asked where it was, let alone what it looked like. Let's get your grandparents and go see it."

But the Halls refused to take them.

"Tomorrow," Anna insisted. "We'll show it to you tomorrow."

"But why not today?" Janet asked.

Amos grinned at her. "If you saw it today, you'd never move in. By tomorrow, it'll be cleaned up and at least habitable."

"But I don't care if it's a mess," Janet protested. "You don't have to hire someone to clean it up. Michael and I can do that."

"Hire someone?" Anna asked. "Why would we do that?" Then suddenly she understood what Janet meant. "This isn't like New York," she said. "Out here, everybody knows everybody else and helps them out. It's just like having one huge family. We'll take care of you. That's what we're for."

Janet's eyes flooded with tears, and she leaned down to hug the elderly woman. "Thank you," she whispered. "You've no idea what all this means to me. Ever since Mark died, I've been so . . . so frightened."

Anna gently patted her back. "I know, dear. I know just how you feel. But everything's going to be fine. Just fine," she said, as her eyes met Amos's beyond Janet's shoulder.

"Do you know Mr. Findley?"

The sun was high, and Michael and Ryan, yesterday's fight forgotten, had taken shelter from the heat under the enormous cottonwood in the Shieldses' front yard. Ryan, to Michael's disappointment, hadn't been at all surprised by Michael's news. In fact, when he'd told his cousin that he and his mother had decided to stay in Prairie Bend,

Ryan had only grinned and said that if he thought that was news, he was wrong—there probably wasn't anyone in Prairie Bend who *didn't* know they were staying. Now, however, he looked at Michael curiously.

"He's crazy," he said at last. "How'd you hear about him?"

Michael ignored the question. "Who is he?"

"He's an old guy who lives all by himself. Everybody says he's crazy and ought to be locked up, but nobody ever does anything about it."

"Crazy how?"

"Just crazy. You know. He talks to himself all the time, and never lets anybody near the place, except Dr. Potter. I heard the only reason Dr. Potter ever goes out there is to see if old man Findley's still alive or not."

"Do the kids ever go out there?"

"What for?"

"Just to see what's going on."

Ryan glanced at his cousin with suspicion. "Nothin's going on. And if you go out there, he shoots at you."

"Bullshit," Michael challenged.

"Bullshit, nothin'. Eric Simpson lives out that way, and he *saw* old man Findley shoot at someone."

"Then how come they didn't arrest him?" Michael demanded.

Ryan frowned. "I don't know," he reluctantly admitted.

" 'Cause he didn't do anything, that's why," Michael told him with a certainty he didn't really feel. "I bet he was just shooting at an animal or something. If he'd done anything, they would have arrested him."

"That's not what Eric says, and he saw it."

"What did he see?"

"Why don't you ask him?"

"I don't know him."

"Well, let's go out there," Ryan suggested. "Then you'll know him."

Ten minutes later they were riding out of Prairie Bend and east along the river road, Michael on an old Schwinn that Ryan had dragged up from the Shieldses' basement. He was straining to match his cousin's ease with the machine, but it wasn't easy. Unlike Ryan, Michael had not grown up on a bike, and the one time he had risked Ryan's no-hands technique, he had nearly lost control.

"Whatcha going to do about school?" Ryan suddenly asked, braking his bike so he fell back alongside Michael.

"What do you mean?"

"Aren't you going back?"

Michael shrugged. "I guess not."

"Then what grade will you be in next year? Will they pass you?"

"Why wouldn't they?"

"Don't you have to take tests?"

"Our school doesn't have tests," Michael replied. "It's an experimental school."

Ryan's look was one of disbelief. "No tests? How do they know who to pass?"

"Everybody passes." Suddenly, Michael slowed the bike and called out to Ryan, "Is that Findley's place?" He pointed off to the right, where an old farmhouse, its paint peeling and its porch sagging slightly, huddled in a grove of scraggly elms at the end of a rutted driveway. A barn loomed twenty yards from the house, and between the two buildings some chickens scratched at the dusty surface of the unkempt and unfenced yard. As he looked at the place, a man appeared on the front porch, dressed in overalls, cradling a shotgun in his arms.

"Let's get out of here," Ryan said. Without waiting for a reply, he pumped hard on his bike, spewing a cloud of dust into Michael's face. Michael paused a moment longer, his eyes leaving the figure on the porch and concentrating on the barn. For a second, he thought he'd seen something— something he couldn't really identify—but as he studied the barn there was nothing. And yet, even as he rode after Ryan, something tugged at him, an ill-formed thought—a feeling, really—that made him look back once more. The man on the porch was gone, and the barn looked exactly as it had before.

He pedaled harder, catching up with Ryan, but it wasn't until they'd passed over a slight rise that Michael's uneasy feeling—that feeling of something pulling at him—passed.

A little further on, they came to another drive, overgrown with weeds. A mailbox dangled from a post by a rusted nail—the only sign that anyone had ever lived there. Ryan pulled his bike off the road. Michael had to slam on his brakes to keep from running into him. He finally spotted the house, nearly invisible in the tangle of weeds that surrounded it.

"Is this where Eric lives?" he asked, his voice reflecting his incredulity at the idea that anyone could inhabit such an abandoned-looking place.

Ryan shook his head, grinning. "This is where you live."

Michael's mouth dropped open, and he stared at the house for a long time. "Mom's gonna croak," he said at last.

Ryan nodded. "I wasn't supposed to tell you, but I couldn't resist. Isn't it something?"

"It doesn't look like anybody's ever lived there."

"Who'd want to?"

"Let's go look at it."

Michael started maneuvering his bicycle up the drive, but Ryan stopped him. "I wasn't even supposed to tell you about it, and if we go look, Mom might see us. She's helping clean it up."

"Why don't they just burn it down?"

"Search me." He paused, then: "You won't tell anyone I showed you where it was, will you?"

"Hell, no." Suddenly Michael grinned. "But I can hardly wait to see the look on Mom's face when she sees it." Then, as he gazed at the old house, his voice dropped to a whisper. "No wonder Dad never said anything about it."

"Hunh?"

"My dad never told us about this place. Mom just found out about it the other night, when Grandpa told her." He was silent for a little while, then turned to his cousin. "Ryan?"

"Yeah?"

"How come my dad didn't like it here?"

Ryan glanced impatiently at Michael. "I already told you I don't know."

"Well—didn't anyone ever talk about him?"

"What do you mean by talk?"

"You know—the way people talk about people."

Ryan thought about it for a little while. "My mom talks about him sometimes. Mom always says he was smart to get out of here, and she wishes she'd had a chance to do it, too."

"How come?"

"I don't know. I guess 'cause it's so small." He gave his bike a push. "Come on, let's get over to Eric's. It's the next place."

The Simpsons' farm, in contrast to the place Michael was going to be living, was well tended, its buildings sitting squarely on their foundations, everything except the house painted the traditional barn red. The house itself, green with white trim, was surrounded by a grove of cottonwoods dotting a neatly trimmed lawn. As they pulled their bikes to a stop near the back door of the house, Eric Simpson, a curly-haired, freckle-faced boy of about Ryan's age, spun the small tractor-mower he was riding around to face them, grinned, and gunned the engine. He expertly cut the throttle and applied the brakes just before the machine crushed Michael's bike.

"Hi."

"Hi," Michael replied. "I'm Michael Hall."

"I know," Eric said as he jumped off the little tractor. "You're gonna live next door." Then, remembering what his mother had told him to say, he scuffed self-consciously at the ground. "Sorry about what happened to your dad," he mumbled.

Michael, still not used to the reality of his father's death, searched for a reply, and found none. An awkward silence fell over them.

"He's not supposed to know about the house," Ryan finally said. "But I knew you'd never be able to keep your big mouth shut, so I already told him."

Relieved, Eric grabbed at the topic. "Did you go inside?"

Ryan shook his head.

"Good thing," Eric said, barely suppressing a grin. "Mom said it looked like some raccoons were living there all winter. There's shit all over the place."

Michael swallowed.

Noting the reaction, Eric pushed on. "And rats, too. Big ones. And then, up in the attic, there's the bats, but at least they don't bite. Much."

Michael caught on. "That's okay. I'm gonna live in the attic, and I had pet rats at home. And I bet there aren't any alligators in the sewers here. You know what it's like to have to beat an alligator over the head before you take a crap?"

Eric grinned slyly at Ryan. "Has he been snipe hunting yet?" he asked. Ryan shrugged, but Michael nodded.

"They tried that at camp last summer, but I already knew about it."

"Michael wants to know about old man Findley," Ryan said. "I told him you saw him shoot at someone, but he didn't believe me. Then just now, he came out on his porch, and he had his shotgun."

"But he didn't shoot at us," Michael argued. "He didn't even point it at us."

"Did you go onto his property?"

"No."

"Well, try it sometime. Me and another guy were messing around there last summer, and we were going to sneak into Potter's Field. So just when I was gonna sneak under the fence, old man Findley came out. He didn't even yell at us. Just blasted at us with his shotgun."

"I bet he was shooting up in the air," Michael suggested. "Just tryin' to scare you. What's Potter's Field?"

"It's down near the river, sort of between your place and old man Findley's, except that he owns it—old man Findley, that is. Hey, you guys want to see my mare? She's gonna foal any day now."

Michael and Ryan followed Eric around to the barn, and a moment later the subject of old man Findley was forgotten. The mare, a large bay, stood in her stall, liquid brown eyes regarding the three boys with benign curiosity. Even Michael could see the swelling of her pregnancy. "Wow," he breathed. "She's really big, isn't she?"

"She was even bigger last time." Eric's voice reflected his pride in the animal, and he pointed to a sleek young horse in the next stall. "That's Blackjack. He was foaled two years ago." Eric's face broke into a grin as he remembered. "That was really something. The same night Magic was dropping him, Ma was having my baby sister, and Doc Potter and the vet were both here. Pa kept running back and forth, so I got to help with the foaling."

Magic, nervously eyeing the three boys, suddenly snorted and reared in her stall. Eric moved forward as the other two boys backed away.

"Easy, girl, easy," Eric soothed her. He continued talking to the nervous mare, and waved Michael and Ryan out of the barn. A moment later the horse calmed, and he joined them. "You guys want to come out when she foals? I'm gonna help the vet, but you could watch."

Ryan shrugged, pretending lack of interest. "I've seen lots of colts being foaled."

But Michael was intrigued. "When's it gonna happen?" he asked.

"Maybe over the weekend, or next week. You want me to call you?"

"Sure. But what if I don't get here in time?"

Eric grinned. "You will. Sometimes it takes all night, but it's always at least a couple of hours." He looked at his watch. "Hey, it's almost three, and I gotta clean up the yard before Ma gets home. You guys wanna help?"

"I can't," Ryan replied. "I gotta be back home by three-thirty."

Eric's eyes shifted over to Michael, but Michael, too, shook his head. "I better not. I have to take the bike back to Ryan's, then walk home."

"Keep the bike," Ryan offered. "You can give it back when you get one of your own."

"Won't Aunt Laura be mad?"

"Nah."

"You care if I stay?"

Ryan shrugged. "All I'm gonna do is go down to the store and help my dad."

Michael made up his mind, and a few minutes later, after Ryan had left, he sat happily on the seat of the tractor-mower while Eric showed him how to work the controls. As he put the tractor in gear and began moving across the lawn, he decided that Prairie Bend wasn't going to be so bad after all. Except that the only reason he was here was that his father had died. His good mood suddenly evaporated, and a stab of pain shot through his temples.

As he rode home through the soft lazy light of the spring afternoon, Michael was unaware of the eyes that followed him. First there were the eyes of Laura Shields and Ione Simpson, looking up from the final stages of their cleaning of Janet Hall's old farmhouse, watching as Michael rode by. Then, a little further on, there was Ben Findley, peering out from behind the heavy curtains that kept his run-down house in constant gloom. As Michael slowed and peered at the Findley place through the darkening day, the old man's hand automatically reached out and clutched the shotgun that stood on its butt next to the front door. But Michael passed on, and Ben Findley relaxed.

CHAPTER 5

The first word that came into Janet's mind was "firetrap," but she made herself deny it, even though she knew it accurately described what she was seeing as the Shieldses' Chevy slewed over the bumpy dirt driveway and the house came into view. Then she got a grip on her emotions and reminded herself that any wooden structure can burn, that this house was no different from any other house. What had happened to the house she grew up in would not happen to this house. She would not let it happen.

Her sudden panic checked, she made herself look at the house objectively.

Objectively, she didn't know whether to laugh or cry.

From what she could see, the building had no discernible color whatsoever. The prairie weather had long ago stripped it of its paint, and its siding was a streaked and dirty gray, far from the silvery color of the salt-weathered cedar cottages of the eastern seaboard.

She'd wanted a red barn.

This barn, crouched almost defensively behind the house, bore the same drab color as the house, but was in an even worse state of disrepair. Its shingles were half gone, and the loft door, visible beyond one of the dormers of the house, seemed to be hanging from only one hinge.

"This place," she declared at last, "lends new meaning to the word 'awful.' "

"Are we really going to live here, Mom?" Michael asked, voicing Janet's own thought. He had been tempted to giggle as he watched his mother's reaction until he realized the terrible truth: this . . . *place* was his new home.

"Maybe it's not so bad, once you get inside," she replied doubtfully.

"Actually, it's worse," Laura told her.

Janet turned to gaze at her sister-in-law. "Worse? What could be worse? It doesn't have dirt floors, does it?"

Laura carefully brought the car to a stop in the weed-choked front yard, and Janet fell silent, studying the house once more. There was something about it that didn't fit. And then she realized what it was.

"My God," she breathed. "All the windows are whole."

Laura gave her a puzzled look. "Why wouldn't they be?"

"But the place is abandoned. What about—well, don't kids like to throw rocks anymore?"

Suddenly understanding, Laura laughed. "Amos fixes them when they do get broken. I'm not going to pretend everybody's perfect around here." She opened the car door and eased her bulk out, smiling wryly at Janet. "I hope you carry your babies more gracefully than I carry mine," she said, then turned her attention to the house. "Actually, it isn't nearly as bad as it looks. It's weathered, and it needs a lot of work, but basically, it's sound. And the floors, believe it or not, are hardwood."

Slowly, the three of them went through the house, and to her own amazement Janet discovered that Laura was right. Though the paint and wallpaper were peeling and the floors needed refinishing, the house did seem to be solid. The floors were level, and the doors square. The plaster had no holes in it, and the plumbing worked.

There were four rooms downstairs—a living room, a dining room, a kitchen, and a pantry; four more upstairs—

three bedrooms and a bathroom, with an attic tucked under
the steeply sloping roof. Each of the upstairs rooms had a
dormered window, including the bathroom. A narrow staircase through the center of the house connected the two
floors, with a spring-loaded pull-down ladder providing
access to the attic.

There was no furniture.

Ten minutes later, Janet and Laura were back in the
living room.

"I know it isn't much," Laura sighed, moving out onto
the front porch and lowering herself awkwardly onto the
top step.

"No, Laura," Janet protested. "You were right. It's
much better than it looks from the outside."

"And it's a lot better than it looked yesterday," Laura
pointed out, brightening a little. "Ione Simpson and I
worked like dogs cleaning out the grime."

"I wish you hadn't," Janet began. "The kids and I
could have done it. And in your condition—"

Laura brushed her objections aside. "You'd have taken
one look and fled. Ione and I almost gave it up ourselves.
But by next week or the week after, you won't know the
place. We'll have all the weeds cleaned out, the buildings
painted, and the fields plowed."

"But I can't afford—"

"Janet," Laura said quietly, "this was Mark's home.
Now it's going to be yours, and we're your family. Let us
do for you what we'd do for each other." When Janet still
hesitated, she added, "Please?"

"But there's so much that needs to be done—"

"And the whole town can do it," Laura stated. "We'll
make a party of it, just like an old-fashioned roof-raising.
Except, thank God, the roof's in good shape."

The two women fell silent, gazing out into the prairie. It
was a comfortable silence, and Janet could feel the quiet of
the plains seeping into her, easing the tension that had
been her constant companion over the last several days. "I

think I'm going to like it here," she said at last. Next to her, she felt Laura shift her position slightly.

"Really?" the other woman asked. Then she laughed, a brittle laugh that made Janet turn to face her.

"It's so quiet. So different from New York. There's a sense of calm here that I haven't felt since I was a little girl. I'd almost forgotten it."

"That's boredom you're feeling," Laura remarked, her voice tinged with uncharacteristic sarcasm. "Right now it seems like peace, but just wait a year or so."

"Oh, come on," Janet cajoled. "If it's that bad, why do you stay?"

Now Laura turned to face her, her large eyes serious. "You think it's that easy?" she asked. "How do you leave a place like this? When you've grown up here, and your husband's grown up here, and you've never been anywhere else, how do you leave? They don't let you, you know."

"But Mark—"

"Mark ran away," Laura said, her voice suddenly bitter. "Mark fled, and I should have too. Except that when he got out, I was too young to go with him. And by the time I was old enough, it was too late. I was already trapped."

"Trapped? What do you mean, trapped?"

"Just that," Laura told her. "That's what a small town is, you know. A trap. At least that's what Prairie Bend is. I used to dream about getting out. I used to think I'd take Ryan and just run away. But of course, I never did." Suddenly her eyes met Janet's. "You won't either, if you stay. They'll get to you, just like they get to everyone."

"Who? Laura, what are you talking about?"

"Father—all of them."

"Laura—"

But Laura pressed on, her words building into a torrent. "I can't get out, Janet. I'm stuck here, trapped by this whole place. I tried to leave once. I really tried. Do you know what happened? Mother just looked at me. That's all she had to do. Just look at me, with those sad, empty eyes.

She didn't have to say a word. Didn't have to tell me that I was all she had left, that Mark was gone, and the baby was dead, and there was no one left but me. It was all right there in her eyes. Ever since that night . . ." Her voice trailed off, and her eyes wandered away from Janet, across the yard, fixing finally on a pair of doors that lay low to the ground, covering what Janet assumed was a root cellar.

"What night?" Janet asked at last. "What are you talking about?"

Laura turned back to her, and when she spoke, her voice was unsteady. "Didn't Mark ever tell you about it?" Then, without waiting for Janet to reply, she sighed heavily. "No, I suppose he didn't. No one ever talks about that night. Not mother or father, not even me. So why would Mark?"

"Do you want to talk about it?" Janet asked, her voice gentle, sure that whatever had happened that night must account for the odd haunted look she had seen in Laura's eyes.

There was a long silence, and then, finally, Laura shook her head. When she spoke, it was in a whisper. "I'm not even sure I know what happened, really. Isn't that strange? I think it was the most important night of my life, and I'm not even sure what happened." Again she fell silent, then finally nodded toward the twin doors she had been staring at a few moments before. "I was in there. Right in there, in the cyclone cellar."

"Here?" Janet asked, her voice reflecting her puzzlement.

Laura's eyes came back to Janet. And then she suddenly understood, and a harsh laugh emerged from her throat. "My God, they didn't even tell you *that,* did they? This was *our* house. This is the house Mark and I were born in."

"But I thought—their farm—"

"*This* was our farm until that night. It was in the summer. I was nine, and Mark must have been sixteen. And mother was pregnant."

"Pregnant?" Janet repeated. "I thought there were only the two of you."

"There were," Laura replied, her voice dropping to a whisper. "The baby—well, mother lost it. At least, that's what they always said." Her eyes clouded for a moment, and she seemed almost to disappear somewhere inside herself, into some dark corner Janet knew she couldn't penetrate. And then Laura's expression cleared again, and she began speaking once more. Something in her voice had changed, though. It was almost as if she was repeating a memorized story, reciting carefully rehearsed words.

"It was hot that day," she said, "and Mother had been trying to do too much, and her labor came on early. Father was furious at her. It was almost as if he blamed her for the early labor. And then a storm came up, and they sent me to the cyclone cellar. And I stayed there. All afternoon, and all night. I stayed there," she repeated. And then, once more, "I stayed there."

Janet wondered what to say. There was more to the story, she was sure. But she was also sure that Laura didn't want to talk about it. Still, she had a certain feeling that she needed to know the whole story of that night, needed to know not only what had happened to Laura, but what had happened to Mark, as well. "And that was the night Mark left home?" she asked.

Laura nodded. "The next morning, Father came for me. He told me the baby had been born dead. I didn't believe him. There was something inside me that didn't believe him, but I don't know what it was." She smiled weakly at Janet. "It's still there," she said. "Even after all these years, I don't believe that baby was born dead, but I don't know why I don't believe it. It's as if there's something in my mind, something I know, but can't remember." She sighed. "Anyway, after that night, Mother was crippled, and Mark was gone."

Janet stared at her, speechless.

"You're still wondering what happened, aren't you?" Laura asked at last. "Well, I can't tell you. I've always wondered, but Mother never spoke about it, and neither did Father. It almost seems as though Mark must have done something, but I know he didn't." Her voice changed, became almost pleading. "I *know* he didn't, Janet. Mark was a wonderful brother, but then, after that night, he was gone." She reached out and took Janet's hand, her eyes taking on the look of a hunted animal. "For a while, I didn't hear from him. Then he wrote to me—he was in college. Just one letter, and then, later, another one, from New York. I wrote back. Oh, I wrote so many letters! No one knew, not even Buck. But he never answered my letters. Maybe he never even got them."

Janet slipped an arm around the distraught woman, cradling Laura's head against her shoulder. "How awful," she whispered. "How horrible for all of you."

Laura nodded. "It was as if our whole family came to an end that night. And I can't remember why. A little while after that, we moved to the other farm, where Mother and Father still live, but it never really made any difference—ever since that night, I've been so terrified. When Ryan was born, I was sure it was all going to happen over again. And now—" Unconsciously, Laura touched her swollen torso.

"It'll be all right," Janet said.

Laura's eyes met Janet's. "If I could only remember what happened that night, what happened to Mother. I—I'm always so scared now, Janet. Every time Buck wants to make love, I'm afraid of getting pregnant. And then, when I do, all I can think of is that horrible night." Suddenly her eyes narrowed. "Did—did Mark ever talk about it?"

Janet shook her head. "Never. Never so much as a word. And you mustn't worry about it, Laura. There's no reason why what happened to Anna should happen to you."

"Isn't there?" Laura whispered. She swallowed once, then spoke again. "Oh, Janet, I wish I could believe that. But I can't. . . . I just can't."

Wordlessly, Janet took her sister-in-law's hand in her

own, and for a long moment the two young women sat
silently, staring at the innocent-looking doors to the storm
cellar, each of them wondering just what of Laura's past
had been hidden away in that dark room beneath the earth
so many years ago.

Michael stood at the window of the smallest bedroom,
his eyes fixed on Ben Findley's barn. If he'd been asked to
describe what was happening to him, he wouldn't have
been able to. But one thing he knew: he was home.

This house, this room, this view of the limitless prairie
from the small dormer window, all of it felt familiar, all of
it right. His father was here; he could almost feel his
presence in the empty room.

And the barn. Old man Findley's barn, clearly visible
from this window. It was almost as if he could see into it,
and yet he couldn't, not really. Still, if he'd been asked
what was inside that barn, he'd have been able to sketch it
out: ten stalls, five on each side, facing each other, none
of them occupied. Two of them, though, seemed to have
been put together into some kind of workshop. Above the
stalls, a hayloft, with a broken ladder its only means of
access. At the back, a tack room, still filled with rotting
leather, bridles and harnesses long ago stiffened and dried
from lack of use and attention. And below the tack room,
something else, something Michael could feel as he could
feel the rest of the barn.

It was as if there were a presence there, calling out to
him, whispering to him in a voice he could feel, but
couldn't quite hear. . . .

"Michael? Michael, are you all right?"

Startled, Michael turned. Standing in the doorway, looking at him oddly, were his mother and aunt.

"Didn't you hear me?" he heard his mother say. He
frowned.

"Hear what?"

"Hear me calling you. We're ready to go."

"But we just got here." He saw his mother and aunt glance at each other.

"We've been here for an hour and a half," his mother told him. "We called you, and when you didn't answer, we thought you must have gone outside. I looked in the barn, the loft, even the tool shed."

"Why?" Michael asked. His eyes drifted back toward the window, and Findley's barn, but though he could still see it, he could no longer *feel* it. Then, as he heard his mother's voice, tinged with anger now, he forced his attention back into the room where they stood.

"Because we couldn't *find* you," his mother was saying.

"I was right here," Michael explained. Why was she mad at him? He hadn't done anything. "I've been right here all the time." And yet, even as he spoke the words, he wondered. *Had* he been there, or had he gone out, gone over to Mr. Findley's barn? Suddenly he was no longer sure.

"Then why didn't you answer me when I called you?"

"I—I didn't hear you." He felt a throbbing in his left temple. "I must have been daydreaming."

"For an hour?" his mother asked.

"It hasn't been that long—"

"It *has*," Janet replied. She saw a flicker of what looked like fear in Michael's eyes, and turned to Laura. "Why don't you wait for us in the car? We'll be right out."

Nodding her understanding, Laura smiled encouragingly at Michael, then disappeared down the stairs.

"Are you mad at me?" Michael asked when he and his mother were alone.

"Well, it seems to me—" She stopped, her eyes narrowing slightly as she looked at him. "Michael," she said, her voice gentle now. "Are you all right?"

The throbbing in his head faded away, and Michael nodded. "I'm sorry," he said softly. "I was just daydreaming, I guess." His eyes roamed over the room, and he smiled. "Can this be my room?" he asked.

"This room?" Janet asked. She looked around the tiny room, wondering why Michael would ask for it. Of the three bedrooms, it was the smallest. "I suppose so, if you want it."

"I do," Michael told her.

From his tone, Janet was sure that something had happened in that room, that it had affected Michael in some way. "But why?" she asked.

Because Daddy's here, Michael thought. He opened his mouth to voice the thought, but then changed his mind. Instead, he glanced around the room, and then, as before, his eyes were drawn to the window. "I like the view," he said. Janet crossed the little room in four easy steps and stood in the dormer, her hands resting on Michael's shoulders as she looked past him out over the prairie vista.

"It isn't much different from the view from the other windows, is it?" she asked.

"It's the barn," Michael said quietly. "I like being able to look at the barn."

"But you can't even see the barn from here—" Janet began, and then stopped as she realized he wasn't talking about their barn, but another barn, one she could see in the near distance. There was nothing special about the structure; indeed, if anything, it was remarkable only for its shabbiness.

"It looks like it's going to fall down," she commented.

Michael said nothing.

"Am I missing something?" Janet asked. "Do you see something about it that I don't?"

Michael hesitated, then she felt him shrug under the touch of her hands. "I just like it," he said at last.

"Well, then, I guess that's that."

Michael turned and faced her. "Then I can have it? This room?"

Janet nodded, the odd tension she had been feeling in the room, and in herself and Michael, suddenly evaporating. She smiled. "And it's a good thing you wanted it. I was afraid I was going to have to fight you for the other big one."

"I'd have lost," Michael replied.

"But you'd have argued," Janet observed.

Michael was silent for a few seconds, apparently thinking about it. Finally, he shook his head. "Maybe last week." His voice was quiet, and Janet tensed, certain that he was about to say something she didn't want to hear. "Last week, you'd have had Dad on your side, but now you don't." His dark blue eyes—Mark's eyes—held her own. "I'll try not to fight with you anymore, Mom."

"Fight?" Janet asked, feeling tears form in spite of herself. "We've never fought."

Michael shifted uncomfortably, and his gaze broke away from hers. "You know what I mean. Arguing, trying to get around you. I—well, I'm not gonna do that anymore."

Janet reached out to her son and took him in her arms, holding him tight.

"Thank you, Michael," she whispered. "We're going to be all right here, you and I. I know it. I can just feel it."

Then, as she felt Michael's arms tighten around her, she glanced once more out the window toward the barn that had so captured her son's attention.

There was a bleakness to it, deprivation and neglect that doused the spark of optimism she had just felt.

CHAPTER 6

Janet hung up the phone, then moved pensively into the kitchen, where Anna, expertly maneuvering her chair with one hand, was sweeping the floor with the other. As Janet watched, Anna moved the pile of dust toward the open back door, then gave the chair a quick spin, catching the screen door with one of its handles and knocking it open. At the same time, a last whisk of the broom sent the accumulated dirt flying into the backyard. As the screen door slammed shut, she turned the chair back to face Janet. "It took me two months to learn how to do that," she said in a voice that carried with it no emotion whatsoever.

Janet shook her head. "I wish you'd let me help—"

But Anna had already rolled across the kitchen to put the broom away. "I've been doing it for years." She wheeled herself over to the table, and gestured for Janet to join her. "Well, is it all taken care of?"

Janet nodded. "I guess so, but I'm still not certain I'm doing the right thing."

Anna shrugged. "It's done, anyway, and believe me, it's a lot easier to go along with Amos than to try to do it your way. Besides, I'm afraid he's right—it doesn't make any sense for you to go back to New York just to pack up. All you'd do is wear yourself out, and we don't want you to do that, do we? Carrying a baby always has its risks, you know.''

Though there was nothing in Anna's voice to indicate that she was thinking of her own last pregnancy, Janet decided to use her mother-in-law's words as an opening. ''Laura told me what happened,'' she said, softly. When Anna made no response, she pressed a little harder. ''The night Mark left—''

Suddenly understanding, Anna's eyes hardened. ''Laura had no right to burden you with that,'' she said. ''Besides, she doesn't know the first thing about it. She was just a child.''

''But she wasn't burdening me,'' Janet protested. ''She's frightened. We were talking about you, and I asked her what happened. So she told me. At least she told me about you losing your baby, and Mark never coming home again.'' Janet's voice dropped slightly. ''And she said that you never told her exactly what happened that night. I think she's been terrified ever since. Terrified that the same thing might happen to her.''

Anna stared at Janet for a few seconds, then shook her head. ''She shouldn't worry,'' she said at last. And then Anna's voice took on the same tone of recitation Janet had heard from Laura. ''All that happened to me was that I overworked myself and brought the labor on prematurely. It was a breech birth, and the cord wrapped around the baby's neck.'' She paused a moment, then: ''That's what they told me, and that's what I believe,'' she finished. The emphasis in her voice, though, only made Janet certain there was something Anna was leaving out, something she was not about to talk about. Indeed, she had already wheeled herself out of the kitchen to the foot of the stairs, and was now calling to her husband and grandson.

''You mean we're not going back to New York *at all*?'' Michael asked. He'd sat in silence while Janet had explained to him that she'd decided to arrange for movers to pack them and let an agent handle the subleasing of the apartment. Now he was on his feet, his eyes stormy, a vein throbbing angrily in his forehead.

"It just seems best—" Janet began, but Michael cut her off.

"Best for who?" he demanded. "What about my friends? Don't I even get to say goodbye to them?"

"But you said goodbye when we came out here—"

"That was different!" Michael's voice began to rise. "When we left, we were coming back!"

Amos rose and moved toward the angry boy. "Michael! Don't talk to your mother in that tone of voice."

With no hesitation, Michael swung around to face his grandfather. "Don't tell me what to do," he said. "You're not my father!" Whirling around, his face contorted with fury, he stormed out of the dining room. Amos started to follow him, but Janet blocked his path.

"Let him go, Amos," she pleaded. "He didn't mean it. He's just upset, and he'll come back down to apologize."

"He can't talk that way," Amos said, his voice firm but bearing no trace of anger. "He can't talk that way to you, and he can't talk that way to me. And he'd better understand that right now." Moving around Janet, he, too, left the dining room. The two women watched each other warily, Janet knowing with all her instincts that Anna would back her husband up. But instead, the older woman seemed to sag in her chair.

"I'm sorry," she said. "I suppose I should have stopped him, but he believes children should be respectful, and even though I know that's old-fashioned, that's the way he is."

And he's right.

The thought skittered through Janet's mind, an alien idea long ago rejected by herself and her husband, and most of their friends. They were modern parents, ever-mindful of the tenderness of the young psyche, ever-striving to allow their son the same freedom of expression they themselves enjoyed. Mark, she knew, would not have reacted to Michael's outburst as his father had. Mark would have taken the time to explain the situation to Michael, and listened to Michael's point of view. And in the end he (and she) would have decided that the trauma of Michael having to leave his friends with no final goodbye outweighed the expense of that last trip to New York, even though logic dictated that they stay where they were.

But here, away from the city and its environment of advanced thinking and experimentation, the same thought kept drumming in Janet's head: *Amos is right.*

These people did things as they had always done them, and if they seemed in some ways backward or reactionary, they had other qualities that made up for it. They had a sense of community, of caring, that refugees to the cities had lost. They retained values that people of Janet's own environment had shed long ago and with no remorse.

There was a solidity to Amos, to all the people of Prairie Bend, that Janet was just beginning to realize she had missed in the years of her marriage.

She stood up and moved around to where Anna still sat, and rested one hand on the older woman's shoulder. "Thank you," she said quietly. "Thank you so much for all you're doing."

Anna covered Janet's hand with her own. "Don't be silly, dear. You're family. We're only doing what any family would do. And it's our pleasure. I lost Mark years ago, but at least now I have you and Michael."

Though neither of them could see the other's face, each of them realized the other was weeping, one for a lost son, the other for—

For what? Janet wondered.

If she'd been asked, which she was blessedly not, Janet would not have been able to say exactly why tears had come to her eyes. Partly for Mark, she supposed, though of that she was no longer sure, but partly for something else, something she was only beginning to discover. Mixed with her sense of loss, there was that something else, a sense of something recovered, a sense of values she had once held, but lost along the way, that were now being restored. She squeezed Anna's shoulder gently, then, wanting to be alone with her thoughts, she slipped out into the fading evening light.

Amos Hall stood at the door to the room that should have been Mark's and was now occupied by Michael, about to put his hand on the knob and open it. Then, out of a sense that he owed the boy the same courtesy he intended to demand, he knocked.

"Go away," Michael replied, his voice tight with anger. Ignoring the words, Amos opened the door, stepped inside, and closed the door behind him. He stood still, saying nothing, waiting for Michael to respond. For several long minutes, the room was still. Then, his movement involuntarily exposing the uncertainty he was trying to conceal, Michael rolled over, propped himself up against the cast-iron bedstead, and folded his arms over his chest.

"I didn't say you could come in here," he challenged. "This is my room."

Amos's brows arched. He moved further into the room, seating himself on a wooden chair a few feet from the bed. "If I ever hear you speak that way to me again," he said, in a tone so low Michael had to strain to hear, "or speak to your mother or any other adult the way you did a few minutes ago, I will take you out behind the barn and give you a whipping such as I haven't given anyone since your father was your age. Is that clear?"

"You can't—"

"And when I knock at your door," Amos went implacably on, "I'm not asking for permission to enter. I'm simply warning you that I'm coming in." Michael opened his mouth once more, but Amos still gave him no opportunity to speak. "Now, three things are about to happen. First, you are going to have an experience I'm sure you've never had before. Ever heard of washing your mouth out with soap and water? Nod or shake your head. I'm not interested in anything you might have to say right now."

Michael hesitated, then shook his head.

"I thought not. Well, you won't like it, but it won't kill you. When you're done with that, you and I are going downstairs, and you are going to apologize to your mother."

Again, Michael opened his mouth, but this time he thought better of it. Instead, he clamped his mouth shut, and his eyes narrowed angrily. In his temples, a dull throbbing began.

"Then, after you've apologized," Amos went on, "this is going to be all over, and we're going to fix some cocoa and forget about it. Do you understand? Nod or shake your head."

For a long minute, as the throbbing pain in his head grew, thoughts tumbled through Michael's mind. His father had never talked to him like that, never in his life. He'd always said what he wanted to say, and his parents had always listened to him. And no one, since he was a little boy, had come into his room without his permission, at least not when he was there. Then why was his grandfather so angry with him? Or *was* his grandfather angry with him? Maybe this was something else. He watched Amos, but could see nothing. The old man just sat there, returning his gaze, waiting. Michael began to feel sure that his grandfather was goading him, pushing at him, wanting something from him. But what?

Whatever it was, Michael decided he wouldn't give it to him, not until he understood what was really happening.

His head pounding, but his face set in an expression that revealed nothing of his growing fury, Michael got off the bed and walked out the bedroom door, then down the hall to the bathroom. He could feel more than hear his grandfather following him.

In the bathroom he stood at the sink, stared at the bar of Ivory soap that sat next to the cold water tap. He reached out and turned on the water, then picked up his toothbrush. Finally he took the bar of soap. Holding the soap in his left hand, he dampened the toothbrush, and began.

The sharp bitterness of the soap nearly gagged him at first, but he went doggedly on, scrubbing first his teeth, then his whole mouth. Once he glanced at himself in the mirror, and watched the foam oozing from his lips, but he quickly looked away from the reflection of his humiliation. At last he dropped the toothbrush into the sink and rinsed out his mouth, flushing it with water again and again until the taste of the soap had almost disappeared. He wiped his face and hands, put his toothbrush away, carefully folded the towel before putting it back on the bar, then wordlessly left the bathroom, his grandfather still following him.

Downstairs, he found his grandmother in the kitchen. Her eyes were flashing with anger, but Michael instinctively knew her fury was not directed at him. Indeed, as she glanced at him, he thought he saw a trace of a smile on her lips, as if she were telling him not to worry, that whatever had happened upstairs, she was on his side. Feeling a little better, he looked for his mother, but she was nowhere to be seen. Then, through the window, he saw her sitting under the elm tree. With his grandfather close on his heels, he went outside.

Janet looked up and saw them coming, but her smile of greeting faded as she saw the grim expression on her father-in-law's face, and Michael's own stoic visage of self-control. At last Michael glanced uncertainly back at the tall figure of his grandfather looming behind him, but the old man simply nodded.

Michael turned back to face his mother. "I'm sorry I spoke to you the way I did." He went on, "If you think we ought to stay here and not go back to New York, then we will."

Janet's eyes darted from her son to her father-in-law, then back to Michael again. "Thank y——" she began, then changed her mind. "That is what I think," she said. Then, softening, she reached out to touch Michael, but got no response. She hesitated, stood up and started toward the house, then turned back. "It's going to be all right, Michael," she said. He glanced at her, anger still clouding his eyes, then dropped his gaze to the ground.

"Go inside and give your grandmother a hand, son,"

Amos said. "And tell me when you're done. We'll make some cocoa."

Knowing better than to do anything except follow his grandfather's instructions, Michael followed his mother into the kitchen and took the dish towel from his grandmother's hands. "I'll do that," he said.

Anna hesitated, then handed him the towel and wheeled herself over to the kitchen table. She busied her hands with some mending, but her eyes, clouded with a combination of love and apprehension, never left her grandson. He was so like his father, she reflected. So like his father—and so unlike his grandfather.

Michael began drying the last of the dishes. His head was still throbbing with pain, and the kitchen seemed filled with the same acrid smell of smoke he'd noticed the other day when he'd been so angry with Ryan. And somewhere, through the fog of pain in his head, he thought he could hear something—or someone—calling to him.

As he worked, he kept hearing his grandfather's words, about how after he had apologized to his mother, it would all be over.

But it wasn't all over.

Instead, he was sure it had just begun.

True to his promise, Amos Hall produced a pot of cocoa that evening, but it failed to serve its intended function. The four of them drank it, but a pall, emanating from Michael, hung over the room, and though Janet and Anna did their best, they couldn't dispel it. By nine-thirty, everyone had gone to bed.

Janet stopped at Michael's room, knocked softly at the door, waited for permission to enter. When there was no response, she hesitated; then, like her father-in-law before her, she opened the door and stepped inside. Michael was on his bed, propped up against the headboard, reading. "May I come in?"

Michael shrugged, his eyes carefully fastened on the book that rested against his drawn-up legs. Janet crossed the small room, sat down on the bed, then picked up the book, closed it, and put it on the nightstand. Only then did Michael look at her.

"Would you like to talk about what happened?" she asked.

Michael's brows knit into a thoughtful frown. He shook his head. "I've got a headache."

Janet frowned. "A bad one?"

"I took some aspirin."

"How many?"

"Only two."

"Okay. About what happened this evening—"

"I don't want to talk about it," Michael interrupted.

"Michael, this afternoon you said you weren't going to argue with me anymore. Do you remember that?"

The boy hesitated, then nodded.

"It didn't last long, did it?"

He shook his head. "I guess not," he admitted.

"Didn't you mean what you said this afternoon?"

"Yes, but—" He faltered, then fell silent.

"But what?"

"But we always talked things over before we decided things. Now it seems like Grandpa is always deciding what we should do."

"*I'm* making the decisions," Janet corrected him. "Grandpa is giving me advice, but I'm making the decisions. And for a while, that's the way it's going to have to be. Once we're settled in our own house we can go back to the old way. But right now, there are too many decisions to be made, and too much to be done, and I just don't have the time to discuss it all with you. And I have to depend on you to understand that."

Michael fidgeted in the bed. "I do. It's just that—"

"That what?"

Michael's eyes fastened self-consciously on the ceiling. "Grandpa made me wash my mouth out with soap."

Janet tried to stifle her laugh, but failed. "Then maybe you won't talk back to him anymore."

"He said it was because of the way I was talking to you."

"Well, maybe it was a little bit of both. Anyway, it's not the end of the world. Lord knows, I survived a lot of mouth soapings."

"When you were eleven?"

And suddenly Janet knew what the real root of the problem was. "I don't think I got one much after I was ten," she said carefully. "But on the other hand, when I was eleven, I'd learned better than to talk back to my elders."

"But you and Dad always let me talk back to you. Even when I was little."

"So we did," Janet said softly. "But who's to say whether we were right or not? Anyway, if I were you, I'd be careful how I talked, at least until we move out of here and into our own place." She stood up, then bent over to kiss Michael goodnight. "How's the headache doing?"

"Still there."

"Well, go to sleep. It'll be gone by morning." She turned off the light on the nightstand, and a moment later was gone.

Michael lay in the darkness, trying to understand what was happening. Brushing his teeth twice had failed to remove the bitter residue of soap in his mouth, and the aspirin had done nothing to alleviate his headache. Furthermore, the smoky odor in the kitchen had followed him upstairs, and as he lay in bed he suddenly felt as if he couldn't breathe.

At last he got up and went to the window. The prairie was lit by a full moon, and as he looked out into the silvery glow of the night, he began to feel trapped by the confines of the house. If only he could go outside. . . .

He knew he shouldn't. He should stay where he was and try to go to sleep. If his grandfather found out he'd snuck out in the middle of the night . . .

That was what made up his mind. There was something about doing what he knew he shouldn't do that made it more fun, that made an adventure out of practically anything. And besides, this wasn't New York. This was Prairie Bend, where no one ever even locked their doors, and the streets weren't filled with strange people. And he wasn't going to be in the streets, because it wasn't the streets that called him.

He pulled his jeans on, and a sweatshirt. Taking his shoes and socks with him, he slipped out of the bedroom and down the stairs, carefully avoiding the third one from the bottom, the one that creaked. He went out the back door, stopping on the porch to put on his socks and shoes. Then, not looking back at the house, he dashed across the yard and around the corner of the barn. He waited there, sure that if anybody'd heard him or seen him, they'd call him or come after him. But after a few seconds that seemed like hours, with the silence of the night still undisturbed, he moved away from the barn, across the freshly plowed field, toward the stand of cottonwoods that bordered the river.

As Janet watched the small figure of her son fade into the gloom of the night, her first instinct was, indeed, to go after him. She put on her robe, hurried down the stairs, and was about to go out the back door when she heard a movement in the depths of the house. A moment later Amos appeared in the kitchen.

"What's wrong?"

Janet shook her head. "It's nothing, really. It's just Michael. He—well, he seems to have decided to go for a walk."

Amos frowned. "In the middle of the night?"

"So it seems. I was just going to go after him—"

"You'll do nothing of the sort," Amos replied, his frown deepening. "In your condition, all you should be thinking about is getting a good night's sleep. I'll go after him myself."

He disappeared back toward his bedroom, and Janet sank down onto one of the kitchen chairs. But as she waited for him to dress, she began to change her mind. A few minutes later Amos returned, dressed in jeans and a flannel shirt. Janet rose once again to her feet as he started out the back door.

"Amos? Maybe—well, maybe we should just leave him alone." The old man swung around, his eyes fixing on her.

"He probably just needs to be by himself and think things over," she said. "Let's give him some time, all right?"

Amos hesitated, his eyes narrowing. "If that's what you want. But he oughtn't to be going out in the middle of the night. It's not right."

"I know," Janet sighed. "And I can't say you're wrong. But just this once, can't we let it go? You go back to bed. Everything will be all right."

"Don't you want me to wait up with you 'til he gets back?"

Janet shook her head. "No."

There was a long silence, and then Amos nodded. "Okay. But I'll have a talk with him in the morning, and I'll see to it that he doesn't do this again."

A moment later he was gone, and Janet started slowly up the stairs to begin her vigil.

Waiting was harder than she'd thought it would be.

The air had shed the cold bite of the month before, but had not yet acquired the soggy heat that would blanket the plains in the days to come, when temperatures of ninety and more would hang over the prairie like a cloying shroud, suffocating people and animals alike with a dank heaviness that was even less bearable than the freeze of winter. Now, at the end of May, there was a briskness to the night air, and the musky odor of fresh-turned earth foretold of the crops that would soon begin to fill the fields. The night was crystal clear, and as he walked, aimlessly at first, Michael gazed up into the sky, picking out the Big Dipper, Orion, and the Little Dipper. Then he came to the stand of

cottonwoods bordering the river, and he paused. There
was a darkness among the trees, where the moonlight was
blocked out by the leaves that had already sprouted from
the heavily intertwined branches. No wonder they called it
the Dismal, he thought. What little light spilled through
from the pasture only lent the woods an eerie look, shadows cast upon shadows, with no easy path apparent.

Shivering, Michael set himself a destination now and
began walking along the edges of the pastures, the woods
on his right, climbing each fence as he came to it. Sooner
than he would have expected, the woods curved away to
the right, following the course of the river as it deviated
from its southeastern flow to curl around the village. Ahead
of him he could see the scattered twinkling lights of Prairie
Bend. For a moment, he considered going into the village,
but then, as he looked off to the southeast, he changed his
mind, for there, seeming almost to glow in the moonlight,
was the hulking shape of Findley's barn.

That, Michael knew, was where he was going.

He cut diagonally across the field, then darted across the
deserted highway and into another field. He moved quickly
now, feeling exposed in the emptiness with the full moon
shining down on him. Ten minutes later he had crossed the
field and come once more to the highway, this time as it
emerged from the village. Across the street, he could see
Ben Findley's driveway and, at its end, the little house,
and the barn.

He considered trying to go down the driveway and
around the house, but quickly abandoned the idea. A light
showed dimly from behind a curtained window, and he
had a sudden vision of old man Findley, his gun cradled in
his arms, standing in silhouette at the front door.

Staying on the north side of the road, he continued
moving eastward until he came abreast of his own driveway.
He waited a few minutes, wondering whether perhaps he
shouldn't go back to his grandparents'. In the end, though,
he crossed the road and started down the drive to the
abandoned house that was about to become his home. As

he came into the overgrown yard, he stopped to stare at the house. Even had he not known that it was empty, he could have sensed that it was. In contrast to the other houses he had passed that night, which all seemed to radiate life from within, this house—his house—gave off only a sense of loneliness that made Michael shiver again in the night and hurry quickly past it.

His progress slowed as he plunged into the weed-choked pastures that lay between the house and the river, but he was determined to stay away from the fence separating Findley's property from their own until the old man's barn could conceal him from the same man's prying eyes. It wasn't until he was near the river that he finally felt safe enough to slip between the strands of barbed wire that fenced off the Findley property and begin doubling back toward the barn that had become his goal.

He could feel it now, feel the strange sense of familiarity he had felt that afternoon, only it was stronger here, pulling him forward through the night. He didn't try to resist it, though there was something vaguely frightening about it. Frightening but exciting. There was a sense of discovery, almost a sense of memory. And his headache, the throbbing pain that had been with him all evening, was gone.

He came up to the barn and paused. There should be a door just around the corner, a door with a bar on it. He didn't understand how he knew it was there, for he'd never seen that side of the barn, but he *knew*. He started toward the corner of the barn, his steps sure, the uncertainty he'd felt a few minutes ago erased.

Around the corner, just as he knew it would be, he found the door, held securely shut by a heavy wooden beam resting in a pair of wrought-iron brackets. Without hesitation, Michael lifted the bar out of its brackets and propped it carefully against the wall. As he pulled the door open, no squeaking hinges betrayed his presence. Though the barn was nearly pitch dark inside, it wasn't the kind of eerie darkness the woods by the river had held, at least not for Michael. For Michael, it was an inviting darkness.

He stepped into the barn.

He waited, half expectantly, as the darkness seeped into him, enveloping him within its folds. And then something reached out of the darkness and touched him.

Michael started, but stood his ground, oddly unafraid. And then he heard a voice, flat, almost toneless, drifting hollowly from somewhere in the depths of the barn.

"Michael."

Michael froze.

"I knew you'd come." There was a pause, then the voice went on. "I have been calling you. I wasn't sure you heard me."

"Who are you?" Michael asked. His eyes searched the darkness, but could find nothing. Nor could he be certain just where the voice came from. As the silence lengthened, he began backing toward the door. "Tell me who you are," he said, more loudly this time.

And then a dog began barking outside with a sharp, staccato sound, once, twice, three times. And somewhere nearby, a door slammed. Michael darted out of the barn, swung the door closed, and dropped the bar back in the brackets. But just before he ran back into the comparative safety of the fields, he heard the voice once more. Its flat atonality echoed in his mind all the way home.

"I am Nathaniel," the voice said. "I am Nathaniel . . ."

CHAPTER 7

Michael came into the kitchen the next morning to find his grandfather waiting for him, sitting at the kitchen table, his back ramrod straight. The old man's eyes fixed on Michael with a coldness that stopped the boy in his tracks.

"Sleep well?" Amos asked.

Uncertainly, Michael edged toward the refrigerator and began rummaging on the top shelf for the pitcher of orange juice he knew was there, well concealed by the masses of leftovers his grandmother always seemed to have on hand. "I guess," he said, finally locating the pitcher behind a bottle of milk. He edged it out of the refrigerator, picked up a glass from the drainboard, and started toward the table.

"I didn't," Amos replied. "I heard your mother moving around, and came out to see if she was all right. She was. But she was worried because you were gone."

"I—I went for a walk."

"I see." Amos stood up. "And you're about to go for another walk. March."

Michael's eyes widened, and he stared up at his grandfather. "Wh-where?"

"To the barn," Amos told him, and for the first time Michael noticed the razor strop clutched in his right hand. "But—"

"No buts," Amos cut in. "You worried your mother last night. You worried her very much. You won't do it again. Now start walking."

Michael's eyes darted toward the door to the hallway, but there was no one in sight, no one to rescue him. Reluctantly, but knowing he had no choice, he followed his grandfather out into the morning sunshine. Only when they were behind the barn, out of sight of the house, did Amos speak again.

"Where did you go?"

Michael hesitated. This morning, what had happened the night before seemed almost to have been a dream. Indeed, as he thought about it, he was no longer sure exactly what had happened. He had gone for a walk, and he seemed to remember having started out toward old man Findley's place. But now he was no longer sure. *Had* he gone there? He tried hard, but all he could really remember was the forest by the river, and the pasture. And a voice. There had been a voice. Or had there?

"N—nowhere," he said at last. "Just down to the woods by the river. I—I wasn't gone long."

"Drop your pants and bend over."

Slowly, Michael unbuckled his belt and undid his jeans. He turned around, then dropped his pants and leaned over, clutching his knees. A second later he felt the first lash of the strop sting his buttocks, and a scream burst from him.

"Don't yell," Amos told him. "If you yell, it will only get worse. Now, tell me where you went."

"I didn't go anywhere," Michael wailed. "I told you, I only went down by the river."

"You were gone for over an hour."

Again the leather strop slashed across his buttocks, but this time Michael was able to choke off his scream.

"I—I didn't know," he pleaded. "I thought it was only a few minutes."

"You shouldn't have gone at all, not without telling your mother."

"I don't have to tell her everything I do—"

The strop whistled through the air this time and seemed to wrap itself around Michael's thigh like a snake.

"From now on, you ask your mother or me before you do anything. Do you understand?"

Michael said nothing, steeling himself against the next slash of the leather. In a moment, it came, and immediately afterward, the sound of his grandfather's voice.

"Did you hear me?"

"Y-yes . . ."

Again the strop whistled through the air and burned into his flesh. "Yes, what?"

Michael thought wildly, clenching his teeth against the pain as tears burned in his eyes. "Yes, sir," he finally cried.

And the whipping was suddenly over.

"All right," his grandfather said. Slowly, Michael straightened up and pulled his jeans up to cover his stinging buttocks. Then he turned to face his grandfather, his eyes blazing with fury and his head throbbing with a sudden ache that overpowered even the pain of the thrashing. "Wait 'til I tell my mom—" he began, but Amos knelt down and took him by the shoulders, his hands gripping him like twin vises.

"Stop that, Michael," he said. "What just happened here is between you and me. You're not to speak to your mother of this. She's been through a lot, and you're not to put her through any more. From now on, you behave yourself. If you don't, you know what will happen. And if you take your troubles to your mother, I can guarantee you they'll only get worse. You're a big boy. I expect you to behave like one."

"But—"

"No buts. Things are different now, and you'd better understand that. I don't like having to do this, but so help me, I'm going to teach you some respect, boy, so that next time you feel like going for a walk in the middle of the night, you'll think twice about it. Understand?"

Michael hesitated, then nodded. But as he followed the

old man back to the house, his headache grew worse, and his mind whirled with confused thoughts. *It's not fair. I didn't do anything. . . . All I did was go for a walk. . . . It's not fair. . . .*

In the kitchen, Janet was at the table, sipping a cup of coffee and making notes on a spiral pad. She looked up as Michael and Amos came through the back door. "Hi. What have you two been up to this morning?"

"Chores," Amos replied before Michael could say anything. He went to the sink and washed his hands; then, drying them on a dish towel, he went around to peer over Janet's shoulder. "What's all this?"

"Things to be done," Janet sighed. "There's so much, and I haven't any idea of where to start. But here're the colors I want for the farm." She tore off the top sheet and handed it to Amos, who studied it for a moment, then passed it to Michael.

"Some imagination your mother's got, huh?"

Michael stared at the old man. It was as if his grandfather had never been angry at all. He was smiling as if the thrashing behind the barn had never happened. And his voice was calm. He was even trying to make a joke: "White paint for the house, red for the barn, with white trim. Now, how do you suppose she came up with something so radical?" His expression turned serious, and he studied Janet's face. "Any problems this morning?"

"You mean morning sickness? Not a trace." Though her stomach was still queasy from that morning's session in the bathroom, she put on what she hoped was a bright smile and rapped the wooden tabletop a couple of times. "I'm hoping it's over with. It was probably just—well, the last few days." She took a deep breath and emphatically returned to her lists. "The problem's going to be the furniture."

"What's wrong with our furniture?" Michael asked, easing himself carefully onto one of the hard kitchen chairs. "I like it."

"There's nothing wrong with it," Janet tried to explain.

"It just doesn't seem practical for a farmhouse in Prairie Bend, that's all."

"Farmhouse furniture is ugly," Michael pronounced; then, realizing what he had said, his eyes filled with fright and shifted to his grandfather.

But the old man only nodded in agreement. "It may be ugly, but it's comfortable," he said just as Anna rolled her chair into the kitchen and brought it to a stop between the sink and the range. Janet started to get up, but Anna waved her back to her chair. She dropped an apron over her lap, then pulled a skillet from a low cupboard and placed it on the stove. "What were you talking about?" she asked of no one in particular. "What's ugly but comfortable?"

"Farmer's furniture," Amos told her.

"According to whom?" Anna demanded, suddenly taking on the look of a ruffled hen.

"According to your grandson."

"Oh," Anna said. She hesitated only a second, then shrugged. "Well, of course he's right. But don't you worry about it," she said, addressing Janet, as she began scrambling a dozen eggs in the enormous cast-iron skillet. "I can furnish that house with a couple of phone calls. Every barn and attic in Prairie Bend is full of furniture, and it won't cost a cent. Besides, you'll spend more money shipping your stuff out here than you'd get if you sold it, so you'll be money ahead even if you have to give it away. Bring me the plates, Michael."

As Michael hesitated, Anna watched him. There was something in his eyes—a hurt—that she had seen before, years ago, in her son's eyes. She had hoped never to see it again. "Michael, are you all right?"

Michael's gaze met his grandmother's, and for a quick moment there was an unspoken communication between the two of them. But then Michael nodded, turning away to move toward the cupboard where the china was kept. Anna's eyes followed the boy, then shifted suspiciously

toward her husband. But if Amos noticed the concealed
fury in his wife's eyes, he gave no sign.

As Michael began putting the breakfast plates on the
table, Janet thought over what her mother-in-law had just
said. It did make sense. Still, there was a faint twinge at
the feeling that by leaving her belongings behind, she
would be shedding still another piece of her old life. But
she quickly shook off her misgivings. After all, she had
made up her mind to start all over again in Prairie Bend.

The sun was high in the sky as Michael carried the pail
of garbage around the corner of the barn. The pigs, milling
around in their pen, immediately began grunting and snort-
ing in anticipation of their midmorning snack. Michael
climbed the sturdy metal bars of the small enclosure, using
only one hand to haul himself up, while he clutched the
bucket with his free hand. The pigs clustered around,
snuffling at the toes of his sneakers, shoving each other
aside in their eagerness to be first at the trough. Finally,
when he was perched on the top rail, Michael grinned
down at the churning animals.

"Okay," he said. "Here it comes!" He upended the
bucket, and the garbage cascaded into the feeding trough.
A boar, the largest of the herd, immediately shouldered his
way between two sows, one of which promptly nipped him
on the ear. The boar squealed in surprise and quickly
backed off. The sight of the immense hog giving way to
the smaller female struck Michael as funny, and he began
to laugh, shouting encouragement to the big pig. "Come
on, don't let her get it all. Get in there and fight for it!"

The hog, as if sensing that he was being mocked,
suddenly turned toward Michael, his small eyes gleaming.
Then, with a speed Michael wouldn't have believed possible from such a clumsy-looking animal, he reared up,
grabbed Michael's foot in his mouth, and gave a quick
jerk.

Michael tumbled into the pigpen, and his laughter turned
to a sudden scream of fright.

The boar backed off for a moment, his front hoof scraping at the ground as his beady eyes fixed upon Michael. Then, grunting angrily, he hurled himself forward.

Michael rolled aside at the last minute and tried to get to his feet, but stumbled over a second pig. Suddenly the whole herd seemed to be on the move, their sharp hooves digging into the ground as they jockeyed for position, half of them attempting to get to the trough, the other half more interested in Michael.

"Help!" Michael screamed. "Someone help me!"

Janet heard Michael's scream and raced out of the kitchen just as Amos emerged from the barn. "What's happened?" she yelled as she dashed across the yard.

"The pigs," Amos shouted back. "He must have fallen into the pigpen." Then he disappeared around the corner of the barn.

By the time Janet reached the hog enclosure, Amos was already using a long pole to poke at the furious animals. "Get up," he yelled to Michael. "Get on your feet boy, or they'll trample you. Get up!"

Suddenly, from around the far corner of the barn, a black dog the size of a large shepherd hurtled into sight, charging straight for the pigpen. With one leap, it was over the top rail, and then it was in the midst of the pigs, snarling and barking, snapping first at one of the sows, then turning its attention to the big boar. The boar, surprised at the sudden attack at its flank, backed off for a moment, giving Michael a chance to scramble to his feet. A moment later, Amos had lifted him up and over the top rail of the enclosure.

As soon as Michael was out of the pigpen, the dog abandoned the fight and leaped out of the pen. A moment later he was next to Michael, who was clinging to his mother, sobbing with fright.

"They were going to kill me," he cried. "They were going to trample me!" The dog, as if trying to comfort the terrified child, licked at his face, his tail wagging. Suddenly one of Michael's arms left his mother to curl around the dog's neck, hugging him close.

Janet stared down at the animal. "Where'd he come from?" she asked. "Whose is he?"

Amos frowned, sure he'd never seen the dog before. If he had, he'd have remembered it. It stood two and a half feet high at the shoulder, with a broad, deep chest and heavily muscled legs. Its coat, coal black without so much as a trace of white markings, was thick, and its eyes, alert and intelligent, seemed to fix on him with a mixture of equal parts of suspicion and hostility. "Don't know," he admitted.

Michael, who had been more frightened than hurt by the pigs, hugged the dog closer. "I bet he followed me home last night," he said. Then he gazed up at his mother. "He saved my life, Mom. Can I keep him? Please?"

Janet felt dazed by what had happened, but when she had assured herself that Michael was, indeed, unhurt, she turned her attention to the dog. The animal seemed to regard her with quizzical eyes, as if awaiting her decision. "I don't know," she said at last. "He must belong to someone," she went on, though she had already seen that the dog wore no collar.

"But what if he doesn't?" Michael asked. "What if he's only a stray? Then can I keep him?"

"We'll see," Janet temporized. "Right now, though, I want you to go in and get yourself cleaned up."

Michael was about to argue, but when he saw the look in his grandfather's eyes, he changed his mind. "All right," he agreed. He started toward the house, and the big dog followed close at his heels. When Michael disappeared into the kitchen, the dog sat by the back porch.

"What do you think?" Janet asked Amos.

Amos shrugged. "I don't know. Never seen him before. But if he's still around when we get back tonight, I don't suppose there's any harm in keeping him."

A moment later, Amos wasn't so sure. As he passed the

dog on his way into the house, it lifted its big head and laid back its ears. A snarl rumbled up from the depths of its throat.

Janet and Michael stared in awe at the little farm, barely able to recognize it even though it was not yet noon and the work had been under way for only three hours. Already the weeds had been cleared from the front yard; people swarmed over the house with scrapers, removing the last traces of paint from the weathered siding, and in the backyard, yet another crew was busy piling brush and weeds onto a smoldering bonfire. Still more people were at work on the barn.

The driveway, barely passable yesterday, had been scraped, and now a backhoe was working, digging drainage trenches along the shoulders of the road. Buck Shields, manipulating its controls with expert ease, brought the machine to a halt and jumped to the ground. "Want to try it?" he asked Michael. Michael immediately climbed up the caterpillar tread of the hoe and perched on its steel seat.

"What do I do?"

"Hold on," his uncle replied, climbing up to stand behind Michael, his work-coarsened hands covering Michael's own softer ones. "It's real easy. This lever brings the hoe up and puts it down, and this one moves it back and forth. See?" He demonstrated the hoe's operation, and another foot was added to the drainage ditch. "We can do about three or four feet at a time, then we have to move the whole thing forward. Try it."

Michael moved one of the levers, and the hoe plunged deep into the earth. "Easy," Buck cautioned. "We want a trench, not a pit." He eased the lever back, and the hoe responded. "Now try moving the dirt to the side, and dumping it." Michael hesitated, chose a lever, and pulled. The claw of the hoe dropped downward and the earth was deposited back into the trench.

"I'm messing it up," Michael said by way of apologizing.

"Maybe we better start you out with the tractor and work up to this. Why don't you see if you can lend a hand out back?"

Michael scrambled down and disappeared around the corner of the house, while Janet walked slowly along next to Anna as she wheeled her chair up the drive. At the foot of the porch steps, the old woman came to a halt and stared silently up at the house.

"You must have a lot of memories of this place," Janet said at last. Anna's eyes flickered, then met Janet's.

"I do," she replied. "But that's all past now, isn't it? For you, maybe this house will be a good one."

Janet frowned thoughtfully. "I don't believe in good houses and bad houses. It seems to me a house is happy if the people who live in it are happy."

"I hope you're right." Sighing, Anna approached the porch steps, then came to another halt. This time, when she looked up it was to Janet, not to the house. "There's some people who can manage stairs in these things, but I'm not one of them."

"I put a ramp for you on the top of my list," Janet told her as she began working the wheelchair up the four steps to the porch, "but I don't know when we'll be able to get it built."

"I'll mention it to Amos," Anna replied. Then, as Janet pushed her through the front door, she seemed to shrink into the chair. Her eyes scanned the foyer and the stairs, then shifted to stare almost fearfully at the closed door to the small room in which she'd delivered her last child.

"If you don't want to be here, I'll understand," Janet said, putting a reassuring hand on the old woman's shoulder.

"No. No, it'll be all right. It's just that it's been so many years." A wry smile twisted her mouth, a smile that Janet had a feeling was forced. "I'm afraid we may not have done you a favor with this place. I had no idea how bad it had gotten."

"But it's *not* bad," Janet protested. "It's going to be

wonderful. Come on. Let's go on a tour, and I'll tell you everything I'm going to do."

They went from room to room, Anna falling silent as Janet explained her plans for each area. At last they came back to the foot of the stairs. Anna gazed thoughtfully up toward the second floor. "Which rooms are you going to use?" she asked at last.

"I'm taking the big one in front. Michael wants the little one."

"The little one?" Anna frowned. "Why the little one?"

"He likes the view. You can see Mr. Findley's place from there."

Anna's expression darkened. "That place," she said. "Ben Findley should be ashamed of himself, the way he's let it go. I swear, I don't know why that man stays around here. If it wasn't for Charles Potter, he wouldn't have a friend in Prairie Bend."

"But doesn't he have family?"

Anna's eyes clouded, and a sigh escaped her lips. "Ben? Not anymore. He had a wife once—Jenny Potter. For a while they had a good marriage, but then—" She fell silent for a moment, then smiled wanly. "Things happen, I guess. Anyway, Jenny left, and ever since, Ben's just gotten stranger and stranger."

"But surely he must have *some* friends."

Anna shook her head. "He doesn't seem to want friends anymore. In fact, I've often wondered why he stays here at all. His life must be so lonely. . . ." Her eyes drifted toward the staircase. After a moment, she turned back to Janet. Suddenly, she nodded her head. "Of course Michael would want the little room." A look that might have been sadness, or something else, shadowed her face. Then she said, "It was his father's."

As his mother had asked his grandmother about Ben Findley, so too had Michael asked Ryan Shields again about the man next door. They were in the barn with a third boy—Damon Hollings—whom Michael had met only today.

"How come he's not here?"

"Are you kidding?" Damon replied, though Michael had directed his question to his cousin. "He never goes out of that weird house, and he never speaks to anyone. And he wouldn't help anyone, even if they were dying on the road in front of his driveway." Damon paused, enjoying the effect his words were having on Michael. "And his place is haunted," he added, his voice dropping to a loud whisper. "There's ghosts there."

"There's no such thing as ghosts," Michael protested, but nonetheless his gaze shifted away from Damon toward the loft door. Beyond, only a few hundred yards away, lay the ramshackle buildings of the Findley farm. And in the depths of his consciousness, a memory—or was it a dream? —stirred. "What kind of a ghost?" he asked, his voice noticeably less certain than it had been a moment earlier.

"It's someone who died a long time ago," Damon told him. "And sometimes you can see it, at night, out in Potter's Field. It looks like lights moving around out there."

"Lights?" Michael asked. "What kind of lights?"

"I—I never saw it myself," Damon admitted.

"You never saw it 'cause it doesn't exist. Right, Ryan?" Michael said, turning to his cousin, but Ryan didn't answer.

Damon shrugged with exaggerated indifference and ran a hand through the tangle of blond hair that capped his mischievous face. "Well, who cares what you think?" he said to Michael. "All I'm telling you is what I heard. And what I heard, and what everybody around here knows, is that old man Findley's place is haunted. So there!"

"Well, I don't believe it," Michael shot back. "I don't believe in ghosts, and I bet there's nothing wrong with Mr. Findley. I bet nobody around here likes him 'cause he's not related to anybody," he said with sudden certainty.

"Well, why don't you go find out?" Damon challenged.

"Maybe I will," Michael replied, taking up the challenge. He turned to Ryan again. "Will you go with me?"

Ryan stared at him, then emphatically shook his head. "And you better not go, either," he said.

Michael's expression set stubbornly as the beginnings of a headache shot through his temples. "I'll do what I want," he said in a tight voice. He turned away from the other two boys and concentrated his attention on the old barn in the distance. As he stared at it, the pain in his head began to ease. From somewhere inside his head, he could almost hear a voice whispering to him. The words were unclear, but the tone was somehow familiar. . . .

By six-thirty the heavy work was done, and only the Halls remained at the little farm.

"Doesn't look much like it did this morning, does it?" Anna Hall commented.

Indeed, it did not. Gone was the tangle of weeds that had nearly hidden the house, and the lawn, mown and trimmed, needed only water and some fertilizer to restore it to the luxuriant green that was the norm in Prairie Bend. The driveway, scraped and graveled, formed a graceful curve to the highway, and the buildings, denuded of the last remnants of their faded and peeling paint, seemed almost to be anticipating the morrow, when a coat of fresh white would restore them to their former respectability. Behind the buildings, forty acres of newly plowed earth awaited whatever plantings Amos eventually decided on. Even Michael had to admit that the place had changed.

"Maybe we really *can* live here," he murmured. Then his eyes shifted westward toward the sagging buildings of the Findley farm, and he fell silent.

Misunderstanding Michael's silence, Amos reached out and drew him close, his arm around the boy's shoulders. "You don't like that place?" he asked, then interpreted Michael's continued silence as assent. "Well, that's just as well. If I'd had my way, I'd have bought Ben's place long ago, but he wouldn't hear of it. Said he'd found the place where he was going to die, and he was too old to change his mind. So there he is, and if I were you, I'd leave him alone."

With an effort, Michael tore his eyes away from the old barn and looked up at his grandfather. "Is there really a ghost there?" he asked.

Janet had not been paying much attention to the conversation. Now she turned to look at her son. "A ghost?" she asked, her voice incredulous. "What on earth are you talking about?"

Michael shifted uncomfortably. "Damon Hollings says Mr. Findley's farm is haunted."

"Oh, for heaven's sake. You didn't believe him, did you, honey?" When Michael hesitated, Janet's voice lost some of its lightness. "There's no such thing as ghosts, Michael, and there never have been." She turned to Amos and Anna, expecting them to support her, but Amos seemed lost in thought, while Anna had turned away and was slowly pushing her chair toward the car. "Amos, tell him there's no such thing as ghosts."

"I'm not going to tell him something I don't know about, Janet," he said at last.

Janet stared at him. "Something you don't know about?" she repeated. "Amos, you aren't going to tell me you believe in ghosts!"

"All I can tell you is that there've been stories," Amos said at last. "So I guess I'll just have to say I don't know."

"What kind of stories?" Michael demanded.

"Things," Amos told him after a long silence. Then he smiled grimly. "Maybe, if you're good, I'll tell you all about them, just before you go to bed tonight."

Michael tried to keep his excitement from showing, tried to keep his expression disinterested. He failed completely.

CHAPTER 8

The prairie was different then; the grass was tall, and in the summer you couldn't even see where you were going. It would grow five, maybe six feet high, and it was like a great sea, green at first, during the spring, and then, in the summer, it would turn brown, and as far as you could see, there it was, waving in the wind just like in the song. Then the cattle came, and the grass started getting more like it is now—still thick, and still tall in the spring, but cut down as the summer goes on. It never used to get cut at all. It would just stand, bloom, go to seed, and die.

And in the winter, the prairie would turn white, and the snow would be so thick no one could go out in it. No one except the Indians, with their travois. And even they didn't travel much in the winter. They'd pitch their tepees, and huddle together, and somehow they'd get through it.

That was what the white people didn't know. They didn't understand the prairie, didn't have any idea of what it could be like. The thing of the prairie is that it just seems to go on and on forever. And there's nothing to measure it by. So what used to happen is that people would lose track out on the prairie. Not of where they were—they always knew that. But they'd lose track of who they were, and what they were.

It would happen slowly, so slowly that most people

105

never knew it was happening to them. They'd come out here from the east, and they'd be looking for land. A lot of them were city people, and what they wanted was to be out of the city. So at first they didn't even have towns. Instead, they'd claim tracts of land—big tracts—and they'd build their houses right in the middle of it, and everything they could see was theirs. And they didn't have any neighbors, not to speak of. Oh, there were other people, but they lived miles away, and the only time you saw your neighbors was during a house-raising or a wedding, a birth or a death. For the rest of the time, you were by yourself, with no one but your family. And sometimes you'd be snowbound for months on end.

It seems like it was the women it got to the most. They'd go on for years, raising their children and taking care of their husbands, and everything would seem to be fine. But inside, they'd start losing their sense of themselves. They'd start feeling like they were disappearing into the prairie. Every day, little by little, getting smaller and smaller, until they'd start to feel like one morning they just wouldn't be there anymore. And then it would happen. One day something would just sort of snap inside their heads.

That's what happened in Prairie Bend. Except that it wasn't called Prairie Bend then, and there was no town yet. Just a few big farms, and the bend in the river. And there was a woman. A woman named Abby Randolph. Her husband had died that fall, and even though she was pregnant, she stayed on, trying to take care of the farm and raise the children.

She seemed fine, the last time anyone saw her, which was in the fall, just before the first snow. And then the snow came, and it kept on coming. The drifts built up, covering everything, and a lot of people died, right in their own houses.

That's not what happened to Abby, though.

Abby started hearing things. At first, she didn't pay any attention to it. She'd wake up in the night, and she'd hear something downstairs, like someone moving around. So she'd get out of bed and go downstairs, but there wouldn't be anyone there. Then she'd check on the children, thinking maybe one of them was playing a joke on her. But they'd be in their beds, sound asleep.

Then one night Abby heard the sound downstairs. It didn't go away. It got louder and louder. Finally, Abby went downstairs.

The noise was coming from the front door. Three knocks, and then a long silence, and then three more knocks. For a long time, Abby just stared at the door, knowing it wasn't possible that anyone could be outside. It was February, and the drifts were ten feet deep, and there was no one else for miles around. But the knocking didn't stop. And then Abby opened the door.

There was a huge man looming in the doorframe, covered with snow, with ice forming on his beard and his eyebrows. Abby stared at him for a long time, and then the man took a step forward and his eyes seemed to flash at Abby. And he spoke.

"I've come for my boy."

The first time it happened, Abby just shut the door, but after that, it happened every night. Every night, she'd wake up and hear the pounding on the door, and every night the man would be there, and every night he'd say the same thing.

"I've come for my boy."

Then one morning, after the man had come the night before, and Abby had shut the door, one of the children was gone. And that night, the man didn't come back. But then, a week later, he came back again, and when Abby opened the door, he smiled at her. "You can have him back in the summer," he said. "You can have him back when the grass is high."

And one by one, that winter, Abby Randolph's children disappeared until there was only one left.

Then spring came, and the snow melted, and people started visiting each other again. When they first came to see Abby, she was sitting on her front porch, with a very *strange look in her eyes. And they found one child upstairs—her oldest son—crouched in the corner of his room. They tried to talk to him, but all he'd do was scream whenever anyone went near him. And the rest of the children were gone.*

They tried to talk to Abby, but she wouldn't say much. All she'd say was that the children's father had come for them, and that he'd bring them back when the grass was high.

The spring passed, and then the summer came, and one day some neighbors went to visit Abby and found her out in the field, digging. When they asked her what she was looking for, she said she was looking for her children.

"The grass is high," she said. "The grass is high, and it's time for them to come back."

The next day, they found Abby. She was in the barn, pinned up against the wall with a pitchfork. Her son was with her, crouched down on the floor of the barn, watching his mother bleed to death. They didn't talk to the boy, didn't bother to give him anything like a trial. They just hanged him, right there in the barn. They say he died even before his mother did. Abby didn't die for hours. She hung on, trying to save her baby. And in the end, she did. The baby was born just before she died. And later on, in Abby's cyclone cellar, they found some bones. They were the bones of children, and it looked like they'd been boiled.

For years after that, people would disappear around Prairie Bend every now and then, just like people disappear everywhere. But around Prairie Bend, they never found the bodies, and they always say it was because of Abby's last son. They said Abby's boy had gotten hungry, and gone looking for something to eat.

And they said that sometimes, when the weather was stormy and the grass was high, you could still see Abby, late at night, out in the field, looking for her children. . . .

*   *   *

Michael stared up at his grandfather, his blue eyes wide and frightened. "That—that's not a true story, is it Grandpa?"

"Of course it isn't," Janet quickly replied. "It's a horrible story, and I wish we hadn't heard it." She turned to Amos, her face pale. "My God, Amos, how could you tell a story like that to a little boy?"

Amos Hall shrugged. "If he hadn't heard it from me, he'd have heard it from someone else. It's been around for years, and it never changes much."

"But surely no one believes it?"

"About Abby? I don't suppose anybody knows the full truth about her and her kids, but it's probably close to the truth. Things like that used to happen around here. Like I said, the prairie would get to people, and they'd just crack up. It could have happened to Abby that winter—"

"No more," Janet pleaded. "I don't want to hear any more about it. I meant the last part, about her son still wandering around and people still seeing her out in the field. Surely no one believes that, do they?"

"I don't know," Amos replied. "Who knows what people see? But I can tell you, people around here tend to be pretty careful about their kids, particularly during summer. But of course, that's only common sense. We get tornadoes during the summer, and they can be nasty. Get caught out in a tornado, and you just have to trust to luck." He stood up, stretching. "Anyway, that's the story. You can believe it or not, as you see fit." He turned to Michael. "And as for you, it's time you were in bed."

Michael got slowly to his feet and kissed his mother goodnight, then his grandmother. He started out of the little parlor, but then turned back.

"Grandpa? What was the name of Abby's son?"

"Nathaniel," Amos told him. "His name was Nathaniel."

Michael climbed up the stairs and went to his room, then undressed and slid into bed. A few minutes later he turned off the light to lie in the darkness and stare out the

window into the night. Far away across the field, he could
see a shape moving through the moonlight. He knew it
was the dog, the dog who had saved him from the pigs,
then waited for him all day, wagging his tail fiercely
when he caught sight of Michael, and not seeming to mind
when he had not been allowed inside the house. But he
was still there, like a shadow in the night, patrolling the
fields while Michael slept.

That's what I'll name him, Michael thought. Shadow.
His name will be Shadow.

But as he drifted off into sleep, it was another name that
kept echoing in his ears.

Nathaniel . . .

CHAPTER 9

"You guys ever hear of somebody named Nathaniel?" Michael's voice betrayed none of the tension he had been feeling as he helped with the painting of the house the next day, glancing only occasionally westward toward Findley's barn. Now, in the bright spring sunshine, the crumbling barn's fascination seemed to have lessened, and Michael had begun to wonder if the sensation of its calling to him—or of something inside it calling to him—had been nothing more than his imagination. But that name kept coming back to him. Nathaniel.

The name he had heard whispered in the barn; the name his grandfather had used last night.

So now, as he diligently helped Ryan Shields and Eric Simpson apply an uneven coat of not-quite-white paint to his bedroom walls, he tried to ask his question with a nonchalance he wasn't feeling.

"Nathaniel?" Ryan repeated. "Where'd you hear about him?"

"Grandpa."

"The story about the kid who killed his mother?"

Michael nodded, and put down his brush. "Is it true?"

Ryan shrugged. "I guess so. Except the part about the ghosts of Nathaniel and Abby still hanging around here.

That's just a story they told us to keep us from shagging out at night.''

"My dad told it to me," Eric offered. "I was only a little kid, but it gave me nightmares."

"How do you know it's not true?"

Ryan gave him a scathing look. "Come on. It's just a ghost story." Then, seeing the look of uncertainty that clouded Michael's expression, he grinned. "You don't believe in ghosts, do you?"

Michael hesitated only a split second. "Hell, no." He picked up the brush once more and began applying more paint to the wall, covering up the thin patches but leaving a series of brush marks. Eric watched him for a moment, then shook his head in disgust.

"You sure don't know much about painting, do you? I bet your mom makes you do that over again." He dipped his roller into the tray of paint, and began going over the area Michael had just done.

"Did Grandpa tell about the knocking at the door, and that weird man all covered with snow?" Ryan asked. "That was the scariest part."

Michael nodded, but Eric looked perplexed. "What man? All I ever heard was that every time Abby ran out of food, she cooked one of her children and fed it to the rest of them."

"Yeah," Ryan agreed. "But Grandpa says she never even knew what she'd done. She always thought a man came for the kids. That's why she's supposed to still be out looking for them."

"Can you believe that?" Eric asked. "Who'd ever believe a story like that?"

"Well, we did," Ryan said, reddening slightly.

"Yeah, but that was when we were little," Eric declared. "I figured out the ghost part of it was just a story when I was ten."

"Sure," Ryan teased. "That's why you're always the one that chickens out when someone wants to sneak into Findley's barn in the middle of the night."

Now it was Eric's turn to redden, but he made an attempt at a recovery. "That place is dangerous. It's gonna fall down any day now."

"You've been saying that since you were ten, too." Ryan deliberately ran a paint roller over Eric's hand. "Oops."

"Cut that out," Eric yelped. "It *is* gonna fall down!" He shook his own roller at Ryan, spattering paint across his friend's face.

Ryan only grinned. "Seems like one of us is still pretty clean, doesn't it?" he said.

Eric nodded, and the two of them turned on Michael.

In seconds the scuffle degenerated into chaos. The sides constantly changed, until all three of them were covered with paint, along with the ceiling, the walls, the floor, and the window. That portion of the window, at any rate, that was closed. Too late, they noticed that the upper section of the casement had been lowered, and the battlefield had not contained the ammunition. And they only noticed that when they became aware of Janet Hall standing in the doorway, her expression of fury carefully masking her urge to laugh.

"What's going on here?"

"Nothing." Though the reply had come from Michael, it was nearly simultaneously echoed by Ryan and Eric.

"Nothing," Janet repeated, her expression darkening.

Michael stooped down to pick up a rag. "I guess we better get it cleaned up before it dries," he mumbled.

"And you'd better get yourselves cleaned up, too," Janet told them. "You can use sandpaper on the floor, and a scraper on the window, but if you don't get that paint out of your hair, it's going to have to be cut off. Now get into the bathroom—all of you—and get those clothes off. Put them in the tub and let them soak. Then get yourselves into the shower—"

"But there's no hot water!" Michael protested.

Janet allowed herself a faintly malicious smile. "You should have thought of that before you started all this. Now get to it. By the time you're done, I'll have some clean clothes for you. Lord knows if they'll fit anyone but Eric, but they'll be here.''

Eric's eyes widened apprehensively. "You're not gonna tell my mom—'' he began, but Janet cut him off.

"Your mother already knows. She was standing right under that window, helping *your* mother—'' she turned her gaze to Ryan, "—paint the shutters downstairs.''

Ryan groaned. "Oh, God. She'll kill me, Aunt Janet.''

"Quite possibly she will,'' Janet agreed, keeping her voice implacable, unwilling to let the children see her amusement. "But before she gets the chance, I want an explanation for all this. Otherwise, you can all work naked for the rest of the afternoon, and go home the same way. Is that clear?''

The three boys nodded mutely and headed for the bathroom. Janet Hall waited until she heard their anguished screams as the icy water began sluicing the latex paint from their skins, then went thoughtfully down the stairs.

She, too, had been under the window, and she had heard the conversation that had led to the paint fight.

"You were talking about Nathaniel,'' she said. Though her eyes were on Michael, Ryan and Eric were clear in the periphery of Janet's vision. Michael nodded, and out of the corner of her eye, she saw Eric echo the gesture. Ryan, however, suddenly looked worried.

"Ryan was teasing Eric about being afraid of ghosts,'' Michael said. "And then—well, it just sort of happened. It wasn't anyone's fault, Mom. We all started it. I just wanted to find out if anyone else heard the story Grandpa told me last night. What's wrong with that?''

"Nothing,'' Janet assured him. "Except that I think it's time you understood that it's only a story. All of it.''

"Grandpa says—'' Ryan began, but Janet didn't let him finish.

"Your grandfather told us a revolting story last night, and I'm sure very little of it is true. The whole idea of that poor woman doing what your grandfather says she did is disgusting, and probably nothing like it ever happened. And as for ghosts, there are no such things, as all of you well know.''

''Then why did Grandpa tell it to us?'' Michael asked.

''Probably for a couple of reasons. Ghost stories are fun. Furthermore, a good ghost story can keep people off property where they're not wanted.'' She turned to Ryan and Eric. ''When you two were younger, did you believe there were ghosts out here?''

Sheepishly, they both nodded.

''And did it keep you off Mr. Findley's property?'' Again, they nodded. ''Then it served its purpose, didn't it?'' She focused her attention on Michael. ''As for why your grandfather decided to tell it to you, I haven't any idea. But it seems to me you're a bit old for that sort of thing. If Mr. Findley doesn't want people on his property, certainly you don't need a ghost story to keep you away, do you?''

''But—but what if it's *not* just a story?'' Michael pressed. ''What if there really *is* a ghost out here?''

Janet saw the glance that passed between Ryan and Eric, and was sure her son had just lost a part of their respect. Michael himself, however, hadn't seemed to notice it. Instead, his large eyes were fixed seriously on her own. ''There are no ghosts,'' she said. And yet, even as she said the words, she wondered if they were true. What about her own ghosts? What about the ghost of Mark that was beginning to haunt her? The doubts about him, the questions about him that were always nagging at the fringes of her mind, demanding answers? Weren't those ghosts? Wasn't she, herself, beginning to wonder what was real and what was not?

Resolutely, she banished her doubts from her mind, and reached out to squeeze Michael's shoulder. ''There are no ghosts,'' she said once more. ''There are ghost stories, but that's all they are. Just stories.'' Then, pointedly eyeing the paint that was quickly drying on the floor and windows, she left the three boys alone in Michael's room.

When she emerged from the house a few moments later,

she found Laura and Anna on the front porch, Laura bent over as if she'd been whispering into her mother's ear. Seeing Janet, she straightened up and smiled, but there was a falseness to her expression that wasn't lost on Janet.

"Has something else gone wrong?" Janet asked, her voice anxious.

"Heavens, no," Anna assured her. "I was just telling Laura not to overdo, that's all. But I'm afraid it doesn't do much good. Sometimes she digs in her heels, and it seems like she's trying to work herself to death. Do you suppose you could find some of that lemonade we had with lunch?"

"I'll look," Janet replied. She went back into the kitchen and found the last of the lemonade, though there was no ice. Still, she rinsed out a glass, filled it with the warm liquid, and started back toward the front porch. Once again, Laura was whispering into Anna's ear, and when Janet made a deliberate sound, there was something furtive in the manner in which Laura looked up. Furtive and frightened. Somehow, Janet had the feeling that it had something to do with the conversation that she and Laura, along with Ione Simpson, had overheard earlier.

The conversation about Nathaniel.

She handed Laura the glass of lemonade.

"You *believe* that crazy ghost story, don't you?" she asked as Laura raised the glass to her lips.

As the color drained from Laura's face, the glass shattered on the floor of the front porch.

Laura Shields was still upset by Janet's accusation. That evening, when she eased her ungainly bulk into the chair that was normally reserved for her husband, she smiled apologetically, hoping Buck wouldn't question her about the nervousness she'd been unable to cover. "I guess maybe I overdid it a little bit today. Women in my condition shouldn't try to paint shutters."

Buck looked up from the paperwork he'd been poring over, and his eyes suddenly hardened. "I told you not to try it. If anything happens to that baby, I guess you know whose fault it will be."

"But I wanted to help Janet with the house," Laura murmured. She settled herself in and sighed.

Buck smiled sourly, and his voice took on a sarcastic edge. "You're just like your mother—if you don't do it yourself, you don't think it'll be done right." He pushed his papers aside. "It never ceases to amaze me that there's a town here at all, considering you weren't even born 'til thirty-one years ago."

"It amazes me, too," Laura said, with careful placidity, determined not to rise to her husband's bait. She reached over to pick up the *TV Guide*, and felt a sudden twinge of pain in her abdomen. Frowning in spite of herself, she waited for the pain to pass, then completed the motion.

"Something wrong?" Buck asked.

"Don't be silly. What could be wrong?" With studied nonchalance, Laura opened the little magazine and began examining the listings. Another pain seized her, and this time she had to bite her lip to keep from crying out. Now Buck rose to his feet, the hardness in his eyes dissolving into concern.

"Something *is* wrong."

"It's nothing," Laura insisted. "It's just something I ate. I've just got a little cramp, that's all."

"Cramp, or contraction?"

"I—I'm sure it's just a—" She jerked spasmodically as another pain shot through her, then, as it eased, she felt a spreading dampness on the chair beneath her. "Damn," she whispered. She looked up at Buck, her expression a mixture of sorrow, pain, and fear. "I'm sorry. I guess I really did overdo it today. You'd better call Dr. Potter." She began to lift herself out of the chair, but another sharp contraction forced her back.

"Ryan? Ryan!" Buck called, the urgency in his voice bringing his son out of the kitchen immediately. "Call Doc Potter, and tell him to get over here right away. The baby's coming."

"But it's not supposed to be—"

"Damn it!" Buck snapped. "Do as I say. Call the Doc while I get your mother upstairs." He slid his large hands under Laura's arms and eased her to her feet. "Can you make it, or shall I carry you?"

Laura took a tentative step, leaning heavily on Buck's arm. "I can make it," she assured him. "But if the baby's going to come tonight, don't you think I ought to go to the hospital?"

Buck ignored the question. "Let's get you upstairs."

"But—"

"Don't argue with me, Laura," Buck told her. "We know what's best for you."

Laura opened her mouth, then closed it again. He was right—argument would be useless; he was just like her father. "All right," she finally whispered. "Just stay with me." She began moving slowly toward the stairs, pausing only to reach out and touch Ryan's hand as she passed him. "Call Dr. Potter, sweetheart. And don't worry. I'm going to be all right, and so is the baby." As Ryan finally started toward the phone, she began climbing the stairs, with Buck beside her.

Three minutes later, she lowered herself gratefully onto the bed, then allowed herself a groan. Another contraction gripped her, and she had to fight not to allow the groan to turn into a scream. She lay still, waited for it to pass, then looked up at Buck, for the first time letting the fear she was feeling show in her eyes.

Ryan appeared at the door, his face pale and his eyes frightened. "Doc'll be here in a few minutes. He said not to worry, that everything's going to be fine."

"Of course everything's going to be fine," Buck said. "You go on back downstairs and wait for Doc. Okay?"

Ryan nodded uncertainly, then opened his mouth to say something, but apparently thought better of it. Laura smiled weakly at him. "What is it?"

"Is—is the baby going to be all right this time?" he asked.

Laura nodded and made herself smile at her son. "This time there isn't going to be any problem at all." But as Ryan left the room, her eyes drifted toward her husband. "There won't, will there? This one will be all right, won't it?" Then, before Buck could answer, another violent contraction seized Laura. This time, she was unable to stifle her scream.

Eric Simpson looked worriedly up at his father.

"Is it time?" he asked. "Is she gonna foal tonight?"

Leif Simpson eyed the mare critically, then nodded. "Looks like it," he said. "Maybe another hour, maybe two. And I bet this one doesn't take all night."

"Should I call the vet?" Eric was standing next to the mare, stroking her head gently. She whinnied softly and pawed at the floor of the stall. "Easy, Magic. Everything's gonna be okay. We'll take care of you."

"You and I can handle this one," Leif told his son. "But if your friends want to watch, you'd better tell them to get on over here." As Eric hesitated, Leif stepped into the stall, gently easing the boy away from the horse. "Go on. You won't miss anything. She's hardly even started to dilate yet."

Moments later, breathless from running from the barn to the house, Eric was on the phone, dialing Ryan Shields's phone number. He listened impatiently as the connection went through, then grumbled to himself as he heard a busy signal. He waited a few seconds, then dialed again. Again, the busy signal.

"Shit," he said softly, but distinctly enough so that Ione Shields, coming through the dining room door, heard him quite clearly.

"Eric!"

"I'm sorry, Ma," Eric automatically apologized. "I gotta call Ryan and Michael, and Ryan's line is busy."

"Then call Michael," Ione suggested.

"I don't know their number."

"Look it up."

"Aw, Ma, I don't have time to do that. Magic's dropping her foal, and I gotta get back out to the barn." As he spoke, he dialed the Shieldses' number for the third time. Still busy. Eric gave his mother an appealing look, one that he was well aware she couldn't resist. "Could you call for me? Please? All you have to do is tell them Magic's foaling, and if they want to watch, they better get out here."

As he was sure she would, his mother nodded. "Run along," she told him. Then, as her son dashed out the kitchen door, she picked up the phone and dialed Anna Hall's number. It, too, was busy.

After four tries, alternating between the Shieldses and the Halls, she finally got through to the latter. The phone rang six times before it was finally picked up.

"Anna? It's Ione. What on earth is going on? Have you been talking to Laura? I've been trying to call them, too, and both your lines have been tied up."

There was a moment's hesitation, then Anna's voice came over the line. "It's Laura," she explained. "It seems as if the baby's decided to come tonight."

Ione paused, the smile fading from her face. "Oh, dear," she said finally. "Poor Laura. Do you think I should go over there?"

This time there was no hesitation from the older woman. "I'm sure if Laura needs any help, Dr. Potter can provide it."

Ione felt a twinge of annoyance at Anna's brusqueness. In truth, she was more than a little hurt. In Prairie Bend, when someone was having a baby, the neighbors gathered around, just as they did when there was illness, or trouble of some sort. It had been that way for as long as Ione could remember—except for the Halls. For some reason Ione had never understood, the Halls tended to keep to themselves.

Oh, they'd accept helping hands to get the crops in, Ione thought, or to fix up that old house for Janet and her son. Ione herself had willingly helped out with that and hadn't begrudged the effort for a minute. But when it came to themselves and their children, the Halls had always been standoffish. Tonight, obviously, was going to be no exception. It occurred to Ione that even with the doctor present, Laura might be able to use the nursing skills Ione had acquired years earlier, before she'd married Leif. But Anna had already made it quite clear that Ione wasn't wanted.

"I see," she said stiffly, making no attempt to mask her feelings. "Well, then, I don't suppose there's much chance of Michael coming over here tonight, is there? Magic's foaling, and Eric promised him he could watch." She paused. "I suppose that'll be out of the question now."

Again there was no hesitation in Anna's reply. "I don't see why. Let me call him," she said.

As she crossed the yard a few minutes later, Ione Simpson paused halfway to the barn to gaze at the newly painted little house that was silhouetted in the distance against the setting sun. In this light, it looked no different from the way it had ever looked, and for a moment Ione wondered if Janet Hall hadn't made a horrible mistake in deciding to move onto the long-abandoned farm. There had been so many stories over the years, so much speculation. . . .

In the end, though, she decided that what Janet Hall did was her own business.

And yet, she knew that wasn't quite true. In Praire Bend, everything that happened to anyone affected everyone else. And something, she knew, had happened in that house that Janet Hall was moving into. . . .

Twenty minutes later, Michael skidded his borrowed bicycle to a halt in front of the Shieldses', sure that Ryan would be waiting for him. With Shadow at his heels, he started across the yard to the front door, but suddenly stopped as he noticed his grandfather's big Oldsmobile parked in the driveway behind his Uncle Buck's car. He

gazed at the Olds for a moment, trying to figure out what
was going on. His grandfather had said he was going to a
grange meeting when he'd left the house a half hour
earlier.

Now, as Michael thought about it, something seemed
odd. Wasn't the grange just for farmers? And if it was,
why would it be at the Shieldses' house? Uncle Buck
wasn't a farmer. And come to think of it, why hadn't his
grandfather said anything about a meeting earlier? In fact,
he'd been watching television when the phone rang, and
then he'd just left, saying something about the grange
as he went out the door. But if he was coming over to
the Shieldses, why hadn't he suggested that everyone
come along? As Michael turned the matter over in his
mind, a pair of headlights glowed from around the bend.
Instinctively, he grabbed his bike and eased himself
behind the hedge that separated the house from the lot
next door.

The car pulled up, and a moment later Dr. Potter got
out, carrying his black bag, and hurried across the lawn
and up the porch steps. The door opened almost immediately,
and Michael saw his grandfather take Dr. Potter by the
arm and pull him inside.

For a moment, Michael was tempted to walk across the
lawn, climb the steps, and knock on the door. But then, as
he stood in the gathering gloom of the evening, his mind
was changed. It was almost as if there were a voice inside
his head, whispering to him, telling him to leave the
house. From beside him, a low growl rumbled from
Shadow's throat, and Michael laid a hand on the dog to
calm him.

Almost against his will, he wheeled the bicycle out from
behind the hedge, mounted it, and started pedaling away,
Shadow trotting along behind. Once, Michael glanced back
over his shoulder, but from the outside nothing at the
Shieldses' seemed amiss. It was just a house, with some
kind of a meeting going on inside.

Except the voice in his head told him there was something else.

Something he didn't understand yet, but soon would . . .

As Michael Hall rode away from the house, Laura Shields gazed up at Dr. Potter, her eyes pleading.

"Can't I go to the hospital? Please, can't you take me to the hospital?"

Potter took her hand in his own, stroking it gently. "It's too late, Laura. The baby could come any time, and the hospital is forty miles away."

"I can make it," Laura whispered, even though she knew she couldn't. Another cramp wracked her body, and she felt the tiny form inside her shift its position. "If I'm in the hospital, I know the baby will be all right. I *know* it."

"Hush," Potter soothed. "Hush, Laura. We're all here, and we're all going to take care of you. You'll be fine. In a few hours, it'll all be over, and you'll be fine." He released her hand, then rummaged in his bag. A moment later he handed Laura a small white pill and held a glass of water for her. "Take this," he commanded. "Take this, and try to get some sleep."

"But the baby," Laura moaned. "What about the baby? I have to be awake when my baby comes."

"You will be," Potter promised. "But right now, you mustn't worry about the baby, Laura. You mustn't even think about it. Not yet."

Not think about it? Laura wondered as she felt the pill begin its swift work. How can I not think about my baby?

And then, as Potter sat gently wiping her sweating brow with a cool washcloth, she began drifting into a fitful sleep. But just before she slipped into unconsciousness, she spoke once again.

"He can't have this one," she whispered. "It's not for him. It's not for Nathaniel . . . it's for *me* . . ."

CHAPTER 10

"Easy, Magic, take it easy."

It had been going on for nearly two hours, and Michael was beginning to wonder if anything was ever going to happen. He was perched on the partition between Magic's stall and the one next to it, while Eric stood at the mare's head, a steady stream of soothing words flowing from his mouth into her ear. His hands roamed over the horse's head and neck, gripping her halter whenever she tried to pull away, but never jerking at the leather straps. "How long does it take?" Michael asked, but if Eric heard his words, he ignored them. It was Leif Simpson who replied.

"Won't know for a little while yet. So far, everything looks all right, and if she can do it herself, we might have a foal in another hour. But if things are twisted around, it could take a lot longer."

"Twisted around? Twisted how?"

"If the colt's in the wrong position," Leif explained. "If it comes out head first, we're home free. But sometimes they don't, and you have to lend a hand."

"How?"

Eric's father grinned at him, his eyes twinkling. "You have to climb right in after the colt. Grab it by the legs, or anything else you can get hold of, and start working it out."

124

Michael wasn't at all sure he believed the man, and the doubt in his eyes was reflected in his words. "But what about wild horses? What happens to them?"

"Wild horses are a different breed of cat, so to speak," Leif told him, "different from domesticated ones. We breed farm animals for traits we want, but sometimes when we breed things in, we breed other things out. So wild horses don't have problems foaling, but on the other hand, they're not as big, and not as strong as old Magic here. Understand?"

As Michael nodded, Magic whinnied loudly, shook herself, and pawed at the floor with her forelegs. "Hang on to her, son," Leif warned unnecessarily, for Eric had a firm grip on the worried mare.

"It's like she doesn't know what's happening," Michael observed.

"Oh, she knows, all right," Leif Simpson replied. "She's been shoving hay around her stall for a couple of days now, getting things ready." He glanced up at Michael. "Sure you don't want to come down here? You can see better."

Michael shook his head. Though he wanted to watch the birth, he also wanted to be safely out of the way if something went wrong. Though he wasn't about to admit it, he had not yet taken on the casual attitude toward horses that the kids in Prairie Bend all seemed to have been born with.

As Michael watched, Leif Simpson frowned, looked closely at the horse, then smiled. "Hang on, Eric," he said quietly. "Here it comes." And as Michael watched, the head of the foal slowly emerged from the mare's womb. "Come on," Leif Simpson urged. "Come on, baby, you're almost there. Easy. Easy . . . eeeeeasy!"

Suddenly the emerging form stopped moving, and Leif Simpson cursed softly. He reached out and began working his hand around the foal, gently pressing with his fingers, feeling his way into the cervical opening.

"What is it, Pa?" Eric asked. Though his hands remained firm on the nervous mare's halter, his anxious eyes were on his father.

"It's a foreleg," Leif replied. "It's not bad. Just got to ease it around so the hoof is loose, and it can slip right out."

Without thinking, Michael slid off the partition and moved closer, staring in fascination at the tiny form that hung suspended, only partially born, its coat matted and damp with the wetness of birth. And then, as he watched, Leif Simpson pulled his hand gently away, exposing a tiny hoof. Almost immediately, the birthing process resumed, and a few moments later the foal dropped from the womb, Leif easing it to the floor of the stall.

"Let her go," he told his son, and Eric released his hold on the mare's halter. Magic, freed, immediately strained her head and neck back, and began licking at the tiny colt. It shivered under its mother's tongue, then struggled uncertainly to its feet, teetered for a few seconds, and dropped back to the floor. It rested; then, once more, it rose to its feet. Instinctively, as Magic still licked at it, it found a teat and began suckling.

"Wow," Michael breathed.

"Neat, isn't it?" Eric asked as proudly as if he himself were the father of the colt. "This one was easier than the last one. Last time, she breeched, and it took most of the night."

"Can I touch it?" Michael asked.

"Not yet," Leif cautioned him. "We want it to get a good fix on Magic. If we start handling it too soon, it could imprint on one of us, and wind up thinking we're its mother. You want to spend the next few months with a colt following you around, trying to get milk?"

Michael cocked his head, gazing in wonder at the tiny form. Unborn only a few minutes ago, the foal was already beginning to take care of itself. "If it were that colt," he eventually said, "I might not mind at all."

"Well, maybe you wouldn't," Leif Simpson replied. "But Magic would be mighty upset." He glanced around the stall, then pointed to the mops and brooms that leaned against one of its walls. "The sooner you two get this mess cleaned up, the sooner you can get back to admiring that little family."

The two boys began working on the stall, cleaning up and disposing of the placenta, removing the soiled straw and replacing it with fresh. But as they worked Michael's eyes kept drifting to the colt.

He wished the colt were his.

Laura Shields woke up, her body wracked with pain. The contractions were coming rapidly now, only a few seconds apart. Dimly, she was aware of people around her: Dr. Potter, standing near the foot of the bed; Buck, next to her, holding her hand. In the far corner, near the door, her father stood, watching her intently. Laura lay still for a moment, waiting for a respite from the pain before she finally spoke, and when it came, her voice sounded distant to her, as if she were far away from herself.

"Go away," she whispered hoarsely. "Go away and leave me alone."

"Hush," Buck told her, his gruff voice distorted with an attempt to be tender. "It's going to be all right. We're all here, and we'll take care of you."

"I don't *want* you," Laura moaned. "Get Mother. I want Mother to help me. Please? If I can't go to the hospital, can't I at least have Mother?"

"Don't, Laura," Buck replied. "Don't talk that way. You know it has to be this way. You know it."

Why? Laura wondered as the pain closed in on her once more. Why does it have to be this way? Why do I have to be alone with the men? Why can't I have my mother with me?

There were no answers to her questions, and all she could do was look up into her husband's eyes. "It's going to be all right, isn't it?" she whispered. "Please, tell me it's going to be perfect, and it's going to be mine, and it isn't going to die. Promise me? Please, Buck, promise me?''

There was silence for a moment as another contraction surged through Laura. Involuntarily, she crushed Buck's hand in her own, but managed to suppress the scream that rose in her throat. "Please," she begged when she could talk once more. "Please promise me."

"I can't," Buck whispered. "You know I can't."

And then the contractions seized her once again, and Laura knew the time had come. Clenching her hands, bracing herself against Buck's strong arms, she bore down, and felt the child within her move, edging slightly downward.

"Good," she heard Dr. Potter say, as if from a great distance. "That's good Laura. I can see the head. Again." Once more, feeling the rhythm of the contractions, she bore down. "Again. Again. Once more . . ."

She bore down hard, and again she felt the baby move. This time, though, the movement was accompanied by a searing pain that sliced through her body, forcing a scream from her throat.

And in her mind, that searing pain cut through her consciousness, peeled away the layers of scar tissue she'd built up over the years, and the memories came flooding back to her. Her brain, muddled with drugs and pain, began garbling memory and reality. As Laura's body delivered her baby into the world, her mind delivered her into the past.

Her father was there, standing at the foot of the bed, staring at her.

"You killed him."

Laura heard the words, but wasn't sure what they meant. And yet, she knew, they were her words, her voice that had spoken them.

Beside her, Potter ignored the tormented words that Laura had uttered, concentrating only on the baby that was slowly emerging from her womb.

Laura's whole body was writhing on the bed now, and

her arms flailed at the air, striking out at something that wasn't there. "My baby was alive," she screamed. "I felt it moving. It was alive, and you killed it!"

Amos Hall's eyes fixed on his daughter. "Stop it, Laura," he said. "You don't know what you're saying. The baby isn't born yet."

Laura's agony only increased. She was moaning now, and her hands twisted at the sheets. Her words became indistinguishable, but in her mind she could see it all. It was her baby, and Dr. Potter was holding it, and it was dead, and they were telling her it had been born dead, but she knew they were lying. She knew it had been all right, and that they had killed it. She knew it. She knew . . .

At the foot of the bed, Dr. Potter held the tiny form that had finally slipped free from the strictures of the womb. Its eyes were closed, and there was a bluish cast to its skin.

Potter held the baby deftly in his left hand, its head down, and with his right hand, he delivered a quick slap to its buttocks.

Potter's eyes met Amos's, and a silent message seemed to pass between the two men. Nearby, Buck Shields stood, watching the doctor, watching his father-in-law, waiting.

"Again," Amos Hall said, his impassive eyes fixed on the baby. "Try again."

Potter nodded once, then struck the baby's rump again, harder this time.

"That's it, then," Amos Hall said softly.

Laura Shields began screaming, and her husband quickly gathered her in his arms, holding her head against his chest, muffling her cries as best he could. She struggled in his arms, trying to work herself loose, trying to reach out for her baby, but it was no use. Buck held her immobile, and after a moment she made herself stop screaming, closed her eyes, and lay back on the pillow, sobbing softly.

Potter sighed. "This can't keep happening," he said quietly, as Amos Hall took the tiny body from his hands. Then he moved to the bed, and reached out, tentatively touching Laura's hair. She jerked away from him.

"Go away," she whispered in a broken voice. "Just go away and leave me alone."

"It was born dead, Laura," Dr. Potter told her. "You have to believe that. Your baby was born dead. You've had a miscarriage."

She opened her eyes and tried to reconcile his words to her memories. "Miscarried?" she asked. "It was born dead?"

Potter nodded. "It was premature, and it was born dead. You have to remember that, Laura. Can you do that?"

"I miscarried," Laura repeated in disbelieving tones. "I miscarried, and my baby was born dead."

A few minutes later, as Potter's sedative began easing her into sleep, Laura Shields repeated the words to herself once more, but she knew she didn't believe them.

The baby had been alive. She was sure it had been alive. And she was sure they had killed it. They had killed it, and they had sent it to Nathaniel.

But still, she couldn't be sure. It had all been so strange, and even as it had all been happening, and the baby was being born, she couldn't be sure of what was real and what was memory. And now, she would never really know.

Then, in her last moments of consciousness, she came to a decision. She would try to accept what the doctor had told her. From now on, when she thought of this night, she'd tell herself that all that had happened was that she'd miscarried.

She'd miscarried, and the baby was born dead.

It would be easier that way.

Eric Simpson cocked his head and stared at Michael Hall. He looked as though he was watching something, but Eric couldn't figure out what it was. "Somethin' wrong?" he finally asked.

Michael started, and then his eyes slowly focused on Eric. "I thought I saw something," he said uncertainly. "Or heard something. And I've got a headache."

Eric grinned. "That's the stuff we slopped down the

floor with. It'll go away as soon as we're outside. Come on.''

It was nearly midnight, and the cleanup from the foaling was finally done. But Michael couldn't quite remember finishing the job. He'd been hosing down the barn floor, and his head had begun to ache, and then he'd seen something. It had only been a flash, and it had seemed to come from inside his head, and yet he was sure he'd recognized some faces.

His grandfather, and Dr. Potter.

And Dr. Potter had been holding something, but Michael hadn't quite been able to make out what it was.

And there had been a sound, high pitched, like the shriek of the wind, or like someone screaming.

Then it was gone.

Now, outside in the cool night air, Michael couldn't even quite remember what it had been like, except for the scream.

The scream was still echoing in his head, and despite what Eric had said, his head still ached.

"It's Nathaniel," he muttered. "I bet it's Nathaniel."

Suddenly the sound of a screen door slamming jarred his reverie, and he heard Eric's mother's voice.

"You boys all done? Want something to eat?"

Michael looked up at Mrs. Simpson. She seemed to be a long way away, and he couldn't really see her very well. He shook his head. "I—I better get back to Grandpa's house."

"Would you like a ride?" Mrs. Simpson asked. "It's past midnight."

Again Michael shook his head. "I can ride my bike. I'll be okay."

His head still pounding with pain and his vision oddly blurry, Michael mounted his bike, whistled to Shadow, and rode off into the night. When he was gone, Ione Simpson put an arm around her son's shoulders and started toward the house. "Is Michael all right?" she asked. "He seemed sort of—odd, just now."

Eric frowned up at his mother. "He was weird," he
said emphatically. "Out in the barn, he started acting
funny, and then he said he had a headache." Michael had
said something else, too, Eric thought, something about
Nathaniel. He considered telling his mother that as well,
then changed his mind. No point in getting his mom all riled
up over that old ghost story. But it really was weird. And a
little scary. Eric felt a shiver start crawling up his spine.

It was as he came around the curve between the Simpsons'
farm and his mother's that Michael first became aware of
the lights.
Far off to the left, dimmed by the distance, he first
thought they were fireflies. He slowed, then stopped the
bike, dropping one foot to the ground to maintain his
balance. Shadow, his hackles slightly raised, crouched
beside him. Michael squinted into the darkness, trying to
determine shapes and forms, but there were none. Only a
faint glow, broken every now and then as something passed
between himself and the source of the lights. Frowning,
the pain in his head increasing by the moment, he started
the bike moving again, concentrating on the lights until the
dark shape of his mother's house cut them off. And then,
as he came to the driveway, they reappeared, and he
suddenly knew where they were.
Potter's Field.
His mind flashed back twenty-four hours, and he saw
what his grandfather had described—a woman, her back
bent as she stooped over, wandering in the night, searching,
constantly searching for what she would never find.
He remembered the tale, and as his headache worsened,
he tried to shake it from his mind. He couldn't.
He dismounted the bicycle, and began walking it up the
driveway until he stood in the shelter of the house, concealed from whatever might be lurking in the field. Still,
whatever was there was too far away for him to see
clearly. He stayed where he was for a moment, indecisive.
Then Shadow, whimpering softly, slunk away into the

darkness. Michael made up his mind, leaned the bike against the side of the house, and followed the dog.

He came to the fence that separated his mother's property from Mr. Findley's. Barely pausing, he slipped between the strands of barbed wire; then, crouching low in the dim moonlight, he scurried across to Findley's barn. His head was throbbing now, but it seemed to him he could begin to make out forms in the faint light emanating from the field.

And then, as he and Shadow slipped into the darkness next to the barn, he heard the voice, the same voice he'd heard before: flat, toneless.

"Michael."

It wasn't a question, and Michael knew it. The possessor of that voice knew who he was. He pressed closer to the barn.

"Nathaniel?" he whispered.

"Come in," the voice urged him. "Come in."

As if in a trance, Michael moved around the barn and lifted the bar from its brackets. Swinging the door open just enough to let himself through, he slipped inside, then pulled the door closed behind him.

"Over here." The voice drifted eerily out of the darkness, seeming to come from nowhere and everywhere. "Over this way."

And then, though the voice had not told him which way to go, though he could see nothing in the pitch blackness of the barn, Michael began moving through the darkness, knowing with the passage of every second that he was coming closer to Nathaniel. It was as if Nathaniel was reaching out to him, guiding him, showing him the way through the darkness with his own eyes.

And Michael's headache was suddenly gone.

He drifted down the aisle between the rows of stalls, his footsteps echoing in the emptiness. Then he paused. Though he could still see nothing, he reached out a hand, and immediately touched a door handle. Lifting the latch, he pulled the door open and stepped into the tack room that lay beyond. He was close now, very close. He could feel Nathaniel's presence.

"Here," the voice of Nathaniel told him. "You can see from here." Michael crossed the room, his senses vibrating with a strange kind of awareness, a feeling of sharing himself with another, and sharing that other as well. Then he was standing near the outer wall of the barn, and Nathaniel was with him.

"Closer," Nathaniel urged him, his voice no longer filling the little room, but seeming to emanate from inside Michael's own head. "Stand closer, and see with me."

There was a tiny gap in the barn siding, and Michael pressed his eye against it. The moonlight outside seemed to have grown brighter, and suddenly Michael could see clearly across the fields to the cottonwoods along the river.

And near the cottonwoods, he could see the lights. Three of them, oil lanterns, their wicks turned low, set in a triangle. And inside the triangle, the form of a man.

"Who is it?" Michael whispered in the darkness.

"My father."

"What's he doing?" he asked.

"Do not speak," Nathaniel's voice commanded. "If he knows you are with me, he will try to kill you."

Michael fell silent, knowing deep within himself that the words, though incomprehensible, were the truth. He waited. In a moment the strangely toneless voice came to him again. "I have been calling you. Why did you not come before?"

Michael was silent, but his mind was working, remembering.

His father's funeral, when he had seen this barn, seen something here that no one else had seen.

Watching the barn from the window of the room that would be his, knowing what it looked like inside, though he'd never been here

Night before last, when he'd come to the barn, knowing that there was something waiting for him.

And now, tonight.

When finally he spoke, he spoke only within himself. "I couldn't hear you. Did you call me tonight?"

And the answer came back, also from within. "Yes. I saw him in the field and felt you near. I called you here so he would not see you."

"But what's he doing?"

"Sending one of us away. One of us was born tonight, and he is sending him away. Just as he sent me away. He does that to all of us . . . if he can." And in those words that sounded only in his head, Michael could feel a terrible loneliness. Then the voice came again. "I have been waiting for you a long time."

"Why?"

"I need you. And you need me. We are alone, Michael. There is no one else. Do you never feel the loneliness?"

Michael trembled in the darkness, but then Nathaniel touched him, and he felt calm again.

"Will you take me outside?"

Michael frowned in the darkness. "Now?"

"Yes."

"He'll see us."

"It does not matter. He cannot hurt us, if we are together. He hurt that one, though."

"Who?"

"The one who was born tonight. I felt it coming, and called out to it. It was a little boy."

"There was a foal . . ," Michael whispered, then fell silent. Once again, that strange vision flashed into his head, only now the faces were clear, and he could see what was in Dr. Potter's hands.

"Not a foal," Nathaniel's voice came. "A boy. A little boy. But he knew that the boy was mine so he brought him here. Now he is burying him. Look."

Michael gazed out into the night, but the light seemed to have faded slightly, and he couldn't see exactly what was happening.

"Take me out there," Nathaniel's voice echoed in Michael's head. "Take me out there, so we can kill him."

"K-kill him? Why?"

"Because he kills. It is for us to punish him, Michael. He hates us, and he fears us, and he will kill us. If he finds us, and if we are alone."

"But—"

The oddly disembodied voice seemed not to notice Michael's interruption. "He does not know about you yet, but if he finds out about you, you will die. Unless you stay with me. Stay with me, Michael."

Michael turned and for the first time saw Nathaniel's face, lit softly by the moonlight filtering through the weathered siding of the barn.

It seemed to be his own face—the same dark blue eyes and wavy brown hair, the same angular cheeks and strong jaw. But the blue eyes were without light, and Nathaniel's skin was pale, almost translucent, like his father's had been at the funeral, and his face was as expressionless as the voice Michael had been hearing in his head.

"How long have you been here?" Michael asked.

"A long time," Nathaniel told him, his voice resonating softly through the large, empty barn. "As long as I can remember. Will you take me outside?"

"Why can't you go out by yourself?" Michael asked with no note of challenge in his words.

Nathaniel stared at him for a long time, his dark blue eyes cold and empty. "I cannot do that," he whispered. "I can never go out by myself. Only with you, or with the others if I find them. Not by myself. It would not be safe."

"Why not?" Though the words formed in his mind, Michael didn't utter them. Nevertheless, Nathaniel answered.

"Only together will we be safe, Michael. Alone we have no power. Alone, they can destroy us. If they find out about me, I will die, and you will die. Unless we are together. Remember that, Michael."

Michael frowned in the darkness of the barn, trying to fathom the meaning of the words, the odd, almost chantlike cadence of the flat-toned speech. Then, as he turned away and peered once more through the crack of the siding, Nathaniel spoke again.

"Never speak of what you saw tonight. If they ask you, tell them what they want to hear. But do not speak the truth. If you tell them the truth, if you tell them of me, you will die."

The moonlight seemed to be fading faster now, and in the distance Michael could barely make out the glimmering light of the lanterns. He strained his eyes against the darkness, and became aware once more that his head was aching. "I—I can't see," he said, turning questioningly to Nathaniel.

But Nathaniel was gone.

CHAPTER 11

By the time Michael left the barn, the moon had disappeared below the horizon, and the night had taken on a
blackness that made the last of the lanterns gleam with an
almost unnatural brilliance. Michael carefully replaced the
bar on the barn door, then with Shadow beside him,
moved slowly through the darkness, his hands extended,
feeling for the barbed wire fence.

He found it. Holding the strands apart as far as he
could, he put his left leg through the fence, then bent
down to duck under the top wire.

A barb snagged the flannel of his shirt, and Michael
reflexively tried to jerk free. The barb worked further into
the material. He reached back with his right hand, feeling
for the wire. A barb pierced his skin, sinking into the ball
of his thumb. Suppressing a cry, he yanked his hand back.
Shadow whined sympathetically and tried to lick the injured hand, but Michael brushed him aside and inserted the
thumb in his mouth, sucking hard on the wound. As the
salty taste of blood filled his mouth, his eyes instinctively
went to the single lantern that still glowed in the field. As
he watched, it went out. With the disappearance of the
light, Shadow's whine turned into a warning growl.

A moment later, Michael heard a car door slam and an

engine grind, cough once, then catch, quickly settling into a reluctant hum.

Ignoring the barbs, Michael forced his torso through the fence, pulling his right leg behind him. The sound of the car was louder now, and even though no lights were showing, he knew the car was coming toward him. He twisted frantically against the fence, but several of the barbs were now firmly embedded in the shredding flannel of his shirt, and he was held fast.

And then, as the engine's drone drew ever nearer, he gave a last lunge against the restraining fence, and his shirt tore free. He dashed across the open space between the fence and his mother's house and dove behind a patch of bushes. A second later, the car—unrecognizable in the darkness—cruised slowly by the house, then down the driveway to the road. Only when it was on the highway did its lights go on.

Michael waited until the car was well out of sight before he emerged from the bushes, breathing hard, his torn shirt damp with sweat. Shadow skittered nervously at his feet. He located his bike, but instead of mounting it, he wheeled it along the driveway, then across the road. He paused there for several more minutes, thinking hard. What was he going to tell his mother? How could he explain his torn shirt?

And then Nathaniel's words came back to him.

"Never tell them the truth.

"If you tell them the truth, you will die.

"Tell them what they want to hear."

Even as fear began to grip him, an idea began to take shape in his mind.

"Laura lost her baby?" Janet asked, the words echoing oddly in the Halls' kitchen. "What are you talking about?"

"She miscarried," Amos Hall replied. He peeled off his jacket and hung it on the hook by the back door, then poured himself a cup of coffee from the ever-present pot on the stove. When he finally sat down in his usual position at the kitchen table, Janet stared at him dazedly. Though his expression was impassive, she could see the pain in his eyes. Then, as if sensing the thought that had immediately formed in her mind, he said, "It didn't have anything to do with her overworking this weekend. The— the fetus was malformed, and Dr. Potter said the baby would have been born dead even if Laura'd carried it to term."

Janet released the breath she'd been unconsciously holding, and sank back in her chair. "But why didn't you tell me what was happening?" she asked. "Why that story about the grange? I'd have gone with you. Anna and I both would have." Her eyes shifted to her mother-in-law for confirmation, but Anna only sat motionless in her chair, her hands folded in her lap, her eyes blank. Janet turned helplessly back to Amos.

"We thought it would be better this way," he said. "We were afraid something like this might happen, and we decided it would be better if you weren't there." His eyes moved toward Janet's torso, and Janet's fingers moved instinctively to touch her abdomen.

"I—I don't understand. . . ."

"This isn't the first child Laura's lost," Amos told her. "She—well, she doesn't have children easily."

"But I should have been there," Janet insisted. "After all she's done for me, the least I could have done was be there."

"No," Anna said, sighing deeply. Janet turned to look at her. A sad, apologetic smile reflected the look in Anna's eyes. "Laura wouldn't have wanted you there," she said. "She wouldn't have wanted either of us there. For me—you know why it would have been painful for me. And for you . . . well, you and Laura are about the same age, and she wouldn't want to frighten you. She wouldn't want you to go through the next few months worrying that what happened to her might happen to you."

"Me?" Janet asked, her bewilderment increasing. "Did she tell you that?"

Anna reached out and took Janet's hand. "She didn't need to. You've been through so much already, dear. And it's not just Laura, you know. We all worry about you. Tonight, Amos decided the best thing to do was wait until it was all over, and hope we'd be able to tell you you had a new niece or nephew." The half smile left her face, and her eyes hardened as they flashed briefly toward her husband. "Things don't always work out the way we want them to," she said.

Oblivious to the look that had passed between Anna and Amos, Janet nodded her head. "It must have been terrible for her," she said at last. "Not even in the hospital, and with nobody there—"

"I was there," Amos Hall corrected her. "And Buck and Dr. Potter."

"I'm sorry," Janet said quickly, immediately contrite. "I didn't mean that. I just meant—"

"Don't worry, dear," Anna assured her. "I know exactly what you meant."

Again, Janet fell silent for a moment, but then she took a deep breath, as a thought struck her. "But what about Ryan? Wasn't he going out to the Simpsons' with Michael?"

Amos shook his head. "He was home all evening."

Janet's eyes darted to the clock on the wall. It was a little past midnight. "But look at the time! Where's Michael?"

"Probably still at the Simpsons'," Anna told her. "A foaling can take all night."

"But what if he's coming home? He's all by himself, and he's only eleven—"

"And he can take care of himself," Amos assured her. "He's like his father—he'll be all right. Just try to take it easy, Janet. Getting yourself into a state won't help."

It was then that they heard the first scream.

Michael had mounted the bike and ridden quickly back toward the Simpsons'. When he was halfway there, he picked the bicycle up and jammed it into the fence between the north side of the road and the field beyond.

When the wheels were securely tangled in the wire, Michael climbed the fence and began walking across the field. In the distance, he could see the faint glow which he knew marked his grandparents' house. Sure of his bearings, he began running, stumbling in the darkness every few yards, pitching headlong into the fresh-turned soil. Each time he fell, Shadow was instantly next to him, nosing at him, snuffling and whining until Michael rose once more to his feet. By the time he reached the far side of the field, with his grandparents' house clearly visible, his hands and face were scratched and bleeding, and what was left of his clothing was covered with grime. He climbed carefully through the last fence and paused to catch his breath.

As his breathing slowly settled into an easy rhythm, he watched the house, but if there was any movement inside, he was too far away to see it. Still, even as he crossed the road to the end of the driveway, he was sure that his grandparents, as well as his mother, were waiting for him.

Twenty yards from the house, he gathered his energy together, and began running.

Running, and screaming. Shadow, as if picking up a cue, added his furious barking to the melee.

"Mother! Grandpa! Help! Help me!"

Still running at top speed, he dashed around the house and hurled himself up the steps of the back porch, his fists pounding on the door. "Help me! Mother, help me!" The door flew open, and Michael threw himself into his mother's arms.

Janet's arms closed tightly around her hysterical son, and she sank to her knees to gather him against her. "What is it?" she asked when Michael's terrified screams finally stopped. "Michael, what happened?"

"My bike!" Michael wailed. "I was coming home, and all of a sudden there was a car behind me. I thought it was Mrs. Simpson, but it wasn't. It—it ran me right off the road."

"Where?" Janet asked. "Where did it happen?"

"Right near the Simpsons'. I hadn't even gotten to our house yet."

Her mind spinning, Janet's gaze drifted up to Amos Hall. He was on his feet now, staring at his grandson.

"Tell us exactly what happened."

They were at the kitchen table now, and Michael was sitting huddled close against his mother, his eyes fixed on the face of his grandfather, who finally reached out to pat his hand. Instinctively, Michael pulled his hand away, but the old man ignored the rebuff. "It's all right. You're safe now. Just try to tell us what happened."

"I was coming home from Eric's," Michael began, letting his voice quaver. "I was coming along the road, and I was looking at our place in the moonlight. And then I heard something. It was a car, and it was coming along the road behind me." He fell silent, as if the memory was too frightening to talk about.

"Go on," his mother said gently. "What kind of car was it? Did you recognize it?"

Michael hesitated, then shook his head. "I don't think it was from around here. And it was coming real fast." He stared up at his mother. "It—it was almost like they were trying to hit me."

"Oh, no . . ." Janet protested, but Michael bobbed his head.

"I got way over, as far as I could, and pedaled faster. I thought maybe I could make it to our driveway, but I couldn't. And then, when it was right behind me, they honked their horn, and I skidded off the road."

"You mean they hit you?" Janet asked, the color draining from her face.

Michael swallowed, but shook his head. "Unh-unh. But then the car slowed down, and I got scared. So I climbed over the fence and hid in the field across the street from our house. And when the car came back, I started running."

"But honey, they were probably looking for you to see if you were all right."

"Maybe—maybe they wanted to kidnap me," Michael suggested, his eyes wide. "Anyway, I didn't even try to go back for the bike. I just started running across the field, but I kept falling and got my clothes all messed up." He looked uncertainly from his mother to his grandfather, then back to his mother again. "Are—are you mad at me?"

Janet hugged him close. "Mad at you? Honey, why would I be mad at you? It was just an accident, that's all. I'm sure no one was trying to run over you, or hurt you at all."

"But—"

"Shh," Janet said. "There isn't any reason why anyone would want to hurt you. You just had a bad fright, that's all. And I think the best thing you can do is go upstairs, take a nice hot bath, then go to bed. By morning you'll have forgotten all about this."

"But what about my bike?" Michael protested.

"Your bike?"

"It's still out there. It got all tangled in the fence, and I was so scared, I just left it there."

"We can get it in the morning," Amos told him. "Now, do what your mother says, and get on upstairs."

"But not before you give your grandmother a kiss," Anna suddenly interrupted. All through the conversation, she had sat in silence, her hands folded in her lap, her eyes shifting constantly between her husband and her grandson. But now she held her arms up, and Michael moved to her side. She wrapped her thin arms around him, and drew him close, so close her lips were at his ear, as if she were going to kiss him. "It's all right," she whispered. "I don't know what happened tonight, but I'll make him believe whatever you say." Then she kissed him on the cheek and released him.

As Michael straightened up, he looked at his grandmother in puzzlement. She knew he had lied. Was she going to tell on him? And then he understood the rest of her words. She was not going to tell on him. Instead, she was going to back him up. Without thinking, he smiled at her.

"I love you, too, Grandma," he whispered, just loud enough for her to hear. Then he turned to his mother. "Mom? Can Shadow sleep in my room tonight?"

Janet smiled and nodded her head. "All right. But just tonight."

His face wreathed in smiles, Michael dashed to the back door and pulled it open. "Shadow! Come on, boy!" Instantly, the big dog loped into the kitchen, then paused to peer suspiciously at the three people who sat around the table. As Michael left the kitchen to go upstairs, the dog hesitated only a second before following. When the boy was out of earshot, Amos spoke.

"I don't like that, Janet. Dogs belong outside. Particularly that dog."

"Oh, Amos, it's only for one night," Janet replied. "Besides, the dog is crazy about Michael. He never leaves his side."

"But we don't know where it came from. For all we know, it could be sick."

"Shadow?" Janet asked. "Amos, that's one of the healthiest-looking dogs I've ever seen. But if it'll make you feel better, I'll tell Michael to make him sleep on the floor."

"I'll tell him myself," Amos said. "As soon as he's in bed, I'll go up."

"I'm *not* lying," Michael protested. He was in bed, the covers drawn tightly up around his neck as if they could protect him from the anger he could see in his grandfather's eyes.

Amos sat on the edge of the bed, and in the corner, his ears up and his eyes alert, Shadow crouched watchfully, his tail curled around his feet, its tip twitching dangerously.

"No one would try to run you down, and no one would try to kidnap you," Amos said once more. "And you didn't just fall off your bicycle, did you?" He spoke in a low voice, his eyes steady on the frightened boy in the bed. "Tell me the truth, Michael," he went on. "Sooner or later, you'll have to tell me the truth."

"If you tell them the truth, you will die."

Nathaniel's words rang in his head, and Michael squirmed further into the bed. "But that *is* the truth," he whispered. "I wouldn't lie to you, Grandpa. Really, I wouldn't."

Amos's hand came up, and Michael was certain his grandfather was about to strike him. But then, from the corner, came a low snarl. Startled, Amos glanced over at Shadow. The big dog was on his feet now. His ears no longer stood up, but were flat back against his head, and his whole body seemed to be a mass of tension. Only when Amos lowered his upraised hand did the dog begin to relax.

"I'm not lying," Michael said once more.

But Amos seemed to have forgotten everything except the dog. "Where'd he come from?" he asked. From his tone Michael knew the old man wasn't asking him a question, so he didn't try to answer it. Then Amos's eyes shifted back to Michael. "We're going to have to get rid of him, you know. If his owner doesn't turn up, we're going to have to get rid of him."

"Why?" Michael demanded. Suddenly, with Shadow threatened rather than himself, he sat up in the bed, the covers falling away from his chest. "Why can't I keep him?"

"I don't like dogs," Amos told him.

"But he's mine! He saved my life, and he's mine!"

"No, he's not. He's a stray, and he doesn't have a home. And tomorrow, if his owner doesn't show up, I'm going to get rid of him."

"No!" Michael's head was suddenly pounding, and his eyes blazed with fury.

Amos's voice dropped dangerously. "Don't argue with me, boy. You know I won't be argued with."

Shadow, sensing the menace to his master in the old man's voice, rose to his feet again, his fangs bared; his snarl barely audible.

For a moment there was dead silence and then, as the dog and the old man watched each other with wary eyes, the tension in the room was broken by a tapping at the door. A moment later Janet stepped inside. Shadow instantly dropped back to the floor, resting his muzzle on his forepaws.

"Is everything all right?" Janet asked.

Amos rose to his feet. "Everything's fine. I was just saying goodnight." He reached down and patted Michael's shoulder. "See you in the morning. And remember what I said." Then he was gone, and Michael and Janet were alone, except for Shadow, who rose and padded over to the bed. As Janet lowered herself to the spot that Amos had just vacated, the big dog rested his head in her lap, and his large eyes gazed up at her.

"He wants you to scratch his ears," Michael said. Janet tentatively touched the animal's ears, and his tail began wagging. Smiling, Janet scratched harder, and the big dog wriggled with pleasure. As her fingers continued to play over the dog's fur, she turned her attention to Michael.

"Does it hurt?"

Michael shook his head. He looked uncertain for a moment, then once more shook his head. "Grandpa didn't believe me."

Janet frowned. "Didn't believe you? What do you mean?"

"He didn't believe someone almost ran over me. And he wants to kill Shadow."

"Michael, what are you talking about?"

"He says we have to get rid of Shadow. We don't, do we? I can keep him, can't I?"

"But what if his owner shows up?"

"He won't," Michael said. "I think he's a stray. Besides, he saved my life. I can keep him, can't I? You won't let Grandpa hurt him, will you?"

"Of course not," Janet assured him. "And if no one shows up to claim him, you can keep him. You may not be able to keep him in the house until we move into our own place, but he won't mind staying outside. Will you, Shadow?''

Shadow sat down and raised one paw, which he offered to Janet. Solemnly, the dog and the woman shook hands. ''See?'' Janet asked Michael. ''We just made a deal. After tonight, Shadow will sleep outside 'til we get moved. Then all three of us will share the house. Now, what do you mean, Grandpa didn't believe you? You mean he didn't believe someone tried to run over you?''

Michael nodded.

''Well, maybe he's right. In fact, he probably is. I'll bet the car was going much slower than you thought, and when you fell off your bike, they just stopped to make sure you were all right.''

''But—''

Janet put a gentle finger to his lips. ''Hush.'' She tucked the covers snugly around him. ''Now, why don't you tell me all about the foaling. Was it interesting?''

A few moments later Michael was excitedly talking about the birth of the colt, describing in detail everything that had happened, everything that he and Eric had done.

''Well, it all sounds fascinating,'' Janet said when he was done. She stood up, then tucked the covers around her son, and leaned down to kiss him goodnight. ''Now you just think about all those things you learned tonight, and in a few minutes you'll be sound asleep. By tomorrow morning, you'll have forgotten all about your accident.'' She started toward the door, but Michael's voice stopped her.

''Mom?''

She turned back.

''Mom, Aunt Laura had her baby tonight, didn't she?''

Janet frowned. ''How did you know that?''

''I—I saw Dr. Potter go into Ryan's house. And I saw Grandpa's car there, too.'' He fell silent for a moment, then his brow furrowed. ''Mom, did something happen to the baby?''

Janet returned to the bed, and sat down again. ''What makes you ask a question like that?''

"Did it?" Michael pressed.

For a moment Janet wondered how to explain to Michael what had happened, then decided to face the question head on. "It was born dead, honey," she said quietly. "Those things happen sometimes. It's called a miscarriage, and all kinds of things can cause it. For your Aunt Laura, it was probably a blessing in disguise."

"Why?"

"Well, sometimes things go wrong with babies, and they just don't develop right. That's what happened to Aunt Laura's baby. Her miscarriage was just nature's way of correcting a mistake." Suddenly she frowned. "How did you know Aunt Laura had her baby tonight?"

Michael hesitated only a moment before shrugging. "I don't know. I guess Mrs. Simpson must have told me."

"All right." Once again Janet kissed her son goodnight. Then she went to the door of his room, turned to smile at him one last time, and switched off the light.

For a long time, Michael lay in the darkness, thinking.

Aunt Laura's baby hadn't been born dead.

He knew it hadn't, because Nathaniel had told him so. . . .

CHAPTER 12

"What am I supposed to say?" Michael asked anxiously as Janet pulled Amos Hall's Olds into the Shieldses' driveway.

"You probably won't have to say anything at all," Janet replied. "You can talk to Ryan while I talk to Aunt Laura. She's in bed, and you won't even have to go upstairs."

Relieved, Michael got out of the car and started across the lawn, his mother behind him. Then, as they mounted the steps to the porch of the white clapboard house, the front door opened and Buck Shields appeared, weariness etching haggard lines around his eyes. He nodded a greeting to Michael, then turned to Janet.

"Thanks for coming," he said. "She's upstairs in our room, the first one on the left."

Janet slipped her arms around her brother-in-law. "I'm so sorry," she whispered. "I wish I'd been here—"

"There was nothing you could have done." There was a flat lifelessness in Buck's voice that wrenched at Janet, and she had to turn her head away as her eyes flooded with tears. Brusquely, Buck extricated himself from her embrace. "Go on upstairs. She's waiting for you. I've got to get down to the store." An uncharacteristic grin played at the corners of his mouth. "My mother's looking after it. She means well, but she never quite manages to make things add up. Can you stay with Laura 'til I get back?''

"Of course," Janet assured him. "I can stay all day, if you need me." Her eyes fell on Michael, who was fidgeting near the front door. "Where's Ryan?"

"Out back, I think. Somewhere around, anyway." He started down the steps, then turned back. "Janet. Laura's—well, she's taking this hard. Don't upset her." Then, before Janet could reply, he hurried down the steps and across the yard. A moment later, he was gone.

As Michael headed around to the backyard, Janet went directly upstairs. She found Laura propped up against some pillows, her pale face framed by her dark hair, her eyes closed.

"Laura?" Janet whispered. "Are you awake?"

Slowly Laura's eyes came open, and she stared at Janet as if she didn't recognize her. Then a soft smile came over her face. "Janet? Janet, is that really you?"

Janet moved across the room, pulling a small chair close to the bed. "Who were you expecting?"

Laura's smile faded away. "Nobody, really," she said. "I've just been lying here, trying to pretend nothing happened." Her eyes met Janet's. "Did you do that when Mark died? Try to pretend it hadn't happened?"

Janet hesitated, then nodded. "It's shock, I suppose. You can't handle the pain, so you deny the injury. But all it does is postpone it." She paused, then: "Do you want to talk about it?"

A sigh escaped Laura's lips, and she turned her face away from Janet to stare at the wall. "I think they killed my baby, Janet," she whispered as her resolve to believe what she'd been told slipped away. "They said it was born dead, but I think they killed it."

Janet's mouth opened, but no words came out. Then, a moment later, she felt Laura's hand in her own.

"Why do they do that, Janet?" Laura continued. "Why do they kill my babies?"

The agony in Laura's voice wrenched at Janet. "Laura. Oh, Laura, you mustn't even think such a thing."

Laura's head turned once more, and Janet could see the tears that streaked her cheeks. "But it was all right, Janet. I *know* it was all right. They said it was born dead, but right up till the end, I could feel it moving." Her voice began to rise, and her grip on Janet's hand tightened. "I could feel it, Janet. If it had been dead, it wouldn't have moved, would it? Would it?"

Janet wondered what to say, wondered if she ought to call Buck or Dr. Potter. "I—I don't know," she said at last. "But sometimes things happen, Laura. Sometimes things go wrong, and there's nothing anybody can do."

Seeming to calm slightly, Laura let her head fall once more onto the pillows, and now her eyes fixed on the ceiling. When she spoke again, her voice was dull. "They wouldn't let me to go the hospital. They wouldn't take me to the hospital, and they wouldn't let mother come. I begged them, but they wouldn't let her come."

"She wouldn't have been able to do anything," Janet said, trying to soothe the distraught woman. "I know how horrible it must have been for you—"

Suddenly the fire came back into Laura's eyes, and she sat straight up in the bed. "Do you?" she demanded, her voice once more rising toward hysteria. "How can you know? Have you ever lost a baby? Have you ever been through what I went through last night? Have you?"

And once again Janet's childhood memory flashed through her mind. But it hadn't been a baby she had lost. It had been her whole family, burning before her very eyes. But she couldn't tell Laura about that, not now.

"N-no—" she stammered.

"Well, just wait, then. Just wait 'til your baby comes. They'll do it to you, too, Janet. Just like they did it to mother when her last baby came. They didn't let mother go to the hospital, either. And they won't let you! When your time comes, you'll be all alone, and they'll do what they want, and you won't be able to do anything about it. Then you'll know how I feel!''

Exhausted, she fell back onto the pillows, and her breathing became a strangling sob. Janet, on her feet now, glanced frantically around the room, her eyes finally alighting on a small vial of pills on the dresser. She picked them up and read the label, but the complicated name of the drug meant nothing to her. She took them to the bed. "Laura? Laura, do you want one of these?"

For a long time Laura was silent, and Janet began to wonder if she'd fainted. Then, once more, her eyes opened, and she stared at the bottle. Finally she shook her head. "No." She hesitated, then reached out to Janet. "I'm sorry," she said. "I shouldn't have said all those things. I must have sounded crazy. It was all just so terrible last night, Janet. It hurt so much, and I was so frightened and confused, and I knew they were killing the baby but I couldn't stop them. I couldn't stop them, Janet." Quietly, she began to cry. "I saw what happened," she repeated brokenly. "I saw it." Then her sobbing overcame her, and Janet took her in her arms, rocking her gently as if Laura herself were the baby she'd just lost.

Michael found Ryan behind the garage, desultorily stacking a pile of split logs. "Whatcha doing?"

Ryan glanced up, then stared openly at the scratches on Michael's face. "What happened to you?"

"I—I fell off my bike. Whatcha doing with the wood?"

"What's it look like? My dad says I have to get all this wood stacked by tonight. Wanta help?"

Michael shrugged, and picked up a piece of wood. Beneath it, something moved, and he immediately dropped the wood back on the pile. "Something's under there."

"Prob'ly a lizard," Ryan told him. "I caught three so far."

"How do you catch 'em?"

Ryan grinned. "Easy. You just hold real still, and pretty soon they think you're gone, so they come out to lie in the sun. Then you put your hand out real slowly, and sneak up behind them, and grab 'em. Wanta try it?''

"Sure."

Cheerfully abandoning work, Ryan picked a likely-looking spot and lowered himself onto a log, Michael taking up a position beside him. For a few minutes, the two of them sat silently.

"Can we talk?" Michael finally asked.

Ryan gave him a sidelong glance. "What about?"

"I mean, will the noise scare the lizards away?"

"Nah. They're deaf." Then: "How long'd the foaling take last night?"

"A long time," Michael bragged. "I didn't go to bed 'til real late." He hesitated, wanting to tell Ryan what had happened the night before, but Nathaniel's strange words still lingered in his mind: *"Never tell them the truth. Tell them what they want to hear."* But Nathaniel hadn't been talking about Ryan, had he?

Michael decided he had not: in his eleven-year-old mind, "them" meant "adults." It was grown-ups you had to keep secrets from, not other kids. "I—I think I saw Nathaniel last night."

Ryan turned to stare at him. "Nathaniel? The ghost?" His tone clearly betrayed his disbelief.

"I think so." Again Michael hesitated. Then: "If I tell you what happened, will you promise not to tell anyone? Anyone at all?"

Ryan regarded him with scorn. "What do you think I am? Besides, who'll I tell?"

"You can't tell anyone."

Ryan shrugged. "Okay. But what's the big deal? There's no such things as ghosts, so you couldn't have seen Nathaniel anyway."

"I didn't say I saw him," Michael argued. "I said I *thought* I saw him."

"Where?" Ryan demanded.

"In—he was in a building."

"What building?"

"A—a barn," Michael hedged.

Ryan's eyes narrowed suspiciously. "Whose barn?" he asked.

"None of your business," Michael said, but when Ryan turned away with an elaborate show of disdain, Michael retreated. "I don't know whose barn it was," he compromised. "But that's where I saw Nathaniel. At least I think I did."

Ryan's curiosity made him face Michael again. "Well, did you, or didn't you?"

"I don't know," Michael said, still not willing to commit himself to telling Ryan everything that had happened. "It was really weird. He—he wanted me to take him outside."

Suddenly something moved in the woodpile, and Ryan tensed, his eyes locked on a dark gap between two logs. Michael fell silent, and a few seconds later, the movement was repeated. Then, slowly, the pointed scaly nose of a small lizard appeared, its tongue darting out every few seconds.

"Don't move," Ryan warned. "If you move, it'll run away." There was a long silence as both boys concentrated on the lizard, while the wary reptile, as if sensing the danger, stayed where it was. "What do you mean, he wanted you to take him outside?" Ryan finally asked. "If he wanted to go outside, why didn't he just go?"

"How should I know? He said he couldn't. But then he—well, he just disappeared. I was talking to him, or sort of talking to him—"

"What do you mean, 'sort of'?" Ryan asked, turning his attention away from the lizard and focusing it fully on his cousin. "Did you talk to him or not?"

Michael wondered how to explain it. "He . . . he sort of talked to me without saying anything. It was like he was inside my head or something."

"That's crazy," Ryan declared. "People can't talk that way."

"I know," Michael agreed. "That's what I've been

thinking about. Last night I was sure I saw him and talked to him, but now I'm not so sure. Do you think—'' He broke off, suddenly sure he knew what Ryan would say if he finished the question.

"Think what?" Ryan pressed.

"Do you think I could have seen a ghost?" he asked, his eyes carefully on the woodpile and away from Ryan.

"There's no such thing as ghosts," Ryan repeated, but with a little less assurance than he'd had earlier.

"I know," Michael agreed. "And last night, I was sure he was real. But this morning, I'm not sure. It's weird."

"*You're* weird," Ryan replied. Suddenly he froze. "Wait a minute. Here comes one. Hold still."

Out of one of the gaps in the woodpile, a lizard appeared, moving slowly, almost as if it were under water. As Michael watched in fascination, its legs began to move, one by one. The tongue, flashing out every few seconds, seemed to be sensing the environment. Once, the lizard froze for a moment, and Michael was sure it was about to scurry back into the dark shelter from which it had come. But instead it started moving in a series of short darts, coming finally to rest on the top of a log, basking in the full sun. Its head was pointed away from the two boys. Michael felt Ryan stir.

"I'm gonna try for him," Ryan whispered. "Hold real still."

Moving as slowly as the lizard had, Ryan began bringing his hand forward, keeping it low down, out of the creature's line of sight. Each time the lizard tensed, Ryan froze, waiting until the lizard relaxed once more before resuming his furtive movements toward it. Finally, when he was only a few inches from the lizard, he made his move.

"Gotcha!" he crowed, cupping his hand over the wriggling animal. A second later, he grinned at Michael. "Wanta hold him?"

"Sure." Michael held out his hand, and Ryan carefully transferred the lizard from his fist to Michael's. For a few seconds it wriggled furiously against Michael's confining fingers, then lay still. Michael looked up at Ryan. "It stopped wiggling. Is it dead?"

"Naw. Open your hand real carefully, and take it in your fingers. Grab it right behind the front legs. If you grab it by the tail, it'll just take off, and grow another tail."

While Ryan supervised, Michael slid a finger into his still-closed fist, feeling around until he was sure he had the lizard trapped between his palm and the finger. Then he opened his fist, and picked up the little creature with two fingers. Its scaly back was the color of wood bark, and there were tiny claws at the end of each of its toes. But when he turned it over, its belly flashed an iridescent blue in the sunlight.

"Wanta hypnotize it?" Ryan asked.

Michael looked dubiously at his cousin. "How?"

"Just hold it upside down and rub its belly a couple of times."

Michael hesitated, then did as Ryan had told him. As he watched, the lizard's torso seemed to arch, and its eyes closed.

"Now put him down."

Carefully, Michael laid the lizard on a log, then stroked its belly a few more times. Finally he drew his finger away. The lizard stayed where he'd left it, its eyes closed, only a faint movement in its throat indicating that it was still alive.

"How long'll it stay that way?"

Ryan shrugged. "A few minutes. You can keep it that way forever, if you rub its belly again every time it starts to wake up. Except if you leave it in the sun too long, it'll get too hot and die." The two boys watched the lizard for a few minutes. Then, without warning, its eyes blinked open. It flipped itself over and disappeared back into the safety of the woodpile.

"Ryan?" Michael asked a few minutes later as the two of them once more began stacking the wood neatly against the back wall of the garage. "Do you think I really could have seen a ghost last night?"

Ryan looked at him disgustedly. "No."

"Then what did I see?"

"I don't think you saw anything," Ryan said. "And I don't want to talk about it anymore."

"But I *did* see something!"

"Bull!" Ryan exploded. "You didn't see anything, and you didn't go into any old barn, and you're just making all this up. All you did was fall off your bike, and now you're trying to make it sound like it wasn't your fault, 'cause you saw a ghost. Well, I don't believe you, and none of the other guys will, either. So if you don't shut up, I'm gonna tell my dad you went into old man Findley's barn. Then you'll really be in trouble."

Michael's eyes blazed with sudden anger. "You said you wouldn't tell anyone! You promised. Besides, I never said it was old man Findley's barn."

"So what?" Ryan sneered. "How was I supposed to know you were going to start trying to con me with a bunch of bull? And I can say anything I want to anyone I want to, so you just better watch out."

Michael fell silent. His head was throbbing with pain, and deep within his mind he thought he could hear a voice whispering to him, urging him to strike out at Ryan. Then, vaguely, he remembered the other day, when he'd suddenly told Ryan to drop dead, and for a moment—just for a second, really—he'd actually thought it was going to happen. He struggled to control himself, afraid of what might happen now if he gave in to that voice inside him, and at the same time knowing that if he kept talking about what he had seen the night before, Ryan would only accuse him of being crazy. But as he went on helping his cousin stack the wood, he kept thinking about the night before. And the more he thought about it, the more everything he'd seen and heard in the darkness began to seem like a dream.

And yet, he *had* seen lights in the field, and he *had* gone into Findley's barn.

He had seen a car, and he had seen someone in the light of the lanterns.

But had he seen Nathaniel?

And how could he have seen what was happening in the field? It had been so dark, and he'd been looking through a crack in the wall of a barn.

And that voice, the voice he thought was Nathaniel's.

It had been so strange, so flat. Had he really heard it at all?

He tried to picture it all in his mind: the blackness of the barn and the faint traces of silvery moonlight that had filtered through the wall.

How *could* he have seen anything? And he hadn't, he realized, really heard anything. That voice had been in his head, like the voice he had heard just now. Besides, he'd had a headache that night, and he could never quite remember exactly what happened when he had one of those headaches.

Maybe Ryan was right. Maybe he was crazy.

He decided he wouldn't talk anymore about what had happened last night, not to anybody. Still, he wished he could talk to his dad about it. His father had always been able to help him figure things out, but now he couldn't do that. Nor could he talk to his grandfather. He shuddered as he remembered the beating a couple of days ago—never his grandfather. But maybe his grandmother. Maybe sometime when he was alone with his grandmother, he'd talk to her about it.

Maybe . . .

As soon as Janet and Michael had left the house that morning, Amos had begun calling around Prairie Bend, trying to find Shadow's owner.

No one, however, was missing a dog, nor did anyone respond to Amos's description of Shadow. He hung up the phone after the last call and turned to Anna. "Well, I guess it's a stray. I'm gonna get my gun."

Anna glared at her husband. "You mean you're going to shoot that dog?"

"That's what I mean to do," Amos replied, his voice grim.

"No."

Amos turned baleful eyes on his wife. "What did you say?"

"There's no reason to shoot it. What's it done to you?"

"I don't like dogs."

"Sometimes I don't like you, either," Anna retorted, her voice low but steady. "Does that mean I should shoot you?"

"Anna—"

"It's not your dog, Amos. It's Michael's dog. It may have saved his life, and if you do anything to that animal, Michael will never forgive you. Your daughter hates you, and your son ran away from you. Do you want your grandson to hate you, too?"

"He'll never know," Amos told her. "By the time he gets home, the dog will be dead and buried. We'll tell him it ran away. He'll believe us."

"He might," Anna agreed. "He might believe us if we both told him that, but if you tell him the dog ran off, and I tell him you shot it, who's he going to believe?"

Amos's eyes hardened. "You wouldn't do that, Anna. You've never gone against my wishes, and you won't now."

"I will," Anna told him, folding her hands in her lap. "This time I will. You leave that dog alone."

Amos left the house without another word, but he felt his wife's eyes on him as he crossed the yard to the barn.

His wife's eyes, and Shadow's eyes.

The dog was curled up next to the back porch, his habitual post when Michael either was in the house or had left him behind. When the kitchen door suddenly swung open, and Amos's heavy tread struck the porch, Shadow's body tensed, and a vaguely menacing sound rumbled from his throat. His hackles raised slightly, but he made no move to get up. Amos regarded the dog with angry eyes.

"Get out of here," he said. He drew his right foot back, then swung it forward. Before the kick could land, Shadow had leapt to his feet and moved a few yards from the house. Amos followed him.

A yard at a time, Shadow backed away toward the barn. Amos kept steady pace with him, softly cursing at the dog, constantly trying to land one of his boots on Shadow's flank. But each time he lashed out with his foot, Shadow dodged away from him.

Suddenly the barn was between them and the house, and Shadow stopped backing away. He crouched low to the ground, and his ears lay back flat against his head. His snarl was loud now, and to Amos it appeared that a cunning had come into the animal's eyes.

Amos tried one more kick.

This time, Shadow made no attempt to leap away from Amos's foot. Instead, he seemed to wait until the last possible instant, then whipped his body to one side, at the same time twisting his neck so he could clamp his massive jaws down on Amos's ankle. With a lunge, he threw Amos off balance, and the big man fell heavily to the ground, grunting in a combination of pain and anger. In another second Shadow had abandoned his grip on Amos's ankle, and was at his throat, his fangs bared, saliva glistening on his tongue. For a long moment, Amos stared into the animal's eyes, only inches from his own, sure that those sharp canine teeth were about to begin slashing at him.

But it didn't happen. Instead of attacking Amos, Shadow suddenly moved forward, raising his leg.

A stream of hot yellow fluid spurted over Amos, drenching his shirt front, stinging his eyes, gagging him as some of it penetrated his mouth to trickle down his throat. And then, when he was through, Shadow moved off to sit on the ground a few feet away, his tail curled around his legs, his ears up, his tongue hanging from his open mouth.

Enraged, Amos lay still for a moment, then rose to his feet and started toward the house. But when he emerged a few minutes later, one hand gripping his gun, the yard was empty.

Shadow had disappeared.

CHAPTER 13

The weeks passed quickly. Janet spent her time working on the little farmhouse that she was fast coming to think of as home. Prairie Bend itself was also becoming home, giving Janet a sense of belonging she hadn't felt since her childhood.

The village seemed to be making a project of her little farm. Every day, as she and Michael worked on the house, people dropped by. Some of them came to work, some of them came bearing supplies.

"Found this linoleum out in the shed. Just been sitting there for a couple of years now. Do me a favor and use it before it rots."

"Got an old wood-electric the missus won't use anymore. Think you might be able to find a place for it? It's not much, but it should last a year or two."

"Thought I'd use this lumber to build a new hog-shed, but I found a prefab I couldn't pass up. Maybe you can use it to brace up that old cyclone cellar. Fact is, I've got some time, and I could show you how it's done." That man spent the rest of the day and half of the next rebuilding her storm cellar with his own lumber, and acted as if she was doing him a favor by "getting him away from work for a couple of days."

And so it went. With each day Janet came to feel more a

163

part of the community, came to feel the closeness of the people in Prairie Bend.

For Michael, though, it was a difficult time. He'd searched everywhere for Shadow, but been unable to find even a trace of the dog. The shepherd seemed to have vanished as mysteriously as it had appeared. Every day, Michael asked his grandfather what had happened, and every day, Amos told him the same thing: "That's the way with dogs. They come and they go, and you can't count on them. Be glad that pain-in-the-neck beast's gone." But Michael was not glad, and no matter how Janet tried to cheer him up, his low spirits persisted.

Amos Hall pulled his Olds to a halt just before the driveway and waved the truck past him. That morning, the moving van had arrived from New York. Finally, after much delay and frustration, Janet and Michael were going to move into their own house. From the back seat, Amos heard Janet's sigh of satisfaction.

"Just look at it," she said. "It's perfect—just perfect."

"It did come out nice," Amos agreed. He glanced at Michael, beside him, but the boy remained silent. "We better get on up there before the movers wreck everything," Amos said. He started to put the car in gear, but Janet stopped him.

"No! I want to walk. I want to enjoy every second of it. After all the work, I just want to soak in what we've done. Come on, Michael!"

While the elder Halls drove on up to the house, Janet and Michael strolled slowly, enjoying the crunch of gravel under their feet.

At the top of the newly installed ramp that paralleled the steps to the front porch, Amos and Anna awaited them, and as Janet absorbed the scene, her eyes filled with tears. "I still can't believe it. Last week it was just a poor decaying wreck, and now it's—well, it's everything I ever dreamed of—"

"Except for the fence," Anna interrupted, her brow

creasing fretfully as she shifted her gaze from the freshly painted house—white with green trim, just as Janet had wanted—to the remnants of the old fence that still stood as a bleak reminder of what the property had been. "I still think you should have gone ahead and let Buck put it in. Post-and-rail would look perfect here."

"It's not practical," Amos interjected, picking up the argument that he and Anna had been wrangling over for days, and which Janet suspected was about more than a simple fence. "What you need is some barbed wire."

Anna opened her mouth to contradict her husband, but Janet stopped her.

"Let's forget about the fence and go look inside before it gets all cluttered up."

Inside, the dinginess and neglect were gone, replaced everywhere with a bright newness that belied the age of the structure. The off-white paint had, as Janet hoped, given the small rooms a more spacious feeling than had existed before. She moved from room to room slowly, placing furniture in her mind's eye, selecting papers for the walls that would bring the rooms to life while retaining their feeling of coziness.

In the kitchen, a blue-painted table with cane-seated chairs, rescued from someone's attic, sat next to the window, and an old, but serviceable, refrigerator purred next to the wood-electric stove that Janet had already come to love. She patted the imposing hunk of cast iron affectionately.

"I haven't seen one of those since I was a child. I'd have sworn they all wound up in the junkyards years ago."

"Out here we still need them," Anna replied ruefully. "When the power goes, sometimes it seems like it's going to stay gone forever." Then she smiled brightly. "But that's mostly in winter, of course. Until November, it's usually back on in an hour or two."

Suddenly Michael's voice interrupted them, shouting from the backyard. "Mom! Mom, come quick! Look!"

Janet stepped out onto the back porch, with Anna and

Amos following behind her. Michael was pointing off into the distance, toward the newly plowed field that stretched away toward the river. Janet's eyes followed her son's gesturing arm, and in a moment she saw it.

It was Shadow, trotting slowly up the field, his tongue hanging out of his mouth, his tail low to the ground.

"Shadow!" Michael yelled. "It's Shadow, Mom! Come on, boy. Come on, Shadow!"

The dog's tail came up and began waving like a banner in the breeze. His trot gave way to a dead run, and he charged up the field, barking wildly. A moment later he'd vaulted the fence separating the field from the barnyard and then was on top of Michael, knocking him off his feet, putting his forepaws firmly on the boy's chest while he licked his face.

As Janet watched the scene in the yard, she heard Anna's voice behind her. "So he ran away, did he? Gone for good, was he?" Then, for the first time, Janet heard her mother-in-law chuckle. "I think I like that dog. Yes, I think I do."

Amos, however, made no reply to his wife's remarks. Instead, he simply turned and wordlessly went back into the house.

A few minutes later, with Shadow on his heels, Michael burst excitedly into the kitchen. "Can I take him upstairs, Mom? I want to show him my room." Then he paused and cocked his head. "Mom? Can we sleep here tonight?"

"Of course," Janet replied. "Where else would we sleep? This is our home now."

"Oh, but how can you, dear?" Anna protested as Michael and Shadow pounded up the stairs. "There's still so much to be done. You don't want to try to live in the middle of all the unpacking, do you?"

Janet stopped her with a gesture. "Anna, if you were in my place, where would you stay tonight?"

Anna hesitated only a moment, then her habitual look of worry gave way to a tiny smile. "If it were me, you couldn't pry me out of here with a crowbar," she agreed.

"I'd be up all night, putting things away, and making plans, and driving Amos crazy." She sighed as they reached the bottom of the stairs, and looked wistfully up toward the second floor, but said nothing about the fact that there was, at present, no way for her to get there. Then, after a moment, she smiled again. "It's a nice little house, isn't it?" she asked of no one in particular. "Such a shame, the condition it had gotten into. All those years, just standing here. And we let it go, too, of course."

Janet, who was already halfway up the stairs, paused and turned back to face her mother-in-law. "It wasn't you who let it go," she said, her voice low and her expression serious. "It was Mark."

Anna seemed to recoil from Janet's words, her right hand reflexively coming up to flutter at her bosom, her eyes clouding over. "Why, Janet, what on earth do you mean?"

Janet hesitated, wondering what exactly she *had* meant by her words. Indeed, she hadn't meant to say them at all. They had just slipped out, unbidden and unconsidered. And yet, as she thought about it, she realized she meant the words, realized that during the past weeks, as she'd worked so hard to restore the house to what it had once been, she'd begun to resent Mark's neglect of the place and, more and more, come to resent Mark himself. Mark, who had lied to her. A feeling had grown inside her that the past was not the only thing Mark had hidden from her and that as she began going through his papers—all the files he'd kept locked away in his office at the university, but that were now packed in cardboard cartons in the little parlor at the front of the house—she'd find more hidden things, find another Mark, one he'd kept as well hidden as this farm, whom she'd never known and wasn't at all sure she wanted to meet. And yet for Anna, there was no hidden Mark. There was only a memory of the boy who had been her son and who had run away from her, who had finally come home only to be taken cruelly from her. How could she talk to this woman who had suffered so, about her own dark feelings?

"Nothing," Janet finally said. "Nothing at all, really. It's just that I don't want you to feel bad about the condition the house was in. After all, you gave it to Mark, didn't you? So it wasn't really your responsibility."

"But Mark was our son," Anna replied. "Everything he was or did was our responsibility, wasn't it?"

Janet met the older woman's intense gaze for a moment, wondering what, if anything, to say. Then, at last, she turned silently away, and continued on up to the second floor.

"It's perfect," Janet repeated an hour later when they were all gathered together again in the little parlor. Her eyes moved from Amos to Anna and then back again. "How can I thank you? How can I ever thank you for all you've done?"

"You don't have to," Amos Hall told her. "We did it because we belong to you, and you belong to us. You're ours, Janet. You must never forget that."

Janet returned her father-in-law's smile. "I won't," she whispered. "You can be sure I won't."

And then, with her son, Janet Hall was alone in her house.

It was late in the afternoon when Janet looked out the kitchen window and, for the first time, saw Ben Findley. He was in his barnyard, throwing feed to the chickens, and as Janet watched him he suddenly looked up, as if he'd felt her eyes on him. A moment later, he turned abruptly and disappeared into his house, and Janet heard the slam of his screen door echo like a cannonshot through the stillness of the prairie afternoon.

She stood thoughtfully at the sink for a moment, then made up her mind. "Michael?" she called from the foot of the stairs. "What are you doing?"

"Nothing," Michael called back. "Just sorting out my stuff. Can I use an old blanket for a bed for Shadow?"

"Okay. I'll be back in a few minutes. I just have to run next door."

Without waiting for a reply, she left the house, crossed the yard, and carefully worked her way through the barbed wire fence that separated her property from Findley's. A few minutes later she stood on his collapsing porch, knocking at his front door. When there was no response, she knocked again, more loudly. Again, there was only silence from the interior of the house. Just as she was beginning to think the man had decided to ignore her, the door opened slightly, and Ben Findley peered at her, his face lost in the shadows of his house, his veined eyes cloudy with suspicion.

"Mr. Findley?" Janet asked. "I'm Janet Hall—"

"I know who you are," Ben Findley cut in. "You're Mark Hall's widow."

Janet nodded, feeling faintly foolish. Of course he'd know who she was. She decided to try again. "I live next door, and when I saw you in your yard, I thought it was time we got acquainted."

"Why?"

"Why?" Janet echoed. Of all the possible responses, this was the last she'd expected.

"I didn't ask you to come live there, and where you live is none of my business," Findley said in a harsh, flat voice. "Just because you live next door, don't think that's going to make us neighbors. It's not."

"But I only thought—"

"I don't give a damn what you thought, young woman," Findley growled. "I know how this town is—everybody knowing everybody else's business, and acting real friendly-like. Well, I can tell you, it's bullshit. Pure bullshit, and I don't want no part of it a'tall. Most folks out here have come to respect that, and they leave me alone."

Reflexively, Janet took a step back. "I—I'm sorry you feel that way."

Findley's eyes narrowed, and his lips tightened. "Don't

be. I don't want your pity. All I want is to be left alone. That's why I have that fence. It's not only to keep the critters in. It's to keep people out. I notice it didn't stop you, though.''

Janet felt the first twinge of anger stab at her. ''Mr. Findley, I was just trying to be friendly. We're going to be living next door to each other for a long time, and it just seemed to me that the least we could do is know each other. So I came over to say hello.''

''You've said it.''

Furious now, Janet glared at the old man. ''Yes, I have, haven't I? And though I'm sure it doesn't interest you, Mr. Findley, I already wish I hadn't wasted my time.'' She turned away and started off the porch, fully expecting to hear the sound of the door slamming behind her. Instead, she was surprised to hear Findley's voice once more.

''Mrs. Hall!''

She turned back. The door was opened wider now. For the first time, she could see the shotgun cradled in Findley's arms. And for the first time, she got a clear look at Ben Findley's face. A shock of recognition surged through her, for what she saw was yet another version of Mark. The deep blue eyes, the strong features, the wavy hair. All of it there, but in Ben Findley, all of it worn and bitter. ''My God,'' Janet breathed. ''You're one of us—you're a Hall.''

Findley glared at her. ''I'm not a Hall,'' he replied. ''We're kin, but I'll not claim to be one of them. I'll not claim to be family with Amos Hall. And if you're smart, you won't, either.''

Janet swallowed, determined to control her temper. ''Amos has been very good to me, Mr. Findley—''

''Has he, now,'' Findley growled. ''Well, it's none of my business. All I want to tell you is to stay away from here, Mrs. Hall. Stay away from here, and keep that brat of yours away, too.''

''Is that a threat, Mr. Findley?'' Janet demanded, her voice icy.

''If you want to call it that.''

"I do, Mr. Findley. And I can assure you that Michael will not be trespassing on your property. But in the event that he does, I will expect you to confine yourself to sending him home."

"I'll do what I have to do," Findley replied, his voice grim. "I don't like people around this place, and I particularly don't like kids. So you keep your brat to home, and everything will be fine. Is that clear enough for you?"

"Entirely," Janet snapped, boiling with fury at the old man. "I'm sorry to have bothered you. I can assure you it won't happen again."

"I'll count on it," Findley said. The door closed in Janet's face.

Seething with anger, Janet turned away once more, and began walking down Findley's driveway. If he didn't want his fence climbed, then so be it! She would damned well walk all the way down his driveway and along the road, to her own house. Her back held ramrod straight, she marched along, feeling his malevolent eyes boring into her every step of the way. Only when she had reached the road did she pause and turn back to glare once more at the rundown shack the old man was so possessive about. And then, allowing herself the luxury of venting her rage in what she knew was a thoroughly childish way, she raised the middle finger of her right hand in a mock salute.

It was nearly eleven before they decided that the house was finally theirs. Their clothes hung in the closets, what little furniture there was had been placed to Janet's satisfaction, and the kitchenware had been stored away in a manner that, though she insisted it was only temporary, Janet knew would probably never be changed. Their beds, made up with the first bedding that had come to light, awaited them upstairs.

Now the two of them sat at the kitchen table sipping the cocoa Janet had made, while Shadow sprawled contentedly on the floor. "Well, what do you two think?" Janet asked, breaking the comfortable silence that had fallen over them. "Did we do the right thing?"

Shadow's tail thumped appreciatively against the floor, but Michael only glanced up at his mother, then away, his serious eyes roving restlessly over the kitchen. "I guess so," he said at last, but his voice betrayed his uncertainty.

"You don't sound very sure. Is something wrong?"

Michael opened his mouth as if to speak, then closed it abruptly. Puzzled, Janet repeated her question. "*Is* something wrong?"

Michael fidgeted in his chair, suddenly interested in the gummy layer that was forming on the surface of his untouched cocoa. He touched it with his spoon, watching it wrinkle, then reached down and carefully picked it up with his thumb and forefinger. "Ryan's mad at me," he mumbled at last.

Nonplussed, Janet stared at her son for a moment. "Mad at you? But why?" Suddenly she frowned, as she realized that it had been a while since she had seen Michael with his cousin. On the occasions Janet had been to visit Laura, still weak and bedridden from the stillbirth, Michael had not accompanied her, and she had chosen not to press the point. Now though, her anxiety was aroused. "Did you two have a fight?" she asked.

Michael shrugged. "I—I don't know," he mumbled. Then he looked up at her. "Is it okay if I go to bed now?" Without waiting for a reply, he scurried out of the kitchen, and she heard him hurtling up the stairs to his room. A moment later, Shadow followed his master.

Janet finished her cocoa, then slowly cleaned up the kitchen. At last she wandered through the downstairs rooms of the little house, locking up, and eyeing the mass of boxes that still waited to be unpacked. Finally turning out the lights, she went upstairs, but paused uncertainly outside the closed door to Michael's room. Though no light showed through the crack at the bottom of the door, neither did she hear the regular sound of her son's breath as he slept. She waited a moment, listening carefully, then tapped softly at the door. When there was no answer, she opened the door and peeped in. Michael, still fully dressed, sat on the floor beside the dormer window, staring out into the night. Shadow lay beside him, his big head cradled in the boy's lap.

"May I come in?"

There was no answer, so Janet stepped into the little room, closing the door behind her. She crossed the tiny alcove and joined her son on the floor. She let her eyes follow his and, in the distance, saw the dark outline of Findley's barn silhouetted against the star-filled sky.

She frowned, remembering her conversation with Ben Findley that afternoon, then decided the view had nothing to do with the crotchety old man. "It's beautiful, isn't it?"

"I like it," Michael replied in a neutral voice.

"Would you like to tell me what happened between you and Ryan?"

"He didn't believe me," Michael said. "He said I was crazy."

Janet's frown deepened. "Didn't believe you about what?"

Michael turned, his eyes searching his mother's face in the gloom. "I saw something that night," he said, and Janet knew instantly the night he was referring to.

"You mean something besides the car that almost ran over you?"

Michael nodded.

"I see," Janet said. "Would you like to tell me what you saw?"

Michael shrugged. "You won't believe me either. It sounds crazy."

"Try me," Janet offered, gently stroking Michael's hair.

"Never tell them the truth."

The words resounded through Michael's mind, and though he tried to ignore them, he couldn't. He wanted to tell his mother what he remembered, but he *couldn't*. Twice, he opened his mouth to tell her about Nathaniel. Each time, he felt Shadow stiffen under his hands, and thought he heard the dog growl softly. Twice, he closed his mouth without speaking, and felt the dog relax.

Finally, an idea came to him. "I—I think I saw Abby out in the field that night."

"Abby? You mean the ghost Grandpa told you about?"

Michael nodded uncertainly. "I—I think so. Anyway, I saw *something* out there."

"Maybe you only imagine you saw something," Janet suggested, but Michael shook his head.

"But I can't remember it very well anymore." He looked puzzled. "I can *sort* of remember what happened, and *sort* of remember what I saw, but I can't really remember how it *felt* anymore. You know what I mean?"

"Of course," Janet told him. "It's like a dream. You can remember every detail when you first wake up, but then, a minute later, it's gone, and all you can remember was whether it was a nice dream or a bad dream. Is that how it is?"

Michael nodded. "And I had a headache that night. But when I saw—" He hesitated as Shadow tensed, then: "When I saw her, it went away." Shadow's body relaxed. "Ryan thinks I'm crazy." He stared at her now, his large eyes frightened and appealing. "I'm not crazy, am I, Mom?"

Janet got to her feet, thinking hard. He hadn't mentioned having a headache before. Could that be the explanation? She reached down and touched his head, stroking his hair with her fingertips. "Of course you're not crazy. Don't ever think that. You just thought you saw something that wasn't there, that's all. It was probably the headache. They can do that to you, you know. Was it bad?"

Michael hesitated, then nodded. "It was a throbbing in my temples."

"Did you take anything for it? Did you ask Mrs. Simpson for some aspirin?"

"No. I didn't get it 'til I was on my way back to Grandpa's house."

"Have you had headaches like that before?"

Again Michael hesitated before he said, "A few. But they aren't too bad, and they don't last very long."

"Well, that's good, anyway. But I think tomorrow we'll go have a talk with Dr. Potter. Maybe you're just allergic to something in the air. In the meantime, you just get a good night's sleep tonight. All right?"

Michael stood up and switched on the light that hung suspended from the center of the ceiling. The glare from the naked bulb filled the room with a harsh light that made Janet squint, but as her eyes adjusted to the brightness, she studied Michael's face. For a moment, his eyes met hers, then drifted away, back to the window.

"You don't believe me, do you?" he said quietly. "You don't think I saw anything."

Now it was Janet who hesitated, and when she spoke, she chose her words carefully. "I believe you *think* you saw something, and that's what counts."

Then, in an instant, a searing pain slashed through Michael's head, and his eyes, frightened only a second earlier, suddenly turned furious. "I saw him," he shouted, his face twisting into a visage of anger. "I saw him, and I talked to him, and he's my friend. I don't give a fuck what anybody says."

Without thinking, Janet stepped forward and slapped her son across the face. "Michael! Don't you ever speak to me that way!" From the corner of her eye, Janet saw Shadow's hackles suddenly rise and felt a sudden pang of fear. What would she do if the dog decided to defend his master?

But as quickly as it had come, Michael's fury was gone, and as he calmed down, so also did the dog. Dazed, Michael stared at his mother, his left hand massaging his stinging cheek. "What did you do that for?" he asked. "Why'd you hit me?"

"You know why," Janet replied, her voice coldly controlled. "Now go to bed and go to sleep, and we'll forget all about this. But it won't happen again. Is that clear?" Without waiting for a reply, she turned and left Michael alone in his room, pulling the door shut behind her.

Michael, his cheek still stinging from the slap, undressed and then turned off the light. But instead of getting into bed, he went back to the window, staring out into the night, trying to figure out what had happened.

She'd said she believed him, and then she'd slapped him and told him not to talk that way again.

But he hadn't said anything. There'd just been a sudden pain in his head, and then the slap.

Still not sure what had happened, Michael crept into his bed. When Shadow climbed up to join him a moment later, Michael slipped his arms around the big dog, hugging him close. . . .

Him. I saw *him.* I talked to *him.*

The words echoed through Janet's mind as she tried to fall asleep, and as she recalled the words, she pictured his face. Her son's clear features had been distorted with rage, his eyes glazed with a fury she'd never seen before.

What had he been talking about? It was Abby he'd insisted he'd seen that night. So who was *he*?

She turned over and closed her eyes, determined to sleep. And yet, sleep would not come.

It was the house, she decided. The strangeness of it, and the emptiness—that was all; that, and her loneliness.

At last, unable to sleep, Janet left her bed and went back to Michael's room. She found him asleep, his face peaceful, one arm flung carelessly over the edge of the bed, the other encircling Shadow's neck. And yet, as she watched his face, she thought she saw something besides peace.

She thought she saw the same loneliness in Michael's face that she herself was feeling.

Gently easing Shadow aside, Janet crept into the narrow bed and gathered Michael into her arms. And then, with her son's head cradled against her breast, she at last drifted off to sleep.

CHAPTER 14

Charles Potter emerged from his office, wiping his hands on a kitchen towel. He smiled at Janet and Michael Hall, who sat side by side on the sofa in the bay window. "My goodness—the whole family today? We're not having some kind of epidemic, are we? Nobody ever tells me anything around here." Then his eyes came to rest on Janet, and his smile faded into an expression of concern. "It's not you, is it?"

"No, no. I'm fine," Janet assured him. "I haven't even had any morning sickness since Monday. It's Michael. He's been complaining of headaches, and I thought you might have a look at him. I—well, I was thinking of allergies, or something."

Potter sniffed disdainfully. "I don't believe in allergies. It's what incompetent doctors diagnose when they can't find out what's really wrong. An allergy is simply an imbalance in the system, and there are remedies for that. Trace elements, we call 'em. Ever hear of homeopathy?"

Janet shook her head.

"Figured you hadn't. Best kept nonsecret in medicine. It's too cheap, and too easy. No money in homeopathy, which is why I'm so poor, I suppose. Well, come on in." Janet stood up and, with Michael trailing her, followed Potter into his examining room.

178

"What kind of headaches are these, son?" Potter asked when Michael had stripped off his shirt and perched himself on the edge of the examining table. Janet leaned against Potter's desk.

"I don't know. Kind of like a throbbing, I guess."

Potter frowned. "Where? In the front? The back? All over? Just the temples?"

"The temples mostly, I guess. I don't know."

"Well, let's take a look at a couple of things." He wrapped the sleeve of a sphygmomanometer around Michael's upper arm. A moment later he began pumping air into the sleeve, his eyes on the pressure gauge, his stethoscope plugged into his ears. Finally he nodded, grinning. "Guess what? You're not dead."

"Is his blood pressure normal?" Janet asked.

Potter shrugged. "Within reason. It's a little high, but that's not surprising. Has he had any nosebleeds?"

Janet turned to her son. "Michael?"

"No."

"Well, you might," Potter told him. "If you do, it's nothing to worry about. Just apply a cold compress, and take it easy for a while. Let's have a look at your eyes and ears, then hit your funny bones."

Ten minutes later, Potter finished his examination, and Michael, buttoning up his shirt, went back to the waiting room. Potter seated himself behind his desk and made a few notes, then peeled off his glasses. As he absentmindedly wiped the lenses with his fingers, only worsening their condition, he smiled at Janet, who was now sitting opposite him. "All in all, I'd say there's nothing really wrong with him. The blood pressure's a little high, but as I say, that doesn't surprise me. The stress of his father's death could have brought that on. And it, in turn, could exacerbate a headache. Has he ever complained of headaches before?"

"Nothing serious. The usual. I've always given him aspirin, and that's taken care of it. But these seem to be different, in a strange sort of way."

Potter frowned. "Different? How?"

Janet shifted uncomfortably. "Well, I'm not quite sure how to say it. A while ago he had one of the headaches, and apparently he thinks he saw a ghost that night."

Potter stopped mauling his lenses. "A ghost?" he asked, his voice betraying his skepticism.

Janet's brows arched, and she shrugged her agreement with his doubt. "That's what he told me. And he was quite adamant about it. Except that now he can't quite remember what happened. But he says that while the ghost was around, the headache went away, and after the ghost left, the headache came back. But everything that happened seems to be kind of fuzzy in his mind."

"I'll bet," Potter replied. Then his forehead furrowed in thought. "Where'd all this take place?"

"Near our house," Janet told him. "He was out at the Simpsons', and it happened on his way home."

"Hmmm." Potter leaned back in his chair and folded his hands over his midriff. He gazed at the ceiling for a moment, then his eyes came back to Janet. "Maybe I'd better talk to him," he said at last. "Whatever he thinks happened, I'd like to hear it firsthand. Do you mind?"

"Of course not." Janet stood up. "Shall I call him in?"

Potter gave her a conspiratorial smile and a wink. "Why don't you send him in, and let me talk to him alone? Sometimes kids talk more freely if their parents aren't around."

Michael sat stiffly on the edge of his chair, regarding Dr. Potter with suspicious eyes. The familiar throbbing was beginning to play around his temples, but Michael tried to ignore it, concentrating instead on what the doctor was saying.

"You didn't see Abby in the field, did you? You saw something else, and you know what it was you saw. Isn't that right?"

"No," Michael replied. "It was Abby, and she was looking for her children, just like in the story."

Potter shook his head. "No, Michael. There's no such person as Abby Randolph. She died a hundred years ago, and she isn't still here, wandering around looking for anything. So you saw something else. Now, I want you to concentrate very hard and tell me exactly what you saw and where you were."

"I was at our house—"

"Why?" Potter interrupted. "It was the middle of the night, and no one was there. Why did you go there?"

"I *told* you. I saw a light in the field, and I wanted to see what it was."

"And you *did* see what it was, didn't you?" Potter leaned forward, the knuckles of his right hand white as he clutched his glasses. "Didn't you?" he repeated.

Michael's headache worsened, and suddenly his nostrils filled with the strange smoky odor that was becoming as familiar to him as the headaches. And then, as if from far away, he heard the voice.

"He knows."

Michael's eyes widened slightly, and his eyes darted to the corners of the room, even though he knew the voice had come from within his own head. Then the voice, Nathaniel's voice, came again.

"He knows, and he's going to make you tell."

"What is it, Michael?" Potter asked, his voice low. "Is something wrong?"

"N-no," Michael answered. "I just—I just thought I heard something."

"What? What did you hear?"

Michael's head was pounding now, and something seemed to have happened to his eyes. It was as if the office had suddenly filled with fog, except that it wasn't quite like fog. And then he knew. Smoke. The room seemed to have filled with smoke.

"I—I can't breathe. . . ."

Potter rose from his chair and moved around the desk. "What is it, Michael? Tell me what's happening."

"I can't breathe," Michael replied. "My head hurts, and I can't breathe."

Again, he heard the voice. *"He knows. He's going to make you tell. Don't let him. Stop him, Michael. Stop him now!"*

Michael's mouth opened wide, as if he was about to scream, but all that came out was a desperate whisper. "No. Stop it. Please stop it."

"Stop what, Michael?" Potter asked. "What do you want me to stop?"

"Not you," Michael whispered. "Not you. Him. Make him stop talking to me."

Potter grasped the distraught boy by the shoulders. "Who is talking to you, Michael?" he asked, his eyes fixing on the boy. "Who?"

"Nath—"

"No! Do not speak my name!"

"Leave me alone!" Michael wailed. "Please . . ."

Potter released Michael from his grip, and as the boy slumped in his chair, he returned to his desk. Silence hung over the room for a few minutes, and then, when Michael's breathing had returned to normal, Potter finally spoke.

"The barn," he said softly. "You were in Ben Findley's barn, weren't you?"

Michael said nothing and held himself perfectly still, terrified of what might happen if he so much as nodded his head.

"It was Nathaniel you saw, wasn't it?" Potter pressed, his voice low but nonetheless insistent. "You went into Ben Findley's barn, and you saw Nathaniel, didn't you?"

Michael shook his head fearfully. "No," he whispered. "He's not real. He's only a ghost, and I didn't see him. I didn't see him, and I didn't talk to him."

But now it was Potter who shook his head. "No, Michael. That's not the truth, is it? Don't lie to me. We both know what you saw and what you heard, don't we?" When Michael made no reply, Potter pushed further. "He looked like you, and he looked like your father, didn't he, Michael?"

Michael bit his lip and squirmed deeper into the chair. Then, as he offered an almost imperceptible nod, Nathaniel's voice whispered to him, no longer loud, no longer threatening. Now it was soft and gentle, caressing. *"Kill him."*

And suddenly, as Michael watched Dr. Potter while Nathaniel whispered to him, he knew he could do it. If he wished it right now, with Nathaniel there inside his head, Dr. Potter would die.

"No," he whispered. Then, again, "No."

"But you will," Nathaniel whispered. *"You must, and soon. You will. . . ."* The voice trailed off, and Michael's headache faded away. As his vision cleared, he frowned uncertainly at the doctor. "Can I go now?" he asked shyly.

Potter said nothing for a moment, then finally shrugged. "We both know what happened that night, don't we, Michael?"

Michael hesitated, then nodded.

"But you won't talk about it, will you?"

This time, Michael shook his head.

"Can you tell me why not?"

Again, Michael shook his head.

"All right," Potter told him. "Now, listen to me carefully. I know what you did, and I know what you think you saw. But you didn't see anything. Do you understand? You didn't see anything in Ben Findley's barn, and you didn't see anything in the field. It was the middle of the night, and you were tired, and all that happened was that you imagined you saw some things that weren't there. They weren't there, because they couldn't have been there. Do you understand?"

Michael hesitated, then nodded. "I—I think so."

"All right." Potter stood up and moved toward the door, but before he opened it, he turned back to Michael. "And one more thing. From now on, you stay away from

Ben Findley's barn. You stay away from his barn, and stay off his property.''

Michael gazed up at the doctor. He knows, he thought. He knows about Nathaniel, and he knows what we saw. And now we're going to have to make him die. He turned the strange thought over in his mind, and wondered why the idea of making Dr. Potter die didn't scare him. Then, while he half listened to the doctor talking to his mother, he began to think about something.

Was making someone die the same as killing them?

He thought it probably was, but somehow, deep inside, it didn't feel the same. Making someone die, he was suddenly sure, was different from killing them. He could never kill anyone.

But he could make someone die.

Janet gazed questioningly at Michael as he emerged from Potter's office, but when he said nothing, her eyes shifted to Potter.

"I don't know," Potter said thoughtfully. "I don't think anything too serious is wrong, but I'd like to think about it and maybe make a couple of calls. Why don't you bring him back tomorrow afternoon?"

A few moments later, after they'd left Potter's house, Michael finally spoke, a fearful note in his voice. "Why did you tell him about—" He hesitated, then finished the question: "Why did you tell him about the ghost?"

"I—well, I was worried about the headaches, and I thought the doctor ought to know what happened when you got them."

"He thinks I'm crazy."

"I'm sure he doesn't—"

"He does too," Michael insisted, his face beginning to redden. "He told me there's no such things as ghosts, and that I couldn't have seen anything out there. Then he wanted me to tell him everything that happened."

"Did you?"

As Michael hesitated, Janet thought she saw a furtive flicker in his eyes, but then he nodded. "What I remember."

They walked along in silence for a few minutes, and Janet had an uneasy sense that Michael had not told Potter all of what he remembered. But before she could think of a way to draw him out on the subject without making him angrier than he already was, she heard someone calling her name. She looked around to see Ione Simpson beckoning to her from in front of the Shieldses' general store.

"Janet, look at this. Isn't it wonderful?" Ione asked as Janet and Michael approached. "Have you ever seen anything like it?"

In the store window, propped up against a galvanized milk can, was an immense Raggedy Ann doll that seemed, somewhere during its lifetime, to have suffered a minor accident. There were a few buttons missing, and one of its shoulders had a tear in it. Looking at it, Janet couldn't help grinning: it was huge and clumsy, and its flaws appeared almost self-induced, as if it had stumbled over its own feet. It was totally irresistible. "It *is* wonderful," she agreed. "But what on earth would you do with it?"

"Peggy," Ione said decisively. Janet stared at her. Peggy, Eric Simpson's two-year-old sister, was only about a third the size of the doll.

"If it fell on her, she'd suffocate," Janet pointed out, but Ione only shook her head.

"I don't care. She'll grow into it. But do you suppose it's for sale? It doesn't look new."

"Well, let's go in and find out," Janet replied. "I've got a whole list of things to get there anyway." With Michael trailing along, the two women entered the cluttered store.

They were greeted by a large matronly woman with a happy face and wide blue eyes, whom Janet recognized but couldn't put a name to.

"Well, now, don't you worry," the woman told them. "You can't be expected to know everybody's name until at least day after tomorrow. I'm Aunt Lulu—Buck's mother?

Isn't that terrible, having a name like Lulu at my age? But what can you do? I've been Lulu since I was a baby, and I'll be Lulu when I die. Now, what can I do for you?''

"I have a whole list—" Janet began, but Ione Simpson immediately interrupted.

"The doll, Lulu. The Raggedy Ann in the window."

Aunt Lulu smiled. "Oh, I didn't put that out there to sell it," she explained. "But it's been in the back room too long, and I thought it might be fun to give it some sunshine, do you know what I mean?"

"You mean it isn't for sale?" Janet asked, feeling Ione's disappointment as keenly as if it were her own.

"Why—well—I don't know, really," Lulu stammered. "It's been here for I don't know how long. It was ordered for little Becky—" She hesitated for just a second, her eyes bulging slightly, and then hurriedly corrected herself. "We ordered it for Ryan, but he didn't want it. I don't see how he could have resisted it, do you? Isn't it wonderful? Just wonderful. And almost as big as a real child—"

"It's bigger than the child I want it for," Ione broke in. "I just have to have it for Peggy. Please?"

Lulu's big eyes blinked. "Well—well, I suppose if it's for Peggy, we'll just have to make sure it's for sale, won't we? I'll have to call Buck and find out what the price is. He's at home, you know, taking care of Laura." Suddenly her happy expression collapsed, and her eyes brimmed with tears. "Isn't it a shame about Laura? So close, and then losing the baby like that." She gazed at Janet, then reached out and took her hand. "But of course, you were there, weren't you? While Laura worked all day in that hot sun? And everything was going along so well for a change. Well, we certainly can't blame you, can we? I mean, if you'd known Laura better, you certainly wouldn't have let her work so hard at your place, would you? I told her she should take it easier, but you know Laura—she won't take anybody's word for anything, and her so small she almost died when Ryan was born, and now this has to happen. I just don't know how much more she can take. I just don't.''

As Michael began edging away from the teary woman, and Ione looked on in what appeared to be horrified embarrassment, Janet tried to understand what the woman was really saying. Though she'd denied it, was she blaming her for Laura's miscarriage? At last though, Lulu's tears began to abate, and her warm smile spread once more over her round face. She glanced around distractedly, then lowered her voice, even though there was no one else in the store. "I do run on, don't I? Well, it's just something everyone has to put up with from us older women. I was a good wife to Fred, and I never talked back to him, not once. But ever since he's been gone, I've found I just love to talk. I suppose it was all those years of not saying much at all. It all just bottles up, doesn't it?''

Janet smiled weakly, wondering if there was a graceful way to end Lulu's ramblings, when Ione Simpson came to her rescue.

"The doll?" Ione asked. "Could we find out how much the doll is?''

"Oh, you just take it, and anything else you want. I'll keep track of it all, and Buck can tell you some other time how much it all comes to. I don't usually work here, you know," she said, turning to Janet again. "Fred always thought a woman's place was in the home, and until he died, that's where I stayed. I'm afraid Buck thinks the same way as his father did. He only lets me in here when he absolutely can't be here himself, and that's only when Laura's having one of her—''

And once again Lulu Shields fell silent, the last, unspoken words of her sentence hanging on her tongue like wineglasses teetering on the edge of a shelf. But in the end, they didn't fall. Instead, Lulu stepped back from Janet, though her eyes suddenly went to Ione Simpson. "You girls just prowl around and find what you need. All right?''

"Fine," Janet agreed, then turned away to begin her

shopping before Aunt Lulu could wind herself up again.
Thirty minutes later she and Ione left the store together,
their arms filled with packages. Behind them came Michael,
totally occupied with coping with the giant Raggedy Ann.

"Do you have a way to get home, or were you planning
to haul all this stuff by hand?" Ione asked as they approached her car.

"Well, we were planning to walk, but I hadn't really
realized how much there was going to be."

"Say no more," Ione declared. Then she suppressed a
giggle. "That's what I should have told Lulu Shields. Isn't
she something else? And don't you believe she never said
a word to her husband. There's a lot of people around
here, me included, who think she talked him into an early
grave, and that he wasn't the least bit sorry to go."

The three of them piled into the front seat of Ione's car.
Raggedy Ann and the groceries occupied the rear. "You
don't suppose she really thinks Laura's miscarriage was
my fault, do you?" Janet asked as they left the village
behind and started out toward their farms.

Ione glanced at her over Michael's head. "With Lulu,
you can count on her not thinking at all. I can't imagine
why she said that." Then: "Yes, I can. She didn't think.
But she didn't mean anything by it, either, so don't worry
about it. She's just a little batty."

"She's weird," Michael said.

Janet frowned at him. "She's just talkative. And don't
you dare start to get in the habit of calling people weird."
She turned her attention back to Ione. "Who's Becky?"

"Becky?" Ione repeated. "What are you talking about?"

"The girl they bought the doll for. That's what Lulu
said before she said they bought it for Ryan."

"I didn't hear that." Ione shrugged. "I'm afraid I
don't hear a lot of what Lulu says. I just tune her out after a
while." Then her brow furrowed. "Are you sure she said
'Becky'? As far as I know, there aren't any little girls
named Becky in Prairie Bend."

"I bet they killed her," Michael suddenly said as Ione turned into Janet's driveway.

Janet stared at her son. "What a terrible thing to say!"

Michael's eyes narrowed. "I bet that's what happened to her. I bet they buried her in Potter's Field."

And then, as the car came to a halt in front of the house and Janet got out, Michael slid off the seat and jumped to the ground. "Is Eric home, Mrs. Simpson?" he asked.

"He's cleaning out the stable—" Ione faltered, shaken by Michael's strange pronouncement.

"I'm gonna go help him. Okay, Mom?"

Janet, as shaken as Ione, nodded her assent, and Michael ran off. They watched him until he'd scrambled through the fence that separated the two farms and disappeared into the Simpson's stable, then began unloading Janet's packages from the back seat of Ione's car.

"What on earth was Michael talking about just now?" Ione asked when they were in the kitchen.

Though her heart was suddenly pounding, and she hadn't the least idea what the answer to Ione's question might be, Janet feigned nonchalance. "Nothing, really. It's probably just an association with that horrible ghost story Amos told him just after we arrived, and the coincidence of names." She smiled weakly. "They used to bury paupers and unknowns in potter's fields, you know."

"Oh, come on, Janet," Ione protested. "There's got to be more to it than that! When was the last time you heard of a graveyard called a potter's field? The term's obsolete! And even so—something like that in Prairie Bend? As far as I know, we've never even *had* a stranger or a pauper here. And the idea of anybody burying a baby out there— well, it sounds crazy!"

Janet sighed heavily, and sank into one of the chairs at the kitchen table. "I know," she agreed. "And I have to confess I'm a little worried." She glanced up, wryly. "In fact, I took him to Dr. Potter this morning." She hesitated. "Michael's been having some headaches. But the doctor couldn't find anything wrong. He says it's probably all a reaction to Mark's death."

Ione's eyes reflected her chagrin. "Oh, God, Janet, I'm sorry. It was stupid of me not to think of that. I must have sounded just like Lulu Shields. Forgive me?"

Janet smiled. "There's nothing to forgive. But you could do me a favor—"

"Anything!"

"Help me out with Michael. I think he just needs some time to get used to things. He's lost his father, and he's living in a new place, and he hardly knows anyone. And I know how kids can be. They can gang up on someone and make his life miserable."

"And you think that might happen to Michael?"

"Apparently Michael and Ryan Shields had an argument. Ryan already told him he's crazy."

Ione's eyes narrowed as she remembered the boy's odd behavior the night Magic had foaled. "Well, we'll just see to it it doesn't happen with Eric, okay?" She paused for a moment, then: "Janet, I don't want you to get upset, but if you think you'd like Michael to talk to someone, I know a good psychiatrist in Omaha."

"A psychiatrist? Come on, Ione, Michael's just a little boy. He doesn't need—"

"I didn't say he does," Ione interrupted. "But you said yourself he's been through a lot, and sometimes children can have problems their parents aren't even aware of."

Janet looked quizzically at the other woman. "Why does it seem to me unlikely that a farmer's wife in Prairie Bend would be acquainted with a psychiatrist in Omaha?" she asked.

Ione burst into laughter. "Because I'm a nurse, that's why! Not everybody in this town never got out. I got out for eight years. But then I reverted to type, and married the boy next door. Anyway, I know someone in Omaha in case you ever need someone for Michael. Okay?"

Janet hesitated, then offered Ione a small smile. "Okay," she agreed. "And thanks." Suddenly she brightened. "I have an idea. Why don't you come over for supper tonight? All of you. It'll be my first party in my new house, and I can't think of better people to have than my neighbors."

"What about your family?" Ione asked. "Don't you think maybe your first guests ought to be Amos and Anna or the Shieldses?"

Janet considered it, then shook her head. "I'll have Laura and Buck as soon as Laura's better, and Amos and Anna must be sick and tired of me by now. Besides, if it's just the six of us, who's going to know? Or care?"

Ione shrugged. "Okay, if that's the way you want it, it's fine with me." A wry grin came over her face. "But I can tell you one thing: everybody in town is going to know we were your first guests. Mark my words!"

Michael stepped out of the sunlight into the shadows of the Simpsons' barn. "Eric?" he called out. When there was no reply, he went farther into the barn. A soft whinny came from Magic's stall, and Michael paused to pat the big mare's muzzle. "Where's Eric?" he asked, and Magic, almost as if she'd understood the question, pawed at the floor of the stall, neighed loudly, and tossed her head. Michael grinned, then called out his friend's name once again, more loudly this time.

"Back here." Eric's voice drifted faintly from the far end of the barn, and Michael abandoned Magic for the tack room, where he found Eric working with a tangle of leather straps.

"Whatcha doin'?"

"Trying to make a bridle for Whitesock."

Michael frowned. "Who's Whitesock?"

"Magic's colt. He's got one white stocking, so we named him Whitesock I found this old bridle, and if I can make it small enough, I can start training him."

"Where is he?"

"Out in the pasture behind the barn."

"Can I go play with him?"

Eric shrugged. "I guess so. But he probably won't play

very much. Today's the first time he's been away from Magic, and he's kinda skittish.''

A few minutes later, Michael was staring over the pasture fence. Just yards away, the colt stared back at him through large, suspicious eyes.

''Hi, Whitesock,'' Michael said softly, and the colt's ears twitched interestedly. ''Come on, boy. Come over here.'' He reached down and tore up a fistful of grass, then held it out toward the colt. ''Want something to eat?''

The colt took a step forward, then quickly changed its mind and backed away. Michael frowned, and shook the grass. The colt wheeled around and trotted across the pasture, then finally stopped to look back at Michael.

Grinning, Michael scrambled through the barbed wire fence and began walking toward the colt, holding the grass out in front of him. ''It's okay, Whitesock. It's good. Come on, boy. I'm not going to hurt you.''

But when he was still a few yards away, the colt once more bolted and ran off to the far corner of the pasture.

Michael was about to follow the horse once again when he felt something brush against him. He looked down to see Shadow, his tail wagging happily, crouched eagerly at his feet. ''You want to help, Shadow?'' The dog let out a joyful yelp and jumped to his feet. ''Okay, let's sneak up on him. Come on.''

Slowly, the boy and the dog approached the colt, and this time Michael was careful to do nothing that might spook the little horse. He moved only a few feet at a time, pausing often to let the colt get used to him. Shadow, seeming to sense what his master was doing, stayed close to Michael, matching his movements almost perfectly.

Finally, when they were only a few feet away from the horse, Michael began speaking quietly, as he'd heard Eric do when he was calming Magic. ''Easy, Whitesock. Easy, boy. No one's going to hurt you. Look.'' Slowly he raised his hand, offering the colt a taste of the grass. ''It's food, Whitesock. Come on. Try it.''

Michael inched closer, and Whitesock tensed, his eyes

fixed on Michael, his right forepaw nervously scraping the ground. Again Michael moved toward the horse, freezing when the colt's head came up and he seemed to be seeking a means of escape.

At last when he was only a foot from the colt, he reached out and gently brushed the grass against Whitesock's muzzle.

And then, from the other side of the fence, Eric's voice broke the quiet Michael had been maintaining. "Hey! Whatcha doing?"

Startled, the colt reared up, his forelegs striking out at Michael. But before the horse's hooves could come in contact with the boy, Shadow had hurled himself against Michael, knocking him to the ground and out of the way of Whitesock's flailing legs. Michael rolled away from the frightened horse, then got to his feet as Whitesock broke into a gallop and dashed across the field, Shadow behind him.

"Shadow!" Michael yelled, and the dog instantly came to a stop, turning to stare back at Michael. "It's okay, boy. Come on. Come back here!" Obediently, the dog began trotting back.

"What were you tryin' to do?" Eric demanded.

"It was your fault!" Michael shot back. "I was just trying to make friends with him. I was giving him some grass, but you scared him when you yelled."

"Well, you shouldn't've been in there at all!"

Stung, Michael glowered at Eric, and his head began to throb with the familiar pain. "You said I could play with him."

"I thought you'd have enough brains to stay out of the pasture. What do you know about horses?"

"I didn't get hurt, did I? And I wasn't even scared!"

"Just get out of the field, and let me take care of him, all right?" Then, ignoring Michael's protestations, Eric climbed through the fence, and holding the bridle in his left hand, started toward the colt.

His headache growing, Michael watched as Eric began

working his way toward the colt, weaving back and forth across the field, countering each of Whitesock's moves with one of his own. Slowly, he began trapping the colt in one corner of the field.

Finally, he moved in on the frightened animal and tried to slip the bridle over the colt's head. Whitesock jerked at the last second and avoided the harness straps.

Once again, Eric made a move to bridle the horse, but again Whitesock ducked away at the last second. But this time, instead of trying to move away from Eric, he reared up and struck out. Eric dodged the flying hooves, but tripped and stumbled to the ground.

Horrified, Michael watched as the colt danced for a moment on his hind legs, then came down to glare angrily at Eric, who was rolling away at the same time he was trying to scramble to his feet.

He's gonna kill him, Michael thought. He's gonna trample him. Suddenly his vision blurred, and Michael's senses filled with the smell of smoke. And he heard a voice in his head.

"Kill him."

Obeying the voice without thinking, Michael focused his mind on the colt.

Die, he thought. *Die. Die. Die.* . . .

The colt seemed to freeze for a moment, then with an anguished whinny, rose up once again on his hind legs, his forelegs flailing as if at an unseen enemy. Finally, as Eric got to his feet and began backing away from the terrified colt, Whitesock crumpled to the ground. He lay still, his eyes open, his breathing stopped.

Michael's vision cleared, and his headache faded away. The smoky odor disappeared, too, and all he could smell now was the sweetness of the fresh grass in the pasture. Shadow sat at his feet, whining softly. Michael gazed across the field, unsure of what had happened.

"Eric?" he called. "You okay?"

There was a moment of silence, then Eric turned around

to stare at him. "He's dead," Eric said. "He's just lying there, and he's dead."

Michael's eyes shifted from Eric to the colt, and he knew his friend's words were true.

And he also knew that somehow he had done it.

Somehow, while his head was hurting and his vision was blurred, he'd made Whitesock die.

His eyes filling with tears, he backed slowly away.

CHAPTER 15

Supper was over, a supper during which much of the conversation had centered on what had happened in the Simpsons' pasture that afternoon. In the end, though, Leif Simpson had put an end to the discussion. "The colt just died," he had said. "It doesn't really matter much why it died. The point is that if it hadn't, it might have hurt Eric pretty bad. So I guess we might just as well chalk it up to providence. It was God looking after Eric, and that's that."

Michael, who had taken little part in the discussion, said nothing, though he didn't believe what Eric's father had said. He'd thought about it all afternoon, and no matter what anybody said, he knew that somehow he'd made the colt die. He hadn't wanted to—all he'd wanted to do was help Eric—but still, he'd done it.

And he couldn't tell anybody. For one thing, no one would believe him. And he couldn't say how he'd done it, because he didn't know. Sighing inaudibly, he decided it was one more thing he could never talk about.

As Janet and Ione attacked the dishes, the two boys headed upstairs toward Michael's room. But when they came to the landing, Eric stopped, gazing up at the trapdoor to the attic. "What's up there?"

"I don't know," Michael replied, his mind still on the colt. "Nothing, I guess."

"Why don't we go up and look?"

A moment later Michael had dragged a chair from his room and climbed up on it. He was barely able to reach the folding ladder that gave the attic its only access. It creaked angrily as he pulled it down, but when he tested his weight on it, it seemed secure enough. He climbed up and pushed at the trapdoor. It stuck for a moment, then gave way, dropping a shower of dust on him. Michael poked his head through the trapdoor.

"Go down and ask Mom for a flashlight," he told Eric. "It's too dark to see anything."

Five minutes later Eric crowded up behind Michael, flashlight in hand. "Let me see."

"Give me the light," Michael replied. "It's my attic, and I get to look first."

Reluctantly, Eric passed the light over, and Michael switched it on, throwing a weak beam into the blackness of the attic. "Wow," he breathed. "It's all full of old crates." He scrambled up into the attic, and Eric followed. "What do you think's in 'em?"

Eric shrugged in the gloom. "Let's get my dad and bring them down."

Fifteen minutes later, the contents of the attic had been transferred to the living room. There were five crates: old pine boxes held together with hand-forged nails, their boards dry and brittle, shrunken with age. The last thing they brought down was an ancient trunk, and when Leif Simpson had deposited it, too, in the living room, the six of them gathered around, staring at the strange collection. Peggy Simpson, with the curiosity of her two years, was busily trying to open one of the boxes with her stubby fingers.

"Do you have a hammer and screwdriver?" Leif eventually asked. "We'll never find out what's in them if we count on Peg."

Michael found the tools in the kitchen drawer that had

already been established as a catchall. "Which one first?
The trunk?"

"Let's save it for last," Janet suggested. "Let's do the
boxes first."

"They're crates," Michael corrected. "Boxes are made
of cardboard."

"Never mind," Janet replied. "Just open them."

One by one, Michael and Eric began prying the lids off
the crates. The first one was filled with old china, thin and
delicate, with an ornate floral pattern done in pink against
a white background.

Janet picked up one of the plates, examining it carefully.
"I know what this is," she said. "It's French. My grandmother had some of this." She flipped it over. On the
back, faint but distinct, was the Limoges mark.

"It's ugly," Michael pronounced, already beginning to
pry at the second crate.

Janet and Ione exchanged a knowing look. "It may be
ugly, but it's valuable," Janet said. Then, as she passed
one of the plates to Ione, the lid came off the second crate,
revealing a cache of battered cookware.

"That's old, but I don't think I'd call it valuable," Leif
Simpson remarked, holding up a badly dented tin coffeepot with a hole in the bottom. "Why would anyone keep
this?"

In the third crate there was a wooden toolchest, bereft of
its contents, and the fourth produced a mass of old linens,
rotted with age, which crumbled in their hands as they
tried to pick them up. Finally Michael pried the lid off the
fifth crate.

"My God," Janet whispered. "Look at it. Just look at
it."

"Wow." Eric reached out and touched an elaborately
tooled coffeepot. "Is it real?"

Inside the box, wrapped in disintegrating paper, was a
large set of sterling: the coffeepot, a matching teapot,
creamer and sugar bowl, and a tray to hold them all.
Below the coffee service they found a condiment caster,

each of its silver-topped glass cruets and pots carefully wrapped. In a separate box, there was a set of silver flatware, all of it as heavily decorated as the coffee set. The value of the china faded into insignificance as Janet assessed the silver.

Suddenly the sound of Michael's voice echoing Eric penetrated Janet's mind. "*Is* it real?"

"It's real," Janet assured them.

"Maybe it's plate," Ione Simpson suggested.

Janet shook her head. "It's not plate. It's sterling, and it couldn't have been made much after 1820."

"How can you tell?"

Janet smiled wryly. "One of my hobbies over the last few years has been drooling over things like this in stores on Madison Avenue. Believe me, I know what this is."

"But whose is it?" Eric suddenly asked.

Michael threw him a scornful look. "It's ours, stupid. It's our house, isn't it?"

Eric ignored him. "But where'd it come from?"

"I don't know," Janet said softly. One by one, she picked the pieces up, examining them carefully. Though they were heavily tarnished, she could find no dents or scratches, and none of the sets seemed to have pieces missing. "But I think Michael's probably right. If they've been in the attic as long as I think they have, they're probably ours." Suddenly, her anticipation heightened by the discovery of the silver, she turned to the trunk. "Pry it open, Michael. Maybe it's full of gold!"

Five minutes later, with some help from Leif Simpson, the old locks gave way, and the boys lifted the lid. Their first feeling was one of disappointment—the trunk seemed to be filled with nothing but old clothing. Carefully, Janet and Ione lifted out garment after garment, all of it seeming primitive in contrast to the silver and china. The materials were coarse homespuns, and much of the stitching was inexpertly done. Below the clothes—mostly dresses and shirts—there was a tray containing some shoes, a few pairs of rotted cotton hose, and some moth-eaten woolen socks. Below the tray, more clothes.

Buried at the bottom, Janet found a book. She took it out of the trunk and held it under a lamp. It was a small volume, bound in leather, with a leather strap held fast by a small gold clasp. The clasp was locked, but when Janet gently tugged at the strap, it easily tore away.

"Damn," she swore softly, immediately regretting the curiosity that had caused her to damage the volume. Gingerly, she opened the cover. The first page was blank, but starting with the second, the pages were filled with an uncertain script, done mostly in black ink. Janet glanced up, but no one seemed to be paying any attention to her. Instead, they were engrossed in examining the contents of the various boxes. Ione was carefully sorting the silver, while her husband unwrapped the china. Peggy had found a wooden spoon, and was happily beating on the bottom of a rusted pan, while the boys examined the trunk, in search of a secret compartment.

Impulsively, Janet turned to the last page of the diary. The script seemed to her to be particularly shaky, as if the writer had been ill or nervous about something. Slowly, she deciphered the old-fashioned penmanship:

14 March, 1884—Spring comes, and it is almost over. Nathaniel and I still live, but when they find out what Nathaniel has done, I am sure they will kill him. In the meantime, though, my baby grows inside me, and it is better that some of us live than that all of us die. I have decided to tell them a man came for the children, and though they will not believe me, and will think me daft, perhaps it will save Nathaniel—all that matters now is that Nathaniel and my unborn child survive.

Janet reread the passage several times, and then slowly closed the little book. She held it in her lap, staring at it. A moment later her eyes drifted to Michael. As if feeling her gaze, he turned and looked at her, as did Ione Simpson. It was Ione who spoke.

"What is it?"

"It's nothing," Janet replied. "Just an old diary."

Janet let Shadow out the back door, and watched as he disappeared into the darkness, intent on making his evening rounds of the little farm. Then, knowing the dog wouldn't be back for a while, she went upstairs, tapped on Michael's door, and stuck her head into his room. He was in bed, his head propped up on his left hand, reading.

"Where's Shadow?" he asked.

"Prowling," Janet told him. She sat on the edge of Michael's bed and took his hand. "I want to talk to you about something," she said.

Michael looked nervous, but didn't turn away. "A-about what I saw?"

Janet nodded. "And about what you said about that little girl—Becky—today. That you think someone killed her and buried her in Potter's Field. What made you say that, honey?"

Suddenly Michael's eyes filled with terror. "I—I can't tell you. I—I promised not to tell anybody."

"Not even me?"

Michael nervously twisted the bedcovers in his clenched fist.

"Please?"

"You won't tell anyone? Anyone at all?"

Sensing that her son's fright was genuine, Janet promised.

"I—I lied to you," Michael said at last, his voice quavering.

"Why would you want to do that?"

"I was scared."

"Of me?"

Michael shook his head.

"Of Grandpa?"

"I—I'm not sure. I guess so."

Janet reached out and gently removed the bedclothes from Michael's hand. "Why don't you tell me what really happened?"

Slowly, Michael began telling his mother as much as he could remember of what had happened that night.

"And on the way home, I saw something," he finished. "But it wasn't Abby."

"Then what was it?" Janet pressed.

"It was Nathaniel," Michael whispered. "I saw Nathaniel, and I talked to him, and I saw someone else, too, but I'm not sure who it was."

Janet swallowed. A knot of tension had formed in her stomach. "You saw Nathaniel, and you were talking to him," she repeated.

Michael hesitated, then nodded in the darkness.

"But Nathaniel's just like Abby. He doesn't exist, honey. He's only a ghost."

"Maybe—maybe he's not," Michael ventured. In his memory, Dr. Potter's words returned, the words with which he'd described Nathaniel: *He looked like you, and he looked like your father. . . .*

"All right," Janet said patiently, still unsure of exactly what Michael was trying to say. "Let's assume Nathaniel isn't a ghost. What did he say that scared you so much?"

Michael racked his brain, trying to remember what Nathaniel had said, the exact words. But they were gone; all that was left were the warnings. And a vague memory.

"He—he said they'd brought us something. A—a baby."

"A *baby*?" Janet repeated, unable to keep her incredulity out of her voice.

Again Michael nodded. "They were burying it out in the field."

Janet's heart began to pound. "What field?"

"The one down near the woods by the river. Potter's Field."

"And you think it was Aunt Laura's baby they were burying?"

Again, Michael's head bobbed.

Janet paused for a long time, then reached out and touched Michael's face, tipping his head so his eyes were clearly visible. "Michael, are you sure you saw any of this?"

"I—I think so."

"You think so. But you're not sure."

"Well—" Michael faltered, then backed off a little. "It was dark, and I couldn't see very well, except when Nathaniel was with me. Then I could see real good."

The knot in Janet's stomach tightened. What was he talking about now? "You could see in the dark when Nathaniel was with you?"

Michael nodded.

"All right," Janet told him. "Now, what about Becky?"

Michael squirmed. "I—I'm not sure. But I bet whoever she is, she's in Potter's Field, too."

"But we don't even know who she is."

Michael swallowed hard, then spoke in a whisper. "I don't care," Michael said, his voice reflecting his misery. "I bet they killed her, too."

Janet gathered her son into her arms. "Oh, Michael," she whispered. "What are you saying? Why are you saying these things?"

Michael met her gaze evenly. "Nathaniel," he said. "I'm only saying what Nathaniel told me."

"But sweetheart, Nathaniel doesn't exist. You only imagined all this."

Michael lay still for a long time, then slowly shook his head. "I didn't," he said softly. Then: "Did I?"

Outside, Shadow began barking.

That night, long after Michael had fallen asleep, Janet remained awake. She read the diary over and over, read all the entries, describing how Abby Randolph and her children had tried to survive the winter of 1884.

How the food had run out, and they had begun to starve.

How one of the children—the youngest—had gotten sick and finally died, and what Abby had done with its remains.

And then, one by one, the other children had died, but

never again was there a mention of illness. And in the end, all of them were gone except Nathaniel, who, along with his mother, survived.

"*. . . Better that some of us live than that all of us die . . .*"

She went to bed finally, but didn't sleep. Instead she lay staring into the darkness, the words drumming in her mind. Perhaps, she told herself, it didn't mean anything. Perhaps it was nothing but the ravings of a woman driven mad by the loneliness of the long prairie winter. Or perhaps it had been written somewhere else, packed in the trunk for shipment, and never unpacked again.

Finally, near dawn, she drifted into half sleep, but even in her semiconscious state she could hear the name:

Nathaniel . . .

She shivered.

There could be no question of the roots of that terrible ghost story now, for she had found its confirmation. Inscribed on the flyleaf of the diary, barely discernible in faded pencil, was the proof: the name Abigail Randolph.

But why were Abby Randolph's things in this house? Who had put them there?

CHAPTER 16

Michael wasn't sure what had awakened him. It might have been the headache that was playing around his temples—not really painful yet, but nevertheless there—or it might have been something else.

It might have been the dream. Though the dream was already fading from his memory as he lay in the darkness, a few fragments remained. His father. His father had been in the dream, and some of the dream had taken place in this room. It had started here, and it had ended here, but part of it had been in the room downstairs, the living room. But it hadn't looked like it did now, filled with packing crates and a few pieces of furniture. In the dream the furniture had been old-fashioned, and his father had been sitting on a sofa—one of those hard sofas with slippery upholstery like some of his parents' friends had in New York.

And his father had looked different. He'd looked young, like Nathaniel, but even though he'd looked like Nathaniel, Michael had known it was his father. And Michael hadn't been there. At least, he hadn't felt like he'd been there. Instead, he'd just been sort of watching, almost as if he was standing in a corner but nobody could see him.

But it had started in the bedroom, the room that had been his father's and was now his. His father had been in

the room, working on one of his model airplanes, when
suddenly the door had opened, and his grandfather had
come into the room. Michael had known right away that
Amos was mad at his father. He'd tried to tell his father,
but he couldn't speak. He'd opened his mouth, but when
he'd tried to speak, his throat had tightened, and nothing
had come out. And the harder he tried, the tighter his
throat got, till he could hardly breathe. And then his
grandfather had hit his father. Suddenly there'd been a
razor strop in his hand, and without saying a word, Amos
had raised it up over his head and brought it slashing down
onto his father's back. But his father hadn't screamed.
Instead, while Michael watched, his father's eyes widened,
and his body stiffened and arched away from the pain. His
hands, which had been holding one wing of the model,
tightened, crushing the balsa wood and tissue paper into a
crumpled mass. Twice more the razor strop had lashed
down, but still his father had said nothing. And then it was
over, and suddenly Michael's father was in the living
room, sitting on the old-fashioned sofa, and though he
couldn't hear anything, Michael knew that somewhere in
the house, someone was screaming.

Then his father was back in the bedroom again, and he
was packing a suitcase, and Michael knew he was going
away and never coming back.

And then, just before he'd awakened, his father had said
something.

"He's alive. I know he's alive."

Now, as he lay in his bed, Michael wondered who his
father had been talking about. Could it have been Nathaniel?
Had his father known Nathaniel, too?

Michael got out of bed and went to the window. The
night was clear, and the moon hung just above the horizon,
casting long shadows over the prairie. Old man Findley's
barn shimmered in the moonlight, its weathered siding
glowing silver in the darkness. Michael stared at the barn
for a long time, feeling it, feeling Nathaniel's presence
there.

And then Nathaniel was once more inside his head, whispering to him.

"It is time, Michael. If we wait, it will be too late."

The night seemed to darken, the moonlight fade away, and for a moment Michael saw nothing. But then his vision cleared, and he saw a house, a house which he recognized, but couldn't quite place. And once again, he felt the familiar throbbing in his temples.

Then he knew. It was Dr. Potter's house. In one of the downstairs windows, a single light glowed. Outside the house, ranging across the yard, he saw a dark shape that he knew was Shadow. . . .

Charles Potter had been sitting alone in the tiny room that was his private retreat. He had been there for hours now, sitting still in his large easy chair, moving only when the fire burned low and demanded more fuel to keep it going. The room was stiflingly hot, but the flames, Potter thought, were helping him think, helping him decide what he must do.

So far, he had done nothing. So far, he had talked to no one about Michael Hall. Nor had he yet decided exactly what had happened in his office that day.

It had been almost as if there were a third person there, a third person invisible to him, who was whispering to Michael. And yet, there had been something about the strange phenomenon that had told Potter there was more to that third person than an invention of Michael's mind.

It was as if Nathaniel had been there, speaking to the boy.

Of course it was impossible, and Potter knew it was impossible. But still, he had sat through the night, wondering if it could have been true, if Nathaniel could, indeed, have been in his office that day.

A sound disturbed his reverie, and Potter stirred in his chair, shifting his attention to the night.

He heard it again, a snuffling sound, as if some animal

were outside. He got up from his chair and went to the window. Outside, he saw nothing but darkness.

The sound came again, and then once more. Frowning, Potter left his tiny den and moved quickly through the house to the front door. He opened it a few inches and looked out.

Suddenly there was a flicker of movement on the porch, and an angry growl. Startled, Potter took a step back, and as his hand fell away from the doorknob, the door itself flew open.

Crouched in the foyer, his fangs bared and his hackles raised, Shadow fixed his glowing eyes on Charles Potter.

Potter stared at the dog, his heart suddenly pounding. He took another step backward, and the dog rose from his crouch, one foreleg slightly raised, his tail slung low.

As he watched the dog, Charles Potter suddenly knew that it had been true.

Nathaniel had been there that day, and Nathaniel was here now.

Charles Potter stared at Shadow, and knew that he was going to die.

Michael stood perfectly still in his room, absorbed only in what he was seeing and hearing within his head.

He was inside Dr. Potter's house now, and Nathaniel was with him. He was watching as Shadow slowly backed the old man through the house until they were in the tiny room where the fire blazed on the hearth.

Michael could smell the smoke of the fire and feel the heat of the room. It was hard to breathe, and the smoke seemed to be drifting out of the fireplace now, filling the room.

"It is time," Nathaniel's voice whispered. *"It is time for him to die. He knows, Michael. He knows about me, and now he knows about you. Help me, Michael. Help me make him die. . . ."*

Michael could see the fear in the old man's eyes, see the

growing terror as the man came to know that there was no place to retreat, nowhere else for him to go. Silently, he released Shadow. . . .

Charles Potter sank back into his chair, his eyes still fixed on the threatening visage of the snarling dog. And then, though he knew this, too, couldn't be happening, he began to feel another presence in the room. It was as if there were eyes on him, blue eyes, intense and angry, filled with hatred. He knew whose eyes they were, and knew why they were there.

His heart was pounding harder now, and suddenly there was a pain in his head, an intense pain—as intense as those staring eyes that now seemed to fill his vision—and he knew what was happening to him.

Then the vessel in his head, filled beyond capacity by his pounding heart, gave way, and blood began to spread through his brain. His face turned scarlet, and his head pitched forward to rest on his chest, as his arms went limp.

Only when the last of Charles Potter's life had drained out of his body did the great black dog let the tension go out of his muscles, let his snarl die in his throat, let his coat smooth down. Then, after sniffing once at the body in the chair, he turned away and trotted out of the house into the night.

In his room, Michael turned away from the window. His headache was easing now, and he was once more aware of where he was. In the back of his mind, there was a faint memory, like the memory of a dream, in which he and Nathaniel had made Dr. Potter die.

But it must have been a dream, like the dream he'd had about his father. It couldn't have been real.

And yet, as he went back to bed and pulled the covers close around himself, he wondered.

It had *seemed* real.

All of it, everything Nathaniel had showed him, had seemed real.

He was still thinking about it when he finally drifted back into sleep.

The sun was well up, promising a beautifully clear day. Janet and Michael, who had been silent that morning, were cleaning up the last of the breakfast dishes when Michael saw the strange truck pull into the driveway.

"Someone's coming, Mom."

Janet glanced out the window, but as the battered old green pickup made its way up the drive, she couldn't place it. And then it came to a stop in front of the house, and Amos Hall climbed out. Seeing Janet watching him from the kitchen window, he smiled and beckoned to her.

"What in the world—?" Janet began, and then suddenly realized she was talking to an empty room. Michael was gone. Assuming he had already headed out to greet his grandfather, she flung her damp dish towel over the back of one of the kitchen chairs, then started toward the front door. But when she reached the front yard, Michael was nowhere to be seen, though Amos still stood by the truck. "Hi," she greeted him, then paused uncertainly. Amos's weathered face wore an uncharacteristic grin. "You look like the cat that swallowed the canary," she said at last.

Amos only shrugged, then stepped back to gaze admiringly at the truck. "What do you think of it."

"Think of what?" Janet replied.

"The truck. Think it'll do?"

Janet stared at it. It was of indeterminate age, though far from new, and it had apparently seen a lot of service. There didn't seem to be a square foot on it anywhere that was free from small dents and scratches, and both the fenders were badly crushed.

"Do for what? It looks like it's ready for the junkheap," she said at last.

Amos nodded. "Inside, though, where it counts, it's

sound as a dollar. It ought to give you a good ten, maybe twenty thousand miles yet."

"Me?" Janet took a step forward. "What on earth are you talking about?"

"Well, you can't spend all your time walking to the village, then begging rides home off the neighbors," Amos replied, his eyes shifting pointedly toward the Simpsons' farm next door.

Instantly Janet realized that Ione had been right yesterday. Someone had apparently seen her getting into Ione's car, and the news had gotten back to the Halls. "But I don't need a truck—" she began.

Amos interrupted her.

"How do you know what you need and don't need? All those years in the city—how would you know what you'll need out here? Anyway, I was up to Mulford this morning, and found this thing just sort of sitting around looking for a new home. So I bought it. What do you think?"

Suddenly touched, Janet went to Amos and slipped her arms around him. "I think you're wonderful, but I think you'd better tell me how much you paid for it, so I can pay you."

Amos self-consciously pulled her arms loose and stepped back. "Don't be silly. They practically gave it to me. You keep your money for other things. You know how to drive a stick shift?"

Janet nodded. "I used to have a VW."

"Then you're all set. This thing might take a little getting used to, but you'll catch right on. Get in."

Tentatively, Janet climbed into the driver's seat. The upholstery had long since given up any notion of holding itself together. Someone, though, had installed seat covers, and though she could feel the springs beneath her, there didn't seem to be any sharp points sticking through. She turned on the ignition, and a moment later the engine coughed reluctantly to life. A red light on the dashboard glowed for a second, flickered, then went out. The gas gauge read empty.

"I'd better get it to a filling station," she commented, but Amos only chuckled.

"She's full up. The gauge doesn't work, and neither does the speedometer or the temperature gauge."

Janet gave him an arch look. "Did they knock the price down for any of that?"

"Can't knock down something that's already collapsed," Amos replied. "Want to take her for a spin? You can take me home and say hello to Anna, and Michael can give me a hand with a couple of things."

Janet thought of all the things she had to do that morning, then quickly decided there was nothing that couldn't wait. "Sure. Michael can ride in the—" And suddenly she fell silent for a moment. "Where *is* Michael?"

Amos shrugged. "Isn't he in the house?"

Janet shook her head uncertainly. "I don't think so. I thought he came outside when you got here. We were both in the kitchen, and I just assumed—"

"He didn't come out here," Amos told her.

Janet shut off the truck's engine and jumped to the ground. "Michael?" she called. "Michael!" When there was no reply, she smiled apologetically at Amos. "He must have gone upstairs. I'll get him."

But he wasn't upstairs, or anywhere in the house. A few moments later, she was back in the front yard, alone. "I can't imagine where he's gone. I *know* he saw you—"

"That's kids," Amos replied. "He's probably out back somewhere, pokin' around. Come on."

They went around the corner of the house, then into the barn. Janet called out to her son, but still there was no answer. And then, as they were leaving the barn and heading toward the toolshed, a slight movement caught Janet's eye. She stopped, and turned to stare thoughtfully at the cyclone cellar. Amos, his eyes following hers, frowned.

"What'd he be doing down there?"

"I don't know," Janet replied. "But would you mind

waiting here while I go see?" Then, without waiting for an answer, she started purposefully toward the sloping door.

She pulled the door open, letting it fall back so that the sunlight flooded into the dimness of the storm shelter. In the far corner, crouched on the floor with his arms wrapped around Shadow, she saw Michael, his knees drawn up against his chest, his eyes wide with trepidation.

"What—?" she began.

"Are you mad at me?" Michael asked, his voice quavering slightly.

"Mad at you?" Janet repeated. "Honey, why would I be mad at you?"

" 'Cause I didn't say hello to Grandpa."

Janet paused. Up until now, she'd assumed that Michael hadn't realized who was in the truck. "So you *did* see Grandpa?"

Michael nodded.

"Then why didn't you say hello to him?"

Michael shrugged unhappily. "I—I had a dream last night," he said at last.

Sensing his fear, Janet sat down on the bench next to her son and put her arm around him. "A bad dream?"

Michael nodded. "It was about Dad. Grandpa was beating him. He was beating him with a piece of leather."

Janet felt her body react to the image that suddenly formed in her mind, but when she spoke, she managed to keep her voice steady. "But honey, you know dreams are only dreams. It wasn't real. Is that why you didn't say hello to Grandpa this morning?"

Again, Michael nodded. He pulled away from her and pressed himself closer to the big dog. For a moment, Janet wished Mark were there. He would know what to say to Michael, how to explain what was happening to him. But if Mark were here, she realized with stark clarity, none of this would be happening; there would be nothing to explain to Michael. "The next time you have a dream like that, I want you to tell me about it right away, all right?

That way, we can talk about it, and you won't have to be afraid.''

But Michael didn't seem to hear her. His gaze seemed far away, and when he spoke, there was a hollowness in his voice. "Why did Grandpa beat Dad?" he asked. And then another vision flashed into his mind, a vision that seemed far in the past. It was the dream he'd had of his father falling from the hayloft, falling onto the pitchfork. Only there was someone else in the loft with his father, and suddenly he could see that person, see him clearly. It was his grandfather.

He looked up at his mother. "Mom, why did Grandpa want to kill Dad?"

Janet's thoughts tumbled chaotically in her mind. Amos beating Mark? Killing Mark? It made no sense.

"They were only dreams, honey," she said, her voice taking on a note of desperation. "You have to remember that the dreams you have don't have anything to do with the real world. All they mean is that something is happening in your mind, and you're trying to deal with it. But the things you dream about aren't real—they're only fantasies."

Michael's brow furrowed as he considered his mother's words. But there were too many memories, too many images. His father, his grandfather . . . Dr. Potter. His frown deepened.

Janet nodded. "I know, honey. Dreams are like that. When you're having them, they seem terribly real. Sometimes they still do, even after you wake up. But in a while, you realize they were only dreams, and forget them." She stood up, and drew Michael to his feet. "I want you to come out and say hello to Grandpa now, and then we're going to go over to see Grandma. Okay?"

But Michael drew back. "Do I have to? Can't I stay here?"

Janet frowned. "No, you can't. Grandpa needs you to help him with some things, and after all he's done for us, I can't see that you wouldn't want to help him."

"But—sometimes he scares me!" Michael protested.

Suddenly Janet reached the end of her patience. "Now, that's enough. Your grandfather loves you very much, and he'd never do anything to hurt you, just as he never did anything to hurt your father. So you're going to pull yourself together, and act like a man. Is that clear?"

Michael opened his mouth, then closed it again. Silently, he nodded his head, then started up the short staircase that led out of the storm cellar, his mother behind him.

Just outside, where he must have heard everything they'd said, they found Amos Hall. But if he had heard them, he gave no sign.

Janet leaned over to give her mother-in-law a kiss on the cheek, but for the first time since they'd met, Anna made no response. Instead, she moved her face away, and continued darning one of Amos's gray woolen work socks.

"It was so good of you to get the truck for me," Janet began, but Anna glanced at her with a look that made Janet fall silent.

"We couldn't very well have you begging favors off strangers, could we?" she said in a distinctly cold voice.

"Strangers?" Janet echoed. "You mean Ione Simpson?"

"I'm sure Ione and Leif Simpson are very nice people, but you do have a family, Janet. If you need something, I wish you'd just ask us."

Janet sank into a chair across from the older woman, barely able to believe that Anna was insulted by what had happened yesterday. "Anna, Michael and I walked into town and had every intention of walking back. But we bumped into Ione, and she offered us a ride."

"So you invited her to dinner? It seems to me that you might have thought of having us first. We've worked so hard on the place, and after all, it *was* our home—"

"—And it's still a mess," Janet interrupted, improvising rapidly. "Last night was hardly what you could call a party. Ione brought over some things she had in the 'fridge, and we just sort of had a picnic." She thought Anna's expression softened slightly, so she pressed on. "It was all very impromptu, but if I hurt your feelings, I'm sorry. Of course, I'll fix my first real dinner for you and Amos, but that's not what last night was. Forgive me?''

Anna's eyes narrowed for a moment, but then she smiled. ''Of course I do. It's just that—well, you know how people gossip in small towns. I just don't want people to start claiming there's trouble between us. And that's what they'd say, you know.''

''Why on earth would they?'' Janet asked, now genuinely puzzled by Anna's words. There had to be more to it than simply an imagined slight.

''They've always talked about us around here, even though we've been here longer than anyone else,'' Anna replied.

''Well, you can believe *I* won't give anyone anything to talk about,'' Janet declared. Then, before Anna could begin worrying the subject any further, she decided to change it. ''I think Michael and I found some of your things last night.''

Now it was Anna who was puzzled. ''Mine? What do you mean?''

''Late last night, we decided to explore the attic.'' She waited for a reaction, but there was none. Instead, Anna only looked at her with mild curiosity. ''We found all kinds of things. I assumed they must have belonged to you.''

Now Anna's brows knit thoughtfully. ''If it was in the attic, it wouldn't have been mine. I don't think I've ever been in the attic of that house in my whole life. And when we moved in here, we brought all our things with us.''

Janet stared at her. ''You were *never* in the attic? But you lived in that house so many years—''

Anna's eyes met hers. ''But I never went to the attic. I started to, once, but Amos stopped me. He told me there was nothing up there, and that it was dangerous. He told me the floor's weak, and if I went up there, I'd fall through and break my neck.''

''And so you never went?'' Janet asked, amazed. ''If

Mark had ever told me something like that, you can bet it would be the first place I'd go." Of course, she thought, Mark never would have told me something like that.

Anna set her darning aside and wheeled herself over to the stove where a pot of coffee was simmering. Picking it up with one hand, she used the other to maneuver herself back to the table, where she poured each of them a cup of the steaming brew. Only when she'd set the pot on a trivet did she speak. "Well, Mark wasn't Amos, and I wasn't you. When Amos told me to leave the attic alone, I did just that."

"But what about the children? Didn't they ever go up there?"

"If they did, I don't know about it," Anna replied. "And I suspect that if their father told them not to, they didn't. Both Laura and Mark had great respect for their father."

"But still, they were children—"

"Children can be controlled," Anna replied, her voice oddly flat.

Suddenly Michael's words flashed through Janet's mind, but when she spoke, she managed to keep her voice light.

"What did he do, beat them?"

Anna stiffened in her chair. "Did Mark tell you his father beat him?" she asked.

Janet shrank back defensively. "No—no, of course not."

"Amos may have used the strop now and then," Anna went on, ignoring Janet's words as if she'd never uttered them. "But I'm not sure I call that a beating." Her voice took on a faraway note that made Janet wonder if the old woman was aware she was still speaking out loud. "A child needs to know respect for his elders, and he needs controls. Yes, controls. . . ." Her voice faded away, but a moment later she seemed to come back into reality. "Amos always controlled the children," she finished.

"But a razor strop—"

"My father used one on me," Anna replied. "It didn't hurt me."

No, Janet thought to herself. It didn't hurt you at all. All it did was make you think that whatever a man told you to do, you had to do. All it did was make you into a nice obedient wife, the kind of wife I could never have been, and the kind that Mark, thank God, never wanted. No wonder he ran away.

But even as she allowed the thoughts to come into her mind, she rejected them. They struck her as somehow disloyal, not only to Anna and Amos, but to Mark as well. Mark, after all, had been her husband, and she had loved him, and who was she to begin questioning the manner in which he had been raised, particularly when the people who had raised him were showing her nothing but kindness. Once again, she retreated to safer waters.

"But what about the things we found in the attic? What shall I do with them?"

Anna's eyes suddenly became expressionless. "I'm sure I don't know," she said. "I don't know what there is."

"There's a lot of silver and china. And there's a—" She stopped short, for Anna's eyes were suddenly angry.

"Don't tell me," Anna commanded. "There are some things I don't want to know about. If there were things in that attic, then Amos knew they were there, and knew what they were. They would have come from *his* family— that house was built by his ancestors over a century ago."

Janet's mind churned.

Abby Randolph's diary, written just a hundred years ago.

But Abby had died. All her children had died except Nathaniel, and then, after that terrible winter, Abby and Nathaniel, too, had died.

"*. . . that house was built by his ancestors. . . .*"

And then she remembered. According to the old legend and the diary, Abby Randolph had been pregnant that winter.

The child must have survived.

It must have been a girl, and it must have survived.

Janet felt a sickness in her stomach as she realized what had gone on in her house so many years ago. She gazed at Anna, who had once more picked up her darning and was now placidly stitching her husband's sock.

How much did Anna know? Had Anna known she was living in Abby Randolph's house, that her husband was a descendant of the only survivor of that long-ago tragedy?

Janet decided she didn't, and knew that she would never tell her. Indeed, Janet wished that she herself had never found the diary. Suddenly, the ghosts of Abby and Nathaniel were very real to her.

CHAPTER 17

Michael followed his grandfather into the barn, then up the ladder to the loft, where the bales of hay—what was left of last winter's supply—were neatly stacked under the sloping roof. He stood back while Amos cut the wire from three bales, and when Amos handed him a pitchfork, he seemed reluctant to take it.

"It won't hurt you," Amos admonished him. "Not unless you get careless and stick the tines through your foot."

Michael took the fork gingerly, then made a desultory stab at one of the bales. A few pieces of hay came loose, but the fork stuck in the bale itself.

"I'll break 'em up, and you pitch it over the edge," Amos offered. He peeled off his shirt, and a moment later set to work, his powerful torso moving rhythmically as he quickly began breaking the neat bales down. Hesitantly, Michael began using his own fork to throw the hay down into the bin below the loft. As he worked, his head began to ache.

He tried to ignore the now-familiar pain, tried to concentrate on what he was doing, but it grew worse, radiating out from his temples and growing into a throbbing that seemed to fill his head. Then the light in the barn began playing tricks, fading away so that the loft seemed to

disappear into a black void, only to come back with a
brilliance that washed the color out of everything.

In his mind, filtered by the pain, he heard Nathaniel
whispering to him, telling him to beware, warning him of
danger.

And then he saw his father.

It was like last night, and though Michael worked on,
doggedly forking the hay over the edge of the loft, he
suddenly was no longer aware of himself. It was as if his
mind had left his body and was now in the far corner,
watching as some other being went on performing his
tasks. But then, as he watched, something changed, and
suddenly he was watching his father.

And his grandfather was there too, breaking up the bales
for his father just as he had been for Michael himself.

And then the two men weren't working anymore, but
were facing each other, and Michael could see the anger in
both their faces. His father was staring at Amos, and there
was something in his eyes that Michael recognized. And
then he knew. His father's eyes had the same emptiness
he'd seen in Nathaniel's eyes. And then he heard his father
speak.

"You killed her, didn't you? You were there when she
was born, and you took her away and killed her."

"No, Mark—"

"I saw it, Pa. I saw what you did. Nathaniel showed
me, Pa. This afternoon, Nathaniel showed me."

Amos's eyes widened. "Nathaniel? There is no Nathaniel,
damn you."

"There is, Pa," Michael heard his father say. "Nathaniel
lives, and he showed me what you did. He wants vengeance,
Pa. He wants it, and he's going to get it."

And then, as Michael looked helplessly on, his grandfather began moving forward, moving toward his father.

Michael knew what was about to happen.

He wanted to cry out, wanted to warn his father, just as
he had wanted to warn him in the dream last night.

In the distance, as if from very far away, he could hear

a dog barking. It was Shadow, and though Michael knew the big dog was nowhere around, he also knew that the shepherd was trying to help him.

Suddenly his voice came to him, and a scream erupted from his throat to fill the vastness of the barn and echo off the walls in a keening wail. The pain in his head washed away, only to be replaced by another pain, a searing that shot up through his body like a living thing, twisting him around so that suddenly he was facing his grandfather, his eyes wide, his face contorted into a grimace of agony.

Then, as he felt himself begin to slip into the darkness that was gathering around him, once again he heard Shadow. The barking grew louder. It sounded furious—as if Shadow was about to attack. . . .

At first he was only aware of a murmuring sound, and was sure that Nathaniel was talking to him again, but slowly the voices became more distinct, and he recognized his mother's voice, and his grandmother's. And there was a third voice, not quite so familiar, but one that he recognized. And then he knew—it was Eric's mother. He opened his eyes to see Ione Simpson smiling at him.

"Well, look who's back," Ione said. "Feeling better?"

Michael tried to remember what had happened, but what he could remember made no sense. He'd seen his father, but that was impossible. And he'd had a headache, and Nathaniel had been talking to him, warning him about something. Slowly, he became aware of a throbbing pain in his right foot, and he struggled to sit up. Ione placed a gently restraining hand on his shoulder.

"Not yet," she told him. "Just lie there, and keep your foot up. Okay?"

Michael let himself sink back onto the cushion that was under his head, and fought against the pain that seemed to be growing every second. He looked around, recognizing his grandmother's parlor. His mother was there, and so were his grandparents, and they looked worried.

"What happened?" he asked at last.

"A little accident," Ione told him. "It seems you aren't quite an expert with a pitchfork yet."

Michael frowned, and another fragment of memory came back to him: his grandfather, moving toward his father. But it hadn't been his father. It had been himself. "I—I didn't—" he began, but his mother interrupted him.

"Of course you didn't, sweetheart," she assured him. "It was just an accident. The pitchfork slipped, and went through your foot."

Now Michael raised his head just enough to gaze at his right foot, which was propped up high on a second cushion, swathed in bandages.

"It isn't nearly as bad as it looks," Ione Simpson assured him. "It looks like the fork went right between the bones, and it doesn't seem like anything's very badly hurt."

Michael stared at the foot for a long moment, then gazed curiously around the room. Something was wrong—if he was hurt, where was the doctor? He frowned worriedly. "Is Dr. Potter here?"

Ione's smile faded away, and her eyes left Michael. Then his mother was bending over him. "Dr. Potter couldn't come," she said. "But it's all right, honey. Mrs. Simpson's a nurse, and she knows what to do."

But Michael's frown only deepened. His mind was continuing to clear and as it did, another memory came back to him, a memory from the previous night. "Dr. Potter," he whispered. "Why couldn't he come? Did—did something happen to him?"

A silence fell over the room, finally broken by the gruff voice of Amos Hall. "He might as well know," he said.

"Amos—" Janet began, but the old man shook his head.

"Dr. Potter died last night, Michael," he said. Michael's eyes widened, and the color drained from his face. "Do you know what a stroke is?" Mutely, Michael shook his head. "It's a blood vessel bursting inside the head. That's what happened to Dr. Potter last night. They found him this morning."

In his mind's eye, Michael had a sudden vision of Dr. Potter, slumped in a chair in front of a fire, his face scarlet, his eyes filled with pain and fear. He shook his head. "I'm sorry," he whispered. "I didn't mean to do it. I didn't mean to . . ." His voice trailed off, and his eyes met his grandfather's. There was a look in his grandfather's eyes that terrified him, and after only a second, he tore his eyes away and listened to his mother's voice.

"It's all right, sweetheart," she was saying. "No one thinks you meant to hurt yourself—it was just an accident. And you'll be all right. The foot will heal right up in no time at all."

Michael started to say something, but then, once again, he saw the strange look in his grandfather's eyes, and he changed his mind.

"Can you tell us what happened, honey?" Janet asked. "Do you remember any of it?"

Michael ignored her question. "Can we go home, Mom? Please?"

Janet's encouraging smile gave way to a worried frown. "Now?"

Michael nodded.

"But Michael, you need to rest for a while."

"I don't want to rest," Michael said. "I want to go home."

Suddenly Amos's voice cut in. "Your mother has some things to do, and you need to rest. And you need to be looked after. You'll stay here."

Now a look of real fear came into Michael's eyes. "Can't I go with you?" he begged his mother. "I can stay in the truck, and my foot doesn't hurt much. Really, it doesn't."

"You need to rest, at least for a little while," Janet said.

"Of course he does," Anna declared, rolling her chair

NATHANIEL   225

close to the couch. "He should just lie here and take it easy, and you should do your errands."

"But I don't *want* to stay here," Michael argued. "I want to go home."

"Hush, child," Anna told him. "Your mother has a lot to do, and she can't do it and take care of you, too. And Mrs. Simpson can't stay here all day either." Suddenly she smiled. "But just because I can't get out of this chair doesn't mean I don't know how to look after someone. In fact, I was thinking of making some cookies."

Michael turned his attention back to his mother. "I don't want any cookies," he said, his voice taking on a sullen tone. "I want to go home."

Janet wavered. She wanted to give in to Michael, wanted to take him home and give him all the attention she thought he needed. And yet, there was something that was holding her back, and she immediately knew what it was. It was that tone of voice he'd just slipped into, the tone of a spoiled child, which Michael had never been. She made up her mind.

"I want you to stay here," she told him. "I won't be gone very long, and you'll be fine. Just stay here, and keep your foot up on the cushion. That way it won't throb so much. I'll be back as soon as I can, and then we'll get you home. Okay?"

Michael hesitated, but finally nodded.

A few minutes later, he was alone with his grandparents.

Janet left the drugstore, then turned the battered green truck away from the square and drove the two blocks to Laura and Buck Shields's house. She parked the car in the driveway and was starting toward the front door when she heard Laura's thin voice calling to her from the upstairs window.

"It's unlocked. Let yourself in and come upstairs." A wan smile drifted across her face, then disappeared. "I'm afraid I'm still not quite up to coming down."

Janet found Laura dressed, but propped on the bed, resting against several pillows.

"I should be *in* bed, but I just couldn't stand it anymore," Laura told her. "So I got dressed this morning, and I'm spending the day *on* bed. At least I don't feel quite so useless this way." She patted the mattress. "Come and sit down and tell me what's happening. I feel like I've been cooped up here forever."

Janet sighed, and lowered herself gratefully onto the bed. "I suppose you've already heard about Dr. Potter."

Laura's gentle eyes hardened. "The only thing I want to hear about him is that he's dead," she half whispered. "I hate him, Janet—I hate him so much . . ."

Janet reached out to touch Laura's hand. "He—Laura, he *is* dead."

The other woman paled, and a tear suddenly welled in her eye. "Oh, God, Janet. I didn't mean—"

"Of course you didn't." She shrugged helplessly. "It was a stroke, I guess. They found him this morning."

Laura fell silent for a moment, then slowly shook her head. "I should be sorry, shouldn't I, Janet? But you know something? I'm not. I just feel sort of—sort of relieved, I guess. After what he did—"

"No," Janet interrupted her. "Laura, stop torturing yourself. Please?"

But Laura only shook her head again. "I can't help it. I believe what I believe, and I believe they killed my baby." Then, seeing Janet's discomfiture, she decided to change the subject. She made herself smile. "Where's Michael?"

"And that's the rest of the news," Janet replied. Briefly, she told Laura what had happened.

"Is he all right?" Laura asked when Janet was done.

Janet nodded. "But it just seems so stupid. And Michael's always been so good with things like that."

"It *is* stupid," Laura agreed. "But I'll bet it won't happen again—one thing about farms: you usually only make a mistake once. After that, you know better. And how are you doing? Is the house all in order?"

"Hardly, but I guess some progress is being made. And last night Michael and I cleaned out the attic."

"The attic? I thought it was empty."

Janet frowned. "You mean Anna was right? You and Mark never went up there?"

"Mark did, once," Laura told her. "Dad gave him a beating he never forgot. Or anyway, one I never forgot. I guess it was one time I learned by someone else's mistake."

"Amos beat Mark?"

Laura gave her a puzzled look. "Of course he did. He'd told Mark never to go up there, and Mark disobeyed him."

"So he *beat* him?" Janet pressed. "Not just spanked him?"

Laura chuckled hollowly. "I wouldn't call a razor strop an ordinary spanking, but it's amazing how effective it was."

"It's no wonder Mark got out as soon as he could," Janet observed, making no attempt to hide her disapproval.

"That wasn't it at all," Laura said quickly. "That had something to do with the night mother had her last baby. By then, Dad hadn't given Mark a beating in—well, it had been a while. What did you find in the attic?"

Janet made an instinctive decision: what Anna Hall wouldn't talk about, her daughter might. "Among other things, I found Abby Randolph's diary."

Laura stared at her. "You're kidding, of course."

Janet shook her head. Then as casually as she could, she said, "Anna told me that the house has been in your family since the day it was built."

Laura nodded. "The old family homestead, and all that sort of thing. But there was never any mention of Abby having lived there. In fact, if I remember right, we were always sort of led to believe that her house had burned down. If it ever existed at all. Personally, I was never sure there ever was an Abby Randolph. And I certainly don't believe she did all the things she's supposed to have done."

"Well, apparently she did exist, and if I read her diary correctly, it seems that she did exactly what the old stories claim she did."

Laura's face paled. "I—I can't believe that."

"It's in the diary," Janet said gently. "Would you like to see it?"

Quickly, Laura shook her head. "And I don't want to talk about it, either. The whole idea of it makes me sick."

Janet wished she'd never brought the subject up. "Well, none of that matters now anyway," she said quickly. "Whatever happened, it's ancient history. But there was a lot of other stuff—china and silver—and I thought we ought to split it between us. I've talked to Anna about it, and she insists it wasn't hers. In fact, she said if it was in the house, it must be mine, since the house is mine. But that just doesn't seem fair.

Laura looked at her curiously. "But if it wasn't hers, then whose was it?" When Janet made no reply, she suddenly understood. "Oh, God," she groaned. "You're not thinking—" Then, seeing that that was exactly what Janet was thinking, she shook her head. "I could never use it. I couldn't look at it, or touch it, let alone eat off it! And anyway, I've got loads of china and silver of my own, which I never use. It came from Mother's mother, and it's all stowed up in the attic. Limoges china, and the most garish silver you've ever seen."

"Limoges?" Janet repeated. "But that's what was in my attic. Maybe it's from the same set."

"I don't see how—"

But Janet was on her feet. "Can I go up and look? Please?"

"Well, if you want to—" Laura told her where the china and silver were stored, and a few minutes later, Janet was rummaging through the Shieldses' attic. She found the trunk Laura had described, opened it, and felt a pang of disappointment. The china and silver were there, all right, but these things bore no resemblance at all to the things she'd found in her own attic. Slowly, she closed the trunk, and was about to go downstairs when something in the far corner of the attic caught her eye.

It was a crib, and though it was not new, neither was it an antique. Indeed, it seemed barely used. And it was not the crib that Laura had set up in her bedroom in preparation for the baby who had died—that crib was still downstairs, a lonely reminder of Laura's loss. Curious, Janet moved toward the crib. Only when she was near it did she see the rest of the nursery equipment.

A tiny rocking chair, painted pink, and hardly used.

A bassinet, used, but, like the crib, in nearly new condition.

Behind the crib, there was a small chest of drawers, just the right size for a three- or four-year-old. Hesitantly, Janet opened one of the drawers. Inside, clean and neatly folded, she found several stacks of clothing, all of it in infant sizes. Tiny dresses, playsuits, blouses, and pajamas, much of it in pinks and whites.

And then, in the bottom drawer, she found an album. Bound in white leather, it was thin and, like the rest of the things in that far corner, barely used. Frowning slightly, she opened it. On the first page, beneath a blank space neatly outlined in green ink, there was a neatly lettered caption:

REBECCA—HER FIRST PICTURE

Janet stared at the odd page for a moment, then quickly flipped through the book. Where the pictures had once been, now there was nothing. Someone had gone through the album, taking out the photographs, leaving nothing but the eerily hollow captions.

She stared at the album for several seconds, wondering what could have happened to the pictures. Should she take it downstairs and ask Laura about it? Then, before she could make up her mind, she heard Buck's voice, his furious tones carrying clearly into the attic.

"She's up there? By herself? For God's sake, Laura, what are you thinking of?"

Startled, Janet closed the album and hurriedly slipped it back in the dresser drawer. Then she moved quickly toward the attic door, opened it a crack, and listened. Now she could hear nothing except indistinct mutterings, muffled by the closed door to the master bedroom. Janet reached up and pulled the light cord, plunging the attic into darkness, then started down the steep stairs to the second floor. Only when she reached the landing, though, could she hear Buck's voice once again.

"But what if she does see it? What if she wants to know where it came from, and why it's there?"

"She won't," Laura's terrified voice replied. "It's way back in the corner, and there's so much other stuff, she won't even notice it. And even if she does, I'll just say we're storing it for someone. Ione—I'll say we're storing it for Ione Simpson. She has a little girl."

"I told you to get rid of it." There was a silence; then, again: "Didn't I tell you to get rid of it?"

"Y-yes."

"Then why didn't you?"

"I—I couldn't."

"You will," Buck said, his voice holding an implacability Janet had never realized was in him before. "As soon as you're strong enough, you'll bring all that stuff down from the attic, take it out back, and burn it."

"Buck, don't make me—"

"It has to be done," Buck said. "Not today. Not until you're well again. But you have to get rid of that stuff. Do you understand?"

Then, as Janet shrank back against the wall, the door to the bedroom opened, and Buck emerged, his face set with determination. Without seeing Janet, he turned the other way and disappeared down the front stairs. A moment later she heard the front door slam.

For a long time, Janet stood where she was, wondering what to do. At last, forcing herself into a composure she didn't feel, she returned to the bedroom, where Laura, still on the bed, was blotting her face with a Kleenex.

"Was Buck here?" Janet asked. "I thought I heard his voice."

Laura nodded. "He just came by to see how I was doing. Wasn't that sweet of him?"

"Yes," Janet agreed. Then: "The china's all different from what I found, and so's the silver. But I found some stuff in the corner. Some nursery furniture." She watched as Laura swallowed hard, then seemed to search for words.

"It—it's Ione Simpson's," she said at last. "It's been there for a couple of years now. She didn't have any room to store it."

Janet hesitated only a moment, then nodded. Laura had lied, just as she'd told Buck she would.

Michael woke up, and for a moment couldn't remember where he was. Then the room came into focus, and he recognized his grandmother's parlor. Drifting in from the kitchen, he could smell the aroma of fresh-baked cookies. Tentatively, he sat up and lowered his bandaged foot to the floor. The throbbing had eased, and when he tried to stand up, he found that the pain wasn't bad at all as long as he kept his weight on his heel. Slowly, he began hobbling toward the door that would take him into the hall and then back toward the kitchen. But when he came to the dining room, he heard his grandfather's voice, and stopped. His grandfather was talking about him.

"There's something about him, Anna. Something in his eyes. I'm sure of it."

There was silence for a moment, and then his grandmother spoke. "Don't, Amos. Don't start. Not on Michael."

"But what about the headaches? He's having 'em, you know. Just like Mark did. And this morning—"

"What about this morning?" Anna demanded, when Amos showed no sign of going on.

"It was in his eyes," Amos finished. "The same look I saw in Mark's eyes. It's Nathaniel. There's the mark of Nathaniel on that child. They told me when I was a boy—"

Suddenly his grandmother's voice grew loud and angry. "They told you a bunch of lies and stories. They ruined your life and my life and Laura's life. The only one who got away was Mark, and now all those old stories have killed him, too!"

"What happened to Mark was an accident."

"If that's what you believe, then believe it. But I don't believe it. I believe you might as well have killed him with your own hands."

Now his grandfather sounded as angry as his grandmother. "Don't say that, Anna. I've always done what I had to do, and nothing more."

"And look at me," Michael heard his grandmother say. Her voice was trembling now, as if she were starting to cry. "Just look at me. Five babies, and all I have left is Laura. And look at her—she's going to wind up just the way I am, and it's going to be on your head. So help me, if you start trying to see your unholy family curse in Michael, I'll see to it that Janet takes him and goes right back to New York. They're stories, Amos! None of it is anything but stories."

"Abby Randolph was no story. And neither was Nathaniel. It won't end, unless I end it."

"Leave it alone, Amos," his grandmother said after another long silence. "There's nothing wrong with Michael."

"We'll see," his grandfather replied. "When Janet's baby comes, we'll see."

Slowly, Michael backed away from the kitchen door, then turned and made his way back to the parlor. With his heart pounding, he lay down on the sofa again and carefully propped his foot back up on the cushion. Then he closed his eyes and tried to make his breathing come evenly, but he couldn't control the terror in his soul: *He knows*, Michael thought. *Grandpa knows about Nathaniel, and he knows about me.*

CHAPTER 18

Janet sat in the small living room, staring apprehensively at the last box remaining to be opened, knowing that its contents were going to be the most difficult for her. Everything else had long since been put away—as spring had given way to stifling summer, she and Michael had spent the long still evenings sorting through the remnants of their lives in New York, putting some things away, consigning others to the trash barrel. Finally there had been nothing left, except this single box which Janet had been assiduously avoiding. It was Mark's box, the remnants of his life, all the things that had been retrieved from his desks—both at home and at the university. Janet had been putting off opening it, working around it, moving it constantly farther into the corner of the room, but now it sat there, conspicuously alone, and there were no more excuses for ignoring it. Unless she put it in the tiny attic, consigned it to that easily forgettable storage room where it might lie undisturbed through several generations.

Like Abby's diary.

She turned the idea over in her mind as she sat enjoying the peace of the midsummer evening. The day's heat had finally broken, and a gentle breeze drifted over the plains. The soft chirping of crickets seemed to fill up the vast emptiness of the landscape, lulling Janet into a sense of peace she hadn't felt in the months since Mark had died. But tonight, with Michael asleep upstairs—apparently peacefully asleep—she began to wonder if she really needed to open that box at all. Perhaps she shouldn't. Perhaps she should simply put it away, as someone had long ago put Abby's diary away, and forget about it.

But Abby's diary had not remained forgotten, nor had Abby herself.

And, Janet was sure, it would be the same with Mark. To her, the plain cardboard container had become a Pandora's box. Despite all logic, she had the distinct feeling that when she opened it, serpents were going to spew forth, devouring what was left of her faith in her husband. And yet, no matter how long she argued with herself, she knew that in the end she would open it. She sighed, and began.

On top, she found all the things she remembered from his desk in the apartment—even the too-short stubs of pencils and the bent paperclips had been packed. She went through things quickly, only glancing at the stacks of canceled checks, the financial records of their life together, the scribbled notes Mark had often made to himself during the course of an evening, only to tuck them away in the desk and forget them.

Only when she came to the contents of his desk at the university did she slow down, pausing to read the files— the notes on his students, the notes on the various studies he always had in mind but never seemed to get around to. And then, at the bottom of the box, she found a large sealed envelope with her name written across it in Mark's distinctive scrawl.

With trembling hands, she ripped the envelope open and let its contents slide onto her lap. There wasn't much there: a copy of Mark's will—the same will that had been on file with their lawyer—and another envelope, again with its flap sealed and her name written on it.

She stared at this envelope a long time, still toying with the idea of putting it away unread, but in the end, she opened it, too. Inside, she found a note in Mark's choppy hand, and yet a third envelope, which had been opened and resealed with tape, this one postmarked Prairie Bend, but with no return address.

She read Mark's note first:

Dearest Janet,

I can't really imagine circumstances under which you would be reading this, but still, I think I'd better write it down. While I'm in Chicago next week, I'm going back to Prairie Bend. There's something that's been bothering me—it goes back many years, and since it's probably nothing, I won't go into it now. There's a lot I've never told you, but I've had my reasons. Anyway, if anything should happen to me, I want you to know that I love you very much, and would never do anything to hurt you. Also, there's something I'd like you to do. I have a sister—Laura—and I'd like you to take care of her. She might not even know she needs help, but I think she does. If you read this, then you'll be reading her letter, too, and perhaps you'll understand. Do whatever you can. I know this note doesn't shed much light on anything, but until I know more, I won't say more.

All my love forever,

Mark

Janet read the note again, then once more. With each reading the tension inside her increased until she felt as if she'd been tied in knots.

"Damn you," she whispered at last. "Damn you for telling me just enough to make me wonder about everything, but not enough for me to *know* anything."

Finally, she picked up the letter from Laura, and feeling as if she were somehow invading her sister-in-law's privacy, she reluctantly pulled it out of its envelope and unfolded it. It was written in a shaky scrawl, and the signature at the bottom was totally illegible. And yet, in spite of the agitation reflected in the penmanship, Janet recognized it as coming from someone closely related to Mark.

Dear Mark,

I know I haven't written to you for ages, and I know you probably won't answer this, but I have to ask you a question. If I don't, I think I'll go crazy. I'm going to have another baby, and after what happened last time, I'm so frightened I don't know what to do. I think they killed my baby. They said it was born dead, but for some reason, I know it wasn't. Mark, I know it wasn't born dead!

I keep thinking about that night—the night you ran away while I was in the storm cellar. I keep thinking I remember something about that night, but I can't quite remember what. Do I sound crazy? Maybe I do. Anyway, I need to know about that night, Mark. I need to know what happened. I keep thinking the same thing is happening to me that happened to Mother. Did they kill her baby? For some reason, I think they did, but I was in the storm cellar the whole night, so how could I remember? Anyway, did you run away because you saw what happened that night? Please, Mark, if you did, tell me. I don't care what you saw, or think you saw—I just need to know. I need to know I'm not going crazy.

As she had with Mark's letter, Janet reread the note from Laura.

There was nothing really new in the note—it was filled with the same illogical speculations Laura had made after her miscarriage, the speculations Janet had attributed to Laura's grief over losing the baby.

Except that when Laura had written this note, she had not yet lost her baby.

But she had lost another one, a little girl, a little girl named Rebecca—Becky? But that didn't make sense either. Becky had lived, at least for a while—there had been pictures of her, neatly mounted in an album and captioned, only to be torn out later, after the child had died. Laura must have torn them out herself, unable to handle the memories of her lost daughter.

And what was there in the note that had brought Mark back to Prairie Bend after all his years away? He could have answered Laura's questions with a letter, however long or short. But he hadn't—instead, he'd come back to Prairie Bend himself, intent on looking for something.

Something, Janet was sure, that was related to the night he'd run away.

Had he found it?

Was that what the letters meant? That if Janet read the letters, it would mean he'd found what he was looking for, and it had cost him his life?

The idea was barely beginning to take hold in her mind when, upstairs, Michael began to scream.

Janet opened the door to Michael's room, and the first thing she heard was Shadow's soft growl. He was next to Michael's bed, his teeth bared, his hackles bristling, and his yellow eyes gleaming in the darkness. But then, as she spoke to him and he recognized her, his fur settled down and his snarl gave way to a soft whimper. A moment later Janet gathered her son into her arms, rocking him gently until his sobbing eased. "What is it, honey? Is it the pain? Do you want one of the pills?"

Michael shook his head, his eyes wide with fear.

"It isn't your foot?" Janet asked. The foot had been slow to heal, and even after eight weeks Michael still had a slight limp. Sometimes, when he was tired, it still ached.

But again Michael shook his head.

"Then what is it, sweetheart? Can't you tell me?"

"Grandpa," Michael sobbed. "I had a dream about Grandpa, and I saw what happened. Just like before, when I saw Grandpa beating Daddy."

Janet had a sinking feeling. She'd hoped the dreams in which Michael saw his father and his grandfather were over and that Michael had forgotten them. "You had another dream?" she asked.

"Only it wasn't really a dream," Michael insisted. "It was like I was there, and I saw it. And this time, I saw what happened when I hurt my foot. I saw Grandpa try to kill me."

"Oh, Michael," Janet breathed. "Grandpa wouldn't hurt you. He wouldn't hurt you for the world. He loves you."

"No, he doesn't," Michael replied, snuggling closer to his mother and twining his arms around her. "I saw what happened! I didn't stab my own foot—it was Grandpa! He was going to stab me. He was trying to kill me!"

Janet gasped. "Stab you? What are you talking about, Michael?"

"W-with the pitchfork. He was going to stab me with the pitchfork, just like he did to Daddy."

A chill ran through Janet, and her arms tightened around the terrified boy. "No, honey. That's wrong. Daddy fell. He fell from the loft, and landed on the fork. It was an accident. Grandpa wasn't even there."

"He was!" Michael wriggled free from her arms and sat up. Even in the dim light, his eyes were flashing angrily. "He was there! I saw him!"

Suddenly Shadow leaped up onto the bed, and Michael slipped his arms around the big dog's neck. "We saw it, didn't we, Shadow? We saw it!"

With a sinking feeling, Janet realized there was going to be no arguing with Michael. "All right," she said softly. "I won't try to tell you what you saw and what you didn't see." Michael seemed to relax a little, and Janet reached out to take his hand. Shadow growled softly, then subsided. "Why don't we put Shadow outside tonight," she suggested. "Then you can sleep with me."

"But Shadow likes to sleep with me—"

"I'll bet he'd like to spend a night outside," Janet countered. "Wouldn't you, Shadow?" The dog's tail moved slightly. "See? He's wagging his tail."

Michael looked at the dog, then reached out to scratch his ears. "Is that okay?" he asked, and as if he understood his master, this time the dog truly wagged his tail. Janet stood up.

"Okay, I'll put him out, and you go crawl into my bed. I'll be there in a minute. Come on, Shadow."

The dog sat up, but didn't move from the bed. Instead, his head swung around, and his eyes fixed expectantly on Michael.

"Go on, boy," Michael said softly. "Go with Mom."

Shadow jumped off the bed and followed Janet out of the little bedroom and down the stairs. Then, when she held the kitchen door open for him, he dashed out into the night. She watched him lope off in the direction of Ben Findley's place, but after a few seconds the blackness of his coat blended into the darkness, and he was gone. Silently, Janet hoped the dog would be as invisible to the cranky old man as he was to her.

She toured the downstairs, turning off lights and checking doors and windows. Just before she put out the last light, she picked up Mark's letter and reread it, then reread Laura's note as well. At last she put both of them back into the envelope she'd found them in, and put the envelope into the bottom drawer of the desk, far in the back. Thoughtfully, she turned out the lights, went upstairs, undressed, and slipped into bed next to her son.

"Are you still awake?" she whispered.

Michael stirred, but made no reply.

"Sleep then," she said, her voice barely audible. "In the morning you'll have forgotten all about it."

"No, I won't," Michael replied, his voice echoing hollowly in the darkness. "I won't forget about it at all. Not ever." He fell silent for a moment, then stirred and turned over.

"Honey? Is something wrong?"

"Unh-unh," Michael replied. "I just have a headache, that's all."

"Do you want me to get you some aspirin?"

"Unh-unh. It's almost gone."

"You mean you've had it all evening?"

In the darkness, Michael shook his head. "I woke up with it," he said. "I had it in the dream, and then I still had it when I woke up. But it's almost gone now."

Janet lay awake for a long time, thinking about Michael. He'd grown quiet over the last few weeks, and even though he'd made up with Ryan, he still wasn't as close to his cousin—or any of the other children of the town—as she wished he were. And his feelings about his grandfather seemed to be getting almost obsessive.

And then, just before she drifted into sleep, she remembered Michael's words the day Ione had bought the Raggedy Ann.

"I bet they killed her. . . . I bet they buried her in Potter's Field."

No, Janet told herself. It's not possible. He's only imagining things. None of it is possible. . . .

It was just after dawn when Amos Hall glanced out the kitchen window, frowning. "There's that damned dog again," he said softly. Anna's eyes followed his gaze, and in the distance she could see Shadow, his tail tucked between his legs, skulking outside the barn.

"If he's after those hens, I'll have his hide," she said, rolling herself toward the door. "You, Shadow, get out of here! Go home!"

The dog tensed, and his large head swung around so that he faced the house.

"That's right," Anna called. "I'm talking to you. Get on out of here!" Then, as Shadow disappeared around the corner of the barn, she turned back to Amos. "What's he doing over here this early? He never leaves Michael. Did you hear Janet's truck come in?"

"I didn't hear it, 'cause it didn't come in," Amos replied. He got up and went into the dining room, then the living room. A minute later he was back. "And Michael's bike's not around either. So he's not here, unless he hiked along the river. I'll go out and have a look behind the barn.''

He left the house and strode across the yard toward the barn, then around the corner. There was nothing behind the barn, neither Shadow nor Michael. Puzzled, Amos came to a halt and surveyed the fields. The ripening grain, nearly three feet high, waved in the breeze, and Amos studied it for a few minutes, trying to find a spot where the boy and the dog could be hiding. And then, as the seconds went by, he began to have an odd sense of eyes watching him.

He turned around, half expecting to see Michael grinning at him, but there was nothing.

Nothing, except—still—the uneasy feeling of being watched. Finally, he looked up.

In the loft door, only his head visible, was Shadow. He was panting, and his mouth was half open, and he seemed to be staring down at Amos.

''What the— You, Shadow! Get down from there!''

Shadow's hackles rose, and a low growl rumbled from his throat. He stayed where he was.

For a long moment the man and the dog stared at each other, and then Amos noticed that the door to the tack room was ajar. And yet he was sure he'd closed it last night, and he hadn't used it today.

Michael *had* to be around, and he must be inside the barn. Amos went inside the tack room, pulling the door closed behind him. ''Michael? You in here, son?''

There was no answer, only a soft scratching sound overhead as Shadow moved across the loft floor.

''Come on, Michael,'' Amos called out a little louder. ''I know you're in here. If you make me come and find you, you're going to regret it. And I want that dog of yours out of the barn right now!''

Still there was no answer, and Amos went on through the tack room and into the barn itself. Something scurried in the silence, and once again he heard Shadow prowling around the loft. Slowly, Amos walked down the center of the barn, inspecting the stalls one by one.

All of them were empty.

At last, when he was at the front of the barn, he turned to gaze upward to the loft.

Shadow gazed back at him.

"I know you're up there, Michael," Amos said. "Someone had to let that dog in here, and dogs don't climb ladders."

Still the silence in the barn was undisturbed.

Amos moved toward the foot of the ladder that led to the loft, and started up it. A second later, Shadow appeared at the open trapdoor at the top of the ladder, a soft snarl escaping his lips as he bared his fangs.

Amos stopped and stared upward, his heart beating a little faster. "Get that dog away, Michael," he commanded. After a few seconds, Shadow backed away from the trapdoor.

Quickly, Amos clambered to the top of the ladder and glanced around the loft.

Shadow had disappeared.

"All right, Michael," Amos said, the softness of his voice concealing his anger. "The joke's over. Wherever you're hiding, show yourself."

Nothing happened.

Amos moved toward the small pile of hay bales. They stood beneath the slanting roof, and Amos had to bend down to peer into the narrow space behind him.

Glaring back at him, his eyes glowing, was Shadow.

Startled, Amos stood up, and his head struck one of the beams that supported the barn roof. He staggered back, and Shadow, as if sensing his advantage, growled and moved forward.

"Get back, damn you," Amos muttered. He glanced around the loft, searching for a weapon, and spotted a pitchfork lying near the edge of the loft.

Moving slowly, his eyes never leaving the dog, he began edging toward the fork.

Shadow advanced, his hackles raised now, and his growl grew into an angry snarl.

Suddenly Amos made his move and had the pitchfork in his right hand. The dog tensed and came to a halt, as if sensing that the situation had changed.

Amos felt his heartbeat begin settling back to normal, and tightened his grip on the pitchfork. He began jabbing it at the dog, and slowly Shadow began to retreat, his growl subsiding into a sullen whimper.

And then Shadow's sinewy rump hit the stacked bales of hay, and he could move no further. His hackles rose once more, and his tail, still tucked between his legs, began to twitch. His yellow eyes, glinting in the shadows of the loft, seemed to narrow into evil slits, and fastened on the fork as if it were a snake.

"Not so brave now, are you?" Amos whispered. "Goddamn cur—lots of courage a minute ago, but look at you now."

Suddenly, Shadow leaped, twisting in midair to clamp his jaws onto the handle of the pitchfork, the force of his weight wrenching the tool out of Amos's grip. Before Amos could react, the dog darted toward the open door to the loft, and a moment later the fork dropped harmlessly to the ground below.

And then, as Amos watched, Shadow turned back, and began advancing on him once more, stalking him as if he were a rabbit, watching him, closing the gap between them, waiting for the right moment to strike.

Once again, Amos began backing away, and once more his eyes searched for a weapon.

There was none.

And suddenly Amos felt the edge of the loft. He came to a halt, glaring at the dog with a mixture of fear and anger.

"Down, damn you," he whispered. "Down!"

Shadow ignored him and came even closer, crouching on his haunches, his eyes glowing malevolently, the snarl in his throat settling into a steady evil hum.

And finally, once more, he leaped. His mouth wide open, he hurled his body forward.

Instinctively, Amos's hands and arms came up to ward off the attack, but he knew it was useless. The animal's jaws were about to close on his throat, its teeth about to sink into his flesh, tearing him apart.

Shadow's weight crashed against him, and Amos lost his balance, tumbling backward off the edge of the loft.

He could almost feel the tines of the waiting pitchfork, feel them plunging into his back, impaling him as they'd impaled Mark.

The split second it took before he struck the bin seemed like an eternity, and he half wished that Shadow's jaws would close on his throat, ripping his life out before the tines of the fork slashed through his body. At least with the dog, death would be quick, and the pain short lived.

And then, just before the fall ended, he blacked out.

The telephone was ringing as Janet returned from feeding her small flock of chickens. She hurried to answer it, but Michael got to it first. A moment later, he called out from the living room.

"Mom? It's Grandma, and she wants to talk to you." Then, as Janet took the receiver, he added, "She sounds real funny."

"Anna? I was going to call you in a few—"

And then she fell silent, lowering herself onto the chair next to the desk. "I see," she said at last. "But he's going to be all right? You're sure?" She listened once again, then hung up the phone and turned to face Michael. "Grandpa's had an accident," she said, reaching for her purse. "We have to go over there right away." Suddenly her eyes darted around the small living room, and she frowned. "Where's Shadow?"

As if in answer to her question, there was a soft woofing at the front door, and Michael went to let the big dog in. He nuzzled eagerly at Michael for a minute, but then, as if he felt Janet's eyes studying him, went to her and laid his head against her side. She hesitated, but finally gave him a tentative scratch behind the ears. As he watched, Michael felt suddenly worried.

"What happened to Grandpa?" he asked, and finally his mother looked at him, removing her hand from Shadow at the same time.

"I'm not sure," she said softly. "Apparently he fell from the hayloft. He's all right, but he says Shadow attacked him."

Instantly Michael was kneeling next to the dog, his arms around the beast's neck. "He did not! Shadow wouldn't hurt anyone. Besides, he was here when I got up, weren't you, Shadow?"

The dog whined happily and licked Michael's face.

"But we've only been up an hour," Janet pointed out. "Your grandfather's been up since dawn. Shadow could have been over there."

"But why would he go to Grandpa's? He doesn't even like Grandpa!"

Janet sighed, and got to her feet. "Well, we don't really know what happened, do we? So why don't we go over there and find out?"

Suddenly Michael stiffened. "No!"

"Michael!"

"I don't want to go over there. Grandpa's going to try to blame everything on Shadow, and it's not fair."

Suddenly Janet's own thoughts from the night before came back to her. *Don't argue with him.* "All right," she agreed. "You can stay here. But I want you to stay in the house, and rest. You still limp, even if it's just a little."

"Can't I even go out to the backyard and play with Shadow? I could just throw sticks for him."

Janet was already at the front door. "Okay, but that's as far as you go. The yard. Understood?"

"Uh-huh."

"I'll be back as soon as I can."

And then she was gone, and Michael and Shadow were alone in the house.

"Did you get him, Shadow?" Michael said softly when the sound of the old truck had faded away. "Did you really get him?" The dog whimpered, and pressed closer. "Good boy," Michael whispered. "Next time, maybe you can make him die."

The scene at the Halls' was eerily familiar: there was Anna, her wheelchair pushed close to the sofa in the parlor, and there was Ione Simpson, doing her best to fill the gap left by Dr. Potter's death, bending over the supine figure on the sofa. But this time, it was Amos Hall, not Michael, on the sofa. Janet paused at the doorway for a moment, but Anna motioned her into the room.

"He's all right," she assured the younger woman. "Nothing's broken, and Ione doesn't think there're any internal injuries. Mostly, he got the wind knocked out of him, and his dignity's taken a beating." Suddenly she frowned. "Where's Michael?"

"I left him at home," Janet replied hastily. "I didn't know what was happening here, and I was afraid he'd just add to the confusion."

"It's his dog, I want," Amos suddenly growled. He struggled a moment, then sat up, fury in his eyes. "That mutt attacked me, and I want it destroyed."

"Now, Amos," Anna began, but her husband cut her off.

"You saw him, Anna. You saw him sneaking around the barn. And then he went for me."

"Oh, Amos, I'm so sorry," Janet said. "What happened? Why did he attack you?"

"How the hell do I know why?" Amos snorted. Briefly, he told them what had happened. When he was done, Janet sighed.

"We'll just have to get rid of the dog then, I suppose."

"Get rid of him?" Ione asked. "What do you mean?"

Amos glared at her. "She means have it destroyed. Don't you understand English anymore?" Ione's lips tightened but she said nothing.

Janet leaned forward. "Amos, I didn't mean that—"

"Well, you should have. The dog's dangerous. I told you that when it first came around, but you didn't believe me. Well, do you believe me now?"

"I—"

But this time it was Ione Simpson who didn't let Amos finish. "Are you sure the dog attacked you, Amos?"

Amos's angry eyes shifted back to the nurse again. "What the hell do you mean, am I sure?"

"We've had a lot of dog bites over the years," Ione replied, keeping her voice calm in the face of Amos's wrath. "Most of them were just nips, but a few of them were good hard bites. And a few years back, a dog about the size of a collie did attack someone around here."

"And?" Amos asked.

Ione shrugged. "At least those people had a break in their skin for their trouble. And remember Joe Cotter? Both his arms were torn up, and he was lucky he survived."

For a long moment, Amos was silent, glowering malevolently at Ione. When he finally spoke, his voice was dangerously low. "Are you accusing me of lying?"

Ione shook her head tiredly, knowing arguing with Amos Hall was useless. "I'm only suggesting you might think it was a lot worse than it was. I mean, where are the bites?"

"Goddamn it, it didn't bite me," Amos roared. "It backed me up to the edge of the loft, then jumped at me and pushed me off."

"Amos, calm down," Anna cut in. "No one's accusing you of anything, and I'm sure you think Shadow attacked you. But couldn't you be wrong? Just once in your life, couldn't you be wrong about something?"

"No," Amos snapped. "I know what happened, and I want that dog destroyed. He's dangerous. Sooner or later he'll attack someone else." His attention turned back to Janet. "How would you feel if he attacked Michael?"

Janet stared at the old man, aghast. "Michael?" she replied. "Why on earth would he attack Michael? He adores him. It's almost as if the two of them can communicate with each other.''

Amos's eyes darkened. ''Well, if something happens to Michael, it won't be my fault.''

Suddenly Janet found herself angry with the old man. ''Amos, stop it,'' she said. ''Nothing's going to happen to Michael, and if it does, it won't be because of Shadow. Right now, that dog is Michael's closest friend, and unless you can come up with something more than talk to back up your claims that he attacked you, I'm not getting rid of him. Ione's right—if he'd attacked you, it seems to me you'd at least have some scratches. I think you simply stumbled off that loft yourself, and you don't want to admit it. And frankly, you should be ashamed of yourself for trying to put the blame on Shadow.'' She rose to her feet and left the front room, followed immediately by Anna, who stopped her just as she was leaving the house.

''Janet? Wait a minute.''

Her anger already spent, Janet turned back to face her mother-in-law. ''Oh, Anna, I'm sorry—I just don't know what got into me.''

''No,'' Anna said softly, shaking her head. ''Don't apologize. It wasn't your fault—none of it. I'm sure you were right about what happened. But Amos has always been that way—he can't stand to be contradicted, or criticized, or made to feel he's wrong. He'll get over it. Just give him a little time.''

Janet nodded. ''Of course.'' She smiled sadly at Anna. ''Is that what happened with Mark? Did he suggest that Amos was wrong about something?''

Anna hesitated a moment, then nodded. ''I suppose you could say that.'' Her eyes met Janet's, and Janet could almost feel the sadness in them. ''Don't you do it, too,'' she pleaded. ''Don't turn away from him—from us. I know he's not always easy, but he loves you, and he loves Michael. I know he does.''

Janet reached out and touched the older woman's cheek.

"I know," she said softly. "And it will be all right. I won't hold anything against him, and neither will Michael."

Anna stayed by the door until Janet was gone, then slowly wheeled herself back to the living room, where Ione Simpson was giving Amos a shot. Anna sat silently in her chair, her eyes fixed on her husband.

But in her mind, she had gone back twenty years, back to the house where Janet lived now, the house Mark had fled from.

She has to know, Anna thought. *Sometime, Janet has to know what happened that night, and why Mark left. And I will have to tell her.* But even as she entertained the thought, Anna was not at all sure she could ever tell the truth about that night and what had gone before. Even after all these years, it was still too painful to think about.

She came back to the present, and focused once more on her husband. Silently, she wondered what had really happened in the barn that morning, wondered if Shadow had, indeed, attacked Amos. Or had it been another accident, like Mark's. Like Michael's.

With a shudder, Anna recalled her husband's words on the day Michael's foot had been hurt. The trouble would go on, she realized. The trouble that had started twenty years ago, then erupted again when Mark finally came home.

And suddenly she knew, with dreadful certainty, that the trouble wouldn't end until Amos was dead. Amos, or Michael. Her husband, or her grandson.

Slowly, Anna turned and wheeled herself out of the room.

"Get it, Shadow! Go get it, boy!" The stick had arced through the air, landing with a thud in the dust near the entrance to the cyclone cellar. Shadow took a few steps away from Michael, then turned back to look uncertainly at his master. "That's right, Shadow," Michael told him. "Fetch. Fetch the stick." The big dog hesitated, then as if finally understanding what was expected of him, trotted off toward the little dugout. But before he got to the stick, he veered off to the right, and a moment later began snuffling around the edges of the closed door. At last he looked back at Michael and barked loudly.

"Aw, come on, Shadow, we're supposed to be playing fetch," Michael complained. He began trudging once more toward the piece of wood which had so far entirely failed to capture the dog's attention. When he had the stick in hand, Michael called to Shadow again. "Come on, boy. Look what I've got!" But Shadow ignored him, his nose still pressed against the crack between the doors of the storm cellar. Frowning slightly, Michael dropped the stick and started toward the dog, and as he drew close to the big animal, he began to feel a slow throb begin in his temples. "What is it?" he asked.

As if in answer, Shadow whined eagerly, and pawed at the door.

"Is something in there?" Michael struggled with the door for a moment and finally succeeded in getting it halfway open. Shadow immediately disappeared into the gloom of the little room, but Michael hesitated, searching the darkness for some hint of what had attracted the dog.

And then he heard the voice.

"Michael."

"N-Nathaniel? Are—are you in here?"

"Go inside," the voice instructed him. "Go inside, and close the door."

As if in a trance, Michael obeyed the voice, moving carefully down the steep steps, lowering the door closed behind him. Slowly, his eyes began adjusting to the darkness. Enough light seeped through the cracks in the weathered doors to let him see Shadow crouching attentively in the corner, his ears up, his tail twitching with eagerness.

"Nathaniel? Are you in here?"

"I am in you, Michael. I am in you, and you are in me. Do you understand?"

In the semidarkness of the subterranean room, Michael

slid his arms around Shadow's neck, pulling the dog close. "N-no."

"We are part of each other," Nathaniel's voice said. "I am part of your father, and I am part of you."

"My father?" Michael breathed. "Is—is that why Grandpa killed him?"

"He found out. He found out, so he killed your father."

Michael's eyes darted around, searching for the familiar face of Nathaniel, but there was nothing in the room, nothing but the coolness and gloom. "What did Dad find out?" he whispered.

"The children. He found out about the children. I told him, and showed him, and he believed. But he was afraid."

"He wasn't!" Michael protested. "My dad wasn't afraid of anything!"

"He was afraid to act, Michael," the strange voice replied. "He was afraid to punish them, even after he saw what they did."

"Y-you mean he wouldn't fight?" Michael's voice quavered as he asked the question, for slowly he was beginning to understand what was going to be asked of him.

"He wouldn't make them die, Michael." Nathaniel's voice took on a strangely compelling quality, and even though Michael was sure he ought to resist the voice, he knew he wouldn't. "Will you, Michael? When the time comes, will you be with me and help me make them die?"

"I—I don't—"

"You do know, Michael," Nathaniel's voice insisted. "You know what you must do. You told us so."

"Told you? Told you what?"

There was a long silence, and then, from inside his head, Michael heard his own words—the words he'd spoken to Shadow that very morning—repeated to him in the voice of Nathaniel: "Next time, maybe you can make him die."

Deep down inside, far down in the depths of his subconscious, Michael understood what was expected of him.

He was to avenge his father's death.

He was to kill his grandfather.

His head pounding with the throbbing pain, Michael tried to drive the voice of Nathaniel out of his mind. His arms dropped away from Shadow, and he hurled himself toward the cellar door, scrambling up the steep steps, bursting out into the morning sunlight. But even then, Nathaniel's face lingered inside him.

"You will, Michael. When the time comes, you will help me. You will make them die, Michael. You will . . ."

CHAPTER 19

Ryan Shields was working on his bicycle, adjusting the seat and the handlebars, when he heard the back door slam. He looked up, then watched curiously as his mother brought a bundle of clothes down the back steps and made her way across the yard to the graveled area where the incinerator stood. "Whatcha doing?"

"Cleaning out the attic," Laura told him. "It's gotten too full, and your father wants me to burn some things."

"Want me to help?" Ryan asked, eagerly abandoning the bike in favor of the prospect of a bonfire. But Laura shook her head.

"I can do it." Carefully, she set the bundle on the gravel, stared at it a moment, then returned to the house. A few minutes later she appeared once again, struggling to maneuver a crib through the back door. Immediately, Ryan recognized the crib.

"You're going to burn that?" he asked. "But that's—"

"I know what it is," Laura said, and there was something in her voice that made Ryan fall silent. "I know what all of this stuff is, and I don't want to talk about it, Ryan." She glared at him for a second. Then: "Don't you have anything to do? Do you have to hang around here all the time? Why don't you go out and see Michael?"

Abashed, Ryan scuffed at the ground for a moment.

"Well?" Laura demanded with a severity that startled her son. "You haven't seen Michael for a long time. Did you two have a fight?"

"Not exactly—"

"Then go," Laura told him.

"But Dad told me not to go anywhere," Ryan protested. "He told me to stay around here in case you needed anything."

"Well, I don't need anything," Laura declared. "And I'm getting tired of having you underfoot all the time." Then, as she saw her son's chin begin to quiver, she suddenly relented. "Oh, honey, I'm sorry. It's just that I'm upset right now, and I have to do something I really don't want to do. It'll be easier if I'm by myself. Do you understand?"

Even though he didn't understand at all, Ryan nodded his head. "But if you don't want to burn that stuff, how come you're going to?"

"Because your father says I have to. I've put it off as long as I can, and I have to do it by myself. All right?"

Reluctantly, Ryan got to his feet. "Okay. Maybe I'll go out and see what Eric's doing. Maybe we can go fishing."

"Why don't you go see Michael? Are you mad at him?" she asked again.

Ryan hesitated, and dug at the ground with the toe of his sneaker. "He's always got his dog with him," he finally said.

"Shadow? Don't you like him?"

"He doesn't like me. He only likes Michael, and whenever anyone else is around, he starts growling. He scares me."

"He's just being protective—he wouldn't hurt you. Now run on along."

When Ryan was gone, she finished bringing Becky's things down from the attic.

She went over them once more—the clothes Becky had never worn, the crib Becky had never used, the mobiles Laura had never been able to hang over Becky's bassinet, and the toys she had never been able to see Becky touch for the first time. Finally there was nothing left except the album, the album which should have eventually filled with pictures of Becky's first years.

The captions were all there: "Her first meal," "Sunning in the backyard," "First step—wobbly, but she did it!"

She turned the pages slowly, as if studying for the last time the pictures that weren't there—had never been there.

She'd nearly lost herself over Becky. She could remember some of it so well, and yet so much of it was a blank.

She could recall the days of waking up and listening for the cries of the baby, only to remember that there would be no cries, for there was no baby. Other days—the worst days—she'd known from the moment she awoke that Becky had died, and those days had been desolate ones.

The best days had been the days—sometimes two or three of them in a row—when she truly believed that Becky was still there in the house, sleeping, perhaps, and would soon wake up and call for her. It was during one of those times that she'd ordered the Raggedy Ann doll, a gift for Becky to make up for her own neglect.

No one had known she'd done it until the doll arrived, and when Buck had asked her about it, she'd blurted out the truth without thinking. "It's for Becky—I've left her alone so much."

That's when they'd sent her away for a while—not very long, really, only a few weeks. And when she'd come back, she'd been all right. Except that every now and then, she still crept up to the attic to go through Becky's things, to pretend, if only for a few minutes, that Becky was all right, that Becky had survived the birth, that Ryan—despite all the love she felt for him—was not her only child.

But she knew Buck was right, she knew she had to get rid of the last of Becky's things and put the child out of her mind, finally and forever. If she didn't, she would destroy herself.

She placed the empty album on top of the heap, then doused the whole thing with kerosene. Finally she stood back and tossed a match onto the pyre. A moment later all that was left of her memories of her daughter began to go up in flames.

For a long time Laura watched the blaze, standing perfectly still, her attention focused totally on the conflagration. When the touch on her shoulder came, she jerked spasmodically, then whirled around to see Janet standing behind her.

"I'm sorry," Janet said. "Are you all right? I spoke to you, but you didn't answer me."

"I—I—" Laura floundered, then fell silent and turned back to gaze once more at the fire which was fast diminishing to nothing more than a bed of glowing coals. "I was just burning some trash," she whispered at last, her eyes filling with the tears she had been doing her best to control.

"Some trash," Janet repeated softly. "It's the stuff from the attic, isn't it? Ione Simpson's stuff?"

Laura hesitated, then nodded mutely.

"Ione didn't want it back?"

Again the hesitation, longer this time, but finally Laura shook her head. "No . . . no, she didn't."

When she spoke once more, Janet was careful not to look at Laura. "I wish you'd called me—I could have used those things for my baby."

At last Laura faced Janet, and when Janet looked into her eyes, she saw a depth of pain there such as she'd never seen before. "Your baby?" Laura asked, her voice as hollow as her eyes. "Did you say your baby?"

Slowly, Janet nodded, and suddenly a bitter smile warped Laura's pretty features. "You really think you're going to have it? You really think they'll let you have it? Go away, Janet. Go away now, while you still can. If you want your baby, go away now, before it's born. They'll kill it, Janet." Laura's voice began rising to that hysterical pitch Janet had heard once before, right after Laura had lost her baby. She reached out to place a calming hand on Laura's arm, but her sister-in-law shrank away from her.

"Who, Laura?" Janet asked. "Who will kill my baby?"

"Father," Laura whispered; then, again, "Father. He'll do it, Janet—he always does it." For a long time she stared into Janet's eyes, as if trying to see whether the other woman believed her, then finally broke her gaze, and glanced once more at the smoldering coals. "That's all that's left of her now. She's gone, Janet. Now, she's really gone."

"Who?" Janet asked. "Please, Laura, who's gone?"

"My little girl," Laura suddenly wailed. "My little girl, my Becky."

And as Laura collapsed sobbing into her arms, Janet once again remembered Michael's words. *I bet they killed her. I bet they buried her in Potter's Field.*

"Come on, Laura," Janet said softly. "I'm taking you home with me. I'm taking you home, so we can talk."

"Is Father all right?" Laura suddenly asked. The two of them were sitting in Janet's living room, and Laura was sipping at the cup of tea Janet had fixed for her. It had taken nearly an hour for her to calm down, but now she seemed better.

"He'll be all right," Janet told her. "He claims Shadow attacked him, but nobody else agrees with him."

"I wanted to go out there, you know," Laura said as if she hadn't heard Janet's words. "When Mother called, I offered to go out and help her take care of him, but she wouldn't let me."

"I'm sure she was only thinking of you."

"No!" Once again Laura's voice rose. "They don't think of me," she said bitterly. "At least not Father. He—he thinks I'm crazy, you know."

"I'm sure he doesn't," Janet protested.

"But he does," Laura replied. "He thinks all women are weak, but especially me. And I suppose he's right. After Becky was born I fell apart."

Janet frowned, remembering the letter Laura had sent to Mark.

"Tell me what happened." But Laura shook her head. "I can't talk about it. If I do, you'll think I'm crazy, too."

"I won't," Janet promised. "Laura, I need to know what's happened here, too. I need to know what happened to you, and to Mark. I don't care what you say, I promise you I won't think you're crazy."

Laura grinned crookedly. "That's what the doctors said, too. But when I told them what happened, they didn't believe me. For a while, I thought they did, but it was only an act. Pretty soon they started trying to convince me I was imagining things. So finally I agreed with them, and they let me go."

"Let you go?"

"I—I was in a hospital for a while. A mental hospital. I finally got out by telling them what they wanted to hear. Do you know how hard it is to do that, when you know all they want to hear is what makes sense, but the truth doesn't make sense? In order to prove you're sane, you have to lie. And that's crazy, isn't it?"

Janet ignored the question. "But why were you there? Because of Becky?"

Laura nodded. "I wouldn't admit she was dead. Even now, sometimes I think she's still alive. I wake up in the middle of the night, and I can almost hear her crying. Then I remember where she is, and I remember what happened. But I didn't used to. Sometimes I'd forget for days at a time. So they sent me away."

"Where is she, Laura?"

"Out there," Laura said. Her eyes drifted toward the window, but when Janet followed her gaze, she saw nothing but the fields: her own fields, the ripening crops beginning to tinge the prairie with a golden hue, and, further away, the overgrown expanse that was called Potter's Field. "Becky's buried out there?" Janet breathed. "But why? Why would she be buried out there?"

Laura shook her head. "I don't know," she whispered. "All I know is that's where they bury them. That's where they see Abby, you know. But it's not Abby, Janet. It's not Abby Randolph looking for her children. It's Father, or Dr. Potter, burying my children.''

Janet shuddered, for Laura's words were too much like Michael's own. For a moment, she had an urge to flee, to take Michael and run away. But she knew she wouldn't—couldn't—until she learned the truth.

Michael, unaware of how long it had been since he'd come out of the storm cellar, stared at the river. It was much lower than it had been in the spring, and its water was getting clearer every day. As Michael watched, he thought he saw a small school of fish swimming against the current. He started walking upstream, toward the village, with Shadow next to him, though the dog stopped every few seconds to sniff at a bush, a small hole in the ground, or a rock. Then, after they'd gone some fifty yards, Shadow suddenly stiffened, and a low growl emerged from his throat. Michael stopped and stared curiously at the dog.

''What is it, boy?''

The dog stood perfectly still, one foreleg slightly raised, his eyes fixed on a point somewhere in the distance. Michael studied the woods, then shrugged and started forward again.

Again, Shadow growled, and Michael turned back to face him. ''Come on, Shadow. There's nothing there,'' he said, his voice implying a certainty he didn't feel.

For a long moment, the dog remained frozen on point, but then slowly began to relax. His growling faded, and the fur on his neck settled back. Finally he went to Michael, sat down in front of him, and licked his hand. Michael patted him on the head. ''See? I told you there was nothing there.'' But a second later, when he started forward once more, Shadow blocked his way. Michael paused, then started to step around the dog.

Shadow countered his move, then nudged at Michael, pushing him slightly backward.

''Stop that,'' Michael said, and once more tried to move

around the dog. This time, a low growl rumbled up from Shadow's throat as once more he blocked Michael's way.

"What's wrong with you?" Michael complained. "Why can't we go this way?"

And then, from a few yards ahead and off to the right, he heard a twig break. Shadow whirled and once more went onto point, his growl turning into a snarl.

Michael peered into the shadows of the forest, but could see nothing. "Who's there?" he called. Then, when there was no reply, he called out again, "Is someone there?"

Another twig snapped, closer this time. Shadow's hackles rose, and his tail dropped slightly, curving close to the ground. Then his snarl escalated into a howl, and he leaped forward, charging into the woods. A moment later he was gone, though his baying filled the woods with an eerie din.

Michael hesitated only a moment, then spun around and ran back down the path, his feet pounding on the ground, the sound of Shadow's fury diminishing in the distance.

At last, out of breath, Michael came to a stop and sank down on the riverbank. From far away, he could still hear Shadow barking. Suddenly, the bark turned into an anguished yelp.

Then there was silence.

Ryan Shields and Eric Simpson saw Michael and came to a sudden halt. They were on their way to their favorite fishing hole, but now, as they watched Michael, they began to wonder if maybe they shouldn't change their minds. They glanced at each other uneasily; then, though neither of them spoke, each of them began scanning the area, looking for the big dog that was always with Michael. Today, Shadow was nowhere to be seen.

"You wanta go somewhere else?" Ryan finally asked Eric, and Eric shrugged.

"I don't know. Maybe he's gone."

"Maybe he's hiding in the woods," Ryan countered.

"You scared of him?"

Ryan hesitated, but finally nodded. "He's always growling, and acting like he's gonna bite."

"But Michael says he never bit anyone."

"So what?" Ryan replied, his voice scornful. "Michael doesn't even know where he came from."

Eric frowned. "Are you mad at Michael?"

"I don't know. He's just sort of—well, he's sort of weird."

Eric nodded his agreement. "But my mom says I ought to be nice to him. Why don't we ask him if he wants to go fishing with us?"

Ryan was about to shake his head when he remembered his own mother's words earlier that day, so he shrugged, then called out to his cousin. Michael looked up, then waved.

"Whatcha doin'?" Eric asked as he flopped down on the riverbank next to Michael.

"Waiting for Shadow," Michael replied, but there was something in his voice that made both the other boys suspicious.

Ryan eyed his cousin. "Did he run away?" he finally asked.

"N-no," Michael stammered. Then he told them what had happened, and finished by asking, "You wanta help me look for him?"

The three boys started slowly back up the path that followed the riverbank, but a few minutes later, Eric suddenly stopped. Michael looked at him curiously. "It was further than this," he said.

"But this is where old man Findley's land starts," Eric replied. "What if he sees us out here?"

Michael's eyes narrowed. "I thought you said you weren't afraid of old man Findley."

Then, before Eric could reply, they heard the sound of an animal whimpering.

"Shadow?" Michael called. "Shadow, is that you?"

From up ahead and off to the right in the forest, came an

answering bark. Michael began running toward the sound.
A second later the other two boys followed him.

Michael found the dog first. Shadow was lying at the
base of a tree, his back curled protectively against a root,
licking at his left forepaw. Michael knelt down and reached
out to touch the injured leg. The dog stiffened for a
moment, then seemed to relax under the boy's gentle
fingers. But seconds later, when Eric and Ryan came into
sight, his hackles rose, and he struggled to his feet, supporting himself on three legs.

"It's all right, boy," Michael whispered. "Lie down.
It's all right."

The beginnings of a growl died in the dog's throat, and
then he eased himself back down to the ground. Warily,
Ryan and Eric approached.

"What's wrong with him?" Ryan asked.

"It's his leg," Michael explained. "Something's wrong
with his leg."

"Is it cut?"

"I don't know. I don't think so—there isn't any blood."

Eric dropped down next to Michael, and reached out to
touch the injured leg, but quickly pulled his hand back
when Shadow bared his fangs.

"No, Shadow," Michael said to the dog. "It's all right.
Eric won't hurt you." Then, keeping his hands on Shadow's
head, he nodded to Eric. "Go ahead—he won't bite you."

Eric still looked uncertain. "How do you know?"

"I know, that's all," Michael told him.

Eric took the dog's leg in his hand, and though a low
rumble came from Shadow, and his eyes fixed balefully on
Eric's, he didn't move. Gingerly, the boy explored the
injured leg, and though Shadow yelped twice, he made no
move either to pull the leg away or to snap at Eric. Finally
Eric released the leg and looked at Michael. "It's swollen,
but there isn't any cut or anything. It's like maybe somebody hit him with a stick or something."

"Is it broken?" Michael asked, his voice anxious.

Eric shrugged. "I don't know."

"I bet it was old man Findley," Ryan said. "I bet he was coming after you with his gun, and Shadow went for him."

The three boys fell silent, staring at each other, and suddenly Michael felt a chill go up his spine as if someone were watching him from behind. His hands fell away from Shadow, and he scrambled to his feet just as Ben Findley stepped out from behind a tree ten yards away.

The old man glared at them for a moment, then his eyes came to rest on Michael. When he spoke, his voice was hard and angry. "You're damned lucky I didn't shoot him," he said. Only then did Michael see the shotgun that he held loosely in one hand.

At the sound of the old man's words, Shadow bared his fangs once more, snarled, and struggled to his feet.

"What'd you do to him?" Michael demanded. Findley grinned, exposing crooked teeth.

"Hit him," he said. "Hit him with the barrel of this here gun, just when he thought he was gonna get me. Now you three get the hell off my land, hear? Get off right now, and don't come back."

As he gazed at the old man, the familiar pain began in Michael's temples, and a thought drifted fleetingly through his mind. *I could make him die . . . right now, I could make him die. . . .* And then, barely discernible in the far reaches of his mind, he heard Nathaniel's voice: *"Not yet. Not now. . . ."*

"I—I didn't know this was your land," Michael stammered as his headache passed. "There wasn't any sign or anything."

Findley fixed him with a hard look, but then nodded. "That's why I didn't shoot the dog," he said. "If it'd been one of theirs," he went on, nodding toward Eric and Ryan, "I woulda shot it. They know where my land starts and where it stops. And now you know, too. So take the dog and get off. And don't come back."

Slowly the three boys began backing away. For a moment, Shadow held his ground, his yellow eyes flashing even in the filtered light of the woods, but then he, too, began backing off, his gait an awkward hobble as he held his left foreleg off the ground. As the three boys watched, Ben Findley moved deeper into the woods, disappearing almost as if he'd never been there.

"C-come on," Ryan whispered, breaking the sudden silence that hung over the forest. "Let's get out of here before he comes back."

As one, the three boys wheeled around and ran back the way they'd come, not stopping until they were well away from Ben Findley's land.

Limping clumsily and favoring his injured leg, Shadow struggled to keep up.

When they finally emerged from the woods at the foot of the Halls' small farm, Michael stopped to stare at the weed-choked acreage of Potter's Field. Eventually, though, his gaze shifted to Ben Findley's ancient barn.

"That's what he really wants us to stay away from," he whispered, his eyes narrowing angrily. "It's not the woods he cares about, it's the barn."

Ryan and Eric stared at him curiously. "How come? What's so special about the barn?" Ryan asked.

Michael turned to the other two boys, an odd smile coming over his face. "You really want to know?"

The boys hesitated, then nodded.

"Maybe I'll show you sometime," Michael said softly. "Maybe when Shadow's leg gets better, I'll show you."

CHAPTER 20

As the summer wore on, the heat of the prairie filled Janet with a languor she was unused to. At first she attributed it only to the weather, but when she finally talked to a doctor in North Platte about it, she was told that she had to expect her body to concentrate most of its energy on the baby growing inside her and that the best thing she could do was listen to the messages her body was sending her, and take life as easy as possible. And for a while, she was able to relax.

The farm needed little attention, and Michael was more than able to feed their few chickens, tend the cow, and keep the barn in order. Janet concentrated on turning the third bedroom into a nursery, and discovered that even that was no trouble. Just as they had for the farm itself, now people dropped by with things they "thought the baby might be able to use."

For a while, Janet kept a watchful eye on Michael, but as July passed into August, and he complained less and less about his headaches, she began to feel that perhaps the worst was over. Even Laura seemed to have been calmed by the summer weather.

Laura and Janet had grown closer. As Laura's strength returned to her, she began spending more and more time at the farm, helping Janet with her first experiments at canning, teaching her the little tricks that made running the farm easier. And she had an endless curiosity about Janet's life in New York.

At first, Janet assumed that Laura's primary interest was in her brother, that she wanted to know what Mark had been like in all the years of their estrangement. But as time went on, it became clearer that for Laura, talking to Janet was the closest she would ever come to the life she had always dreamed about, and when Janet described the rhythms of the city, told her about the galleries and museums, the shows and the parties, it was almost as if Laura was experiencing them herself.

It was on a day in late August, when the prairie was shimmering with heat and they were sitting on the front porch whiling away the afternoon by talking about all the things they should be doing—and would do, once the heat broke—that Janet finally asked Laura why she had stayed in Prairie Bend.

Laura smiled, a soft smile that reflected both sadness and longing. "By the time I knew what I wanted, it was too late," she said. "I was already married, and Ryan was born, and I just let myself drift along. For a while, I thought about taking Ryan and just leaving, but I always seemed to get pregnant just when I had my mind made up. When you're pregnant, you may feel like running away from home, but it just isn't practical, is it?"

Janet let one hand fall to the swelling in her torso, then brushed a damp strand of hair from her brow. "Not practical doesn't begin to express it. It's funny—when I was pregnant with Michael, I had so much energy I used to frighten Mark. He was always telling me to slow down—take it easier. He was sure I was going to lose the baby. But this time, it's all different. I don't even feel like getting up from this chair."

"You're not as young as you were then," Laura pointed out.

"But look at you," Janet argued. "You weren't taking it easy in May, and you're not that much younger than I am." Then, as Laura's smile faded away, Janet started to apologize for her careless words, but Laura stopped her.

"It's all right, Janet," she said. "And you're right, I wasn't taking it easy. But it wouldn't have made any difference. They would have killed my baby anyway. That's one of the reasons I didn't take it easy—sometimes I can pretend that what happened to the baby was my fault. Isn't that silly? It's easier for me if I can pretend that the baby would have lived if I'd just done something differently. But it isn't true. With Becky, I was so terribly careful, and then—well, I won't go into that anymore." Suddenly she stood up and went to the end of the porch. Though Janet couldn't see her face, she knew that Laura was gazing at Potter's Field.

"I keep thinking I ought to go out there," Janet said when the silence at last became unbearable. "Sometimes I wake up in the middle of the night, and think I ought to go out there and look around that field."

Laura turned around to face her once more, and when she spoke her voice was low, and slightly trembling. "Do you?" she asked. "Or are you just saying that? Do you really believe what I've told you about what's happened to my babies, or are you just like the doctors, only pretending to believe me?"

Janet had been hoping this confrontation would never come, hoping that her failure to argue with Laura would be enough. But now the question had been asked, and she had to answer it.

"I don't know," she said. "It seems totally illogical. I just can't imagine Amos and Dr. Potter doing such a thing. Amos seems so—well, so steady—and so did Dr. Potter."

"Then you don't believe me," Laura pressed.

Janet sighed heavily, and before she replied, she looked around for Michael. But neither he nor Shadow were anywhere in sight. "Michael believes you," she said, her voice low.

"Michael?" Laura replied, her voice sounding dazed.

"What do you mean, Michael believes me? Have you talked to him about it?"

Janet shook her head. "I didn't have to. He talked about it himself." Briefly, she told Laura what had happened at the dry goods store the day after they had moved into the little house.

"And then when Ione Simpson said there weren't any little girls named Becky around here, Michael said he bet Becky had been killed, and buried in Potter's Field."

Laura's face paled, but Janet pressed on. "He seems to think his grandfather killed your baby. Not only that, but he thinks Amos killed Mark, and wants to kill him as well."

"Dear God," Laura whispered. "But how does he know?"

"It sounds crazy," Janet replied, then smiled in spite of herself. "There's that word again. Anyway, he claims he saw Amos kill Mark in a dream, and he claims he saw something happen to your baby the night it was born."

"But he wasn't there—"

"No, he was out here that night—out at the Simpsons'. Eric's mare was foaling, and Michael was watching. And then on the way home, something happened. He said he fell off his bicycle, but when he got back to the Halls', he was incredibly upset. He wasn't hurt, except for a few scratches, but he seemed terrified by something. And then there were the headaches," she added, though her mind was already on something else. It was only a fleeting memory, an image of Michael, bent over Anna's chair, while Anna kissed him goodnight.

Except Anna hadn't been kissing him. She'd been whispering something to him, her voice so low that no one but Michael had been able to hear her.

"Laura," Janet asked, the memory of that brief whisper refusing to disappear, "what about Anna? Does she know what you think happened to your babies?"

Laura's face set in bitterness. "She knows. But in the

end, she always believes whatever Father tells her. Out here, that's the way it is. No one believes me, Janet.''

"Except Mark. Mark believed you, didn't he?"

Laura's pallor increased, but she said nothing.

"It's all right," Janet told her. "I read the letter you wrote him. He left it for me, along with a note." She fell silent, wondering how much to tell Laura. "The note was strange, Laura," she said carefully. "It was as if he knew he might die if he came back here."

"And he did, didn't he?" Laura replied, her voice lifeless. "It's my fault, isn't it? I should never have written to him at all. But I was so frightened. I put that letter off for so long, but then, after I got pregnant again, I just had to write to him. I *had* to, Janet. I never wanted him to come out here—I just wanted him to tell me what happened the night he ran away. But I guess he thought I was crazy, didn't he?"

Janet nodded. "That's what I thought, when I read the notes. But now I'm not so sure. What if he believed you? What if he came out here because he believed you?"

"But—"

Janet ignored the interruption. "Your mother, Laura. Let's go talk to your mother. She must know something."

Anna's gaze wandered from Laura to Janet, then returned to her daughter. "I've never spoken about that night to anyone," she said finally. "Why should I tell you about it now?"

Laura's eyes brimmed with tears. "Because I *have* to know," she pleaded. "Can't you understand, Mother? I've been terrified most of my life. And my babies. What about my babies, Mother? What really happened to them?"

Anna's eyes narrowed. "Your babies were born dead, just like mine."

"Were they, Anna?" Janet asked. "Laura doesn't think so, and I don't believe Mark thought so, either."

"How do you know that?" Anna's voice rose, and her hands gripped the arms of her chair. For a moment, she seemed about to lift herself up, but then she slumped back. "Did Mark say something?" she asked. "Did he ever talk about the night he left?"

"No," Janet replied. "But he left me a note. And a letter he'd gotten from Laura."

"You wrote to him?" Anna demanded of her daughter. "After he abandoned us, you wrote to him?"

Laura hesitated, then nodded her head. "He was my brother. I loved him. And I needed to know why he went away. But now he's dead, Mother, and so you have to tell us. You *have* to."

"I don't have to," Anna replied, her voice low. "I've never talked about that night because I don't know what happened that night." Her voice broke, and her eyes filled with tears. "It's been the same for me as it has for you, Laura. Don't you understand? I—I thought they killed my baby, too."

"Dear God," Janet whispered. "But why? Why would anybody want to kill a baby?"

"I didn't say they did. I said I thought they did. But I could never prove it. They told me the baby was born dead, and I could never prove it wasn't. But I felt that baby. I felt that baby alive inside me, and deep inside, I've never been able to convince myself that Amos didn't kill it. And I've never forgiven him for it, even though I don't know if he did it." Suddenly a twisted smile distorted her face. "Maybe that's what crippled me," she whispered. "Maybe this is my punishment for my evil thoughts about my husband." Her voice turned wistful. "I want to walk, you know. Maybe if I knew myself what happened that night, I might be able to walk again."

There was silence in the room for several long seconds, a silence that was finally broken by Laura. "Maybe Michael knows what happened that night," she said at last. Anna stared at her with disbelieving eyes. "He—he knows what happened to my baby, Mother," she went on. "He told Janet he saw them kill it—"

Anna swung around, her eyes locking on Janet. "That's

impossible," she said. "He wasn't there that night. He couldn't have seen anything."

"I know," Janet agreed, her voice reflecting her own disbelief. "But he says he saw it." She hesitated, then went on. "He says Nathaniel showed him what happened."

"Nathaniel?" Anna repeated. "But there is no Nathaniel—"

"Michael says there is," Janet replied.

"Do you believe him?"

Janet shrugged helplessly. "I don't know what to believe anymore—"

"I want to talk to him," Anna said suddenly. "Alone. I want to talk to him alone. And I want you to tell me everything else Michael has said."

Michael stared down into the depths of the swimming hole, and saw the collection of boulders that choked the bottom. Here and there, the larger ones rose nearly to the surface, and not more than five feet from the place where he had dropped into the water only three months ago, a broad flat plane of rock had replaced the water entirely. He looked up, and met his cousin's gaze.

"I said you were lucky," Ryan told him as if he'd read the thoughts in Michael's mind.

But Michael shook his head. "I knew I wasn't going to get hurt," he said.

"Bullshit," Ryan replied. He gave Eric a disgusted look. "You shoulda seen it—it was all muddy, and you couldn't see anything. And he did a backflip off the tire."

Eric turned suspicious eyes on Michael, but when he spoke, it was to Ryan. "Maybe he came down here earlier and found out where the rocks were."

"I did not," Michael protested. "I'd never even been here before. But I knew I wasn't going to get hurt."

"How did you know?" Eric demanded.

Michael knew he couldn't explain it. How could he tell them what it had been like, when he couldn't really figure it out himself? Still, Ryan and Eric were staring at him, and he had to say something.

"It—it was like somebody was there, whispering into my ear, telling me where to dive. I wasn't even scared. I just sort of knew that nothing could happen to me."

Ryan stared at him with scorn in his eyes. "If nothing can happen to you, how come you managed to stick a pitchfork through your foot?"

"I didn't do that. Grandpa did that."

"Aw, come off it, Michael. Grandpa didn't do it. You're so full of shit!"

"I am not!" Michael flared.

"You are too," Ryan shot back. "Like remember that day old man Findley caught us in the woods, and you said what he was really worried about was the barn?"

"Y-yes—" Michael admitted.

"Well, you said you'd show us what he was so worried about sometime, but you never did. You're just as scared of him as everybody else is."

"I am not!"

"Are too!"

Michael's eyes narrowed. His head began to ache, and in the depths of his mind, he heard Nathaniel's voice, warning him. But it was too late. If he backed down now, Ryan and Eric would never let him forget it. Besides, it would be an adventure, and a forbidden adventure at that.

He ignored Nathaniel's warnings. "All right then, let's go over there "

Shadow suddenly stirred from his position at Michael's feet, and a low growl rumbled up from deep in his throat. Michael reached out and scratched the dog's ears, and the growl faded away.

"When?" Eric challenged.

Michael shrugged with feigned nonchalance. "Tonight?"

Ryan and Eric exchanged a glance, each of them waiting for the other to call Michael's bluff. "Okay," Eric said at last. "But I bet you don't show up. I bet you chicken out, and then claim your mother stayed up late and you couldn't sneak out.''

"Mom goes to bed early," Michael argued. "And even if she doesn't, I'll still get out."

"But what if she sees us?" Ryan asked.

"She can't," Michael replied. "Her bedroom's on the other side of the house. She can see Eric's house, but she can't see old man Findley's at all."

"What if she sees Eric?"

But Eric shook his head. "She won't. There isn't any moon tonight."

Ryan, though, was still uncertain, and his brows knit into a worried frown. "If my dad catches me, he'll beat the shit out of me."

Eric shrugged. "Then stay at my house tonight. My room's downstairs, and I can sneak out any time I want to. I never get caught."

A little later the three of them started home, but as they ambled through the woods and across the fields, none of them said much. Each boy was thinking of the night's adventure, Eric and Ryan with anticipation, but Michael with a strong sense of unease. Maybe, he decided as he and Shadow turned up the driveway to his house, it would have been better to have let Eric and Ryan think he was chicken. But it was too late now.

Shadow barked happily and dashed ahead. Michael looked up and saw his grandmother seated in her wheelchair just in front of the porch. As he watched, the big dog bounded up to her and reared up to put his paws on the old woman's lap, his tongue licking at her face.

"Get down," Michael yelled, breaking into a run. "Shadow, get down!"

"It's all right," Anna assured him. "He's a good dog, aren't you, Shadow?" She patted him on the head, then began to ease his weight off her lap. The dog quickly settled down at her feet, though he kept his head high enough so she could scratch his ears. Anna smiled at

Michael. "I thought it was time you and I had a good talk."

Michael glanced around uncertainly. "Where's Mom?" he asked. "And Grandpa?"

"Your grandfather's at home, and your mother and Aunt Laura had some errands to run. But I wanted to talk to you, so here I am."

"T-talk to me?" Michael asked. "About what?"

"All kinds of things," Anna replied. "For one thing, why don't we talk about why your grandfather killed your father?"

Michael stared at his grandmother. Her eyes were on him, and though he expected them to be angry, instead he saw only a soft warmth. And she was smiling.

"D-did Mom tell you that?"

Anna hesitated, then nodded. "She told me that's what you think. She told me you saw him do it."

Michael swallowed, then nodded. "Mom says it was only a dream, though."

"I know," Anna said. "And I didn't argue with her. But what if it wasn't a dream? What if you really did see it?"

"You mean you believe me?"

"I don't believe you're a liar, Michael. As far as I know, you've only lied once, and I believe you had your reasons for that lie." She paused a moment, then went on. "It was the night Aunt Laura's baby was born," she said. "You saw them bury her baby out in the field, didn't you? Out in Potter's Field?"

Michael froze, a wave of fear washing over him.

"Is that what happened, Michael?" Anna pressed.

"I—I'm not supposed to tell. I'm not supposed to tell anybody. H-he told me—" Michael broke off, already sure he'd said too much.

"But you didn't tell me," Anna reassured him. "I told you, didn't I? I told you what happened."

Uncertainly, Michael nodded.

"And what about that day in the barn, Michael, when

your grandfather stabbed your foot? Are you allowed to tell me about that?''

"Mom said that was an accident—" Michael began, but Anna held up a quieting hand.

"I'm sure your mother thinks it was an accident. But I want you to tell me what really happened. Can you do that?''

Slowly, Michael told his grandmother what had happened in the loft. When he was done, Anna sat silently for a long time. Then she reached out and took Michael's hand. "Michael, do you know what it was your father thought your grandfather had done? What Nathaniel had shown him?''

"N-no."

"Well, don't you think we ought to find out?"

Michael frowned. "But Mom says I only imagined it all. Mom says I only dreamed the things I saw.''

"But what if you didn't, Michael? What if you really saw it all?''

"You mean you believe me? You don't think I'm crazy?''

Anna put her arms around the boy and drew him close. "Of course you're not crazy,'' she told him. "And you mustn't be afraid of what you know. It's what you don't know that's frightening, Michael. That's the way it always is,'' she said, almost to herself. "The things that you don't know about are the most frightening.'' She let her arms fall away from the boy, and straightened herself in her chair. "Now, let's you and I go and find out just what's in Potter's Field, all right?''

Michael's eyes widened apprehensively. "But Mr. Findley—''

"Ben Findley won't stop us,'' Anna replied. "I've known Ben Findley most of my life, and he won't do anything. Not to me. Not when he knows I'm sitting right there, watching him. Now, help me with this chair.''

With Michael behind her and Shadow at her side, Anna Hall moved across the yard. Then she started out through the pasture toward the barbed wire fence that surrounded Potter's Field, her chair fighting her every inch of the way.

"Leave me here," Anna said. She gazed at Ben Findley's ramshackle house, partly hidden from her view by his barn. A few feet away lay the barbed wire, and beyond it the tangle of brush and weeds that choked the abandoned field. "You and Shadow go out into the field, and see what you can find." When there was no reply, she twisted around in her chair.

Michael's expressionless eyes seemed fixed on a point in the distance. Anna followed his gaze, but all she saw was the barn. "Michael? Michael, is something wrong?"

Michael came out of his daze, and his eyes shifted to his grandmother. "But what if old man Findley—"

"He won't come out," Anna told him. "He might try to scare children, but he won't try to scare me. Now, go on."

As Anna watched, Michael made his way carefully through the fence, the big dog following close behind him. Once, Michael glanced up toward the barn, but then he concentrated on the ground in the field. He moved slowly, knowing he was looking for something, but unsure what it might be.

For ten minutes, the boy and the dog ranged back and forth across the field, finding nothing. Then, suddenly, Shadow stiffened and went on point.

And at the same time, a headache began to form in Michael's temples.

There was a stone on the ground, a stone that didn't quite seem to belong in the field. Though it was weathered, it seemed to have been purposely shaped, flattened and rounded as if it was meant to mark something. As Michael stared at the stone, Shadow moved slowly forward, his nose twitching, soft eager sounds emerging from his throat.

"*Here.*" Though it was only one word, the voice inside his head was unmistakable. The word resounded in his head, echoing, then gradually faded away. As it died, the headache cleared.

Michael knelt on the ground and carefully moved the stone aside. He began digging in the soft moist earth beneath the stone.

Six inches down, his fingers touched something, and after a little more digging, he was able to unearth the object.

It was a piece of bone, thin and dish shaped, and even though Michael had never before seen such a thing, he knew at once what it was.

A fragment of a skull.

In twenty minutes, Michael and Shadow found five more of the flat, round stones, and beneath each of the stones, there were pieces of bone.

At last, Michael returned to his grandmother and told her what he'd found.

"What are we going to do?" he asked as they began making their way back toward the house.

For a long time, Anna was silent, but when they were finally back on the front porch, she gazed into Michael's eyes. "Michael, do you know how you see the things you've seen?"

Michael nodded.

"Can you tell me?"

Michael gazed fearfully at his grandmother. "I—I'm not supposed to tell. If I tell, I'll die."

Anna reached out and touched Michael's cheek. "No," she said softly. "You won't die, Michael. Whatever happens, I won't let you die."

Michael paled slightly. "You're not going to tell Grandpa, are you?"

Anna drew the boy close. "I'm not going to tell anybody, and neither are you. Until we decide what to do, this is our secret. But you mustn't be frightened. Do you understand that?"

Michael nodded silently, then pushed his grandmother's chair through the front door. When his mother and his aunt arrived a few minutes later, neither he nor his grandmother said a word about what had transpired between them.

It was their secret, and, Michael decided, he liked having a secret with someone else. Since his father had died, there had been no one to share secrets with.

No one except Nathaniel.

Ben Findley let the curtain drop back over his window as the woman and the boy disappeared into the house next door. For a long time, he thought about what he ought to do, wondered if, indeed, he ought to do anything at all. In the end, though, he went to the telephone, picked it up, and dialed. When it was finally answered, he explained exactly what he'd seen. "I don't want them there," he finished. "I don't want your family snooping in my field."

All right, Ben," Amos Hall replied. "I'll take care of it."

VISA

HALLMARK
#5114

12-20-84

4 Tx	16.99
4 Tx	16.99
2 Tx	3.99
1 Tx	2.50
1 Tx	2.50
	42.97 ST
	3.01 TX
	45.98 CH

5 %

1001 0150
21-50

CHAPTER 21

Michael lay in bed, wishing he'd never promised Ryan and Eric that he'd take them into old man Findley's barn. This afternoon, when they'd been at the swimming hole, it had seemed like it might be a great adventure. But now he wasn't so sure—ever since he'd been in Potter's Field and his head had started hurting, he'd begun to remember Nathaniel's warnings once again. Now, in spite of his grandmother's words, he was frightened, but he'd told Eric and Ryan he'd meet them, and if he didn't, they'd think he was chicken.

At last, when he was sure his mother was asleep, he slowly began getting dressed. Only when he had double-knotted his tennis shoes and checked his pocket for his house key three times did he finally open the door to his room and whisper to Shadow, "Go on." The dog obediently slipped through the narrow opening and padded silently down the stairs. Closing the door, Michael went to the window and peered out into the darkness. As Eric had said, there was no moon, but the night was clear, and the soft glow of starlight softened the blackness. Michael opened the dormer window, then climbed gingerly out onto the steeply sloping roof. A shingle cracked under his weight, and Michael froze for a moment, listening for any slight

279

movements from within the house. When he heard nothing, he began making his way carefully toward the eave.

He crouched at the edge, his eyes fixed on the rain gutter. The pipe seemed as if it was about to collapse under its own weight, and finally he decided not to risk it. Surely his mother would awaken if the gutter pulled loose, and the jump looked pretty easy. He lowered himself to a sitting position and let his legs dangle over the edge. A moment later he launched himself off the roof, letting his knees buckle as he hit the ground so that he rolled into the kind of somersault he'd seen his father use when he was skydiving. He lay still for a moment—something else his father had always done—and then stood up to brush the dust off his jeans. Then he went to the front door, unlocked it, and let Shadow out.

Ryan and Eric were waiting for him next to the storm cellar.

"How we gonna do it?" Ryan whispered. "Old man Findley hasn't gone to bed yet. There's a light on in the downstairs window."

"Maybe we better not try it," Michael suggested.

"You chickening out?" Eric asked.

"N-no. But what if he catches us?"

"If we do it right, he won't," Eric said. "We can cut down to the river, then come back through Potter's Field. That way the barn'll be between him and us. Come on."

They moved out of the shelter of the storm cellar's slanting roof and began zigzagging down the length of the pasture, hunched low, pausing every few seconds to watch and listen.

Except for the soft chirping of insects and the lowing of cattle floating over the prairie, the night was silent. They came to a stop at the fence separating the pasture from the wheat field beyond, and Michael peered intently into the darkness. The night seemed to thicken over Potter's Field, just to the west. Shadow, crouching at his master's feet, whined softly.

"What is it?" Ryan asked, his voice barely audible.

Michael said nothing. His head was beginning to hurt, and in the darkness he was almost sure he could see a slight movement. And as if from a great distance, a voice—Nathaniel's voice—was whispering to him. The words were indistinct, but Michael knew it was a warning.

"Something's out there," he said at last. "In Potter's Field. I can feel it."

"Come on," Eric said. He climbed the fence and began making his way down the wheat field toward the woods next to the river. Ryan followed him, and, a moment later, so did Michael. But even as he came to the strip of cottonwoods and stepped into the near-total darkness beneath the trees, Michael's headache grew worse, and the voice in his head became more urgent.

Their progress slowed. They moved with all the care their imaginations demanded, and every time a twig snapped under their feet, they came to a halt, waiting for an answering movement that would tell them they were not alone in the woods. After what seemed an eternity, they emerged from the forest, and found themselves at the south end of Potter's Field. They gazed out at it. In the gloom of the night, its growth of tumbleweeds seemed to have turned threatening.

"Maybe Michael's right," Ryan whispered. "Maybe we ought to go home."

"You scared?" Eric asked.

Ryan nodded.

"Well, I'm not," Eric declared. "Come on." He started to worm his way through the barbed wire fence that surrounded the field, but suddenly Michael's hand closed around his arm.

"There's something out there."

Eric hesitated. "Bullshit." Then: "What?"

"I—I don't know. But I know there's something in the field. I can—I can sort of feel it."

The three boys, their eyes squinting against the darkness, peered into the field, but saw nothing more than the blackness of the night and the strange forms of the tumbleweeds etched vaguely against the horizon.

Suddenly Shadow tensed, and a low growl rolled up from the depths of his throat.

"Oh, Jeez," Ryan whispered. "Let's go home."

And then, in the distance, a light appeared, and Shadow's growl turned into a vicious snarl.

"It's Abby," Ryan breathed. "It's gotta be Abby, lookin' for her kids."

"M-maybe it's not," Eric said, but his voice had suddenly lost its conviction. "Maybe it's old man Findley—maybe he saw us."

Only Michael remained silent, his eyes concentrating on the light, his ears hearing only the words that were being whispered within his head.

"If he finds you, you will die."

The light moved, bobbing slowly through the field, stopping every few feet. With every movement, it seemed to come closer, almost as if whatever was in the field knew the three boys were there, and was searching for them.

Shadow, too, seemed to be concentrating on the light. Every muscle in his body was hard with tension under Michael's hands, and the end of his tail twitched spasmodically. A menacing sound, barely audible, welled up from deep within him, and his ears lay flat against the back of his head.

And then, as if he'd responded to the hunter's instinct buried deep in his genes, he shot off into the night, disappearing almost instantly, as his black fur blended into the darkness.

The dog's sudden movement triggered Ryan and Eric, and suddenly they were running, oblivious now to the sounds of their feet pounding through the underbrush as they dashed back into the cover of the forest.

Only Michael, his head throbbing, stayed where he was, peering into the darkness, searching the field for someone —or something—he knew was there, but couldn't quite find. And then, following the voice that seemed to come from within, he carefully crept through the fence and began making his way across Potter's Field toward the barn beyond.

Amos Hall had been making his way carefully through the field. He knew where each of the markers lay, which were the stones that marked the children's graves. He paused at each of them, though only for a second at the ones that still lay undisturbed.

The stones that had been turned over that afternoon took more of his time, for when he came to those, he knelt in the earth, carefully sifted the soft soil through his fingers, smoothing it as well as he could, then replacing the stone markers with an odd sense of reverence.

He'd been in this field only four times since the day when he was a young man and his father had brought him out here, shown him the stones, and told him the story of Abby Randolph.

"And our children still die," his father had told him. "It's as if there's a curse on us, almost as if Abby and Nathaniel want us to remember how they felt, want us to feel the pain they must have felt that winter." Amos had started to protest his father's words, but his father had stopped him. "It'll happen to you, too, Amos. You'll have children, and some of them will be all right. But there will be others who will be born dead. Bring them here, Amos. Bring them here and bury them with Abby's children."

Amos hadn't believed it at first, not until the first time it had happened. He and Anna had been young then, and as Anna's belly swelled with the growing child they had made plans for it, begun to love it, cherishing it even before it was born.

And then, finally, one night it had come.

And it had been dead.

Amos remembered that birth still, remembered being in the little downstairs room with Anna, helping her as her labor began. And then the child had emerged from the womb, and he had known immediately that it was dead.

Anna had denied it.

It couldn't have been dead, she'd said. It couldn't have been dead, because she'd felt it moving inside her, right up until the very end. If it had been alive then, how could it have died?

Amos hadn't been able to tell her. He'd tried, done his best to make her understand the tragedy that had befallen their family so many years ago, but in the end, he'd failed. Stories and old wives' tales, Anna had insisted.

Despite what Anna had thought, Amos had brought the child out to this field and buried it with Abby's children. And when he'd returned, Anna had changed. A hurt had entered her soul, a hurt that had never healed. Slowly, over the years, she'd come to think he had killed her child.

When it had happened again, her bitterness had only increased. And once more he had come to Potter's Field, burying what he had come to think of as Nathaniel's child near its brother.

Then there had been Mark. And Laura. Healthy children, who had lived though both had seemed frail at birth.

With Anna's last child, it had been different. Amos still could not bring himself to remember that night. On that night, he had not come to the field. That night, Charles Potter had done it for him, and Amos had never even asked where that child lay.

He didn't want to know, for it was after that night that Mark had left, and Anna had retreated to her wheelchair, and Laura's mind had begun to weaken.

Laura.

He hadn't even tried to explain the truth to Laura. Instead, he'd merely been there, as he'd been there for Anna, to help her with her labor, and take away the tiny bodies when she inevitably gave birth to one of Nathaniel's children. For Laura, he'd been here twice.

If other people ever came to Potter's Field, Amos Hall had never known about it.

Except for Mark.

Mark had come to the field twice. Once, the night Anna's last child had been born. That night, he'd said nothing. Instead, he'd simply disappeared. But then, last spring, he'd come home, and once more he'd come to Potter's Field. And after that night in Potter's Field, he'd sought Amos out, confronted him with wild ravings about dead children who still lived, shouting about Nathaniel and punishment.

Amos had tried to explain the truth of what had happened so many years ago. But Mark hadn't wanted to hear. Instead, he'd only stared at Amos with hate-filled eyes. "I was there, Pa," he'd said. "I was there the night my brother was born. You thought you'd killed him, didn't you? And you gave him to Doc to bury. But he wasn't dead, Pa. I could hear him, crying out, calling to me. I followed him that night, Pa. While Doc carried him into the field, I followed him, and I watched what happened. Doc buried him, Pa. The baby wasn't dead, but Doc buried him anyway. And he's still not dead, Pa. He's alive. Nathaniel's alive."

Mark had been shouting, shouting and screaming, and then, Mark had died. And Amos, in his own mind, was still not sure if it had been an accident, or if he had meant to kill Mark. All that had mattered was that suddenly there was silence in the barn. Silence and peace. There had been too many years of pain, too many years of misunderstandings. Now, all that mattered to Amos was that Potter's Field lay undisturbed, that Nathaniel's children have their peace.

But today, Anna had come, and Michael, and Michael had prowled the field, turning over the stone markers, disturbing the soil that covered Nathaniel's children.

Tonight, carefully, reverently, Amos was repairing the damage.

He worked slowly, moving from grave to grave, checking each stone.

Twice, he thought he heard sounds in the night, sounds

that didn't fit. Twigs snapped, and he knew well that the creatures of the night moved silently, never betraying their presence with more than a rustling of leaves that could be mistaken for the wind. Tonight, there was no wind.

He paused each time he heard a sound, and listened, but all he heard was silence, and after a few moments he returned to his work.

Then, as he was replacing the sixth stone, he felt something. It was a presence, and it was near him. And suddenly the night was filled with sound—the sound of running feet, human feet, fleeing into the woods by the river. And yet, despite the sounds, Amos still had the feeling that he was being watched. Nervously, he cast the beam of light in a circle around him, and finally saw them. Two yellow eyes gleaming in the darkness, and beneath them the bared fangs of Shadow, his lean body slung close to the ground in readiness for the attack.

His rifle. Amos had to find his rifle. He groped around in the dark, but it wasn't there. Finally, in desperation, he used the flashlight. The gun lay on the ground a few feet away, just out of reach. As Amos moved toward it, Shadow launched himself into the air.

Neither the man nor the dog uttered a sound, and for Amos the dog's silence was the most frightening thing about the attack. Shadow's first lunge knocked him off his feet, and he tumbled to the ground, expecting the dog's fangs to sink into his flesh immediately. It didn't happen.

Instead the dog placed himself between Amos and the gun, his cold yellow eyes fixed on the man, his teeth bared. For several seconds, Amos lay still on the ground, waiting for the dog to renew his attack.

Then, when Shadow made no move toward him, he pulled himself up onto all fours. Shadow watched him, but still made no move.

But when Amos started forward, moving slowly and carefully, Shadow tensed, and his tail began to twitch.

Amos backed off, and Shadow's tail stopped moving, but he inched forward, closing the distance between himself and Amos to what it had been before.

Every time Amos tried to move toward the gun, it happened again. The bared fangs, the dangerously twitching tail, the tensing of the body.

Slowly, Amos began backing away, and just as slowly Shadow closed on him, never crowding him, but never letting the distance between them increase.

Then Shadow began playing Amos, moving him slowly across the field, circling him slowly, guiding him toward the fence that separated the field from the woods. At first Amos rejected what was happening, but each time he tried to define the direction of his own retreat, Shadow countered him.

And still there was no sound, either from the man or from the dog.

Minutes later, Amos felt the sting of barbed wire as the lowest strand of the fence gouged into his leg. He stopped, sank into a crouching position for a moment, then finally stood up. Shadow, too, came to a halt, as if sensing that for the moment the man could go no further.

After a few seconds had passed, Amos took a step to the left. For the first time, Shadow growled, then countered the move. Amos tried going to the right. Again, the growl, and the counter.

"Goddamn you," Amos muttered. Carefully, he made his way through the fence. The moment he was free of it, Shadow slipped easily beneath the bottom wire and began relentlessly driving the old man through the woods toward the river beyond.

CHAPTER 22

Michael made his way slowly across Potter's Field, carefully avoiding the worst of the undergrowth but nevertheless having to stop every few yards to free himself from the weeds and vines that seemed to grasp at his ankle with every step. For a while he kept a careful watch on the light that still bobbed in the darkness fifty yards away, but even as he watched it, he knew it posed no threat: Shadow was out there, and Michael was certain that the dog was stalking whatever was in the field. Soon he shifted the focus of his attention to the barn.

His headache began to ease as he drew close to the looming structure, and by the time he had come close enough to touch it, his mind was clear, and the pain was gone.

And all his memories of Nathaniel had returned. He could remember everything he had talked about with Nathaniel, every word Nathaniel had told him.

And he knew he had disobeyed Nathaniel.

He moved slowly around the corner of the barn to the side door. When he had achieved his goal, he stopped for a few moments and gazed out into Potter's Field, but the light was gone now, and the darkness of the night was once more complete. All he could see was the silhouette of the forest against the night sky, and even that was little more than a vague line across the horizon. Above, he could see the stars; beneath, there was nothing but blackness.

Creeping as quietly as he could, he slipped through the darkness to the front of the barn.

Mr. Findley's lights were still on, and once, through the curtains, Michael saw the form of the old man himself, pacing restlessly across his kitchen floor. But no dogs barked, and the silence of the night remained undisturbed. Michael returned to the side door, removed its bar, and slipped inside the barn.

The barn was filled with a musky odor that made Michael want to sneeze, but he resisted it. And even though he could see nothing, he moved through the blackness with the same confidence he would have felt if it had been broad daylight. Somewhere in the darkness, Nathaniel was waiting for him.

And then came the words, whispered in that odd toneless voice that seemed to originate deep inside his own head.

"Outside, Michael. I want to go outside."

Michael froze in the darkness, knowing that Nathaniel was close to him, very close.

"Wh-where are you?"

"I am here, right next to you. Now we will go outside."

As if an alien force was moving him, Michael started back toward the door. A moment later, with Nathaniel beside him, he was outside again in the fresh night air.

"It smells good." For the first time that night, the voice came through Michael's ears, and he turned to face Nathaniel. Suddenly the night seemed brighter, and he looked curiously at Nathaniel's clothes.

They looked old-fashioned, and they didn't seem to fit very well.

"Where'd you get those clothes?" he asked. "Are they from a store?"

Nathaniel looked puzzled. "Someone made them for me," he said as he carefully placed the door bar back in its brackets. Then, before Michael could ask him another question, Nathaniel started off into Potter's Field.

"They are here," Nathaniel said softly, pointing to one of the stones that marked the children's graves. "Can you feel them, Michael? Can you feel the children around you?"

And strangely, Michael realized that he could feel something. It was almost as if he and Nathaniel were not alone in the field; all around him he could feel strange presences, and on the edge of his consciousness he thought there were voices, voices he couldn't quite hear. They weren't like Nathaniel's voice, clear and strong even when Nathaniel wasn't speaking out loud. These voices were soft, indistinct, but there was something about them that made Michael feel sad. They were lonely and abandoned, and Michael wanted to help them.

"Who are they?" he finally asked.

"My mother's children," Nathaniel whispered softly. "Abby's children."

"But why are they here?"

"My father kills them," Nathaniel replied. "My father comes for them, one by one, and brings them out here. But tonight we will kill my father."

"Kill him," Michael repeated, his voice suddenly as toneless as Nathaniel's.

"If we don't, he will kill us," Nathaniel whispered. "And he is here, tonight. He was looking for you, Michael. He knew you were coming tonight, and he was looking for you. The light in the field, Michael. It was my father." He stopped talking and crouched down for a moment. When he straightened up, there was a rifle in his hands. "He was going to kill you with this," he said.

Michael stared at the gun, and knew immediately where he'd seen it before. Still. . . . "He won't—" he protested, but even as he uttered the words, he knew they weren't true.

Nathaniel had been staring off toward the river, but now

his head swung around, and his blue eyes fixed on Michael, holding him in their grip.

"He killed your brothers and sisters, Michael."

Michael felt fear begin to grow in him. "I—I don't have any brothers or sisters," he whispered.

"Here," Nathaniel breathed. "Here around you are your brothers and sisters. And there will be more."

There will be more.

His mother. His mother was pregnant; very soon she was going to have a baby—a brother or a sister for him. So Nathaniel was right. In the darkness, he nodded. Nathaniel's powerful eyes released him from their hold, and he turned away once again.

They moved quickly now, and Michael had no trouble avoiding the tangle of vegetation that overran the field. Though he was seeing with his own eyes, it was as if Nathaniel was showing him the way. They climbed over the fence. Silently, confidently, Nathaniel stepped into the trees, with Michael close behind him. And even here, though nothing in the quality of the starlight had changed, Michael found he could see clearly.

Then, from close by the river, he heard a low growl and knew without being told that it was Shadow. Ahead of him, Nathaniel came to a stop. He turned around to face Michael once again, his hypnotic gaze drawing Michael's spirit close.

"Will you help me?" he asked.

Almost unwillingly, Michael nodded.

"He's nearby, Michael. Ahead, by the river. Come."

They moved slowly now, slipping from tree to tree. Every second Shadow's menacing snarl grew louder. And then, through the trees ahead, Michael saw his grandfather.

Amos felt his heart pounding, and tried to think how long he had been here, trapped against the river, held at bay by the dog who never made a move to attack him, never came close enough for Amos to strike out at him with the flashlight, yet never dropped his vigilance, but instead paced back and forth, his head low and his tail drooping, his eyes flashing in the starlight, a steady snarl raging in his throat.

In the darkness behind the dog, Amos sensed a movement. "Who's there?" he called out. "Is someone there?" Then, sure that he knew who it was lurking in the woods, he forced his voice into a tone of command. "I know you're there, Michael. Come out and call off your dog."

In the woods, Michael stiffened as he heard his name, but suddenly he heard Nathaniel's voice, heard it as he had heard it so many times before, emanating from within his own head.

"Say nothing. Say nothing, and do nothing."

But he knows I'm here, Michael thought. He called my name, and he knows I'm here.

"Wish him dead."

Nathaniel moved forward through the darkness, and Michael stayed where he was, watching and listening, watching with the strange clarity of Nathaniel's vision, and listening to the soft sounds of Nathaniel's instructions.

"Wish him dead."

The seconds crept by—each of them, to Michael, an eternity.

An unnatural silence seemed to fall over the night. Shadow, his growl dying on his lips, suddenly lay down on the ground, his ears up, his eyes still fixed on Amos.

Amos, too, sensed the change in the atmosphere, and suddenly felt his skin begin to crawl. Whatever was out there, he was suddenly certain, it was not Michael, and it was coming for him.

With shaking fingers, he pressed the switch on the flashlight and began playing its beam over the forest.

And then Amos saw him.

Standing perfectly still, his face a pale mask in the white light of the torch, his blue eyes wide and steady—the same blue eyes of all the Halls—the figure of the oddly dressed boy seemed to Amos to have about it the calmness of death.

"W-who are you?" he asked, forcing the words from his throat. Suddenly he was having difficulty breathing, and his heart was pounding with a fury that frightened him almost as much as the visage that glared at him with malevolent eyes from a few yards away.

The words suddenly filled the night.

"I am Nathaniel."

Amos staggered. "No," he gasped. "No. Nathaniel's dead. Nathaniel's been dead for a hundred years. Who are you? Tell me who you are!"

Again, the same words: "I am Nathaniel."

Amos staggered, and the flashlight dropped from his trembling hands.

Michael, still rooted to the spot where Nathaniel had left him, watched as his grandfather sank to his knees, and listened as Nathaniel whispered to him once again:

Wish him dead.

Then, as Amos clutched at his chest, his terrified eyes still fixed on the spot where the apparition stood, Michael began to feel Nathaniel's power within him.

Die. Die. Die.

The word echoed in his mind, his lips silently formed it, the thought transfused his soul, and as he watched, his grandfather sank slowly to the ground.

You killed my father. Die. Die. Die.

And then, as the night sounds slowly began again, Michael knew it was over. Shadow rose to his feet and padded over to sniff at Amos's body. He whined a little; then, wagging his tail, he trotted toward Michael, sat at his feet, and licked his hand.

In the darkness, Nathaniel smiled at him.

"Go home now, Michael," he heard Nathaniel say. "Go home, and wait."

Michael hesitated uncertainly. "But what about Grandpa?"

"They will come and find him," Nathaniel said quietly. "It will not be very long. Go home and wait, Michael. I will tell you what to do."

With Shadow beside him, Michael turned and started

back through the forest. Suddenly he turned back.
"Nathaniel?"

But all Michael saw was the blackness of the night.
Nathaniel was gone.

Michael slipped his key in the lock of the front door,
twisted it, then gently pushed the door open, silently praying
that the hinges wouldn't squeak. As soon as Shadow scuttled through the narrow opening, Michael followed, and
closed the door as carefully as he had opened it. Then he
made his way up the stairs, testing each tread before
putting his weight on it. After what seemed to him to be
forever, he made it to the second-floor landing, and paused
to listen. From behind the closed door to her room, he
could hear the even sound of his mother's breathing. A
moment later, he was safe in his own room. He undressed,
then slipped into bed, where he lay wide awake listening
to the night and waiting.

Suddenly he heard Nathaniel's voice whispering inside
his head, and at the same moment, the quiet of the night
was shattered by the sound of a gunshot. Obeying Nathaniel's
instructions, Michael leapt out of bed, and ran to his
mother's room. He pounded on the door, then burst inside.

"Mom! Mom, wake up!"

Janet's eyes flew open, and she sat up, reaching instinctively for the lamp next to her bed. As light flooded the
room, she heard a sound, then another.

Two shots.

"There was another one," Michael told her, climbing
onto her bed. "It woke me up, Mom. Someone's down by
the river, and they're shooting at something."

Janet swung her legs off the bed, struggling to drive
away the last vestiges of heavy sleep. A moment later she
was at the window, peering out. All she could see was
darkness, suddenly pierced by a light from the Simpsons'
house, a few hundred yards away. A moment later, the
phone started ringing.

"Go answer it, honey," Janet told Michael as she struggled to find the sleeves of her bathrobe and pull it on over her ungainly bulk. As Michael jumped off the bed and dashed out of the room, Janet followed him as quickly as she could. Another shot rang out as she took the receiver from Michael.

"It's Mrs. Simpson," Michael told her.

"Ione?" Janet asked. "Ione, what on earth is going on?"

"Then it's not coming from your house?" Ione asked.

"Our house? Ione, Michael and I were both sound asleep. And I don't even own a gun. Michael says it sounds like it's coming from down by the river."

"That's what Leif thinks, too."

"Maybe it's hunters," Janet suggested.

"In the middle of the night? Don't be silly."

"Then what could it be?"

Ione hesitated a moment, then: "Janet, did you say Michael was asleep?"

Janet frowned, and her eyes went automatically to Michael. "Yes."

"Didn't Michael go out tonight?"

"Go out? What are you talking about?"

"Boys," Ione said in a weary voice. "It seems Eric and Ryan decided to have themselves a little midnight adventure. But I caught them at it. They said Michael was with them. Was he?"

Janet was silent for a moment, then: "Just a minute." She covered the receiver with her hand. "Michael, did you go out with Ryan and Eric tonight?"

Michael opened his mouth to deny it, but then changed his mind. "Yes," he admitted. "We—we were just messing around."

Janet spoke once more into the phone. "He was with them," she told Ione. "But what's that got to do with the shooting?"

"I don't know," Ione replied. "But the boys said they saw someone in Potter's Field. They—well, they thought it was Abby. But I've never heard of a ghost carrying a gun before." Then, before Janet could make a reply: "Hold on, Janet." There was a murmuring, then Ione came back on the line. "We're coming over there, Janet. Leif thinks it might be Ben Findley shooting, and he wants to find out. There've been stories of Ben shooting at kids before, but so far, no one's ever heard the shots." Ione's voice hardened. "I don't care what old Ben does, but if he was trying to shoot at the kids, he's in big trouble. And while we're at it, we might as well find out from all three of the boys exactly what they were up to. Okay?"

Janet sighed. "Okay. I'll put on some coffee." She hung up the phone, and turned to confront Michael. "You are in trouble, young man," she told him. "You know better than to go out by yourself at night, and if you were trespassing on Mr. Findley's property, you should know that he would have been perfectly within his rights to shoot you." Then her worry overcame her anger. "My God, Michael, you could have been killed! Why did you do it?"

Suddenly Nathaniel's warning voice sounded in his head. *"Not yet!"*

"I—I don't know," Michael stammered.

Janet glared at him. "Well, you'd better figure it out," she told him. "And whatever you have to say had better match pretty well with whatever Ryan and Eric have to say. Understand?"

Michael nodded; then, as Janet started toward the kitchen, he sank down to the floor and slipped his arms around Shadow. "I'm scared," he whispered to the big dog. "What'll they do when they find Grandpa?"

Shadow nuzzled at his master, and his tail thumped against the wall as he wagged it. Then, once more, Nathaniel's voice came to him. *"It will be all right. In a little while, it will be all right."*

When the knock came at the front door, Janet hurried to answer it, opening the door wide in the expectation that the Simpsons and Ryan Shields would be on her porch.

Instead, it was Ben Findley.

His hooded eyes were glowering, and his threatening demeanor was made no less frightening by the shotgun in his left hand.

"Where's that brat of yours, Mrs. Hall?" he demanded.

Janet ignored the question. "Was that you shooting just now?"

"That wasn't no shotgun," Findley growled. "That was a rifle. Is your kid here?"

"Of course he's here," Janet finally replied. Then her eyes narrowed. "I just talked to Ione Simpson," she told him coldly. "Her husband thinks the shooting might have been you."

Findley hesitated a moment, then nodded his head. "Can't say as I blame him for that," he said.

Janet was about to demand that the old man leave her property when a car turned into the driveway and the porch was suddenly flooded with the glare of headlights. A moment later, the Simpson family and Ryan Shields piled out of the car. But when they saw who was on the porch, their words of greeting died on their lips. It was Leif Simpson who finally broke the silence.

"What're you doing over here, Findley?"

"Checkin' up," the old man replied, his voice sullen. "I came over to make sure her kid was here where he belongs."

Leif's eyes narrowed. "What made you think he might not be?"

Findley's rheumy eyes shifted toward Janet, then went back to meet Leif's steady gaze. "Why don't you and I have a little talk, and let the ladies go inside?" he asked.

Leif nodded his agreement, and Janet held the door open while Ione, carrying Peggy, followed the two boys into the little house. Janet hesitated a moment, then closed the door, leaving the two men on the porch.

A few minutes later, Leif joined them in the kitchen. "You'd better call Buck," he told Janet. "It seems Amos Hall was out here tonight, and Findley thinks it must have been him shooting. But he hasn't seen Amos's light for a while, and he and I are going to go down toward the river and have a look around."

"Amos?" Janet repeated. "Why would Amos be out there? Where was he?" And then she remembered Ione's words. "Potter's Field?"

"That's what Ben Findley says."

"But—but why?"

"Don't know," Leif replied. "But he also said it might be a good idea if you got hold of a doctor."

Janet made the calls, then joined Ione and the children at the table. "All right," she said softly. "It's time for you three to tell us what you were up to tonight."

One by one, the three boys recounted the story of the evening.

Each of them told about sneaking out, and each of them told about making their way down the Halls' pasture, across the field, and into the woods.

Each of them told about seeing the light in Potter's Field.

Ryan and Eric talked about losing their nerve, and running pell mell back the way they had come, and bursting back into the Simpsons' house, too frightened to worry about the noise they were making.

At last Janet turned to Michael. "What about you, Michael?" she asked. "Did you come home when you saw the light in the field?"

Michael shook his head. "I—I went into Mr. Findley's barn," he said softly.

Janet frowned. "Weren't you frightened, too?"

Again Michael shook his head.

"But why not?"

Michael hesitated, and then he heard Nathaniel's voice: *"Tell them. Tell them now."*

"Because of Nathaniel," he breathed. "Nathaniel and I killed Grandpa."

Janet stared at her son, his words battering at her mind. But Michael's face was placid, and his eyes were calm.

"Nathaniel said we had to," he went on. "Grandpa was going to kill us, Mom. He killed Daddy, and he was going to kill me, too."

A wave of dizziness swept over Janet, and suddenly the lights in the room seemed to go out.

CHAPTER 23

Janet opened her eyes and stared without comprehension at the unfamiliar face that loomed over her. But then, as she came totally awake, she remembered what had happened. She struggled to sit up, but the stranger put a restraining hand on her shoulder.

"Don't," he said. "Just lie there, and try to take it easy. You very nearly lost your baby a little while ago. You didn't, but you're not out of danger yet. I'm Dr. Marsden," he added.

A small groan escaped Janet's lips, and she sank heavily back onto her pillows. "Amos," she whispered. "Did they find Amos?"

Marsden nodded. "He's downstairs." But then, as Janet sighed with relief, he went on: "They found him by the river, Mrs. Hall. I'm not sure exactly what happened, but your son couldn't have had anything to do with it."

Janet gazed at the doctor for a moment, then looked away, her eyes fixing on a point somewhere near the ceiling. "You mean he's dead?" she asked, her voice hollow.

"It looks like a heart attack. His gun was right next to him, and one of his hands was still on the stock. He must have been shooting at something, but whatever it was, it doesn't look like he hit it. Anyway, the men didn't find anything out there except Mr. Hall. In the morning, they'll look again.''

''But Michael said—''

''I know what the boy said,'' Marsden interrupted. ''Mrs. Simpson told me. But you heard the shots yourself, didn't you? Wasn't your son here at the time?''

''But you said they found him down by the river. That's where Michael said—''

''That's where the shots came from, Mrs. Hall. Now, I want you to rest. If I have to, I'll give you something—''

''No! I don't want anything, Dr.—'' She struggled to remember his name, but couldn't. ''I'll be all right. But I want to see Michael. Can I? Please?''

Marsden hesitated, then finally nodded. He left the room, and a minute later Michael appeared in the doorway. ''Mom? Are you okay?''

Janet beckoned him over to the bed. ''I'll be all right,'' she assured him. She reached out and took Michael's hand. ''Honey, what you said just before I fainted. About killing Grandpa?''

''Uh-huh,'' Michael mumbled.

''What did you mean by that?''

''I already told you,'' Michael replied. ''It was me and Nathaniel. Nathaniel told me I should wish him dead, so I did. And he died.''

Janet fought the wave of dizziness that threatened to overwhelm her. ''But that's not possible,'' she told him, her voice unsteady. ''You can't wish someone to death. You were here when Grandpa died. You were with *me*.''

Michael shook his head. ''I was with Nathaniel,'' he said. ''I had to talk to him tonight. Grandpa wanted to hurt us. He wanted to kill us, just like he killed Daddy, and Aunt Laura's babies.''

''No, Michael,'' Janet wailed. ''Grandpa didn't do any of that.''

Michael's face set stubbornly. ''Yes he did,'' he replied. ''I saw him. Nathaniel showed me. And besides, the night Aunt Laura had her baby, I saw them. I saw them kill the baby, and then I saw them out in the field. They were burying Aunt Laura's baby. I was with Nathaniel that night, and we both saw it."

"But Michael, Grandpa was home that night, remember? When you came home, Grandpa was there."

"I don't care," Michael said. "I know what I saw, and I'm not lying."

Suddenly Janet wanted to shake Michael, as if somehow she might physically shake his impossible ideas out of his head. Where had they come from? What did they mean? Then her weakness overcame her, and she collapsed back onto the pillows. "Tomorrow," was all she could say. "We'll talk about it tomorrow. . . ."

Michael got off the bed and started toward the door, but then turned back.

"Mom?"

Janet opened her eyes. Michael was studying her with an intensity so great she had to look away.

"Everything's going to be all right now," he said softly. "I don't think I'm going to have my headaches anymore. I think they only came when Nathaniel was showing me things." He paused for a moment, then went on. "We had to make him die, Mom. He was going to kill the baby. Even if he didn't kill me, he would've killed the baby."

Janet's head turned, and she stared at Michael. "Stop it," she whispered. "Just stop saying those things." Her voice rose to the edge of hysteria. "They're not true, Michael. *They're not true!*"

Michael returned her gaze, his face suddenly angry. Then he left her alone, closing the door behind him.

Anna Hall was dozing in her chair, her ever-present mending on her lap, her head lolling on her breast.

In the hall, the clock began to strike, and Anna came half awake, certain that Amos had finally come home.

"Amos? Is that you?"

There was no answer, but even as silence settled once

more over the house, Anna had a strange sense that she was no longer alone.

She tried to clear the fogginess from her mind, and opened her sleepy eyes to peer around.

Then, at the window, she saw it.

A face, a face she recognized.

It was Mark's face, but younger than he'd been the last time she saw him, almost as young as he'd been when he ran away so many years ago.

And yet it wasn't Mark's face. It was a face like Mark's, but different.

Then she heard the voice.

"He's dead, Mama. He's dead."

The words struck Anna almost like a blow. For a moment she wasn't certain she'd heard them at all. There was a flat atonality about them that made her wonder if the face at the window had spoken the words, or if she'd only imagined them.

Then the voice came again. *"He's dead, Mama. You must not be frightened anymore."*

Then the face disappeared from the window, and once more Anna felt the solitude of the house.

She sat for a long time, listening to the soft ticking of the clock, amplified by the night, trying to decide what had really happened to her. Had it been real, or had it only been a dream?

Then, as the hours wore on, a sense of peace slowly settled over her, a sense of peace she hadn't felt in years, not since before the night so many years ago when she had given birth to her last child. Suddenly she smiled. That was who the face had reminded her of. The face at the window had looked like her last son, just as she'd always imagined he would look—if only he had lived.

And with the sense of peace came something else.

It was Amos of whom the boy had spoken. As the night wore on, and Anna waited, she became increasingly sure that Amos was not coming home that night, that he would never come home again.

At last, as the clock was striking two, she heard a car pull up the drive. She rolled herself over to the window and stared out into the night, squinting against the darkness as she tried to make out the face of her visitor.

And then, as the figure of a man emerged from the pickup truck in front of the house, Anna gasped.

It was Ben Findley.

Trembling, Anna slowly backed away from the window. Her eyes searched the room as if looking for a place to hide. But there was no place to hide, and in the end she let the chair drift to a stop in the center of the room. A moment later she heard the front door open, and then Ben Findley stood framed in the doorway, his gaunt figure looking like a ghost from the past.

"Hello, Anna," he said at last.

The seconds ticked by, and Anna felt the color draining from her face, felt her whole body, even the legs that had been lifeless so long, trembling.

"You," she breathed at last.

Ben Findley nodded. His eyes left Anna for a moment and drifted slowly over the room. He nodded almost imperceptibly, then turned back to Anna. "Amos is dead, Anna. Leif Simpson and I found him down by the river."

"The river?" Anna asked blankly, her mind reeling not only at the confirmation of her strange sense that her husband was dead, but at the presence of Ben Findley in her house. "What was he doing down at the river?"

Findley shrugged. "I called him today. I saw you and the boy this afternoon, and I told Amos I didn't want anyone poking around that field."

Anna's eyes narrowed. "What happened, Ben. Did you kill him?"

Findley shook his head; then, without asking Anna's permission, he came into the room and lowered himself onto the sofa. Slowly he told Anna what he and Leif Simpson had found. When he was done, Anna fell into a reflective silence for a few moments. Then her head came up, and her eyes roved to the window and the blackness of the night. "Perhaps it was the children," she said in a voice that was only partially audible. "Perhaps the children finally got their revenge." Suddenly she looked at Ben Findley. "Ben, do you believe in ghosts?"

Findley looked puzzled for a moment, then shook his head. "No, I don't. Why?"

Anna shook her head, as if trying to clear her mind. "I don't know. I just thought I saw one tonight, that's all." She paused, then went on. "I knew Amos was dead, Ben. I wasn't waiting for him to come home. I was waiting for someone to come and tell me what I already knew."

Findley's body tensed, and his hooded eyes darkened. "How?" he asked. "How did you know?"

Anna shrugged. "I told you—a ghost."

"Nathaniel . . ." Findley said softly.

Anna's head came up angrily. "Nathaniel!" she echoed, her voice suddenly regaining its strength. "Don't be a fool, Ben. There is no Nathaniel. There was never a Nathaniel. All my life, since I married Amos Hall, I've heard of nothing except Nathaniel. He doesn't exist, Ben. He was never anything but a fantasy of Amos's."

"No, Anna—"

"Yes! He killed my children, Ben. He killed my children, and somehow, in his twisted mind, he managed to blame it on his holy Nathaniel. But it was a lie, Ben! Amos was insane, and a murderer. I could never prove it, but I knew. I always knew."

"How?" Ben Findley suddenly demanded. He rose to his feet, towering over Anna, his blue eyes blazing. "How did you know, Anna?"

Anna cowered in her chair, her burst of strength suddenly deserting her. "I knew," she whispered. "That's all. I just knew."

"And is that why you stayed with him?" Findley asked. "Is that why you stayed with him all those years, Anna? Because you knew he'd killed your children? It doesn't make sense. If you truly knew, you'd have left him, left him and gone away. If you truly thought he'd

killed your children, you never would have stayed with
him.''

Anna shook her head helplessly as her eyes flooded with
tears. ''No,'' she protested. ''You don't understand. I—I
couldn't walk, Ben. I couldn't walk, and I couldn't prove
what he'd done.'' Suddenly she looked up at him implor-
ingly. ''Don't you understand, Ben? Don't you understand
at all?''

Findley ignored her question. ''And what about our
child, Anna?'' he asked softly. ''Did Amos kill our child,
too?''

Anna recoiled from his words. ''No . . .'' she whimpered.
''No, don't talk about that. Please . . .''

''Tell me, Anna,'' Findley pressed, his voice relentless.
''Tell me what you think you know about our son.''

''Dead,'' Anna whispered. ''He was born dead. That's
what Amos always told me. But I never believed him,
Ben. I never believed him. Amos killed our baby that
night, just like the other two. He killed him, and they
buried him in Potter's Field.''

''No, Anna,'' Findley told her. The anger drained out of
his voice, and Anna responded to his sudden gentleness,
gazing at him with frightened eyes. ''He didn't die, Anna.
He wasn't born dead, and he didn't die. Potter brought
him to me that night. He brought him to me, and I've had
him ever since.'' He paused, then, ''I named him Nathaniel,
Anna. That's who you saw tonight. You saw Nathaniel,
and he's our son.''

A terrible silence fell over the house as Anna tried to
comprehend Ben Findley's words. The room seemed to
turn around her, and her mind reeled as twenty years of
her life shattered into meaningless pieces.

And then, gathering her strength, Anna Hall grasped the
arms of her wheelchair. ''No,'' she breathed. ''No. None
of it's true!'' Her voice pitched to a scream, as slowly,
supporting herself on trembling arms, she began to rise
from the chair. ''Why are you lying to me?'' she wailed.
''Why? Why?'' She took a halting step toward him, and

suddenly her fists came up. "Lies," she screamed. "It's all lies! I know the truth, Ben. I know it!" She began pummeling at his chest, her legs wobbling, but still somehow supporting her.

Ben Findley's arms went around Anna, and he held her tight. "No, Anna, I've told you the truth. It's all over now. Amos is dead, and he can't hurt you anymore. It's all over. Amos is dead, and our son is alive, and it's over."

But Anna shook herself loose. "It's not over," she hissed. "I wasn't wrong, Ben. I wasn't! You're lying to me, but I'll find the truth! So help me, I'll find the truth!" Then she turned, and with an effort of sheer willpower, she walked slowly across the room and disappeared into the tiny room that had been her private retreat for the last twenty years.

A moment later, when Ben Findley tried to follow her, he found the door locked. When he called to her, Anna Hall refused to answer him.

The next morning, Anna began to hear the rumors. People called—nearly everyone in town—to express their sympathies, and Anna listened to them, and made all the proper responses. But some of them didn't stop with condolences about Amos's death. Some of them made oblique references to Michael:

"Such a terrible thing for a boy his age—"

"Of course, losing his father must have been a terrible trauma for him, but to blame his grandfather—"

"Of course, he couldn't have seen a ghost, but he must have seen *something*—"

"Of course, I can't believe it's true. Why would a little boy want to do a thing like that—"

Anna listened to it all, and slowly pieced it all together. Finally she turned to Laura, who had arrived during the night, after Ben Findley had left. She hadn't seen Laura last night, but she'd told her through her closed door that she was all right and that she needed to be alone for a while. Laura had accepted it, as Laura always accepted everything. Only this morning, when Anna had slowly and shakily walked out of the tiny room, had Laura tried to confront her.

Anna smiled grimly at the memory.

Laura had stared at her, speechless, then finally opened her mouth to protest. "Mother—you can't—"

Anna had silenced her. "Obviously I can," she'd said. "Since I am."

"But—but—how?"

"I don't know," Anna admitted. "Something happened to me last night. I'm not sure what it was, and I won't talk about it. But after I found out your father had died, something inside me changed." She'd smiled sadly at Laura. "Maybe I've stopped punishing myself. Or maybe I could have done it long ago," she said. "Maybe my chair was nothing more than my own way of running away from things. I've been thinking about it all night, Laura, and that's the only thing that makes sense. Charles told me that years ago, you know. From the very beginning, he told me there was nothing wrong with my legs, that I'd just decided I didn't want to walk." A tear welled in her eye, then ran slowly down her cheek. "And it worked, you know," she whispered. "Your father used to beat me, years ago—"

"Mother!"

"He did, Laura. But then he stopped. When I couldn't walk anymore, he stopped."

Then, with a strength she hadn't felt for years, Anna had begun taking charge of her own life, a task she'd ceded to Amos on the day she'd married him.

"I want to go to Janet's," she said now.

"But mother, Janet's in bed. The doctor's ordered her to stay in bed for at least a week."

"Then she'll need help," Anna replied. "I can at least take care of the cooking. I won't have my grandson rummaging around eating God only knows what."

"Mother, no one expects you to do anything right now.

Ione Simpson's looking after her, and Michael can spend the nights with us, if it's too much trouble for the Simpsons."

Anna's face set. "Laura, I know you're trying to do what's best for me, and I appreciate it. But I'm not senile, and if I have to sit here listening to idle gossip about my grandson—"

Suddenly Laura's expression turned wary. "Gossip? What gossip?"

"It seems," Anna replied, "there are some people in town who think Michael might have had something to do with Amos's death."

Laura paled. "I know what they're talking about, but it isn't true, mother. It isn't possible—"

"I'll decide for myself what's possible and what isn't," Anna snapped. "Now, will you take me over there, or do I have to learn to drive again the same day I have to learn to walk?"

"Mother, you really should stay home—what will people think? And Father—think of Father."

Anna made no reply. Instead, she simply began making her slow way to the front door, then out onto the porch. She was starting down the steps when Laura finally decided that she was not bluffing. "All right, Mother," she said, and followed the older woman out to her car.

Ione Simpson looked up in shocked surprise, then got quickly to her feet as Anna Hall, leaning heavily on Laura's arm, walked slowly into Janet Hall's small living room. "Anna! What are you—" She paused, floundering, then recovered herself. "I'm—I'm so sorry about Amos."

Anna nodded an acknowledgment, and quickly scanned the room. "Is Michael upstairs?"

Ione hesitated, then shook her head. "He's in the kitchen, I think."

Wordlessly, Anna turned toward the kitchen. Laura moved quickly to help her, but Anna brushed her aside. "I want to talk to him alone.'' Slowly, but with remarkable steadiness, Anna walked out of the living room.

She found Michael at the kitchen table, staring sightlessly at a bowl of cold cereal. As if coming out of a trance, his eyes suddenly focused, and he looked at her. ''Aren't you going to give your grandmother a kiss?'' she asked.

With obvious reluctance, Michael got up from the table and approached her. ''I—I'm sorry, Grandma,'' he whispered. Anna put her arms around him.

''It's all right, Michael. I know it's hard, but he was an old man, and whatever happened, it wasn't your fault.'' Then she held him at arm's length and looked directly into his eyes. ''It wasn't your fault, was it?''

Michael trembled slightly, then nodded his head.

''I see,'' Anna breathed. She let her hands drop from Michael's shoulders and moved to the table, where she carefully lowered herself into a chair. ''Sit down, Michael,'' she said softly. ''Sit down and tell me what happened. Can you do that? Can you tell me all of it?''

Slowly, Michael recounted his story of the night before, and when he was done, Anna slumped tiredly in her chair. ''You wished him dead,'' she whispered. ''You and Nathaniel wished him dead.''

She reached out then, reached out to comfort the sobbing boy who sat across from her, his head buried in his arms. At her touch, he looked up.

''I'm sorry, Grandma. I'm sorry!''

''Michael,'' Anna said almost fearfully. ''There's something you haven't told me.''

Slowly, Michael's sobbing subsided, and at last he looked up at his grandmother, his eyes red, his cheeks splotched with tears.

''Who is Nathaniel?'' Anna asked. ''You haven't told me who Nathaniel is.'' She hesitated, then asked the question she'd been dreading. ''He's—he's a ghost, isn't he?''

Michael's eyes widened, and for a long moment he stared at his grandmother in silence. At last, he shook his head.

''No, Grandma,'' he said softly. ''He's real.''

CHAPTER 24

Ben Findley stared at the tray of food that still sat where he'd left it on the table in the little room beneath the barn.

It was untouched.

He hadn't really expected anything different, not since he'd come down here late last night to find the room empty. That, too, had not been unexpected, but still he'd gone over the barn carefully, inspecting everything. Everything had been as it should have been. The door to the tack room, as always, was barred from the outside. The planks that formed the siding of the barn were as solid as ever, despite their appearance from the outside. Upstairs in the loft, the door was still nailed shut.

Yet despite the fact that the security of the barn did not appear to have been breached, Nathaniel was gone. He was gone, and he had not come back.

Findley picked up the tray and, balancing it expertly on one hand, used the other to steady himself as he climbed the ladder out of the tiny cell. He left the barn, not bothering to lock it, and quickly crossed the yard.

Inside his house, he put the tray on the sink and stared idly at his little kitchen. A puddle of coffee had spread across the kitchen counter, and he automatically moved to wipe it up before the stain could penetrate the butcher-block top.

He and Nathaniel had made that top together, and he wasn't about to let it be ruined.

Impulsively, he decided to inspect the entire house, and he began moving slowly through its few rooms, examining everything, making sure everything was in the perfect condition he had always maintained.

The interior of the little house was in remarkable contrast to its ramshackle exterior. The hardwood floors gleamed under his feet, their mellow oaken planks polished to a soft glow. The walls were lined with leatherbound books, stored in cases he had built himself, all the joints carefully dovetailed so that as the years went by they would remain as true as they had been the day he and Nathaniel had put them together.

The furniture was sparse. Two chairs—one his, the other Nathaniel's, for the times, much more frequent than Charles Potter had ever suspected, when Findley had felt safe enough to have Nathaniel inside the house.

At times, Ben Findley had wondered if he'd begun taking a perverse pleasure in keeping the interior of the house in such perfect contrast to its exterior, but deep inside he knew he had not. It was just that he liked things to be right, and over the years he had come to want them to be as nice as possible for Nathaniel.

At first, of course, it had not been for Nathaniel at all.

It had been for Anna.

For a long time after that night when Nathaniel was born, Ben Findley had hoped that Anna Hall would finally leave Amos and come to live with him. Him, and Nathaniel.

He had fantasized in those years, picturing the light that would come into Anna's eyes when he told her that their son was alive. That fantasy had kept him going those first years, after Jenny had left him.

Even twenty years later, he could clearly remember that night. It was the night Nathaniel had been born, and Charles Potter had brought the baby to him, meeting him in the field, while a storm howled around them.

"Amos thinks he's dead," Potter had told him that

night. "I made him think so, or he might have killed him. He knows the child's yours." He'd handed the blanket-wrapped infant to Ben. "Amos thinks I'm burying him. I'll stay here for a while, in case he's watching."

Ben had peeled a corner of the blanket back, and gazed down into the face of the son that Anna Hall had borne him, the son that his own wife had never been able to conceive. "What about Anna?" he'd asked, but Potter had shaken his head.

"I don't know. It was hard, and she thinks the baby's dead." Then he'd met Ben's eyes. "He's yours, Ben. Yours and Jenny's."

Except that Jenny hadn't wanted the child, wouldn't even look at it.

"Anna's?" she'd demanded. "You expect me to raise a child you had by Anna Hall? Never! Never, Ben!"

That night, she, like Mark Hall, had gone away.

Unlike Mark, she had never come back.

And so Ben had begun to raise the child himself, hoping, at first, that Anna Hall would one day recover from the child's birth and walk again.

He'd hidden the child, knowing that he had no reasonable explanation for its being there, and slowly, over the years, his life had changed.

For a long time, he'd whiled away the time by preparing the house for Anna, but when he'd finally come to accept that Anna was never coming, he hadn't stopped working on the interior of the house.

By then, he was doing it for Nathaniel.

Nathaniel became the sole focus of his life. Ben Findley became consumed with the need to provide whatever was necessary for the little boy who was growing up in his house.

What was needed for Nathaniel was isolation, for isolation meant safety. So Ben constructed his shield, and made himself into the town recluse, the rundown appearance of his farm discouraging most visitors, his surly façade—a façade that had finally become his true personality—repelling those few who braved the tangle of overgrowth of the yard to knock on the peeled and weathered boards of the front door.

It had worked. Years ago, people had stopped trying to be friendly toward him, and he had ended up being as trapped as Nathaniel within the limits that he had set for them.

The limits had been simple: No one must know, or even suspect, that Ben Findley was not living alone.

At first it had only been temporary. When Anna came, they would bring Nathaniel out in the open, and live as the family they were.

But Anna hadn't come.

Instead, she'd retreated to her wheelchair, and soon moved away from the little house where the two of them had loved. She had wiped Ben Findley from her life.

Ben had resented that, and he knew that there had been times when he'd taken Anna's rejection of him out on little Nathaniel. Sometimes, for no reason at all, he'd found himself punishing the child, beating him.

But as the years wore on, he'd come to care totally for the boy. And so he'd raised him, isolating himself along with Nathaniel. He'd done what he could to make Nathaniel's life comfortable, and if it wasn't enough, Ben was sorry.

He knew the boy was peculiar, but he also knew there was nothing he could do about it. Nathaniel's oddness, he was sure, was only a result of his isolation.

And he'd taught the boy, taught him everything he knew. What he did without in the way of human companionship, he tried to make up for with books. Ben clothed Nathaniel, making the boy's garments himself; buying clothes in Prairie Bend was out of the question, and doing it through the mails was equally risky. Catalogs would begin coming, catalogs of children's clothes and toys, and the woman at the post office would begin to wonder why Ben Findley was getting such things. And if she wondered, she'd talk, and then she'd want to know. So he took no risks.

Still, Ben knew it hadn't worked. Nathaniel was different from other children, ill-equipped to deal with the world. There had been times when Nathaniel had seemed to drift off into a private world of his own, and Ben had been unable to reach him. It was as if he'd been listening to voices only he could hear. But it didn't happen often, and he always came out of it. And there had been the other times, the times when the children—what his cousin Amos had always called "Nathaniel's children"—had been born. Those nights, Ben had sometimes heard Nathaniel in the barn, moaning softly, almost as if he were in pain. Sometimes he'd tried to comfort the boy, but he'd never been able. Nathaniel had never even seemed aware of his presence.

By the mornings after those terrible nights, though, Nathaniel had always seemed to be all right, and Charles Potter—still the only other person who knew of Nathaniel's secret existence—had maintained that the odd spells meant nothing.

And then, last spring, Mark Hall had come home.

Ever since then, Nathaniel had been different.

He'd become odder, and seemed to disappear deeper into his private world every day.

He'd stopped speaking to Ben, preferring to spend his time alone in his room beneath the barn, lying on his cot, his eyes wide open but blank, staring at something Ben could never see.

His voice, never expressive, had taken on an atonality that sometimes frightened Ben, and when he looked at Ben now, it always seemed to be with anger.

And when he'd spoken, he'd said strange things.

"I know what happened," he told Ben once. "I can see it now, and I know what happened."

That was all he'd said, but in his words, and in his eyes, Ben had sensed danger.

Then, last night, Nathaniel had disappeared from the barn.

And Amos Hall had died.

*   *   *

It wasn't until dusk that Findley went back to the barn. He carried Nathaniel's dinner with him, not because he expected Nathaniel to be there to eat it, but because he had taken Nathaniel's dinner to the barn every night for so many years that when he'd fixed his own meal that evening, he'd automatically cooked for them both. He opened the barn door, slipped inside, and pulled the door closed behind him.

And then he felt it.

Nathaniel was there.

Nathaniel's presence was in the atmosphere of the barn, just as his absence had been palpable the night before.

Findley paused, then spoke softly into the gloom of the building. "Nathaniel?"

There was no answer. Ben started toward the tack room, but had taken only a few paces when suddenly he felt something behind him. He turned slowly, and stared at the glistening tines of a pitchfork hovering a few inches from his chest. Beyond the cold, glittering metal, his hands grasping the fork's handle, Nathaniel's eyes blazed at him, penetrating the deep shadows of the barn. The tray clattered to the floor. "Nathaniel—"

The finely honed points of the fork inched closer to his chest. "Where are they?" Nathaniel demanded.

Ben frowned. "What? Where are what, Nathaniel?"

"The children. The children in the field. Where are they?"

"Nathaniel—"

A single tine of the fork touched the skin of Ben Findley's throat, pierced it. A drop of blood began to form, then slowly ran down the inside of Ben's shirt.

"Tell me where they are. I have to find them."

"I don't know what you're talking about, Nathaniel," Ben said softly. "Now put down the fork, and tell me what you mean."

But it was too late. The look was in Nathaniel's eyes, the look Ben Findley had seen before, and he could almost imagine he heard the voices himself, the voices Nathaniel was listening to.

He's going to kill me, Findley thought. He killed Amos, and he killed Charles, and now he's going to kill me. Then another thought came to him: Why shouldn't he kill us? One way or another, all of us killed him.

He felt the tines of the fork pressing against his throat again, and began backing away. Behind him, he suddenly felt the wall of the barn, and there was nowhere else to go. He stopped, his eyes fixing on Nathaniel's.

"I'm sorry," he whispered, even as he knew it was too late. "I'm sorry I took your life away from you."

Nathaniel nodded, then hurled his weight against the pitchfork.

Ben opened his mouth to scream, but no sound came out, as two of the tines plunged through his flesh, then on into the soft pine planks of the barn wall.

A stream of blood welled up from his torn throat, then overflowed and began pouring down the front of his shirt.

A few seconds later, his eyes rolled backward and his body went slack.

Nathaniel stared for a moment at the man who had raised him, and killed him, then went out into the gathering night.

CHAPTER 25

Janet awoke with a start, her heart pounding. The dream had come again, the nightmare in which she stood helplessly by and watched as flames consumed the house she'd grown up in. Only this time, the dream was different. This time, as she cowered in the night, transfixed by the smoke and flames, it wasn't her brother who was calling to her.

This time, the voice she heard was Michael's, and the face she saw at the upstairs window was Mark's.

And in the background, barely audible, was another voice, a voice she recognized as that of her unborn child.

This time it wasn't her parents and her brother who were dying. This time it was her children and her husband.

She shook off the remnants of the dream and lay in the gloom, listening to the throbbing pulse of her heart, staring at the ceiling where strange shadows were cast by the soft glow of her nightlight. Inside her, she could feel the baby stirring—that was good, for as long as the baby moved it still lived, and for a while during the past twenty-four hours, she was sure she had lost it. Then, as her pulse slowly returned to normal, she shifted her attention, listening to the sounds of the house. Voices drifted up from downstairs. Though she couldn't make out the words, the murmuring itself was comforting to Janet.

She knew who was downstairs: her mother-in-law, her son, and Ione Simpson.

Earlier in the day, when she'd first mentioned that Ione had volunteered to stay with them and look after them, she had expected Anna to object. But she'd been wrong. Anna, without Amos and without her chair, had literally changed overnight.

"She has a level head," Anna had said of Ione. "And I don't feel like talking tonight. With Laura, I'd have to talk. But with Ione, I can just sit and think. I need to think, Janet," she'd added in a tone that had almost frightened the younger woman. "I need to think about a lot of things." And then, sounding more like her usual self, she'd glanced pointedly at Janet's belly. "Aren't you supposed to be staying in bed?"

Janet nodded. "But I feel so useless up there. And the baby's all right. The doctor said—"

Anna's eyes flashed with sudden anger. "Doctors are fools! Never believe what they say. Never! I believed Charles Potter once."

The force of Anna's words struck Janet almost physically. She sank back against the cushions of the sofa. "Anna, what are you saying? He was your doctor for years—"

"Amos's. He was Amos's doctor, Janet. To me, he was—" Suddenly she fell silent, but Janet had the distinct feeling there was something the older woman wanted to talk about.

"He was what, Anna?"

Anna's eyes suddenly shifted away from Janet, and she appeared to be trying to come to a decision. Finally, her empty eyes met Janet's. "I don't know what he was," she said at last. "I don't know what's the truth, anymore, and I don't know who lied to me all my life. I don't know anything anymore, Janet. For twenty years, I sat in a wheelchair, but at least I thought I knew why I was there. I thought it was Amos's fault. I thought he'd done something to me when my last baby was born, thought somehow he or Charles Potter had hurt me when they killed my baby.''

"Anna," Janet pleaded, "don't say that."

"Wait," Anna said quietly. "I'm not saying what I believe, Janet. I'm only telling you what I thought." Suddenly she seemed to straighten up. She took a deep breath. Then she said: "Ben Findley was the father of my last child."

Janet stared at her mother-in-law, unable to make any reply at all.

"It's true. Ben was different then. Not like he is now. In some ways he was very like Amos—like all that family— except there was nothing of Amos's cruelty about him. Amos *was* cruel. He beat the children, and he beat me. And he was absolutely convinced that some awful curse had been placed on his family. It all went back to Abby Randolph, and Nathaniel, and the child that survived."

"But you said—"

"I know what I said." Anna sighed, then went on talking. "I think Amos killed two of my children. I don't know anymore. Not after last night. But what's important is that I *believed* he did. That's one of the reasons I fell in love with Ben Findley. I blamed Amos for so much, and in Ben I found the parts of Amos I was attracted to, without the parts I hated. Can you understand that?" She paused, but Janet made no reply. "Anyway, I fell in love with him, and I got pregnant by him. And Amos knew." Slowly, her voice trembling with the pain she felt at reliving the story, Anna told Janet what had happened twenty years ago, when her last child had been born. "He had sworn he'd kill it," she finished. "He'd said he'd kill it, but then, when it came, he told me it was stillborn. He told me, and Charles Potter told me. But I didn't believe them. I believed they killed it, just as I believed Amos had killed my other children. I believed they killed it. And later on, I believed they killed Laura's children."

"But if that's what you believed—"

"Why did I stay? Because Amos was my punishment, and I deserved to be punished for my . . ." Her voice faltered. "For my sins. I stayed out of my own guilt, Janet. I hated Amos, but I stayed."

Janet felt sick. Sick and betrayed. "And you didn't warn me, either," she said, her voice suddenly bitter. Her eyes turned angry. "What about Michael? Did he beat Michael, too? And would you have stood by when my baby came, even though you thought Amos might kill it?"

Anna shook her head helplessly. "I don't know," she whispered. "I just don't know. But it's over now, Janet. Nathaniel—" She fell suddenly silent.

"Nathaniel!" Janet demanded. "What about Nathaniel? That's only a ghost story."

"Is it?" Anna broke in. Then her body seemed to droop. "Maybe it is, at that. But Michael doesn't think so. Nor do I. Nathaniel is real, at least in some ways. For me, he's real, and he's bringing me an odd kind of peace." She fell silent, then smiled softly. "I'm going to have another grandchild, Janet. I'm going to see Mark's second son, and Amos isn't going to kill him. It will be almost like having my own son back."

Janet had gone upstairs then, trying to puzzle out the meaning of all that Anna had told her. She had fallen asleep for a while, then awakened. Now, as she listened to the calming drone of voices from below, Anna's words seemed to fade from her mind. Perhaps, as Anna had said, everything would be all right now.

And then came the scream.

Anna jerked out of the half sleep she'd fallen into, and stared at the contorted face of her grandson. Shadow, his tail twitching nervously, was licking at Michael's face, but the boy didn't seem to notice. "What is it?" Anna asked, her eyes leaving the screaming boy and fixing on Ione Simpson. "My Lord, what's wrong with him?"

Ione had been sitting on the floor studying the chessboard between herself and Michael, but was now crouched beside the boy, cradling him in her arms. "It's all right," she told Anna. "It's going to be all right."

Michael's screams subsided, and as he calmed down, so did Shadow. Finally, his weight still resting against Ione's breast, his eyes opened and he looked up into his grandmother's face.

"He killed him," he whispered. "It happened just now. He killed him."

"Who?" Ione asked. "Who killed someone, Michael?"

"Nathaniel," Michael whispered. "I saw it. Just now. I saw him in the barn, and he was hiding. And then Mr. Findley came in. And—and Nathaniel killed him."

Instinctively, Ione glanced toward the window, but the rapidly gathering darkness revealed nothing of what lay beyond the glass. Whatever Michael was talking about, he hadn't seen it with his eyes.

"All right," Ione said, automatically reverting to the soothing voice she'd cultivated during her years of nursing. "Tell us what happened. Tell me what you saw, and how you saw it. Can you do that?"

Michael gazed up at her for a moment, then his eyes shifted back to his grandmother.

"It's all right," she assured him. "Whatever you tell us, we'll believe you. Just tell us what happened."

Michael swallowed. "I was looking at the board," he said. "I was trying to decide whether or not to move my bishop, and then all of a sudden I got a headache. And I heard Nathaniel's voice."

Ione frowned and started to say something, but Anna silenced her with a gesture.

"Only he wasn't talking to me," Michael went on. "He was talking to Mr. Findley. He was asking about the children. He wanted to know where the children were, and Mr. Findley wouldn't tell him. So Nathaniel killed him."

"How?" Anna asked. "How did Nathaniel kill him?"

Michael's voice shook. "The way Grandpa killed Dad," he said softly. "With a pitchfork."

Suddenly, from the doorway, they heard a low moan, and both Ione and Anna turned to see Janet, her face pale, leaning heavily against the doorframe. "I can't stand it," Janet whispered. "I just can't stand it."

"Ione, help her," Anna said, but the words were unnecessary: Ione was already on her feet, offering Janet a supporting arm. But Janet brushed her aside, her eyes fixed on Michael.

"It isn't possible, Michael," she said. "You couldn't have seen anything like that." Hysteria began to edge her voice. "You were sitting right here. You couldn't have seen anything. You couldn't!"

Michael stared at his mother, his eyes wide and frightened. "I did, Mama," he said. "I know what I saw."

"No!" Janet screamed. "You're imagining things, Michael! Can't you understand?" Her eyes, wide with distress and confusion, flicked from Michael to Anna, then to Ione. "Can't any of you understand? He's imagining things! He's imagining things, and he needs help!" She broke down, her sobs coming in great heaving gulps, and now she let herself collapse into Ione's arms. "Oh, God, help him. Please help him!"

"It's all right, Janet," Ione soothed. "Everything's going to be all right. But you have to go back up to bed. You have to rest." Without waiting for her to reply, Ione began guiding her back up the stairs.

Suddenly alone with his grandmother, Michael looked fretfully at the old woman. His hands played over Shadow's thick coat, as if he were seeking comfort from the dog. "Why doesn't she believe me?" he asked. "Why doesn't she believe I saw what I did?"

"Maybe she does," Anna told him. "Maybe she does, but just doesn't want to admit it to herself. Sometimes it's easier to pretend things aren't happening, even when you know they are. Can you understand that?"

Michael hesitated, then nodded. "I—I think so."

"All right. Now, would you do something for me?"

"Wh-what?"

"I want you to call Aunt Laura and ask her to come out here. And have her bring Buck and Ryan, too."

Michael's brow knitted into a worried frown. "Why?"

"To help Mrs. Simpson take care of your mother. You and I and your Uncle Buck are going to go over and have a look at Ben Findley's barn."

The enormous barn door stood slightly ajar, and an ominous silence seemed to hang over the unkempt farm like a funeral pall. The little group stopped in the center of the barnyard, Michael on one side of Anna, Buck Shields on the other, supporting her with his arm. Shadow, his tail between his legs, whined softly.

"He's gone," Michael whispered. "Nathaniel's gone."

"There's no such person as Nathaniel," Buck Shields said, his voice angry. Anna silenced him with a glance, then switched on the flashlight she held in one hand, playing its beam over the walls of the barn. Nothing showed, nothing moved.

"Stay here with your grandmother," Buck said. "I'll go have a look inside."

"No!" Anna's voice crackled in the darkness. "We'll all go inside. Whatever's there, Michael's already seen it. And whatever's there, I want to see it."

They started toward the barn, and suddenly Shadow stiffened, then a growl rumbled up from the depths of his throat.

"Someone's there," Michael whispered. "Someone's inside the barn."

As if in response, Shadow whimpered, then leaped forward into the darkness, disappearing into the building. There was a scuffling sound, and Shadow began barking. Then his barking subsided into a steady snarl, and Buck Shields moved forward, taking the light from Anna Hall's hands.

He slipped through the door, then paused. Shadow's snarling was louder, coming from the far end of the barn. Buck made his way slowly along the inside of the door, then felt on the wall for a light switch.

The blackness of the barn's interior was suddenly washed away with a brilliant white light from three overhead fixtures. Buck blinked, and shaded his eyes with one hand.

Sixty feet away, at the far end of the barn, he could see Ben Findley, his eyes still open, his clothes covered with blood, held upright only by the pitchfork that impaled his throat, pinning him to the wall. Buck stared at the dead man for a few seconds, trying to control the churning in his stomach that threatened to overwhelm him. Then his eye was caught by a flicker of movement.

Slowly, Buck started down the center aisle of the barn, approaching Ben Findley as if he were some grotesque religious icon hovering above an altar.

Like a supplicant at Ben Findley's feet, Shadow was crouched low to the ground, his tail sweeping the floor in slow movements, his eyes fixed on the dead man's face.

Nathaniel lay in Potter's Field, his eyes fixed on the barn. Light glimmered through the cracks in the barn's siding, and it almost looked as if the building were on fire.

He knew he should get up and move. Soon, he was sure, people would come looking for him, and when they found him—

Not yet. They couldn't find him yet.

Even though the three of them were dead now—the one who had wanted to kill him when he was born, and the two who had kept him a prisoner all his life—there was still something he had to do.

He had to go home. His eyes turned away from the barn, and focused on the little house where he'd been born.

With his mind, he reached out to it, exploring it.

There were people in it tonight. His sister—Laura—was

there, and Michael's mother was there. And someone else, a stranger. So he couldn't go there tonight. Tonight, he must hide, and stay hidden until it was safe. Softly, inaudibly, he sent out an urgent signal.

In the barn, Shadow suddenly rose from his position at Ben Findley's feet and trotted out into the night.

CHAPTER 26

There was no funeral for Amos Hall, none for Ben Findley. Anna had forbidden it.

"I won't do it," she'd said. "I won't pretend to shed tears for Amos, and as for Ben Findley—well, he lived alone for twenty years, and he can be buried alone, too."

She'd told no one of her conversation with Ben Findley the night Amos had died, and now she knew she never would. There was no point, she'd decided. There was no one left who knew the whole truth of what had happened all those years ago. And she'd decided it no longer really mattered. Finally, it was over. They were all dead, and even though they could no longer give her the answers to her questions, neither could they hurt her any more than they already had.

They'd talked to her about Ben Findley, of course, when they came down from Mulford to investigate his death.

She hadn't told them about Nathaniel. That, too, was something she'd decided never to speak of again. So when they'd asked her if she had any idea who might have killed Ben Findley, she'd only shrugged. "A drifter, I suppose. Ben didn't have any friends, but he didn't have any enemies, either. So it must have been a drifter."

No one else in Prairie Bend had been able to offer a

better idea, nor had anyone given credence to Michael's insistence that Nathaniel had killed the recluse.

The investigators went over Ben Findley's farm, but paid scant attention to the little room below the barn, dismissing the cell as nothing more than the storm cellar it appeared to be. In the end, they went back to Mulford, sure they would never find Ben Findley's killer, and equally sure that no one in Prairie Bend would care.

For Janet, the days following the deaths were increasingly difficult. She found herself watching Michael closely, guarding herself against the moment when he would suddenly be attacked by one of his headaches, then insist that Nathaniel had shown him something both hideous and impossible. Even as the days went by, and nothing happened, she did not calm down. Instead, she only grew more nervous, sure that whatever was happening to Michael had not yet ended.

Part of her certainty that things were not over involved Shadow.

Since the night Ben Findley had been found dead in his barn, the huge black dog had not been seen. Nor had Michael seemed upset by his disappearance.

"He's helping Nathaniel," Michael had said. "He'll come back. Nathaniel will bring him back."

And so Janet was waiting.

It was on the fifth day, near dusk, that Shadow returned.

Janet and Michael were in the kitchen. Michael was at the sink, doing the last of the supper dishes, while Janet sat at the kitchen table laboriously attempting to master the basic manipulations of the knitting needles that Anna had given her that afternoon. "Learn now," Anna had told her. "In the winter, it will help pass the time." And so she was trying, but it was not going well. In fact, Michael could already do it better than she could.

"I just don't get it," she said at last, dropping the work on the table. "I can't keep the same number of stitches in a row, and they just keep getting tighter and tighter." Then, when Michael made no reply, she looked up to see him staring out the window. His right hand was raised as he rubbed at his temples. "Michael?" When he still said nothing, Janet rose to her feet. "What is it, honey? Is something wrong?"

Then her eyes followed his, and in the distance, in Potter's Field, she saw the familiar black mass that was Shadow.

"He's looking for the babies," Michael said in a far-away voice. "He's looking for the babies that Grandpa killed."

Holding her emotions tightly in check, Janet slipped her arms around her son. "No, Michael. There's nothing out there. . . ."

"There is," Michael repeated, his voice growing stronger. "Shadow's out there looking for them, helping Nathaniel find them."

"No!" Janet exclaimed.

Michael pivoted to face her, glaring at her with furious eyes. "Yes! They're out there, and Nathaniel has to find them, and I have to help him."

He began struggling in her arms, trying to wriggle free, but Janet hung on. "No!" she screamed. "There's nothing out there, and there is no Nathaniel, and you have to stop pretending there is! You have to stop it, Michael! Do you hear me? *Just stop it!*"

Michael was still in her arms, but suddenly his eyes, blazing with fury, gazed into hers.

"You don't know," he whispered. "You don't know, because you don't know Nathaniel."

For several long minutes the two of them stood frozen in a contest of wills. Then, at last, Janet knew what she had to do.

"All right," she said, letting go of Michael. "Let's go find out. Right now, let's go find out what the truth is."

Taking Michael by the hand she left the house and strode across the yard to the toolshed. Seconds later, Michael's arm still firmly gripped in her right hand, a shovel in her left, she started toward Potter's Field. "We'll dig them up," she told Michael as they climbed through the barbed wire. "If there are any bodies in this field, we'll dig them up right now, and look at them."

Shadow's head came up, and he watched them as they approached. Then, as he recognized them, he bounded over, his tail wagging, a happy bark ringing out over the prairie. Michael threw himself on the dog, scratching him and petting him, but Janet stood still and silent. Finally, when Michael had begun to calm down, she spoke.

"Where are they?" she asked. "Where are they buried?"

Shadow's ears suddenly dropped flat against his head, and his joyful barking faded into a wary growl.

"It's all right," Michael soothed. "It's all right, boy. We're gonna help you." Then, slowly, Michael began moving through the field with Shadow at his side.

"Here," Michael said.

Janet moved the stone at Michael's feet aside, and plunged the shovel into the earth. She worked silently, not heeding the stress she was putting on her body, caring more about proving to Michael that there was nothing in the field than about any danger to her unborn child.

And then, a moment later, the bone fragments appeared.

Janet stared at them, then reached down to pick one of them up. She studied it a moment, then handed it to Michael. "Look at it," she said. "It's old and crumbling, and it could be anything. It might be human, and it might not. But whatever it is, it's far too old for your grandfather to have buried it here."

Michael's temples were pounding now, and he glowered at his mother with barely contained fury. "There's more," he whispered. "All over the field, there's more."

"Where?" Janet demanded. "Show me where. You keep telling me Aunt Laura's babies are buried out here, Michael. But where are they? If they're here, show them to me."

Trembling, Michael glared at her, then silently hurried away. He moved across the field, then finally stopped.

"Here," he said once more. "If you want to see it, it's right here."

Wordlessly, Janet began digging once more.

Nathaniel watched for a few moments, then turned away and moved slowly through the barn, looking at it all for the last time. The little room beneath the trapdoor where he'd spent so many years; the tack room, from which he'd watched the burials on those strange nights when the children had been born and then died.

His children, the children he could reach through the powers of his mind. There hadn't been many of them, but he still thought of them as his.

There had been his brother. On the night Nathaniel was born, he had called out to his brother, and his brother had answered him. But then he'd gone to sleep, and when he woke up, his brother was gone. For a long time after that, Nathaniel had called out to his brother, called to him for help, but his brother had never come to him.

There had been two others since then, two others that he had felt, but in the end, they had brought them to the field, and buried them.

And then, a few months ago, his brother had come back. Nathaniel remembered it so well—he'd awakened one morning and sensed that he was no longer alone, that at last his brother had returned to help him avenge all the wrongs that had been done. For a long time, he and his brother had talked, and his brother had promised to come for him, to take him outside, to help him destroy their enemies.

But then his brother had died. He'd tried to warn Mark, but he couldn't. Mark was older than he and had ignored his warnings. And the old man had killed him.

And then, a few days later, Michael had come. He'd called out to Michael, too, and Michael had answered him.

And with Michael's help, he had destroyed his enemies.

And now, Michael and his mother were in the field, and would find the children, and know the truth.

Now, at last, Nathaniel could go home.

He left the barn and in the gathering darkness crossed the yard. He ignored the house—the house that had been part of his prison through all the years of his life, but that had, in these last days, been his secret refuge. Instead, he concentrated his mind on his goal: the house where he'd been born.

He moved quickly, slipping easily through the barbed wire, and in a few seconds, he was there. . . .

Janet's shovel struck something, something that stopped the blade's penetration of the earth, but was too soft to be a rock. As Michael stood by, with Shadow quivering at his side, Janet lowered herself to her knees, and began digging with her hands.

A moment later she felt the soft folds of a blanket.

Her heart began to beat faster as she worked, and then she pulled the object she had uncovered free from the earth that had hidden it.

She stared at it for a long time, afraid to open it, afraid it might actually be what she thought it was.

But she had come too far to turn back now. With a shaking hand, she folded back one corner of the blanket.

She could only stand to look at it for a second. Already, the flesh had begun to rot away, and the skin was entirely gone from the skull. Her stomach lurched, and involuntarily, Janet dropped the tiny corpse back into its grave. Her face pale, her whole body trembling now, Janet turned to gaze at her son.

"How did you know?" she breathed. "How did you know?"

"Nathaniel," Michael said, his voice steady. "Nathaniel told me."

"Where is he?"

Michael fell silent for a moment, then his eyes filled with tears.

"He's gone home," he said. "He's gone home to die."

*   *   *

Michael stopped, his eyes fixed on the window of his room. Janet, too, stopped. Following Michael's gaze, she looked up. The house was dark except for a single, oddly flickering light that glowed from Michael's window. Shadow bounded ahead to scratch eagerly at the back door.

"What is it, Michael?" Janet asked.

"Nathaniel. He's here. He's in my room."

"No," Janet whispered. "There's no one here, Michael. There's no Nathaniel." But even as she said the words, Janet knew she no longer believed them. Whatever Nathaniel was, whether he was someone real, or a ghost, or no more than a creature of Michael's imagination, he was real. He was as real to her now as he was to Michael, and to Anna.

Slowly, Janet moved toward the back door of the house. Michael followed her, his face suddenly gone blank, as if he was listening to some being that Janet couldn't see.

She pulled the door open, and reached for the light switch. Nothing happened. Shadow slipped inside, immediately disappearing through the kitchen and up the stairs.

Janet could sense the presence in the house now, and her instinct was to flee, to abandon the house to whatever had invaded it, to take Michael and run out into the darkening night.

Instead, she went into the living room and picked up the poker that hung from the mantelpiece. Then she turned, and as if in a trance, moved toward the foot of the stairs, and started up.

Michael followed. Once again, his head was pounding, and once again, his nostrils seemed filled with smoke. And once again, Nathaniel's voice was whispering in his head.

"This is my house, and I have come home."

Michael moved on, his vision starting to cloud.

"This is my house, and I will never leave it. Never again."

They reached the landing. The presence of Nathaniel was almost palpable. Shadow, too, was there, his great body stretched on the floor in front of Michael's door, a strangled whimpering coming from his throat.

"This was my mother's house, and this is my house. I will not leave my house again."

Michael stopped, staring at the closed door, listening to Nathaniel's voice, knowing what Nathaniel was going to ask him to do.

Janet, too, stopped, but then she moved forward again, and put her hand on the knob of the door to Michael's room.

She turned it, then gently pushed the door, letting it swing open.

In the center of the room, his empty blue eyes fixed on her, his ashen face expressionless, Nathaniel stood, illuminated by the soft light of an oil lamp.

"This is my house," he said. "I was born here, and I will die here."

Janet recognized them all in the strange face she beheld. It was an ageless face, and it bore no emotion, and all of them were there.

Mark was there, and Amos.

Ben Findley was there.

And Michael was there.

For endless seconds, Janet searched that face, her mind reeling. Even now, as she saw him, she still was uncertain if he was real or only an apparition.

"Who are you?" she breathed at last.

"I am Nathaniel."

"What do you want?"

"I want what is mine," Nathaniel replied, his toneless voice echoing in the small room. "I want what was taken from me. I want—"

"No!" Janet suddenly screamed. All the torment that had built inside her over the last months, all the tensions, all the fears, overwhelmed her now, focusing on the strange being in Michael's room. "No," she screamed once again. "Nothing. You'll get nothing here."

She raised the poker, swinging it at Nathaniel with all

the force she could muster. Nathaniel staggered backward under the blow, and then Janet dropped the poker, hurling herself forward.

"Help me, Michael!" The words thundered in Michael's head as he watched his mother throw herself on Nathaniel. Then, again, Nathaniel's words came: *"Help me!"*

Everything Michael saw was fogged now, fogged by the smoke that was choking him, and by the sound of Nathaniel's words ringing in his head.

"Help me, Michael. Please help me . . ."

His mind began to focus, and Nathaniel's wish began to take shape within him.

And then, as Michael silently commanded him, Shadow suddenly rose to his feet and launched himself into the room. To Michael, it was as if he was seeing it in slow motion: the dog seeming to arc slowly through the air, his lips curling back to expose his gleaming fangs, his ears laid flat against his head, droplets of saliva scattering from his jowls.

"Help me!" Nathaniel's words filled the room now, battering Michael's ears as well as his mind.

Then Shadow reached his target, his body twisting in midair and knocking over the little table that held the oil lamp as his jaws closed firmly on a human throat.

A scream filled the room as the oil lamp burst, and flames suddenly shot in every direction. The bedcovers caught first, and then the curtains.

Suddenly the room was filled with real smoke, and Michael understood with certain clarity that this was the smoke he'd been smelling all along, that Nathaniel, while showing him the past, had been showing him the future as well. And now he could hear his mother's terrified screams drowning out Nathaniel's bellows of pain and anguish.

His fogged mind cleared, and he watched for a moment, frozen to the spot, as his mother began flailing at the quickly spreading fire.

On the floor, his throat bleeding, Nathaniel lay calmly beneath the still attacking dog.

"No," Michael screamed. He hurled himself into the room. "No, Mom. Stop it—it's too late! Out! We've got to get out!"

Without waiting for her to reply, Michael grabbed her arm and began dragging her from the burning room.

For Janet, none of it was real anymore. Not Nathaniel, not Michael, not even the fire. She was caught in her nightmare again, but this time, she had to save them. Her family was going to die, and she had to save them.

She fought against the hands that restrained her, tried her best to stay in the burning room, tried to combat the growing flames.

Then, out of the smoke, a great weight hurled itself against her, and she fell to the floor. She recovered herself and got to her knees, then once again regained her feet.

But the weight was pressing at her now, pushing her toward the door, while the insistent hands still pulled.

And then she was out of the burning room and on the stairs. Her mind began to clear, and she recognized Michael in front of her, pulling her along. Behind her was Shadow, barking furiously, prodding at her, his large body preventing her from going back up the narrow stairs.

Then they were out of the house, huddled together in the yard, watching as the flames consumed the tinder-dry wood. Once, as she looked up, Janet thought she saw a face at Michael's window, but a second later it disappeared as the house crashed in on itself.

Then people began to gather around her; first the Simpsons, then the Shieldses, and then others, until soon most of Prairie Bend was there.

No one tried to save the house, no one tried to save anything that was in it: as the house burned, Janet's labor began.

EPILOGUE

"We'll take her to our house," Leif Simpson said.

Janet lay on the ground, her head cradled in Laura Shields's lap. Her face, glistening with a film of perspiration, was a mask of pain made grotesque by the orange light of the fire. The first violent contraction of her premature labor had wrenched a scream from her lips, and only Buck Shields's strong arms had kept her from collapsing. But now she drew on what few reserves of strength she still had. "No," she whispered. "Anna's . . . I want to go to Anna's."

"But there's no time, Janet," Ione protested.

"There is," Janet gasped. "I'll make time. But I want to have my baby at Anna's. Please . . . please." Another contraction seized her, and she moaned.

"I'll take her," Buck Shields said. "We'll put her in the back of the Chevy. It won't take more than an extra minute or two." He glanced at Ione Simpson. "Can you meet us there?" As soon as Ione had nodded, Buck leaned over and picked Janet up in his strong arms. "It's going to be all right," he told her. "We're taking you home." Janet sighed, and let her eyes close, blotting out the sight of the smoldering farmhouse, giving in to the pain that was wracking her body.

As Buck carried her to the car, she numbly tried to

337

remember what had happened that night, how the fire had started.

But all she could remember was being at the kitchen table, then going upstairs to bed. A few minutes later, the house had burned.

She had no memory of going out to Potter's Field that night, no memory of what she had found there.

She had no memory of seeing Nathaniel that night.

For in dying, Nathaniel had taken her memories of him with him.

Ten minutes later, Ione Simpson arrived at Anna Hall's house, a determinedly cheerful expression masking the dread she was feeling. Janet's baby, she knew, was at least a month early, possibly more. And from the look in her eyes, Ione had known that Janet was in shock even before she went into labor. Nonetheless, she did her best to ease the fear that was plain in Michael's eyes as he sat in Anna's parlor, staring up at her. "Isn't this going to be exciting?" she asked. "Just like Magic foaling last spring, except this time you're going to have a baby brother or sister." Then, when Michael failed to react to her words, her tone changed. "Where's your mother?"

"Upstairs," Michael replied in a dazed voice.

"All right. Now, I want you to do something for me. I want you to find all the clean towels you can, and bring them into your mother's room. Okay?"

Michael seemed to come out of his trance, and nodded.

A few minutes later, his arms filled with folded towels, he appeared in the doorway of his mother's room. He stared at Janet, who was propped up against the pillows, her face drawn, lines of pain etched around her eyes. "Are you okay?" he asked, his voice filled with anxiety. "Does it hurt?"

Janet said nothing, but Laura Shields took the towels from Michael and eased him out of the room. "She's going to be fine, Michael. She and the baby are both going to be fine."

Michael gazed at the faces around his mother, but in none of them could he see anything to give him a hint about what was going to happen to his mother. His grandmother was sitting beside his mother, gently wiping her face with a damp cloth, while his uncle hovered in one corner. At last, understanding that right now no one had time for him, Michael went back downstairs to wait.

It was just after midnight, and Michael was in the parlor doing his best to shut out the sound of his mother's labor as it echoed through the house. Outside, the wind had begun to rise. He was alone—had been alone for hours as everyone in the house gathered upstairs to help with the delivery. Michael had wanted to be there, too, but his wishes had been denied. It would be easier for everyone, particularly his mother, if he stayed downstairs.

He was lying on the sofa now, staring out the window into the darkness, listening as the wind rose, howling around the house. Then, slowly, in the back of his mind, he felt something reaching out to him. It was a voice, and though the words were unclear, he understood the meaning.

Someone, somewhere, needed his help.

There was something oddly familiar about the sensation. It seemed like something that had happened before, but that he had forgotten about.

Then, as the wordless pleas for help became more insistent, the sounds of the wind and of his mother's agony began to grow dim. Unconsciously, Michael folded his arms over his chest, then drew his knees up, curling himself into a tight ball.

There was something surrounding him. Something damp and warm, and very comforting. And then, slowly, he began to feel pressure on his head, and the damp warmness around him began to move, producing an undulating rhythm that seemed to rock him gently.

The pressure on his head increased, turning into pain, and suddenly Michael moaned, a soft cry muffled by the damp folds that bound his limbs. The pain sharpened, and he felt as if his head was being crushed. Then the moist strictures of his bonds suddenly tightened around him, squeezing him, moving him. . . .

"It's coming," Ione said. "I can see the top of its head now. Bear down, Janet. It's almost over—just bear down hard."

Janet, sweat running off her body to soak into the already damp sheets, groaned softly, and tried to comply with Ione's instructions. But it was hard—so hard.

Suddenly Michael's bonds closed tightly around him. He felt as if he were being crushed, and he tried to fight against the restraints, but he had no strength. He screamed now, a long, high-pitched howl of agony.

Shadow, who had been asleep on the floor, suddenly awoke and rose to his feet. He moved to the couch, paused a moment, whimpering, to lick at Michael's face, but if Michael was aware of the big dog's presence, he gave no sign. Then, with Michael's next scream, Shadow turned and trotted upstairs to lie by the door to Janet's room, his ears laid back against his head, his tail twitching nervously, an odd sound halfway between a whine and a snarl drifting up from his throat.

In the parlor, the terrible pressure on Michael's head suddenly stopped. He tried to move his body, but couldn't. And then there was something else.

Something seemed to be twisting itself around his neck, making it hard for him to breathe.

He began struggling, fighting against the new restraint, but he couldn't get loose, couldn't throw it off. He could feel himself choking, feel himself beginning to gag.

Then, in the distance, he heard a voice.

"Here it comes," the voice whispered. "Here comes the pretty baby." Then: "Once more, Janet. Just once more."

Suddenly the pressure on Michael's body increased,

squeezing, squeezing him ever harder, and he could feel himself being moved forward.

But with each forward motion, the pressure on his throat increased. There was no air now, and he could feel something strange happening in his brain. His sensations were growing dim, and his pain was easing.

There was a blackness around him, a gathering darkness that threatened to swallow him up. For a moment, he fought the blackness, tried to fight his way into the light. In the end, though, the darkness won, and he gave in to it.

"The umbilical cord," Ione Simpson gasped. The baby had stopped moving, only its head having emerged from the womb, and she knew instantly what had happened. "The cord's wrapped around his neck. It's strangling him. Hard, Janet. Bear down hard. Now!"

With a final effort that was more sheer will than strength, Janet forced the last of her energy into her torso. Her body heaved on the bed, and she cried out in exhaustion and agony. But slowly, the baby moved.

"Now," Ione whispered. "Now . . ."

With sure fingers and strong hands, she grasped the baby's body and drew it forth from the womb. Working as quickly as she could, she cut the umbilical cord away from the child's neck, then gave it a gentle thump on the back.

Nothing happened.

She tried again, a little harder, then felt for a pulse.

There was nothing.

Her eyes left the baby for a moment and scanned the room. Anna still sat by the head of the bed, her face pale and impassive. Laura Shields, her eyes fixed on the motionless infant, was crying, shaking her head in apparent disbelief. In the far corner, Buck Shields stood, his lower lip caught between his teeth, his entire body quivering with tension.

"Like Laura's," he said softly. "It's like Laura's."

Then, though she knew it was too late, and that there was nothing that could be done, Ione tried once more to bring the baby back to life.

Michael opened his eyes in the dimly lit room. Upstairs, he knew, his brother had been born, and he'd helped in the birth. Already, he understood that the odd voice he'd heard in his head a little while ago had been his brother's voice, and that his brother had needed his help. And he'd given his help, taking on the pain of the birth as he would take on whatever other pain his brother ever felt.

His brother, he knew, was his responsibility. It would be up to him to take care of the tiny child, comfort him when he was unhappy, tend to him when he was sick.

And protect him from evil.

Michael got up from the sofa and started slowly up the stairs. As he approached the landing, Shadow got to his feet, then moved slowly toward Michael, his tail low. He whimpered softly, then licked at Michael's hand.

Michael opened the door to the room in which his mother lay, and stepped inside.

His gaze roved through the strangely silent room, drifting from one face to the next. Finally his eyes fell on the tiny bundle that was cradled in Ione Simpson's arms.

"Let me see him," Michael whispered. "Let me see my brother."

Ione hesitated, then slowly shook her head. "I'm sorry, Michael . . ." she whispered.

"Let me see my brother," Michael repeated.

Now it was Anna Hall who spoke. She rose to her feet and moved slowly across the room until she stood in front of Michael. "He's dead, Michael," she said quietly. "Your little brother was born dead."

Michael's eyes widened, and he backed away from his grandmother. "No," he said. "He wasn't dead. I know he wasn't dead." His voice began to rise. "I could feel him. I could feel him, and he was alive!"

Turning away from the people in the room, the people

he knew had killed his infant brother, Michael fled from the house, out into the night and the shrieking wind. He ran aimlessly, scrambling through fences, stumbling in the fields. At last, exhausted, he collapsed to the ground, where he lay sobbing and panting. Shadow crouched beside him, licking at his face.

He didn't know how much time passed by, but when he looked up, the night had grown even darker. The wind had ceased. All was silent.

In the distance, there was a soft reddish glow, and slowly Michael came to realize that he was seeing the dying embers of the house that had burned that night.

And then he saw another light, the yellow flame of a lantern, looming in the darkness. He watched it for several long minutes, and when it didn't move, he began creeping forward, huddling low to the ground, Shadow beside him.

And then, in the darkness, he could see.

There was someone there, working in the dim light of the lantern, and Michael knew what they were doing.

They were burying his brother, burying the brother he knew they had killed, but who was not dead.

As he watched, Michael knew what he must do.

In his own mind, his brother was Nathaniel, and his brother still lived.

Now, it was for Michael to avenge Nathaniel.

ABOUT THE AUTHOR

JOHN SAUL's first novel, *Suffer the Children*, was published in 1977 to instant bestsellerdom. *Punish the Sinners, Cry for the Strangers, Comes the Blind Fury, When the Wind Blows* and *The God Project*, each a national bestseller, followed. Now, John Saul's trademark setting, a sleepy, isolated town where suddenly no one is safe, forms the background for this master storyteller's most chilling novel yet. John Saul lives in Bellevue, Washington, where he is at work on his next novel.

RELAX!
SIT DOWN
and Catch Up On Your Reading!

☐	24607	**LINES AND SHADOWS** by Joseph Wambaugh	$4.50
☐	23845	**THE DELTA STAR** by Joseph Wambaugh	$3.95
☐	20822	**GLITTER DOME** by Joseph Wambaugh	$3.95
☐	22750	**THE KINGMAKERS** by Arelo Sederberg	$3.95
☐	24493	**DENNISON'S WAR** by Adam Lassiter	$3.50
☐	24172	**NATHANIEL** by John Saul	$3.95
☐	23336	**GOD PROJECT** by John Saul	$3.95
☐	24234	**MAY DAY IN MAGADAN** by Anthony Olcott	$3.50
☐	24116	**A CONSPIRACY OF EAGLES** by Bart Davis	$3.50
☐	23792	**THE COP WHO WOULDN'T QUIT** by Rick Nelson	$3.95
☐	22753	**THE GUNS OF HEAVEN** by Pete Hamill	$2.95
☐	23709	**OMEGA DECEPTION** by Charles Robertson	$3.50
☐	24646	**THE LITTLE DRUMMER GIRL** by John Le Carre	$4.50
☐	23987	**THE TAKERS** by Wm. Flanagan	$2.95
☐	23577	**THE SEEDING** by David Shobin	$2.95
☐	23678	**WOLFSBANE** by Craig Thomas	$3.95
☐	23420	**THE CIRCLE** by Steve Shagan	$3.95
☐	22746	**RED DRAGON** by Thomas Harris	$3.95
☐	23838	**SEA LEOPARD** by Craig Thomas	$3.95
☐	20353	**MURDER AT THE RED OCTOBER** by Anthony Olcott	$2.95
☐	24606	**THE SWITCH** by Elmore Leonard	$2.95
☐	24609	**THE TENTH CRUSADE** by Christopher Hyde	$3.25

Prices and availability subject to change without notice.

Buy them at your local bookstore or use this handy coupon for ordering:

Bantam Books, Inc., Dept. FL, 414 East Golf Road, Des Plaines, Ill. 60016

Please send me the books I have checked above. I am enclosing $_____
(please add $1.25 to cover postage and handling). Send check or money order
—no cash or C.O.D.'s please.

Mr/Mrs/Miss_____

Address_____

City_____State/Zip_____

FBB—12/84

Please allow four to six weeks for delivery. This offer expires 6/85.

DON'T MISS
THESE CURRENT
Bantam Bestsellers